BEFORE I FORGET

André Brink is the author of fifteen novels in English, including *A Dry White Season, Imaginings of Sand, The Rights of Desire* and, most recently, *The Other Side of Silence*. He has won South Africa's most important literary prize, the CNA Award, three times and has twice been shortlisted for the Booker Prize. His novels have been translated into thirty languages. André Brink is Professor of English at the University of Cape Town.

André Brink

BEFORE I FORGET

VINTAGE

Published by Vintage 2005

2 4 6 8 10 9 7 5 3 1

First published in Great Britain in 2004 by
Secker & Warburg

Vintage
Random House, 20 Vauxhall Bridge Road,
London SW1V 2SA

Random House Australia (Pty) Limited
20 Alfred Street, Milsons Point, Sydney
New South Wales 2061, Australia

Random House New Zealand Limited
18 Poland Road, Glenfield,
Auckland 10, New Zealand

Random House (Pty) Limited
Endulini, 5A Jubilee Road, Parktown 2193,
South Africa

The Random House Group Limited Reg. No. 954009
www.randomhouse.co.uk/vintage

A CIP catalogue record for this book
is available from the British Library

ISBN 0 099 47752 1

Papers used by Random House are natural, recyclable
products made from wood grown in sustainable forests.
The manufacturing processes conform to the environ-
mental regulations of the country of origin

Printed and bound in Great Britain by
Bookmarque Ltd, Croydon, Surrey

Thank you

S

for the little blue bus

Rompre avec les choses réelles, ce n'est rien. Mais avec les souvenirs! . . .
Le coeur se brise à la séparation des songes.

Jean d'Ormesson, *C'était bien*

If we cease to grieve we may cease to remember.
Plutarch, 'Letter of Consolation to his Wife'

. . . love is immortal though the body is not
Nicholas Gage, *Greek Fire*

You DIED AT seventeen minutes to ten this morning. I was of course with you; no one else. The last love of my life? I will soon be seventy-eight, after all. Beyond the age of redemption. There may still be years ahead of me, especially if I've inherited Mam's genes – she turns a hundred and three in late August, three weeks after my own birthday – but duration is, regrettably, not all that matters; and you, more than anyone else, with all the joy you have brought me, have also made me only too aware of my waning powers, desire brought on but performance taken away. I know that Goethe, at seventy-five, still had an affair with a seventeen-year-old, to whom he wrote one of his most beautiful poems. And there are the lustrous examples of Chaplin and Picasso and Bertrand Russell and Chagall and Karajan and Mandela, or even, way back, of Father Abraham, not to mention Methuselah who begat and begat and begat until an unspeakable age. But in due course, sooner for some, later for others, all good things of day begin to droop and die; and not just women, but men too, succumb to the dark forces of gravity. Ever since that first day, on New Year's Eve, fifteen months ago, something inside me, something well beyond reason or practicality, knew that after you there could not be another woman. There was nothing melodramatic about the acknowledgement: it was very calm, unemotional, and precise. Like a last boundary stone on an ancient road. After this, *ultima Thule*. Or whatever.

Have you changed the substance of my life, or just the contours? Whatever it might be, you have given meaning to it at a time when I was beginning to sink into despondency about my waning powers – intellectual, moral, physical and (undoubtedly and regrettably and shamefully) sexual.

That evening, after all the upheaval in the street with my stalled car, our hands and faces still showing traces of grease and oil, you invited me in for a drink. From that humdrum beginning all the rest flowed, fifteen months of exploring unexpected tracts of the topography of heaven; with, for fair measure, a stretch of purgatory and the odd corner of hell thrown in.

It is still a pulsating, living memory inside me. As the long December twilight darkens almost imperceptibly over the glimmering surface of the southern ocean, you sit cupping in two slender hands a large glass of red wine.

I sniff appreciatively. 'Cabernet Sauvignon,' I say. 'About 1995? Paarl region rather than Stellenbosch.'

Your eyes widen. 'Spot on. Where did you learn to do that?'

'One of my passions,' I explain. 'It's fun trying to identify all the elements that speak to the palate and the nose.'

'Like what?'

I swirl the deep red wine in its glass, and take a small sip, slipping into a pretentious pose: 'Like, in this one, the complex flavouring of cedar wood, blackcurrant, mocha and vanilla, all of them tinted with suggestions of mint and chocolate, of sun-ripened sweet berries and subtle tannins which precede the medley of darker berries, wood spice and toasted coconut that tease the palate.'

'My God,' you exclaim. 'You're either a barefaced liar or a pretty formidable connoisseur.'

'A matter of practice. And picking up the jargon.' I wink. 'The real fun starts when one tries to puzzle out people in the same way.'

'Do you do it with everybody you meet?'

'No, no. Only those who seem worth the effort. I must admit I find a particular challenge in reading women in that way.'

'How do you do that?'

I hesitate, and decide to let it go. (Already, in my mind, I could imagine reading you, unique and euphoric: not a dark heavy red wine this, but a white, a Sauvignon Blanc perhaps, from a cool *terroir*, fresh and bright but without any tartness or greenness, with an intense straw-like and green-peppery and lemon-grassy bouquet, and hints of asparagus and gooseberry, a fleeting farmyard presence, a complex fruitiness that lingers in the aftertaste, beautifully balanced for perfect ageing?)

All you do is dip the tip of your tongue into your wine and point it wet and glistening in my direction. At last you ask, 'Are you in the wine business?'

'Strictly as a drinker.'

'Then what are you? You're definitely not a mechanic – I could see that.'

'I'm supposed to be a writer. But I haven't written anything for years.'

Sudden enlightenment dawns in your eyes. 'Jesus, you're not *the* Chris Minnaar?'

'Guilty as charged.'

'Well! I'm sorry, I should never have taken up so much of your time.'

It is a moment of choice. Without trying to unravel it, I sense that everything may be at stake here. I look very intensely at your face: the contrast between the not-quite-blonde hair and the very dark eyes set wide apart; the small mole on one high cheekbone, the generous mouth. There is something that puzzles me, tugs at memory: I'm sure I have seen a face like this before, but where, but how? And I know I cannot let go until I have traced it.

'I'm not in any hurry,' I say, willing to compromise not just the night ahead but, for all I know, the future. 'I don't really have anything else to do.'

'It's New Year's Eve!'

'It doesn't seem to bother *you* much.'

'To tell you the truth, I've been invited to a party. I was actually on my way there, remember, when I found you. But I don't feel like going any longer.'

'I'm also supposed to go out. But I'd much rather stay here.'

'Think of your reputation.'

'I am doing just that.'

That was the beginning of it all. You didn't go to your party, and I skipped mine. We spoke for fourteen hours without coming up for air. In the high morning, you fell asleep on the old sagging couch with the broken springs. I remained sitting beside you, looking down at your face, serene in sleep. It was frank and innocent, hiding nothing from me, and yet the purest mystery.

THERE ARE TWO moments in the relationship with every woman I have known in my life, which have brought me closer to understanding — even if it was without ever fully getting there — what it means to be alive. One is the moment of orgasm. Not my own, but that of the woman I am with. Because it is immeasurably more wonderful than anything I could hope to feel myself. Seeing – hearing, feeling, knowing – her in the throes of ecstasy, does not primarily bring a sense of achievement, the Little Jack Horner syndrome (*Look what a clever boy am I*), but a sense of awe: this is what a human individual – this *she* who is *you* – is capable of. It is an unfathomable combination of two sensations which ought to be essentially different, and yet are merged: it is a sharing, almost a fusion, which leaves me with a feeling of unspeakable joy, even of gratitude (*Thank you for allowing me to be with you in the ultimate moment*); but also a feeling of utter solitude. I can see it, hear it, feel it, taste it – but I can never be on the inside of it with you. I cannot even be sure whether I really know what it is like. Is it 'like' my own? Or incomparable? Just as I can never know if what you see at any given moment is exactly the same as what I see. We look at a colour. We both call it red. But it is only because we have been taught to call it by that name. There is no guarantee – not ever – that we *see* it in the same way, that your red *is* my red. How much more momentous is something like orgasm. But for that very reason your solitude, your quite literal wrapped-upness in it, cannot but bring that experience of what for lack of a better word I call awe.

The other moment is very, very different. And yet not, if one really thinks about it, so different at all. It is the moment when I wake up with a woman in my arms, and see her still sleeping. I raise myself on an elbow. I gaze. I gaze at her without even for a moment being able to understand anything at all of what I see. You: sleeping. The one I have shared a special experience with; the one I have shared hours, days, months, perhaps years of my life with. Yet, here, in this instant, so utterly confirmed in your youness that you are turned into a mystery, I am conscious of being on the outside of it: it actually makes me feel an intruder, someone who should not be here at all, should not be allowed to gaze upon you in this ineffable moment of sleep. Because here you are totally vulnerable, you have no protection against the world. Except the protection of your own self. Which, being unfathomable, leaves you so naked that you may just as well have been peeled from your skin, a grape, a transparent fruit, light in the heart of light. And that *is* a mystery, for ever.

And yet by falling asleep beside me, you have sanctioned, silently, this intrusion and this gaze. To sleep with someone can be more intimate than making love. It is a yielding, and a trust, that cannot be compared to anything else. You have granted me this. Can I ever be worthy of it? This is the moment I come closest to understanding something of that overused and misunderstood word: love.

AFTER A LONG time of gazing at you, I got up, taking care not to disturb you, and tiptoed to a narrow divan in the corner, from which I stripped a brightly coloured spread – it looked Spanish, perhaps Mexican – which I draped over you. You shifted to find a comfortable position, uncovering one foot. I went to the kitchen to drink a glass of water, and in the too-bright New Year's morning washed the dishes from the slap-up meal you had prepared sometime during the night without interrupting the conversation. After that I returned to watch you sleep until, like a cat, you stretched and yawned and woke up to resume the talk.

All of this happened fifteen months ago. And now it comes tumbling back, clamouring to be remembered, without form and void. My love, and all the other loves of my life. Into the emptiness your death has left behind, this absence of everything that used to spell not just your life, but life itself. At my age one should be used to death and dying. In the terse and moving Afrikaans expression: they are chopping in our wood. And have been at it for a long time now. But one never quite gets used to it. You never know when the axe will bite into your own bark and let the white splinters fly.

Throughout last night I lay awake — I knew what was coming; I knew exactly how it would happen, and yet was wholly unprepared. I lay in bed watching the television. Staring mesmerised at the images of war. What everybody had been predicting for months, had now begun. The bombing of Baghdad. Spectacular flares in the night sky, like Guy Fawkes, the sound of explosions which might be crackers but were not. America on its collision course with Iraq, one face of evil seeking out another. Saddam, Bush. For months the world had been teetering on the edge of this chicken game, wondering whether the US (Britain is merely a snotty little brother running after the big bully in this equation) was really going to plunge in. Now it had begun. Saddam and his sons hopefully killed, the TV said, in a bomb raid on a bunker.

Since no convincing reasons have been advanced at any stage — least of all in Secretary Powell's recent song and dance in the Security Council — one is left floundering among wild and wilder theories. I know of few more damning and devastating comments on the philosophy of war than this paragraph by Chris Hedges, war correspondent of the *New York Times*:

> The enduring attraction of war is this: Even with its destruction and carnage it can give us what we long for in life. It can give us purpose, meaning, a reason for living. Only when we are in the midst of conflict does the shallowness and vapidness of much of our lives become apparent. Trivia dominate our conversations and increasingly our airwaves. And war is an enticing elixir. It gives us resolve, a cause. It allows us to be noble.

If this is what it is about, if this is an acceptable assessment of the US in the wake of 9/11, then the West has truly come to the edge of the abyss. It is in the face of the Void that humanity has always undertaken its most profound philosophical probings. I must confess that looking at my whole life and all my loves, I can possibly see it as nothing but a response to the 'trivia' Hedges talks about: an attempt to find the 'purpose, meaning, a reason for living' he now discovers in war. Somewhere, something has gone unimaginably wrong.

All of it remained unreal on the stark screen of the television set, a spectacle, a show put on for our diversion in the night hours. And yet real people were really dying, might still die in their hundreds or thousands, who could tell? That was the true obscenity. While in the hospital, less than half an hour away from here, you too were waiting for death, for the release from the coma in which you had been lying for almost a month now, ever since your birthday on the last day of February when you went out to buy cigarettes at 'our' little super-market and did not come back.

At seventeen minutes to ten this morning you died. I was there. Oh yes, I was there. I left soon after. I had no stomach for the formal-ities to follow: there were doctors and nurses and registrars enough to deal with that. They had all the facts on file since the first day I was brought there by the police. Somewhere in the midst of the breaking war in Iraq was George, your husband, presumably taking photo-graphs: a call with destiny he could not possibly miss. But there would be friends who could be summoned to fill in the details. I no longer belonged with you; if I ever had. As far as the hospital was concerned, I am only your employer and your friend. Was.

All I can think of for the time being is writing in this new black book with the red spine, bought especially for the purpose: writing, compulsively perhaps, but redeemingly – writing, writing, writing, unable to stop. For it is in the gaps and silences in between that you insinuate yourself. You. Rachel.

To remember you. In and through every loop and line my hand traces on the page, to recall you, like Eurydice, from the dead. What else does one write for? What else could possibly drive us so? Whence this unnatural urge? To defy death, like Scheherazade? No. I think there is one thing above all. Only one. To hold on. To have and to hold. Before it slips away. Before I forget.

But as I write about you, others are bound to follow, flowing across the pages like ink, like water, like the menstrual blood of death and life, unstoppable. A test of memory, or of invention, as the case may be. All those others, the women, who have marked my life, every beginning and turn and ending, every curve or darkness of my body. A commemoration of whatever women have shared with me – or added to me? or taken from me? – over my already too numerous years. I've always had a passion for organising, systematising, patterning. (The persistent push of my father, the lawyer, the rigid, driving man of my early years?) Paging through all the old journals that have accumulated dust and fish moths and mouse or gecko shit for so long, I shall try to find, from all those bygone years, whatever still makes sense. No, not a record of victories and conquests, not that at all. God forbid. Many of them could not be termed 'victories' by any criteria whatsoever; on the contrary. In moments of ebullience before I met you I might have been tempted to think that I have tasted every form of success in my life, including failure. Now, after your death, it might be equally true to say that, with women as with much else besides, I have tasted every kind of defeat life has to offer, including success. In love, these distinctions do not come so readily to hand. Let it be a kind of harmless adventure in its own right, as I stumble along.

It was Jenny who told me about the curious custom, which apparently was spread across all the old cultures of Europe, known as the *moon-cloth*. In some cultures, she said, it was known as the *blood-cloth*, in some as the *woman-cloth,* but its function was the same everywhere – and Jenny was a cultural anthropologist, she should know. (I shall never forget the light in her eyes, particularly in the moment of orgasm – she was one of the rare women I have known who keep their eyes open when they come – as if there was a candle burning deep inside her, behind them, a luminosity from within, not a reflection of anything outside. And I remember what they looked like as she spoke to me about this moon-cloth, which was, for us, the preferred term: it was not just a point of information she imparted, but a peculiar excitement, a prelude to sex.) In one way or another, this cloth, it seems, figures in most of the great quests and journeys of our civilisation: Marco Polo took with him on his voyage to the Great Mogul, the moon-cloths of his wife and his three daughters; Columbus took one from the virgin Juana de Concepción, the young woman who had promised to wait for him. (There is even a hint, said Jenny, of such a cloth being entrusted to him by Queen Isabella, but this might be difficult to substantiate, for obvious reasons.) Sir Francis Drake had such a cloth, and so had Vasco da Gama. Jenny had a Greek scholar working on the *Odyssey*, and she was confident that an obscure passage in the First Book might be found, upon retranslation, to confirm that Penelope had provided her Odysseus with such an amulet. In the work of the French anthropologist Lucien Lefèvre she had found exciting indications, from tombs in the Valley of the Kings, that even the illustrious dead in Old Egypt were supplied with such a moon-cloth to accompany them on the long journey towards the realm of Osiris. Most earlier researchers had missed the references, for the simple reason that they had not been looking for them. But working back from Columbus and Marco Polo, all the way to Gilgamesh, it would now seem that these cloths fulfilled a crucial function, linking later voyages of discovery to primordial religious rites.

What at first may sound crude, really contains a very basic and profound wisdom. For the moon-cloth was in fact nothing but a piece of fabric, a bandage, or a rag used by a woman during menstruation. Much still needs to be clarified about its function: was it a means of keeping the absent woman present in the wandering hero's mind during his travels, and perhaps ensure that he was brought home safely to her? Or just a mnemonic device? A form of protection for the hero against harm that might befall him on his way, an exorcism of evil, or a simple token or pledge of love? What makes it particularly significant, Jenny pointed out, is that it runs against the grain of most anthropological views on early cultures, where menstrual blood is generally regarded as negative, a form of defilement, even pernicious. But her research was impeccable and her findings beyond reproach. She often spoke about this phenomenon, and I invariably found something particularly stimulating in these discussions — starting quite matter-of-factly, but leading to some of the most highly charged sexual encounters of my life. (And always those eyes to remember her by.)

So I think of these notes as a collection of moon-cloths garnered along the way, and taken with me to wherever the journey may take me. Somewhere else. Somewhere not here. Perhaps no more than an old man's fancy. Never without a smile, mind you, perhaps like Mam's on that distant day when she tried to persuade me, without believing it herself, that sex was sinful. I think of it as a private celebration. Or could it be to ask some kind of forgiveness? I am not sure about that. Remorse, said Spinoza, is the second sin. Perhaps it is a kind of homage. In praise of women. What would I have been — how could I have been *me* — without each and every one of them?

TO BEGIN WITH: the bright little Katrien, when I was barely eight years old and she was, at eleven, very much the older woman, my cousin, deposited in our house by the Great Drought of '33 that swept away her parents, Mam's sister and her hangdog husband, from Victoria West where they had farmed with dust and stones for much too long; and while they were scouring the streets of Johannesburg in search of work, part of the new wave of poor-whites, Katrien and her two older sisters, Marie and Annie, were dumped on us. ('What else is family for?' asked Mam, folding the sheets.) The older sisters were put in the spare room; Katrien was deemed young enough to share my room, which had two single beds. But on a shiversome and scary winter's night she crept in beside me and, giggling and whispering wetly in my ear, took my hand and introduced me to an undreamed-of foreign land. An only and lonely child, I had no inkling of the way a girl was made, and the discovery left me breathless.

That was how Mam found us in the morning, as we'd simply fallen asleep, exhausted with excitement, at an ungodly hour of the night, still in some kind of prelapsarian embrace, legs entwined, her long white flannelette nightie up to her neck and my blue-striped pyjama pants lost in the bedclothes. I mean it literally: the pants were lost and never found again. Pure mystery. That night brought home to me two miracles of love that are always to be borne in mind: it giveth and it taketh away. What was given was the discovery that a tiny part of my anatomy, an insignificant pink worm, had the mysterious propensity to jump to attention at almost double its customary size (something I must have noticed before, but which only hit me with its full significance that night); what was taken away was my striped pyjama pants, a loss I blithely accepted.

Mam prudently chose to deal with the matter without informing my father, who might have maimed me for life in his righteous rage; and with a great show of piety (yet accompanied by the mysterious smile which set me wondering) she impressed upon me that the body was a sinful thing, inclined to all evil, undertook personally to intercede with God to fend off the dire wrath that would otherwise descend on me, and supervised the regrettable process of moving Katrien's bed into the spare room with her sisters. I was made to swear an oath on the black Bible, a promise I had no intention whatsoever of keeping, that I would thenceforth avoid any repetition of such perfidious enterprises. Eight years old: and already I decided that if that really was what God thought of the body, He had no idea of what could make life worthwhile, and was not to be trusted. For the time being the sin remained unspeakable, without a name.

It was at least a year before a name became attached to it. I had picked up at school the word *cunt*, without the vaguest idea of what it meant, but sensing it was better than most for swearing; and one weekend after the cousins, Marie and Annie and the unforgettable Katrien, had joined their parents in Sodom, Gomorrah or Johannesburg, and erupting in a rage when Thys, one of the rare friends who were sometimes allowed to come and play with me, broke a little green wagon I had been given the previous Christmas, I yelled at him, 'You cunt, you cunt, you bloody cunt, now look at what you've done!' My father, working on the chicken run at the bottom of the garden, overheard. Thysie was sent away, blubbering, with a few smart slaps on the rear, for having broken the wagon, and then I was hauled into the house by the left ear. I was told to go and put on my church clothes, shoes and tie and all.

Father was a ferocious disciplinarian, and there was a set formula for punishment. I would be taken to his study, and Mam would be summoned. Then a passage would be read from the Bible – usually something from Proverbs (*He that spareth his rod hurteth his own son: but he that loveth him chastiseth him betimes*; or – with an admonishing look at Mam – *The rod and reproof give wisdom: but a child left to himself bringeth his mother to shame*) – followed by a prayer, from the length and histrionics of which I could gauge pretty accurately how grave the impending beating was going to be. After a drawn-out *A-a-a-men* we would all be expected to remain kneeling in silence while God provided him with the details of the chastisement to follow. Whereupon I would be instructed to fetch the instrument of torture – belt, strap, wire coat hanger, or a switch from the pepper tree – remove my pants and bend over the edge of his desk, which was by far the most humiliating part of the entire process, and count out aloud the number of blows administered. When at last it was over, I was expected, for some unexplained reason, to kiss Mam, and to thank him (any lack of sincerity perceived in my expression of gratitude, might result in a continuation, even a doubling, of the punishment).

On that particular day the instruction to put on my church clothes was daunting enough; but at least I wasn't ordered to take off my pants. Unless he'd decided, I thought in trepidation, that putting on my Sunday best would make the taking off that much more momentous. Mam was summoned, and we all gathered in the study. This was evidently too serious for any ordinary hiding. My heart was quaking like a bird taken from a trap. I thought it might escape through my throat and fly away.

My father read a very long passage from the Bible. Mam, who had been informed in an ominous whisper of the nature of the crime, sat noisily blowing her nose into her handkerchief. Only years later it occurred to me that she might have been smothering secret laughter.

I was closely questioned about the word I had used: where I had heard it, who had used it to whom, what I knew about its meaning. Then we all had to kneel for the torture by prayer. The final *Amen* was followed by a long silence. We all sat down again.

At last my father said, 'Now, Chris, God has made it clear to me that you have spoken that word in ignorance, and that you have no idea of the magnitude of what you have done.' I could not believe my ears. He went on: 'The word you used, and which you are never, ever, to use again, whether in my presence or not – and don't forget that God will always be there to listen – is one of the most evil and terrible words on this earth. It comes straight from hell and smells of fire and sulphur.' I sniffed involuntarily, but caught no whiff. He went on, working up steam: 'The reason why it is so terrible,' he said, 'is that it refers to that part of a woman's body we do not mention by name.' He cleared his throat, and hesitated, his face turning a deep purple, like the wattles of a turkey cock, which suddenly brought to mind an image I would have preferred not to think about just then, and concluded in a near whisper: 'It refers to a woman's *filimandorus.*' He paused, allowing the word to sink in, before repeating it, slowly, emphasising each syllable, almost with relish. '*Fi-li-man-do-rus.*' Then he got up, clutching the Bible in his big hand with the dark bristles between the joints, and Mam rose to her feet with flushed cheeks, and they both looked down at me, and he said, 'Now you may go. Think about it.'

For the rest of my life I have seldom been thinking about anything else.

THIS AFTERNOON I went to the old-age home to visit Mam. Even though I knew she was unlikely to understand what I wanted to tell her, I had to speak to her. For a few minutes I remained at the door of her room, with sudden misgivings about the decision to come, and staring, with all the familiar pain, at the ancient, ugly little garden gnome huddled in the chair beside the tall hard bed. Her head looked like a decorated egg gone wrong, small tufts of hair stuck randomly to the fragile, bird-like skull. The bird image was enhanced by the beak of the nose. I know I'm beginning to look more like her by the day now, with most of my hair gone too. (And yet she had been beautiful. Everybody spoke about it. In past centuries men would have fought duels over her, or hanged themselves. But we live in less dramatic times.)

A nurse pushed past me. 'Look who's here, Auntie Minnaar,' she said brightly, hurrying to the chair to straighten the mohair rug on the little rag doll's lap and pat the knees with a proprietorial air, like a girl trying to show off a Christmas doll which is not exactly the one she was hoping for.

Eagerness lights up the faded eyes behind the daunting glasses. ('You must have very good eyes, Auntie Minnaar,' a nurse once told her, 'to see through such thick glasses.') 'Is that really you, Boetie?' she asks in her small dry voice which sounds like a crumpling of paper. (The patronising endearment irks me, but I know she means well.) 'I have been waiting for you.'

'Sorry, Mam.' I bend over to kiss her, stung briefly by her old sour breath. 'I've been hellishly busy.'

'I know, I know.' She smiles happily. Then her eyes, momentarily so blue and bright, begin to fade again.

I settle on the high bed. 'I have bad news, Mam.'

'Oh, that's nice,' she says.

I sigh, and wonder whether there is any point in going on. Wonder, too, as often before, whether she can turn her lucid moments on and off at will.

'Tell me?' she says eagerly.

'Rachel died this morning.'

'I see.' She sounds disappointed. After a moment she asks, 'And who was Rachel?'

'A friend. A special friend. I told you about her many times.'

'Of course you did.' She nods several times. 'Well, I'm happy for you, Chris. You know you've always been my favourite child.'

'I am your only child, Mam.'

'Is that so?' Another series of pensive nods. 'A difficult birth, you know. And I had no milk for you, poor little darling.' Then a bright smile. 'But then there was that girl, you remember, the one who had the baby they gave away. So she took care of you.'

Nannie, her name was; I was told many years later. Sixteen years old, and disowned by her family. Perhaps, it has sometimes occurred to me, that is why I've had my lifelong penchant for small breasts.

'I came to tell you about Rachel,' I remind her.

She looks up at me through the layered dust on her glasses.

'She died,' I repeat.

'Yes, of course. You told me.' A sigh. 'They always do, don't they? It is in their nature to die.'

'Mam.'

'I'm the only one who cannot die,' she says with sudden vehemence. 'You know what, Boetie? I think God has forgotten about me. And it isn't fair. I don't mind if He hears me. He has been very inconsiderate to me lately. After everything I've done for Him.' Another sudden, disarming smile, her mouth a slightly deeper, moister wrinkle among the many others. 'But I've been thinking a lot, Boetie. For how long was I married to your father?'

'Thirty-five years, I think. But . . .'

'That's it. And that was enough, wasn't it? Glad to see him go. Randy old goat to the end. Come to think of it, perhaps that's why God is keeping me alive, out of harm's way. I really can't bear the thought of all eternity with your father.'

'Were you happy?' I ask.

'Of course we were happy. We were married.'

'That's not what I asked.'

'Well, that's all I can tell you.'

'I've so often wondered about you. He had this habit of going for endless walks every day, remember? Rain or shine. Sometimes he was barely home, when he would set out again.' It was like a compulsion. As if he couldn't bear to be home. And yet neither of them ever said a word about it. He would invariably go out in the evenings too, I remember. But that was different: then he would go to meetings of the Church Council, or to make house visits with the dominee, or attend secret gatherings of the Broederbond or the not-so-secret meetings of the party. Or he would go back to the office to catch up with work. (How many years did it take me to discover that many – most? – of these nocturnal excursions involved women?)

'Is that why you came?' Mam interrupts. 'To talk about your father's walks?'

'I came because Rachel died,' I say through clenched teeth.

'Did she? When?'

'This morning. At seventeen minutes to ten.'

'A strange time to die. But then she always was a bit perverse, wasn't she?'

'No.'

'How old was she?'

'She turned thirty-seven a month ago.'

'You always went for the young ones.'

Perhaps. Nannie again? But I think that has changed. My scope has widened. Or perhaps at my age one simply has less choice; you have to settle for what is on offer. If anything.

'So your wife died?'

'Not my wife, Mam. Rachel. She was married, but not to me.'

'You never mentioned that to me.'

'I did, Mam. I discussed everything with you. Don't you remember?'

'Of course I remember. And it means so much to me, Boetie, that even as a boy you always came to ask for my advice about girls, and sometimes my help.'

That is true. I could not have wished for a stauncher or more helpful ally. This she would never broach with Father. It seemed to give her vicarious pleasure to pave my way towards seemingly unattainable girls, later women. Even when my entanglements became more serious. It never ceased to surprise me, given the curtailments marriage to my father had imposed on her, how much she seemed to know about relationships; even about sex. How much of it was intuition? How much based on the pure pleasure she seemed to have derived, especially in her early years, from making love with a man as dour and patriarchal as my father? (Unless I had totally misread him? There was so much misunderstanding and antagonism between him and me.)

'Ever since that first time you did things with a little girl, you remember?' Mam interrupts the pleasurable flow of my thoughts.

'Katrien?'

'No, the other one. What was her name? Driekie, I think. Uncle Johnny and Aunt Bella's little daughter. A precocious little thing, if ever I saw one. In the fig tree, wasn't it? You were such a sweet boy. So innocent. Even when you used such bad words, sometimes.' She chuckles. 'And I had to tell you about everything. Flowers and bees and people and girls and things.'

Yes, I remember. Everything that is so inconclusively referred to as 'the facts of life'. About 'the union of the bodies'. An act, I gathered at the time, which tended to procure some satisfaction for the male of the species, while generally leaving the female unimpressed. But then, with that enigmatic little smile, she would add quite primly, 'I guess I have been blessed in that regard.'

We sit in silence for a long time. I don't know what to say next. I may simply start the conversation all over again; she won't know. To fill the silence, I reach over and remove the heavy glasses from her nose. She makes a vague clasping motion with one hand as if to catch a fly, then gives it up. Naked, her eyes are an amazing childlike delft-porcelain blue. I breathe on the lenses and wipe them clean, repeat the process, then replace the glasses on the bridge of her bony beak.

'All your girls,' she repeats contentedly, momentarily screwing up her eyes. 'I always enjoyed hearing about your doings. You came to me with all your loves, you remember? Every little one of them.'

'Not all,' I venture gently, embarrassed.

'You kept secrets from me?' I cannot fathom her eyes through the glasses. Is there reproach in them? Or a glint of glee? 'I suppose I deserve it,' she resumes without warning. 'I kept secrets from your father too.'

'What were they?'

'I can't remember now.'

I try not to show my irritation. 'Now Rachel's gone,' I say.

'You said she was a married woman?'

I should not have told her; I never thought it would stick. 'Yes,' I say tersely. 'But that has nothing to do with it.'

'Did he kill her then?' she asks unexpectedly.

'Who?'

'Her husband.'

'Of course not! What makes you say a terrible thing like that?'

'Did you?' she persists.

'That is a preposterous idea.' I half rise from the bed to go.

'In love no question is ever preposterous.'

I make an effort to contain myself. 'I can assure you George and I were the best of friends.'

'Who is George?'

'Her husband.'

'He trusted you?'

'Of course he did.'

'Silly boy.' I cannot make out whether she is referring to George or to me. She reaches out to put her hand, like a chicken's claw, on my wrist. 'Don't go. I need you, Boetie.'

I hesitate and sit down again.

'So what are you going to do about it?' she asks anxiously. 'What about the children?'

'We don't have children, Mam,' I say. 'We weren't married.'

'That didn't stop your father.'

I feel a cold hand clutching my guts. 'What do you mean? Did he . . . ?'

'I really don't know what you're talking about,' she says primly.

I give up. 'I was just trying to tell you about Rachel, Mam. Who was married to George.'

'You can never trust a woman,' she says with surprising emphasis.

'I trusted her with my life.'

'You've trusted too many women with your life, Boetie.'

'I've never regretted it,' I assure her. It comes out more strongly than I meant it to.

'You must have had children,' she says, a reproachful whine now adding an edge to her voice. 'I'm quite sure you did.'

'Helena and I had a little boy when we were married. Don't you remember? Pieter. But that was over thirty years ago.'

'Then where is he now?'

'There was the car accident, Mam. Both of them died.'

'You were always a reckless driver.'

'It wasn't my fault. I told you so many times.' But perhaps it was? Helena and I were quarrelling, Pieter was crying on the back seat, pleading with us to stop.

'So they're all dead now,' she sighs. 'But that is the price one pays, isn't it? You will be quite lonely now, I suppose.' She sounds almost happy at the prospect.

'I will, Mam. But there are memories.'

'Indeed there are,' she says brightly. 'I remember so well how you used to save little frogs from the pond. You were afraid they'd drown.'

ANOTHER SLEEPLESS NIGHT in front of the television. There's something obscene in the mere act of watching. War as spectacle, as entertainment. *The Rocky Horror Iraqi Show. Baghdad on Ice.* (Except it's on fire now.) The big chains must be pushing up their rates. And what they're showing tonight is not just a sequel to last night. It also, somehow, cancels it. Already the earlier truths or affirmations now seem superseded. Saddam and his sons were not killed in the bunker after all, it would appear. We cannot be sure of anything we see with our own eyes.

An American soldier has gone berserk, throwing grenades into the tent where his companions slept. A helicopter has been downed by friendly fire. If they just give the allied forces enough time, they might wipe themselves out, no need of an enemy. But even this may be a fiction thought up by – or dictated to – 'embedded' journalists. There was a time when embedding was a literary conceit. We are swept along by narrative invention. The Middle East is the home of Scheherazade. The patron saint of us writers. One of my earliest and most passionate – and most abiding – loves. And don't forget the little sister, Doniziade. Ah, Doniziade. I can imagine her huddling on their bed, listening to the stories as she becomes involved in the unfolding relationship between her sister (herself a just-nubile seventeen or thereabouts) and the insatiable King Shahriyar, bent on revenge for all the wrongs, real and imagined, done to him by women. Doniziade is the indispensable catalyst. Without her, no stories. Without her, who knows, no sexual charge, no love. What she has shown me is that there is *always* a third presence in the embrace of two lovers: I do not mean the memory of an earlier love, or the dream of a future one, not any corporeal being, but simply the image of a *possible* other. The image of an innocence, which is by definition already lost. It is never just you-and-me. Doniziade is the observing *other* who makes love possible.

At the end of it all Scheherazade has produced three children. Storytelling can be a risky business. There is darkness on either side. I can see the little sister there with them, thin arms clasping tomboy knees, her small face rapt. Her grave, big, dark eyes miss nothing.

DID IT REALLY begin with Nannie's small, tight, milk-swollen breasts, or Katrien's enthusiastic explorations, or Driekie in the fig tree? Or, much more likely, during Mam's long illness in my first year of life, when the old housekeeper carried me swaddled in a cloth on her broad back, humming to me, singing stories to me, in her own language, Xhosa, insinuating the rhythms and cadences into me long before I could understand a word. The safety of that solid back, the softness of her ample buttocks, *Tula, tula*, little baby. We called her old Aia, for me she had no other name. Woman and story merging in that first awareness of being protected, sheltered, safe, blissful, sleepy, happy.

Even if those were the beginnings, the first intimations of femininity in my mind, there was never any straightforward sequence. Chronology is boring at best. This, then that, then something else. That is not what matters to me. The eating of the fruit of knowledge does not introduce history, but discovery. And mostly one goes forward blindly. Or, as the Greeks had it, backwards: we don't see the future approaching, only the past receding, learning to understand as we move further away from the event. In a way you, Rachel, predate Scheherazade and Katrien; Driekie follows conversations with Anna, or making love with Daphne. Time, the Italian writer Luigi Malerba says somewhere, is merely an expedient invented by man so as to stop everything happening at the same time.

What seems to me to make more sense is that every turning point of the country's history over the past three-quarters of a century, seems to be marked by a woman in my life. And others in between, to consolidate or divert, to reveal or affirm or entertain. Kathy of the tapered fingers, Jenny of the limpid eyes, Marion with the sand in her pussy, Mia of the deep navel, dancing Daphne, freckled Frances, the wordless intensity of Helena, Maike shouting obscenities at the top of her voice when she comes, Anna under the stars. And you, Rachel. Always back to you. But no chronology; it doesn't work like that. They all merge into one another, yet each one is very distinct. Together, they spell me.

I have read of a Frenchman who was asked by the members of his family on his deathbed which of his long life's memories he would want to take with him, the best, the most cherished; and with a small smile of contentment, without any hesitation, he replied, 'I have eaten well.' When my time comes, I hope I'd be able to say with equal satisfaction and equal conviction, 'I have loved well.'

*　　*　　*

WHERE DOES THE dancing Daphne really fit in? 'Before' Helena, 'after' Anna? She *doesn't* fit in, that is the point. Not one of them does. That may be the only clue, if clue there is, to their mystery, if mystery there be. In a way, like all of them, she was just there, for a moment and for ever. Which is also why I'm wary of distinctions: one-night stands, lifelong loves. Where's the difference? Which of these is Daphne? (Which of these, Rachel, is you?)

Daphne fascinated me from the first time I saw her on stage, long-limbed and lithe (all the clichés which she imbued with new meaning), with a shower of blonde hair down to the curve of her buttocks. A dancer's body, and a mind like a scalpel. I was hooked immediately. And it was a constant challenge to be with her. She could talk about a stunning range of subjects – the ice ages of Europe, bisons in America, colonial exploitation in Africa; and unfailingly she would return to the political situation in the country and her acute sense of implication in it – but her passion was dancing, whether classical ballet or flamenco or Latin American extravaganzas. And she was proud of her body, with reason. She enjoyed showing it off, whether on the stage or alone with me. But no sex. Strictly no sex. That, she believed in total earnest, would dissipate her energy and make her lose her focus. Yet in every-thing but the ultimate act of consummation she was as ardent as a flame, as articulate as a dervish. How many times did she writhe in my arms, nearly sobbing with passion, pleading, 'No, Chris, no. Please! I don't think I've ever wanted something as madly as this, but I daren't. You must help me to say no. Please help me.'

And then, at the same time, her weird, almost religious, fanatical castigation of the same body which could bring her to the edge of ecstasy, or move in the spotlight on a stage like a firebird, a feather in a high wind. Around her waist I discovered, the first time she allowed me to remove her top, a coarse knotted rope, tied so tightly that it left unsightly marks of many colours on her smooth skin: deep reds and purples, which in the older bruises had begun to edge into greens and yellows.

At first she refused to talk about it. But I persisted. Was it some-thing religious? A St Teresa of the stage?

'No. It's nothing of the kind. I don't even believe in God.'

'Then what is it?'

'It has nothing to do with you.'

'I really don't understand you, Daphne.'

At long, long last, perhaps in desperation, she told me. 'It's this country,' she unexpectedly confided, as if that would clear up everything. 'Don't you see?'

'I'm afraid not.' Of all imaginable excuses, this surely was the most far-fetched.

But she continued, deadly serious. 'Every morning when I come to work, I drive past the black townships from my parents' plot. I see the children begging in the streets. The papers are full of reports about forced removals, about all the misery around us. And it gets worse every day. Ever since Sharpeville I have the feeling that the country is sinking deeper and deeper into a morass all the time. There is so much suffering, and so much anger.'

'That I can understand,' I agreed. 'It was Sharpeville which plunged me into writing.' I remembered so well: I'd been writing ever since I was twelve or thirteen; but then Father had intervened. One evening he summoned me to his study where he held up an exercise book in which I'd been writing a 'novel' and which he'd confiscated while going through my drawers in my absence. 'What is this?' he demanded. Flushed with embarrassment, but perhaps also with a touch of pride, I tried to explain. He flung down the book on his big desk, which had so often been my site of punishment and humiliation. 'I have read what you wrote,' he said in a frosty voice. 'I'm afraid there is only one word for it, and that is *shit*. You understand me? I won't have a son of mine spend his time on such nonsense. You must be bored, as you obviously have nothing better to do. From now on you will do more sport. And I shall make arrangements for extra lessons in Latin. If you want to follow in my footsteps and become a lawyer, you can never start too early on Latin. Don't let me catch you wasting your time and mine again like this. Is that understood?' He patted the edge of the desk with a meaningful gesture that made my little balls contract. And that was that. I did not stop writing: I only went to more trouble, helped in no small way by Mam, to keep it concealed. Through the rest of my school and university career, and later following in Father's awe-inspiring footsteps as a lawyer, I kept my writing strictly to myself. She hid everything I produced in her stocking drawer. Until the explosion of Sharpeville shocked me so deeply that I could no longer be silent. (By that time the irrevocable break between me and Father had already led to his premature death, which as it happened coincided with a premature ejaculation – or so Mam learned, much later, from the shamefaced secretary who had been at the receiving end of it.) And under the influence of Marlene, the young auburn-haired woman I was with at the time, I wrote *A Time to Weep*, which caused an unexpected furore and decided my future as a writer.

I turned back to Daphne and her murderous rope. 'I understand what it does to you. But what has that got to do with this ghastly rope around your body?'

'It's because there's nothing I can do about what's happening. Nothing at all. At least you can write, you can make sense of it. You wrote *A Time to Weep*. It's an amazing book. But what about me? I'm a dancer. What difference can I make? Most people just look the other way when they see what is going on. That's why I thought: at least I can make sure that I keep myself aware. Even if I can't change anything, I can keep myself from forgetting. I want to make sure that with every move of my body, on stage or off, I won't ever allow myself to ignore what is happening beyond my own little world.' She clasped one of my hands in both of hers. '*Now* do you understand?'

'It sounds pretty barmy to me.' But then I nodded slowly. 'Perhaps, in a way, I see what you mean. But even so . . .'

'Just try. Because I'm asking you. Do it for me.'

I sighed. 'I'll try.'

In spite of my promise, I could not stop imploring her, hoping against hope, fired by the fierce conviction that a body like hers could not be allowed to remain unfulfilled – and for such a nebulous, absurd, outrageous cause. However serious she was about it, however noble her intent, it served no purpose whatsoever, it made no sense, it was a criminal waste. My God, the nights I spent in passionate pleading, as I removed one after the other of Salome's separate veils, until the last, the obdurate last. 'No, no, no, please, Chris. If we do this I may just as well give up dancing. Don't you understand?'

No, the hell I didn't. There were times when I was driven to such an extreme that I would shout at her, the worst obscenities. 'You're a fucking tease, Daphne. You're a fake and a phoney. You're a selfish, twisted bitch.' Which she seemed, in fact, to enjoy.

And once, when my desire was driven beyond endurance, I found myself ejaculating in rage and despair.

Her reaction was wholly unexpected. 'You poor, poor darling. What has happened? I didn't mean to torture you. Was that terrible? I feel just awful, I'd never ever want to hurt you.' And then the ultimate twist, as she suddenly went down on her knees in front of me: 'Chris, may I taste it? Please. Just once?'

I was in such a state that I could not refuse. She unzipped me and took out my still half-tumescent member, and started to lick the sticky moisture, which in spite of the copious emission of only moments before, brought me back to rampant urgency. I wanted to stop her, but couldn't. And she, I presume, in that strange, intense innocence which characterised her whole relationship with me, had no inkling of what was happening and inevitably still going to happen. Until I came in her mouth and she gurgled in surprise, though not in dismay, and swallowed it to the last drop.

At least, I thought, this would point a way to the future. If intercourse was ruled out, this was a not altogether unacceptable substitute. But Daphne stood fast. This had happened, and could not be undone. In a way it had been a learning experience. A kind of illumination. It had revealed to her new possibilities, and perhaps new frontiers, of the human body, of male and female endurance. But the risk was too big. The next time she might be tempted to go further. And then everything would be wrecked. So it should never, never be allowed to happen again. Promise?

I wanted to tell her as finally and furiously as possible, to fuck off. But of course I couldn't. A bird in hand and all that.

For how long it could have gone on in this way, I really cannot tell. But then came that evening.

I'd gone to the theatre with her. She danced. One of the most sensuous performances I'd ever seen her in. When we came out, she was on a high. We celebrated in a restaurant. We both drank too much, which in itself was something exceptional for Daphne. Afterwards she made me drive her to her parents' home. Only when we got there did she confide in me that they had gone to Durban for the weekend. But there had been no lewd purpose to the invitation, absolutely not. She wanted, she said very simply, very directly, to dance for me. For me alone. Outside in the garden.

There is a full moon. The night is unreal. And we are both far gone.

In the shadows of some tall shrubs, her back turned to me, she takes off all her clothes. It is a while before I realise what is happening. I half rise from the garden bench where she has made me sit; but she swings round to me and fiercely orders me back. Crestfallen, but not entirely surprised, I comply.

She undoes, with considerable effort, the coarse, thick rope around her waist and flings it into the bushes. Even in the moonlight the angry dark circle of bruising across the gentle swelling of her stomach is visible; and in a way it fascinates me even more, certainly more morbidly, than the small dark patch below it, which I have never been allowed to see before.

Daphne begins to dance in the moonlight. Something eerie about it, as she moves from patches of stark white light into the pitch black of the shadows. There is no sound. Even the usual shrilling of crickets and insects in the grass and frogs in the invisible stream that gurgles past the bottom of the garden with its shrubs and trees and flower beds and gnomes and nymphs, is hushed. And Daphne dances. Initially there is grace in her motion, the fluid marvel of her movements I've seen so often on the stage, as she flits across the lawn, makes her dazzling pirouettes, flings out her arms, kicks up her legs.

But gradually the mood of the dance changes. It is no longer pure fluid grace, aesthetic agility, a moving demonstration of supreme artistry, but slowly, almost imperceptibly, it slides into defiance, challenge; it becomes more jarring, more raw, rude, angular, as if she were driven now by a kind of earthy rage. Now she is clearly *wanting* to shock me, to provoke me, to dare me, to anger me. Perhaps she wants to punish herself (but for what?), to drive herself to excesses she has never attempted before, as if to avenge some imaginary outrage by humiliating me, and herself. She becomes a creature possessed, a frightening, demonic thing that hurls itself into the shrubs and bushes, runs headlong into trees, stumbles and falls over rockeries and water features, trying more and more purposefully to hurt herself, to maim herself.

Caught in the terrible spell of it, I stare at her in horror and fascination. Until at one stage she runs into a murderous thorn bush and gets caught there, and tries to struggle free like some terrifying night bird with flapping wings, and falls to the ground. I can hear the breath tearing from her lungs, gasping and moaning. And that is what finally releases me from the evil spell. I jump up and hurry to her, and pick up the dead weight of her. She is sobbing now, and trying to fight me off – 'No, no, no, let me *go!*' – and kicking and flailing about. But I hold on. Just hold her, very tightly, until the raging sobs subside and she goes limp in my arms.

I carry her inside and lower her on to the thick carpet in the lounge with its forbiddingly formal middle-class Pretoria furniture. Here in the flat disillusionment of the light I can see that she is streaked with blood, all over her face and perfect body. Her long hair is matted, with burrs and thorns and twigs and moths and insects knotted into it. Her nose is bleeding. I find her frightening, hideous. And unbearably beautiful.

Leaving her there, spreadeagled and trembling on the Vandyke carpet, covered with a woven cloth I'd stripped from a table, I go in search of a bathroom, and fill the tub nearly to the brim. Then go to fetch her and slide her into the warm water. She moans. I kneel beside the bath. Wait until slowly her body relaxes and she stops shaking. At last I start washing her, with infinite care, trying to move the sponge as gently as possible over the deeper cuts and bruises. From her face, all the way to her feet. Washing and spongeing and daubing her shoulders and her tiny breasts with the lovely long pale nipples, her slender arms, each finger joint separately, bending her forward to reach the back with its muscles now relaxed and supple, and then the legs, the feet, the toes. And finally, at first almost too awed to touch, but with growing intent, her thighs, her sex like the imprint of a small antelope's elongated heart-shaped hoof in the dense dark undergrowth of her pubic hair.

At last I pick her up, and dry her, thoroughly but reverently, in a huge white towel from the rail; and then carry her through the house to a bedroom, where I lay her down on a big bed. She opens her eyes, and half smiles, and says, 'I'm glad you're here, Chris.'

And then I make love to her. Very slowly and carefully at first, taking an infinite time to caress and explore every part of her, first with my fingers, then my lips, then my tongue, leaving snail tracks of saliva all over her. More and more passionately as I feel her body responding. As my tongue probes between the complicated folds of her sex, she starts to make small whimpering sounds and they increase in intensity until the night is ringing with her love-calls. At some stage it is over, I don't remember when or how. I must have fallen asleep on her, still embedded — that word again — in her, in a state of near oblivion. But when I wake in the morning she has somehow shifted from under me and gone.

I discovered her in the kitchen, dressed in fresh clothes, making toast.

I swept away her hair to kiss her nape from behind; but when I tried to put my hands on her breasts she pulled away.

'No, Chris.'

Exactly like a hundred times before. I lowered my hands. Around her waist, under the thin plaid shirt, I could feel the knotted rope.

'Come on,' I said, teasingly. 'Don't pretend nothing happened.'

She looked round at me with a blank, lovely face. 'What do you mean?' she asked.

'Now come on, Daphne . . .'

But not once, neither that morning nor at any time during the few weeks our relationship still limped along to its now inevitable end, did she give the slightest intimation that she had an inkling of what had happened that night. The eyes she had fixed on me all the time I was inside her, wide open even in the moment of orgasm, were devoid of consciousness or conscience, a cloudless, birdless sky. To Daphne, that night had simply never happened. And with the passing of time I started wondering whether it could have been *my* imagination. Perhaps it had been the magic of the moon. But that was impossible. There were small crescents of bite marks on my body for days afterwards, a numbness in my tongue, luxurious little aches and stiffnesses all over my body. Surely I could not have imagined *that*?

When at last we parted. I had the feeling that I would never know her, had never known her.

WITH GEORGE LOMBARD it was as if I'd always known him, as if we'd been to school together – even though he was at least thirty-five years my junior. It was a month after that New Year's Eve when I'd met you. Since then it had become a daily routine to speak to you on the telephone, seldom for less than an hour. This time it was in the middle of January. All you wanted to say was, 'George is back.' Your voice suddenly different, full of joy. And then silence for almost a fortnight. Until you called to invite me over for a meal.

'Are you sure I won't intrude?' I asked cautiously.

'Of course not. George wants to spoil us, he's a great cook. Besides, he told me he's been a fan of yours for years. I believe he's read everything you've ever written.'

'Poor man.'

'So will you come?'

'If you really think so.'

'Yes, I do. I've missed you. And George can't wait.'

And so I returned to Camps Bay, where on New Year's Eve you had first found me, desperate and smudged with grease. The driveway to your house dips steeply into the paved entrance, which is really the back door, as the front overlooks the sea. It is an area of sprawling villas, ostentatious hanging gardens of the Babylonian kind, pretentious columns and wraparound balconies, of glass and marble and stainless steel and wrought iron. But your house surprised me, as on the first night, with its ordinariness. A small old-fashioned seaside home that had somehow been overlooked by the developers and the nouveaux riches, and sat in a tumult of greenery like a little old woman in a floppy hat doing her shopping among the lapdog ladies of Constantia. And inside (although that first time I had barely taken notice: I was too rapt in our endlessly unfurling conversation), the happy mess I would get to know so much better during the fifteen months that followed. Tables with books and dishes and CDs stacked on them, chairs in the most unlikely spots, a few curtains half taken down (or half hung?), paintings lined up on the floor along the walls. And your sculptures everywhere, some in resin or plaster, but most of them in clay, fired and unfired.

Even before I could knock, George came to the door with you. He seemed huge beside you (and when I first met you I thought you were tall!). His mop of greying blond hair was unkempt as if he'd been streaking his long fingers through it repeatedly; and his face wore an expression of permanent happy bemusement. He looked like a big, huggable bear. Next to him you seemed like a girl, your short dark-blonde curly hair as unruly as I remembered it. There was something easy and relaxed about both of you; from the way you moved and occa-sionally touched it was obvious that you were at ease within yourselves, your bodies comfortable and happy with each other. Yes, I felt a touch of jealousy. Whenever I'm faced with a disproportionate couple like that, no matter how I try to suppress the thought, I cannot help trying to visualise how they would make love. In this case, I may as well say it, I imagined you straddling him. Your long athletic legs; your head thrown back, the expression in your wide-set black-chocolate eyes, the light caressing your cheekbones, the line of your breasts. Stop it. For heaven's sake, stop it. You're supposed to be dead, I am in mourning. George is somewhere in the Middle East, taking photographs.

But that evening he was home, and the three of us were together. Except that the obvious closeness between your bodies, as he enfolded you protectively, lovingly, somehow set me apart.

Yet both of you are eager, without in any way appearing to be forcing it, to overcome the first strangeness. In spite of the gentleness of his appearance, his easy movements, his handshake is pleasantly firm; in fact, it makes me wince. Which turns him humorously apologetic. Soon we are all laughing and joking together. Almost immediately you slip back into the uncomplicated sharing of our New Year's Eve conver-sation; and from George's interventions it is clear that you have already told him all about it. Instead of making me feel slightly embarrassed, the openness with which you draw our first talk into this one, brings with it a feeling of generosity; we are really like old friends meeting again after a long absence. And once George starts talking about his recent photographic trips – the war zones of the Democratic Republic

of the Congo, Rwanda, which brought about his absence over New
Year; a new twist in the Pinochet saga in Chile; the state of Ground
Zero in New York; and on the way back the penis museum in Reykjavik
and the aurora borealis in Tromsø – the evening becomes a roller
coaster that carries us at constantly varying speed along its loops and
ups and dizzying downs. It is a repeat of that first night, only this time
there are three of us talking together, not two.

You are the one who tries to introduce some shape into the exhilarating confusion. 'We still have to eat, guys!' you call us to order.

'It's nearly done,' George reassures you. 'I'm going to the kitchen
in a minute.'

'What about the wine?' you ask. 'My throat is parched, and we have
a guest, remember.'

'He's not a guest,' says George. 'He's one of us.'

'He still needs wine. And so do I.'

'Pronto.' He opens the best of white wines. A Mulderbosch Sauvignon
Blanc. George raises his glass. But you quickly interrupt the ceremony.
'Wait,' you cry. 'This is a special moment. Let Chris taste it first and
tell you what he finds in it. You won't believe this, George.'

I try to protest, but you are not to be denied, and not wanting to
spoil your fun I do my bit, like a circus dog you are putting through
his hoops. (But then, you are doing the same with him, all evening.
And somehow we are both eager to perform; and you are of course
a superb ringmaster.)

After I've said my lines about 'a fresh fig-varietal fruit, green pepper
and gooseberry, combined with an earthy straw-like flavour', you
applaud spontaneously, and George joins in.

'Where did you learn all that?' he asks, clearly impressed.

'From many people over many years in many places.' I pause. 'But
it was my uncle Johnny who started it all. After that, I topped up on
experience in France – Burgundy, Bordeaux . . . It was a long haul.'
My thoughts wander back over the years as I tell you about that early
beginning. Yes, Uncle Johnny. Who must have been one of the first
South Africans to go to France to study oenology, in the early years
of the last century. When he came back after God knows how many
years to take over the family farm in the Franschhoek valley he acted

as guru to all the vintners in the area, at a time when hit-and-miss plonk was the staple drink. He became famous overnight. But then he married the wrong woman. Aunt Bella, Father's younger sister, beautiful to behold, but as staid and God-fearing as they come. Which in due course she tried her best to inculcate in all her daughters, no fewer than five of them.

My bewitching cousin Driekie told me how her mother had grimly warned them that until the day of his marriage a man should firmly be made to believe that a woman's legs were joined together from the knees up. It was on that never-to-be-forgotten Sunday afternoon in December of 1938, the year of the centenary of the Great Trek, in the fig tree at the bottom of Uncle Johnny's orchard, behind the house. When I assured Driekie that I already knew better, she smiled knowingly, and shrugged, and said, 'Oh well, then . . .' The grown-ups were all comatose following the gargantuan Sunday meal, so we had all the time in the world. And when we went home much later her legs, from her knees up, were streaked with the sticky juice of dark red Adam figs.

It nearly ended in catastrophe when her dour mother waylaid her in the kitchen and demanded to know what had happened. (I was following at a safe distance, ready to bolt.) But with all the wily innocence of her twelve years Driekie was a match for Aunt Bella. 'It's blood,' she said without batting an eyelid, and without realising what interpretation, at her precarious age, might be attached to it.

'Oh my God,' gasped Aunt Bella, not intending it as an exclamation but quite literally as a call for help to the Almighty. And turning to some of the other girls who were, as always, in the vicinity, she sobbed, 'Our Driekie has just become a woman in the fig tree.'

'I fell and got scratched by the branches,' Driekie tried to explain. 'I'm just lucky I didn't break anything. I think God sent an angel to save me.'

At that stage, I must confess, I had only a confused idea of the mysteries surrounding the female rites of passage; all I knew was that this was no time for me to be around. I didn't mean to leave Driekie to her fate, but right then there was nothing I could do or say without further complicating everything. I blurted out the first thing that came to my mind: 'I must take Uncle Johnny his coffee. He called me.'

Avoiding the throng of chattering girls who were falling over their own feet in their eagerness to escort Driekie to the bathroom I blindly poured some coffee – the pot was always simmering on the Dover stove – and scurried off to my uncle's secret chamber.

This requires some explanation. From the beginning of their marriage Aunt Bella had complained to Uncle Johnny that, much as she loved him, his involvement with the products of the vine was a source of profound concern to her and an abomination in the eyes of God. There was ample evidence on all the farms around them, she argued, of the iniquities and destruction flowing from the abuse of alcohol. But not, Uncle Johnny reminded her, from proper use. What about Jesus himself who had turned water into wine? This made her withdraw for a while; but she soon called upon a daunting new phalanx of biblical references to flatten him. Uncle Johnny, a man of humour and understanding, weathered the storm. When it came to matters of the flesh, he'd already, in a manner of speaking, made some headway. ('Look what happens to women joined from the knees up,' he is reported to have told her once. 'You have five daughters to show for it.') But he hadn't counted on Aunt Bella's perseverance or the power of her convictions where vines and wine were concerned. In the fullness of time her onslaught acquired a momentum that was irresistible. When my valiant uncle tried to use the cultural argument about the noble state of the civilisation of France, where he had been taught his skills, she withered him with a tirade about all the naked women, let alone those evil French kings, a heathen lot, Catholics all, and an insult to the name of God. He turned a slightly paler shade of white, but still stood fast. Wine was his passion, he proclaimed; he'd spent years of his life, and most of his father's savings, on preparing himself for his vocation, and he'd be damned if he were to give it all up now. But Auntie Bella persisted as only she could. She knew how to wear him down, ignoring even his shrewd quotes from the Bible to counter her tireless campaign (*A continual dropping in a very rainy day and a contentious woman are alike* . . .). And in the end there was no way out. He had to have all those hectares upon hectares of vineyard uprooted, every last stump. That the grapes could still be delivered to the table market carried no weight with her. Even the metonymy of evil had to be avoided.

That was when he moved out of the conjugal bedroom and withdrew to the little room which used to be his study and where he slept on a single bed for the rest of his natural life, which was a hell of a long time; and hardly ever spoke a word to man or beast again. To ward off Aunt Bella's predictable campaign of criticism and interrogation, he told her that he had resolved to immerse himself in the study of the Bible. When she reminded him of his responsibilities to his family, he quoted the wisdom of Solomon to her: 'It is better to dwell in a corner of the housetop, than with a brawling woman in a wide house.' That shut her up.

Only on rare occasions did he ever leave the little room again, for the odd mysterious trip to Cape Town, once every month or two. 'To see a man of God,' he laconically explained whenever he was asked about it; and that was enough to keep Aunt Bella happy. In fact, she seemed to draw a morbid inspiration from his silence. (He was 'in a struggle', she happily explained to the rest of the world. 'He is communing with God.') She stomped through the house singing hymns without stop; she took over the farm, replaced the lost vineyards, all those fallow fields of sin, with orchards of peach and apple and quince trees, and made them unbelievably rich.

What she never knew was that on those secret outings to Cape Town he would fill the boot of his massive old Chevrolet with bottles of the best wine he could find, mostly French, which he would smuggle from the securely locked and bolted garage into his little room at night, where he could taste them in peace.

This was how I found him on that memorable day while Aunt Bella and her daughters, in a state of collective hysteria, were arguing about female blood, the curse of womanhood, and the will of God the Father. Uncle Johnny was drinking from an exquisite crystal glass. He hadn't thought of locking the door as everyone knew it was his sanctum and no one (except on the rarest of occasions, after God had personally spoken to her, Aunt Bella) would ever dare to go in there. I had no idea of what to expect. For all I knew this might be a worse option than facing the female fury in kitchen or bathroom.

In total silence we stared at each other. It was the first time in years that I had seen him: I must have been six or seven when he went into seclusion; I was thirteen now.

Then, to my utter surprise, a smile flickered across his pale face. 'So,' he said. 'And who are you?'

'Ch-Chris,' I stuttered, ready to turn on my heel and flee.

'You're Hendrik's son, are you?'

I nodded, spilling some coffee into the saucer.

'Your father chose himself a handsome woman.'

I didn't know what to say to that.

'What brings you here?' he resumed.

'It's . . . well, you see, Driekie and I . . . I mean, in the big fig tree there at the back . . . we didn't *do* anything, really . . . it's just . . .' And then I gave up. 'Oh shit,' I said.

'I'm absolutely sure you didn't do anything,' he said, still smiling. 'Shall we celebrate?'

'Celebrate?'

'There's always something to celebrate,' he said jovially. 'Today we shall celebrate whatever you didn't do in the fig tree.' Very slowly he drained the glass, held it up, filled it halfway, then offered it to me.

I hesitated, gulped, then took the glass and swallowed it all, still in a state of shock.

'No, no, no,' said Uncle Johnny. 'That's not the way to do it at all. Allow me.'

He showed me how to hold the glass, how to sniff at the rim, to tilt and lightly twirl it, to sniff again, and then to taste with almost religious devotion. I learned about the mystery of the *caudalie* produced in the mouth within exactly thirty-six seconds of tasting a good wine.

But my tongue was blunt and stupid. What I do remember is the patience with which he persisted.

At one stage I said in despair, 'I don't know *how*!'

Out of the blue he asked, 'Out there in the fig tree, did you get a taste of Driekie?'

My face was burning. I couldn't get a word out.

'Uncle Johnny . . . ?'

'I just want to know if you got a taste of Driekie. Can you remember what she tasted like?'

By this time my whole body was on fire. 'Like . . . like sherbet, Uncle Johnny.'

He frowned, then broke into laughter. 'That's a beginning, I suppose. But I can see we still have a long way to go.'

'Yes, Uncle Johnny. I'm sorry, Uncle Johnny.'

'Listen to me, Chris. What I'm trying to teach you is for your whole life. Do you understand?'

'No, Uncle Johnny.'

'A man who cannot taste his wine properly, will never understand a thing about women. Will you remember that?'

'Yes, Uncle Johnny.'

'Right, let us try again.'

Exactly what I tasted on that first afternoon, I really cannot tell today. I had no idea at all what to look for. Uncle Johnny kept mumbling about gooseberries or guavas or straw or, yes, figs, ripe and green.

At the end of our long session he said, 'All right. Enough for one day. Come back tomorrow.' During the rest of our visit I was invited to his hideout every day, and my education in tasting slowly went its way.

The idea was that my course was to be resumed the following summer. But such a long interval was most unsatisfactory. Later, by the time I went to study at Stellenbosch, and during the five years I spent there, he regularly summoned me for weekends and holidays. Aunt Bella came to dislike me thoroughly. Whether she mistrusted the nature of our clandestine dealings, or perhaps still nursed a lingering suspicion about what had or hadn't happened between Driekie and me on the day of the blood, I could never be sure. The problem was that she couldn't very well confront me openly about the nature of my arcane dealings with Uncle Johnny. (Certainly, however exuberant and thorough my initiation may have been, he took great care never to make me drunk.) Oh, she did her best to waylay me whenever I approached the study or came from it, offering whatever bribery she could think of to find out the subjects of our discussion. But I just told her cryptically that we were doing Bible study. I'm not sure that even she always believed it. But in the end she was given no choice. And at least she had the grace to know when she was defeated. She withdrew, with God in tow (He, too, obviously knew when to desist); and as time went by, I had the satisfaction of knowing that I had brought a little ray of light to the darkness into which Uncle Johnny had been banished; while he, in turn, took pleasure in opening a worthwhile new corner of the world to me.

By the time I reach the end of my story we are ready to start on George's main course, a delectable seafood dish of prawns, mussels, and an astounding variety of subtly interacting fish textures and flavours, for which a new bottle is opened, tasted, commented upon (George is hilarious in inventing bouquets and aromas no *tastevin* has ever dreamed up) and consumed. And with the dessert, clean and slightly tart on the tongue, there is a Vin de Constance, many years old and probably as good as anything exported in the early nineteenth century to please the palates of Napoleon in exile, Jane Austen at her not-so-private escritoire and, later, Baudelaire amid the flowers of evil.

'I once took a photo of Driekie,' George announces unexpectedly.

We stare at him in surprise.

He smiles. 'Well, perhaps not *your* Driekie,' he says. 'But a little girl in a tree, peering through the leaves. Terribly sentimental, I'm afraid – it was in my early years – but we all go through our phases.'

'Some of us never get past them,' I assure him. 'At least, that is what people tend to say about me.'

'My little girl looked like Lewis Carroll's photos of his Alice, dressed up as a beggar waif. Wait, I think I can find it.' And off he goes to what I presume must be his studio.

'He must have millions of photos,' I comment to you. 'He cannot possibly find the one he's looking for.'

'George has a great system,' you smile, with obvious pride. 'And it's all on computer now.'

'When did he find time for that?'

'That was my contribution,' you admit. 'Took me the better part of our marriage. Which is four years old today.'

'You never told me.'

'It was meant as a private celebration. But too good an opportunity to pass by, don't you agree?'

'Then I'm deeply honoured. By both of you.'

You raise your glass; the dessert wine gleams a deep amber against the light. 'Let's drink to many more.'

George comes back as we clink. He gives us a quizzical look.

'We're drinking to your marriage,' I explain. 'And lots of children.' A cloud briefly passes over his large face. 'No such luck,' he says. There is a momentary uneasy silence. Then he laughs, seemingly care-free, and makes a cutting gesture with the edge of one hand across his crotch. 'Unfortunately, I took some too exaggerated precautions against the hazards of my job. Quite a few years before I met this one.'

'Now, George,' you gently reprimand him. It could have been a quite embarrassing moment. But somehow you manage to turn it into a subject of banter, and soon only the merest shadow remains in the background of the conversation.

He puts a photo on the table in front of me, obviously a printout he has just made. 'Isn't this Driekie?' he asks, beaming.

The girl looks very different, but the atmosphere is perfect: the strong contrast of light and shadow in the abundant foliage, the sugges-tion of depth behind the leaves, and the small figure huddling in the shadows, only one naked shoulder and half of her face visible, staring straight into the lens, impish and challenging, yet strangely grave for such a small child. As if in that fleeting instant from a childhood now for ever lost she already possesses all the consciousness of woman-hood, of its suffering and its silences, its fears and uncertainties, its unabashed affirmations and exultations. Little Alice indeed.

'You have a wonderful way of using the light,' I say.

'Any photographer can use light,' he replies with a grin. 'What I am trying to do is to *provoke* the light.'

'You also provoke the spectator.'

'If I couldn't do that I should put away my cameras.'

'Does this photo have a title?' I ask, almost reverently.

'*Eve*. What else?' And then, in his characteristic way, he bursts out laughing. 'Only seconds after taking it I lost my balance – I was sitting on a branch right opposite – and fell like a rotten apple. Which I prob-ably was. And broke my leg. And very nearly my camera too. A leg can be mended but a Leica cannot be replaced. I tell you, photography is a hazardous business.'

'I gather you always head for the hot spots – war, disaster, God knows what?'

'Like you in your books?'

'Touché,' I admit. 'But isn't that inevitable? Somehow the dark things reveal more about us. The light is less interesting. Even your little Eve lurks in the shadows.'

'Ah, but only the light can *discover* her.'

'*You* are a creature of light,' you say, placing your hand adoringly on his. The contrast etches itself into my mind: yours so slim, the line of the fingers clean and strong, as if they can register the lightest vibration; his large and broad and powerful, the fingers stubby and thick. (Yes, I can imagine those fingers . . .)

'But you do go in search of the dark and terrible places,' I persist.

'Only because it is necessary for *someone* to report: I was there, I saw it, it happened. The tree falling in the forest and all that. The unrecorded life.'

'Do people pay attention?'

'That is *their* responsibility. Mine is to make sure it is recorded. Otherwise it is just too easy for people to say they didn't know.'

And from there the conversation meanders across some of the most dramatic experiences of his career.

'I think the toughest moment of all was in the late eighties,' he says, smiling with boyish pleasure at the recollection. 'I was on the way back from a funeral in Soweto. In those days . . .' He shakes his head. 'In Orlando I stopped for a moment to reload my camera. And suddenly my car was surrounded by a crowd of demonstrators on their way from a gathering. I only found out later that they'd been attacked by police less than half an hour before. Several youths had been killed. And they were in a foul mood. Blocked me in from all sides and started rocking the car. It felt like a ship tossed on a bloody stormy sea. I saw some of them bending down to pick up stones. This is it, I thought. I'm not going to get out of this place alive.'

'Then what happened?' I ask.

You are staring at him in admiration; you've obviously heard this story before.

'I had one secret weapon,' he beams. 'I was never without it. Always in my breast pocket. So I rolled down my window and took this photo out and flashed it at them.'

'What was it?'

'A shot taken by a colleague, of Winnie Mandela and me. Her arm round my shoulders. And she'd inscribed it. *To George Lombard, with fond wishes, Winnie.*'

'That did it?'

'You bet. It was like the Israelites marching through the Red Sea. And the rage turned into jubilation. I waved my clenched fist at them, and shouted, *Amandla!* And off I went at speed.' He becomes reflective for a moment. 'Ja, in those days . . . There was only one person in the world who could have saved me that day, and that was Mama Winnie. Her name was magic.'

'And today . . .'

Briefly, he becomes deadly serious. 'How sad. How terribly, terribly sad. All those years while Madiba was in jail, she was the one who carried the flag.'

There is a silence. Then you say, 'And then she had to learn to walk in the shadow of a man.' Another pause. You add, 'It's always the women, isn't it?'

'*You* don't seem to be suffering too badly,' I gently mock.

'Ah, but George and I walk together,' you reply. 'I'm not carefully stepping in his footsteps.'

'You seem loving and caring enough,' I insist.

'Surely love and care are not ruled out!' you say sharply, leaning your head against George's shoulder that looms like a comfortable and comforting mountain beside you.

George gives you a laborious hug; I wince as I think of bones crunching. 'Never underestimate this one,' he warns me, winking. 'You know, she was the one who asked *me* to marry her.'

'Only because you would never have made up your mind,' you tease.

'My mind was made up long before you asked me,' he protests. 'I was thinking about *you*. I'm still not convinced you knew what you were letting yourself in for.'

'You're having regrets now?'

'I'm just not sure about your sanity. Everything else is okay.'

'Perhaps two mad persons make one sane one.' You take one of his hands in both of yours. 'Shall I tell Chris why you held back for so long?'

'No.'

'Right, then I will.'

'You may invite retaliation as soon as I'm alone with you again.'

'I'll hold you to it,' you promise. And then proceed to tell me about his first marriage, which lasted for seven years. ('So we're not out of the danger zone yet, you see.') His wife, Louisa, used to be his dark-room assistant, taking over more and more of his administrative duties and responsibilities. But above all she insisted on accompanying him on his trips. 'We're a team,' she would say whenever he tried to object. 'You need me, I need you, right? So stop complaining.' Then, one January, came their final, fatal mission, to a region in Mozambique ravaged by freak floods. George didn't give personal safety any thought; when he was working, his only concern was the photographs he had to bring back. On that particular afternoon a whole village was swept away by the churning flood. He paid no heed to the warnings of police and safety personnel, venturing to the very edge of the raging waters. Four or five members of a family, most of them small children, came past, swept along on an uprooted tree stump in the orange-brown torrent. George was transfixed by what he could see in the viewfinder of his Leica. Louisa became hysterical. 'You can't just stand there taking photos!' she screamed at him. 'Those are *people*! We've got to help them.'

'There's a whole cordon of police just a hundred metres down-stream,' he shouted back. 'They're equipped to help. We'll just kill both them and us in the process.'

But she was beyond reasoning. By the time he realised what was happening, she had already thrown herself into the flood, trying to swim to the family on the tree stump in the swirling waters. Without stopping to take off his boots or anything he rushed in after her. At the next bend in the river, as he'd told her, there was a team of helpers tied to ropes, ready to help. All but one of the members of the embat-tled family were brought to safety. So was George. But Louisa had gone under. They could only presume that her head had hit against a log, or a submerged rock. Her body was never found.

'For more than a year after that he didn't take a single photo,' you tell me quietly.

He merely looks at me, with such pain in his eyes that I have to turn my head away.

'Until I realised that my duty to bear witness was more important than my own grief,' he says at last. 'Certainly more important than silence.'

'And that is why, to this day, he doesn't want me to go along when he goes on a shoot,' you say.

'Can you blame me?' he asks.

'Nobody ever blames you for anything, George.'

'Perhaps that is the problem,' he says wryly.

And after that? I'm no longer sure about what came next. (After I went home that night, I stayed up, listening to music, making notes, as is my wont, about our whole conversation. I need to hold on. My safety rope, I suppose, in the swirling waters of my own life.) I know we had more to drink. Cognac, I seem to recall; but perhaps we returned to wine. And then, presumably apropos of some turn in the conversation, he wanted to listen to *Don Giovanni*. Wasn't it too late? you asked cautiously. Wouldn't that be asking too much of your guest?

'*Don Giovanni* isn't asking too much of anybody. Chris, of all people, should know that.' (Whatever that might mean.)

And so we listen to *Don Giovanni,* all two hours of it – after a long argument about which recording to choose. (He has at least five of them.) In the end it is the Colin Davis, with Kiri Te Kanawa – though George has reservations about Martina Arroyo's Donna Anna. 'That's the problem with *Don Giovanni*,' he argues. 'In an opera with so many plum parts, you're bound to be dissatisfied with one or two. But Kiri's Donna Elvira will do it for tonight.' (Let me state for the record that I did not agree with George about Arroyo: especially in the final scene, she is sublime.)

We listen with rapt attention. But at Leporello's aria listing his master's conquests – six hundred and forty in Italy, two hundred and thirty-one in Germany, a hundred in France, and already a thousand and three in Spain; including country wenches, maids-in-waiting, city girls, countesses, baronesses, marchionesses, princesses – you cannot help interrupting.

'Poor man!' you comment. 'I'm beginning to feel sorry for him.'

'That's fatal,' I assure you. 'The moment a man succeeds in making a woman feel sorry for him, she is lost.'

'There's nothing pitiful about Don Giovanni,' protests George. 'Don't let the music seduce you either. Surely, what needs to be cleared up is *why* he has become such a compulsive seducer.'

'Because he's lonely,' you answer without hesitation. 'And that's why I feel sorry for him.'

'Anyone can play the lonely card,' I object.

'Then what do *you* think drives him?'

'I don't think it's always the same thing,' I argue. 'In his youth I'd say it is the urge to make a statement: *I am here*. The need for affirmation. But as he approaches middle age, who knows, it may simply be the need to be reassured. About his waning powers. About himself.'

'Isn't it pure arrogance?' George challenges me. 'Too much self-assurance, rather than too little?'

'For me, there's a kind of absurd courage about Don Giovanni,' I maintain. 'He might have been one of Camus' heroes. And Mozart understood it perfectly.'

'Not Mozart,' you remind me. 'The librettist, da Ponte.'

'No, listen to the music. The libretto is just the story of Don Giovanni's loves. It's the music that looks into the heart of the man behind the loves.'

George shakes his head. He is still smiling, but his eyes are deadly serious. 'I don't think *Don Giovanni* is about love at all. It's about freedom.'

'Now you're sidestepping the issue,' I say.

'Just wait,' he says. 'We're getting there.' And he makes us wait for the last scene of Act One, when the Don's house is invaded by the revelling peasants from outside. Then he says, 'Why would they all suddenly break into song about *viva la libertà*?' he asks. 'To me, this is the key to the whole opera. And if you listen carefully, you'll hear how Mozart anticipates this music through scene after scene that leads up to it. And how he keeps on reminding us of it until the very end.'

'At the bitter end Don Giovanni goes to hell,' you interrupt him. 'Not much freedom in that, is there?'

'Except if you see the Don's freedom in the very fact that he has the *choice* to go to hell, and freely chooses it. In which he finally affirms his nobility in opposition to poor Leporello whose only choice is to find a new master.'

'But surely you cannot exclude love from the story!' I exclaim.

'Of course not. But for Mozart love is only the litmus test. To determine whether one is truly free or not.'

'Must it really end in hell?' you ask. 'That's a terribly dark way of looking at love.'

'Quite. But don't you think there *is* a terrible darkness about love?' asks George.

'I thought you were the one who argued for light earlier in the evening,' I joke.

It is his turn to say, 'Touché.' But then he adds, 'Perhaps in the end there is not all that much difference between light and darkness. The problem lies in our way of seeing. As Rachel has suggested.'

About so much of our conversation that night I had occasion to think back on later, much later. Not least, two days ago when I stood looking down at your face pale in death.

It was almost three o'clock before I left your house; and on the dark way home it all continued to whirl about in my mind. I needed time to sort it out. And when I got home, I went to my study and took out my recording – the Riccardo Muti – and played right through *Don Giovanni* once again as I made my notes. I was no closer to a solution for the turbulence in my thoughts. All I knew, and *that* at least came to me like an illumination, was that I had gone to Camps Bay to visit a woman with whom I had fallen in love on New Year's Eve; but that when I came home I left behind two very dear friends.

No. This won't work. It avoids the real issues. Listening again to *Don Giovanni* in my home after coming back from you and George (as I am listening to it once more as a background to these notes), I returned to our conversation, and realised that what we had discussed, the words we'd used, had little to do with the real conversation taking place *behind* the talk. Perhaps we ourselves had not sensed clearly what that 'real' conversation had been about. But if I honestly wasn't sure then, I want to know *now*. Evasion will no longer do, now that you are dead.

What I believe I was thinking was this: that on New Year's Eve I had been moved so profoundly by something in you that I'd left with a feeling that, yes, I could fall in love with you. Nothing final or definitive, but it was a distinct possibility. A feeling in my spine, or in what the more vulgar among the romantics might call my 'heart'. I knew you were married – you'd spoken such a lot about George – yet as a person, as an entity, he had seemed unreal, absent. I have not had too many scruples about love in my life; yet in my dealings with women I have always tried as much as possible to avoid married women. (Not necessarily a decision on moral grounds. But on the purely practical level, think of it: if a woman has a big husband, he may beat you to a pulp; if the man is on the small side, he may shoot you – neither of which particularly appeals to me.) However, on that first New Year's Eve, in the eagerness and newness of the discovery, which I felt was mutual, George never seemed wholly real to me, and so I was beginning to prepare myself for possibly making an exception. It is, after all, the privilege of age to find exceptions to most rules; and for all I knew this might be my last chance.

But now I had met George. And found in him – what? – more than just a friend. Would it sound too melodramatic to say 'a brother'? The brother I would have had if my mother hadn't lost her first child whom she had told me about, not so much nostalgically as reproachfully, so often throughout my childhood. Someone close and intimate I know I've always missed. *You* had recognised the loneliness in me; thank you for that. (Why else would you have diagnosed Don Giovanni the way you had?) Now, suddenly, there he was. My lost older brother, almost forty years younger than myself. Weirder things can happen. And thinking of him as someone so close, drew you into the equation as well. I could no longer think of you simply as *you*, as Rachel Lombard. (The very fact that you bore his surname, now marked you as part of him, and him as part of you.) You were no longer imaginable without George. Which made you no longer a potential lover, but a friend; my brother's closest ally. Suddenly love was no longer an option. (At least not without the taboo of incest. But I'm not sure I was, as yet, conscious of that.) For the moment you were a dear and lovely friend, part of the new couple in my life, Rachel-and-George. Does that make sense?

THERE WAS, ON my way home from your house that New Year's morning, a disturbing memory suddenly rising up inside me like a bubble from some submarine plant. How could I have forgotten about it? Now, after all these years, it returned, unsettlingly. I was back in the famous tree of knowledge at the bottom of Uncle Johnny's orchard, that Sunday afternoon. And Driekie was telling me of her mother's sermonising about a girl's legs being joined from knee to hip. But there was something else too, and that was the part I had forgotten.

Some time before we had arrived on the farm in that distant December of 1938, she and her four sisters had gone for a walk to the farm dam one afternoon. They were alone, it was fiercely hot, and on a wild impulse, as they reached the farm dam, they'd stripped off their clothes before plunging into the muddy water, wonderfully cold below the warm surface on that blistering day. There was nothing unusual about that. But when they stepped out of the water again and went to lie on the steep bank to dry their bodies in the sun, she heard a rustling in the bushes nearby, and when she went to investigate, a young coloured boy – about my age, she said – the son of one of the labourers, came scuttling from the undergrowth and fled like a hare towards the labourers' little hovels. She recognised him, his name was David.

They were annoyed at being spied upon, but it was not really anything to be unduly upset about. Boys are boys. ('If it were you,' she told me in the tree, shuffling and blushing, 'I wouldn't have told anybody.') But that evening at supper they couldn't stop giggling and fidgeting, and when Aunt Bella demanded to know the reason, Driekie was finally persuaded to tell her.

Their mother flew into a worse rage than anything they had ever witnessed before. 'A *Hotnot!*' she exclaimed in horror. 'Spying on *my* daughters! You could all have been raped.'

'He ran away the moment I saw him, Ma,' she tried to explain. 'And we all know him. He's always fetching and carrying for us. And sometimes we even help him in the kitchen with his school work. He's actually quite clever. And very polite.'

'A *Hotnot!*' was all she kept saying. Like one of their old 78 records with the needle stuck in a groove.

Immediately after supper she marched to Uncle Johnny's inner sanctum to inform him of the outrage. All the girls remained huddled on the doorstep behind her in trepidation, expecting some kind of apocalyptic eruption. But Uncle Johnny remained lying quietly on his back, his eyes staring at the ceiling.

Perhaps that, more than anything else, caused her to explode.

It was midsummer; it was still light outside. Aunt Bella slammed the study door behind her, summoned her daughters to follow her, and strode out of the house, down the slope of the hill from where they overlooked the whole glorious valley, to the row of dilapidated labourers' shacks.

From the yard, where a few mangy dogs glowered at them and some late chickens were still scratching among the discarded parts of an old broken-down wagon, Aunt Bella shouted at David's parents to come out. They were briefly, and rather incoherently, informed of what had taken place. In the meantime a small throng of other labourers, in worn overalls or hand-me-downs (at least Christmas was near, when they would all be given their annual set of new clothes), had gathered at a safe distance to find out what the commotion was about. Once again the tale of horror was repeated, gathering size and momentum with every retelling.

In the end little David was dragged from the house where, expecting the worst, he had been hiding under a bed (an unmistakable sign of guilt). His father and two of the other men were ordered to bring him to the barn where apricots and early figs and peaches were drying in their large wooden trays. Aunt Bella ordered the girls inside, to take up position against the wall. An old wine-barrel was hauled from a distant corner and rolled to within a few feet of the girls as they gazed in horrified fascination. And then David was dragged inside. Aunt Bella, who seemed to be possessed by now of some evil force beyond her own control, gave a series of brief orders. Her voice came in short barks, and she was breathing deeply. David's clothes were torn from him, his wrists and ankles were tied with thongs hanging from a hook in the corner, and he was drawn spreadeagled over the barrel. Tears and snot were streaming from him.

And then the three men, the father and his two helpers, were ordered to flog him. Two of them had lengths of hosepipe, the third a halter.

At this point of her story, that Sunday afternoon in the tree, Driekie couldn't go on. She just shook her head. By now her own face was streaked with tears.

'It just went on and on, it didn't stop. In the beginning David screamed at every blow, but later he just whimpered, he had no voice any more. It wasn't like crying, it was like an animal. And still they went on and on and on.

'And then, sometime, I heard myself shouting, I wasn't even sure it was me, but I think it was. "You're killing him!" And then they stopped. It was as if they'd forgotten what they were doing, or why. Then Ma said something to the men and they went out and brought a pail of water and threw it over David and he started making sounds again. By that time it was dark outside. But the barn was locked up for the night and David was left there until morning. And then my ma told him to wash up the blood.'

This, as I seem to recall it now, was what had, in its inscrutable and terrible way, inspired Driekie and me to do what we did. I still don't want to think of it. But now, I know, I won't ever forget it again. What upsets me is that I'm not sure of what it says about Aunt Bella. Or about Driekie. Or, perhaps more disturbingly, about me.

MY NIGHTS, LATELY, are often shaped like doughnuts, with a hole in the middle. Usually I simply remain lying in bed, largely at peace with myself and the world, until I drift off again. Or I put on a CD and listen to music. Or, if sleep really seems out of reach, I turn on the light and read for an hour or two. But over the last few nights there is a new diversion: the war in Iraq. It steadies the nerves and calms the senses. The soporific effect is guaranteed, because it is all so very far away, and endlessly repetitive, and much less real than a war movie. The Iraqis have now begun to show dead or captured enemy soldiers. Saddam is reported to have left Baghdad in an ambulance. Which remains, in every sense of the word, to be seen. In Nasiriyah there has been heavy fighting, quite spectacular; but Mr Bush or his many advisers could take a leaf from the book of the people who organise Bastille Day fireworks in Paris.

A little over a month ago there was the depressing symbolic moment when General Colin Powell stood up at the Security Council to declare war on Iraq. Behind the podium the huge tapestry of Picasso's *Guernica* had, inexplicably, been covered with a blue cloth. It was as if history itself was hiding its face in shame. And now we are watching the consequence.

This war comes with so much baggage on both sides, so many lies told, so many atrocities committed, so many strings attached, that nothing can be clear any more. All is suspect. It is itself an atrocity and an act of terrorism, the latest chapter of the West's interminable crusades against the Saracens. (And one cannot but remember that already in the Middle Ages Arab historians referred to the Crusaders as barbarians, who knew nothing of medicine, culture or civilisation.)

So many reasons have been advanced for this enterprise. But ultimately it is war for the sake of war. A no-strings war, as one sometimes — too rarely? — encounters the no-strings fuck.

THE NO-STRINGS fuck. A consummation devoutly to be wish'd. But realistically attainable? I'm not too concerned, in these notes, about finding reasons for links or sequences: why this, now, and not something else? But perhaps it is Melanie who comes back to me now because of a need to return, from the complications of the present, to a moment that seems totally straightforward and unambiguous and simple. But how trustworthy is the recollection?

I met her shortly before my marriage to Helena. They were best friends, Helena an assistant to an architect, Melanie an actress. Helena was the quiet one, intense, private, devoted. Exactly what I needed at the time, I believed. It was in the mid-sixties, not too long after my spell with Daphne, and back in Cape Town I was doing a fair amount of work for the theatre; I had made my first splash as a writer and was basking in the publicity, but wanted to get back into a more secluded existence and Helena provided the shelter and security I craved. Melanie was the wild one, the flamboyant and unpredictable one, the bohemian. When I met her there was electricity in the air. The sexual tension must have been obvious to all but Helena — which makes me wonder: how well did I really understand Helena? But it was a month before the wedding. (How we finally decided to get married is another story.) Helena and I spent a weekend at Umhlanga Rocks with Melanie and her current boyfriend: she used to go through men as if she were trying on clothes in a shop, without even bothering to retire to a cubicle or draw a curtain.

This one was a total mismatch, a very beautiful but shy young man (I cannot even remember his name) who seemed to spend all his time drawing. Inevitably, he and Helena turned out to be wholly in sync, as they say, and spent most of the time together comparing patterns and designs and textures. On the last evening the four of us went for a walk along the sea. There was a heavy fog through which, from time to time, the moon briefly showed itself in an impossibly romantic, silvery light shimmering like ectoplasm. No one spoke. Helena and I were holding hands; so were Melanie and her young man. But she and I were in the middle and from time to time as we walked our hands would touch or her hip would briefly press against mine as she moved her legs. Entirely by accident, of course. I had such an erection that it was difficult to walk, but everything was mercifully obscured by the night. After we got back to the beach flat we had rented, Helena and the boyfriend huddled together at the dining table over a set of drawings. I was not in a mood for socialising, preoccupied as I was with a new novel, and emotionally perturbed by Melanie's proximity. Her physical closeness during the walk, the memory of her lovemaking with the boyfriend the night before: long low moans and whimpers coming through the thin wall that separated their room from ours, and gradually increasing to a scream of ecstasy ringing and ringing in the night like a siren. (It had charged me up unbearably; but it totally switched off Helena. And after she had fallen asleep I had to masturbate on my side of the bed to calm myself down. By which time Melanie was starting again next door. What had her young man done to deserve such largesse?)

With these memories still a turmoil in my mind, as Helena and the artist huddled over the drawings on the dining table in their pool of light, I went outside and found a secluded spot among the rocks where I could nurse my desire and try to tame my thoughts. Occasionally the spray from a crashing wave would break exhilaratingly right over me. And suddenly Melanie was there beside me. We didn't say anything, we removed only the most obstructive bits of clothing and went for each other like two cats. But even before I could enter her we heard Helena calling from behind through the silver fog.

'Let's just hide here, no one will find us,' Melanie gasped in my ear.

But the call was repeated, this time from much closer. And as if in response to an executioner summoning us to the block, I called back, 'We're here at the rocks. Come and join us.'

The three of us sat there for another while; then the boyfriend, too, approached through the dark. And soon we all returned home, much subdued, for a couple of nightcaps and bed. Within minutes the sounds next door began again. This time, curiously, Helena was the one who responded with rare passion; and I had a hard time trying to concentrate.

A month later we were duly married and were, I suppose, happy. Once or twice during the following years the women exchanged letters, promising to set up a meeting, and then it petered out. It must have been six months or so after the accident in which I lost both Helena and little Pieter – something which even after all these years I am reluctant to return to – and was leading an unusually monastic life of contrition and penance, when a letter came from Melanie. She had been married twice, and twice divorced, in the interim; she'd heard about the accident and offered her condolences. She was wondering how I was doing. I could detect no hidden subtext to the letter, and of course after those five years everything might well have dissipated. But on an impulse I dashed off a telegram: *We have unfinished business.*

I was placing everything on the line.

She replied the next day: *When do you want me?*

Who was I to say no? I telephoned. Trunk calls still had to be booked in advance, and it took an hour and a half to get through, on a very bad line. But the key words were audible enough, and on the Friday morning I went to fetch her at the airport.

With the exception of my period in Paris, it was the most concentrated bout of fucking in my life. Just as well we had only a long weekend; any longer, and you could have hung me over the washing line to dry. Still, I do think I lived up to her expectations; these days I couldn't possibly have lasted the course. We drove to deserted beaches and made love; we drove into the mountains and made love; we followed the overgrown courses of rivers and made love in thickets or clearings; we wined and dined in restaurants and fondled; in between we dashed home and made love.

And that was the pure joy of it: that neither had come with any hidden expectations, but purely to drain the cup of love to the dregs and then to pour another. And another. It couldn't go on for much longer, the body can do only so much before it reaches – at least temporarily – the limits of its resources and possibilities. I was aching for a week after that, barely able to move; and then began to wish for more. And so did Melanie. We made telephone calls to and fro, and promised each other repeats and encores but we never did. One should not try to improve on perfection.

But was that the real reason? I tried to persuade myself of it at the time. Now, with the unclouded vision of my old age, I know there was something else. Something which suddenly, without any warning, on our last day together, came to the surface. Just for a moment, but that was enough to make me wonder with a pang far beyond the delightful sufferings of the body, whether in the ultimate analysis the no-strings fuck is possible.

We had driven to Kleinmond in the morning. She was to catch her plane in the early evening. It was still a nearly deserted place in those days; there were long stretches of white sandy beach on which one could walk naked for hours without encountering a soul. And we did just that. From time to time we would simply sink down on a towel and make love, then go on, then make another stop. Once we fell asleep, totally spent, on the firm sand. The tide was out. When we came to again, it was from the water lapping at our feet. I woke up first, and impulsively, like a puppy driven by instinct to find its mother's teat, returned to the over-and-over explored yet still secret depths of her to probe the flanges and folds of her sex. And then I slid my body over hers, and into hers, and we rose together like the tide. It came washing right over us, half drowning us, as we came together.

We walked back hand in hand, still naked, at the lace-edge of the tide. The salt water stung sharply where our passion had bruised and chafed and broken our skins and mucous membranes. But there was something ecstatic about it, a new awareness of our bodies, as if they had been newly shaped by love, by exquisite pain.

We didn't speak. I felt no need for it, I was so completely sated. But once, when we stopped briefly to look out across the sea, I saw that she was crying.

'What's the matter?' I asked with a sharp intake of my breath.

She just shook her head and tried to turn away.

'Tell me,' I said, feeling an unfamiliar distress rising in me; confronted unexpectedly by a whole wide landscape within her of which I had no understanding, not even an inkling.

'Melanie?'

Again she shook her head, and withdrew her hand from mine, and started walking on alone. I could see her shoulders shaking.

'Melanie!' I called after her, trying to catch up. 'Please tell me. Talk to me.'

She kept ahead of me. After a long time a sprinkling of houses came into sight again and we stopped to put on our clothes. Suddenly, dressed, we felt shy and couldn't look each other in the face. I made to speak, but she quietly lifted a finger and pressed it against my lips. She was no longer crying.

By the time we got back to the car she was very composed. But we still had nothing to say. And when that evening we said goodbye at the airport, our kiss was brief and almost perfunctory.

In our telephone conversations, even as we tried with a kind of desperation to rekindle from the cold embers a little flame that had died, neither of us ever spoke of that moment again. In due course the phone calls came to an end. We never broke up, we just did not go on.

IT IS TIME to return to you. I have been avoiding the memory of that first meeting on New Year's Eve. Not that there is anything to be scared or diffident about in the memory itself. It is not even a matter of being reluctant to remove the scabs and reopen old wounds. Perhaps I am just afraid that touching it in any way would diminish or spoil whatever had made it unusual, unique. Even at my age I believe in some kinds of magic.

It is the search for this uniqueness, or at least the illusion of it, which has driven me throughout my life. When I find myself with a new woman, the magic moment is the first unveiling. That moment when she is lying beside me and I bend over her and touch her through her underwear, and she raises her hips so that I can take it off. That moment remains for me the most deeply moving. That is the threshold, the moment she announces her decision: *Yes, you may, I consent, I want you, I want you to want me.*

Of course, I know what I will find, but not *how* it will be. The larger scheme is familiar, but not the detail. And *this* is the mystery, this is what it is all about. Oh, I know in advance that she will remind me of other women – a nipple or a knee or a toe, the little mole just here, a certain way of smiling, a gaze through half-closed eyelashes, a small gesture, how she tosses her hair back or moves her hand through it, a wrinkle in the tiny pointed hood of her clitoris, the intake of her breath as I enter her, the sounds she makes. Yes, yes, many reminders, all the time. (Only with little Katrien there could have been no reminders, it was the purest of beginnings, innocent of memory; even with Driekie in the fig tree there were already fleeting moments of comparison or recognition.) But the point of being with *this* woman, here, now, is that she is *not* any of the others, not *anyone* else in the whole world or in the history of the world, but only *she*. Later, yes later, as familiarity increases, as newness wears off, and that which she has in common with others begins to outweigh what is unique in her, the relationship will change, sadly and fatally, inevitably. For the moment it is the discovery and acknowledgement of her *in*comparable quality which overrides all else. This is *you*; and the youness of *you* makes it possible for me to be *me* in relation to you. So the occasion to enter her, not just her vagina but her *self*, her thoughts, her memories, or that part of her she offers to make available to me, while at the same time she enters into *me*, a subtle osmosis . . . can there be anything more miraculous than that? On the level of the body I have often wished I could momentarily change places with a woman, to know, truly, if fleetingly, how it feels to be entered like that; but beyond the body, in the commingling of mind and memory, there is no strangeness, no distinction between self and other.

And that is why I love them, the women, every individual one of them: each one has been adored, each one has been necessary. I have always been *there* in the bed of love, fully present, loving the reality of *this* body, every quirk and detail of it, every quivering sign of life. In this togetherness our bodies are us, but they are also more and less than us. Do they take us with them, or are we taking them with us? To wherever they can go, to wherever it is possible for us to go. Beyond words, even beyond music. Certainly beyond what we have known before or could possibly have known. This is the place of knowledge, and it enfolds us like a fig tree burning, it sets us free into an almost unbearable light.

Each separate limb, as it touches or responds to touch, becomes a miracle beyond flesh and blood, illuminated by its own light, its own lambent fire, but without being consumed. I know that I can name each one of them individually, and that each name will mean more than it has meant before, each will be a *sesame* and a *shibboleth*, each one a candle of meaning, and perhaps a damnation which I am happy to accept. *Eye, mouth, ear, shoulder, elbow, hand, hip, back*, each the opening line of a poem, casting a spell, lifting a veil. *Toe, foot, ankle, knee. Thigh*. I pronounce you. You utter me utterly. And now I whisper it, holy of holies, going back to that word from my childhood: *Filimandorus*. But I go beyond it too, to the more ancient exorcising word – this *is* a return to origins – reclaiming it from insult or profanity, and calling it, simply: *Cunt*.

There is a world around us, of violence and fear and deception and misery. There is a past behind us, a future ahead. But here, while we are here, it is just now, it is us: you, I, slick with sweat, indivisible, yet for ever separate.

This, I should have told George, is where I believe I am most unlike Don Giovanni. He played the arithmetic game, he was fucking by numbers ('In Italy six hundred and forty, in Germany two hundred and thirty-one . . .'); to me it is the glimpse of a woman's uniqueness, her unrepeatability, which drives me on.

This is threatening to become unbearably heavy-handed. And I remember something Lawrence Durrell once said in an interview: 'The French know that love is a form of metaphysical enquiry; the English think it has something to do with the plumbing.' Let us not underestimate the plumbing; no home can function without it. And I have done my own fair share of plumbing, no doubt – and no shame – about that. There is something very sane and healthy and basic about it. Plumbing the depths. But it is only the enquiry which takes one beyond plumbing which makes it memorable. Here endeth the lesson.

All of this to explain why I have been so reluctant to write about you, and our first night together, that New Year's Eve: I have simply been afraid of revisiting it to find your uniqueness diminished or somehow faded. To be forced to acknowledge that what was so very special about it is the naked fact that there *is* nothing special.

But now you are dead. And in a way I owe it to you, and perhaps to myself, to revisit it and affirm, or reaffirm, both its uniqueness and its commonality.

It could not have begun in a more mundane manner. I was feeling low and lonely, an end-of-year feeling: another year gone and nothing new to show for it, after too many years of writer's block. (After *Radical Fire* in the mid-nineties I haven't been able to finish anything.) I couldn't face spending the night alone, and I resented the idea of a jolly party surrounded by people beaming goodwill. But in the end I succumbed to what seemed the lesser evil and accepted an invitation from two old friends in Llandudno who thought it would be fun to see the New Year dawn together. Charl and Bridget. I set out early, much too early, from my home in Oranjezicht. As it was a glorious day I decided to take a leisurely drive along the beach road. Three Anchor Bay, Sea Point, Bantry Bay, Clifton, Camps Bay, Bakoven. The sun had about an hour to go before it would dip into the inky Atlantic, and the whole bay was shimmering like quicksilver. I had to stop for cigarettes. (How curious, it now strikes me, that cigarettes should have triggered it, as they brought about the beginning of your end, just over a year later.) I'd given up smoking fourteen months and three days before; but I knew Bridget always ran out of supplies during a party and thought I should make timeous provision. There was no parking at all along the beach road, so just after Blues I turned into Camps Bay Drive to find a café higher up. Soon I turned off when a shady little lane seemed more appealing, and then again and again. ('You have a novelist's way of driving,' someone once said: Andrea, I think. 'Never straight from A to B, always looking for the turn-offs and byways, enough to send anyone up the wall . . .' 'I always get there in the end,' I retorted.) Gradually my mood lifted; but solitude still weighed on me, even after so many years on my own. But then, usually when I was alone in my life, it had been my own choice; now my choices were beginning to run out.

At last I found a small supermarket in a deserted street, where I stopped for the cigarettes. And then, when I got into the car again, it wouldn't start. Just my sort of luck: and I really know nothing about the insides of a car. After five minutes of more and more furious efforts, I was still stuck. Whenever I turned the ignition key there was only a disheartening click. The sun, now ponderous and red, was already touching the horizon like a big bloated balloon. With all the male self-assurance I could muster I opened the bonnet and started tugging at wires, first tentatively, then with more and more panicky rage, returning to the driver's seat at irregular intervals to try the ignition again. Click. My hands were getting filthy; in the rear-view mirror I could see that my face was streaked with grease. That only made me more frantic.

And then, out of the blue, I heard a rising volume of music approaching, and in a volcanic eruption of Beethoven from a car radio you stopped on the opposite side of the road and shouted something. At first I couldn't hear what you were saying, and you had to turn the music down.

'Do you need help?' you asked.

I was flabbergasted. People no longer do this kind of thing. I myself have given up stopping for strangers. Years ago I often did, particularly if an attractive female was involved. Not necessarily with any ulterior design: I might have been prompted by purely aesthetic reasons. On a few occasions it did have consequences, nothing very profound, but invariably entertaining. Once or twice it was the beginning of something more durable. Then, sometime in the eighties, I picked up a febrile sprite who called herself Claudia – I had reason not to believe her – with whom I spent a couple of nights, only to wake up one morning to find that she had cleared out, taking with her a large suitcase full of my possessions. And that was the end of another Good Samaritan.

But you stopped for me. And you loved Beethoven. *And* you had these haunting looks. (The strange feeling of someone else looking at me with those eyes, through a glass darkly.) What more could I wish for in this world, right then?

There was something dramatic about the contrast between your very dark eyes and your almost-blonde, rather dishevelled hair. As you got out of your car, a not-so-young, bright blue Golf, I saw the rest of you. You wore a dark red, full-length dress of some flimsy silky material that clung to your contours. You were barefoot. I am particularly susceptible to young women with bare feet.

You gave me a quick, searching look as I got out. Then, presumably reassured by my age, you streaked your fingers through your hair, and said, 'May I try?'

'There's no life in here,' I said. 'But by all means try.'

You tried.

Click.

You said, 'Fuck.'

I'm old-fashioned enough to disapprove of strong language in women, but somehow, coming from you, it was so unexpected, and sounded so sincerely meant, that I couldn't help laughing.

'What's so funny?' you asked, in a tone of dark suspicion.

'You,' I said. 'Sorry. I didn't mean to offend you. But I wasn't expecting you to run down the alphabet to F so quickly.'

A slight grin. Your wide eyes the colour of bitter chocolate. The suppleness of your long body as you got out again and ducked under the bonnet.

'I just stopped here –' I pointed at the small supermarket on the corner – 'to get cigarettes for a party, I was dawdling on the way and I'm already running late and everybody's waiting – and now the car won't start.'

'Have you checked the battery?'

'Do you know about cars?'

'Not a thing.'

That strangely reassured me. 'There was nothing wrong until I stopped,' I told you.

'It happened to me the other day. That's why I think it is the battery. Shall we have a look?'

'We haven't even met yet.'

You stretched out your hand, noticed how dirty mine was, hesitated, and then took it regardless.

'Chris,' I said helpfully. 'Chris Minnaar.'

'I'm Rachel Lombard.' There was a pause. What next? Then you asked, 'Shall I check your water?'

'I'll check the car's battery,' I said with a straight face.

That was exactly where the problem lay. All the cells were dry. You offered to give me a lift to a nearby garage.

'Are you sure it's safe?' I asked.

'I won't harm you,' you said.

'I was thinking of you.'

'I'll take the chance.' This time the smile was wider. 'I wouldn't normally, but you won't believe this: I went to a star-woman this morning, an astrologer, and she said I'd have an opportunity to help somebody today and if I didn't, I might lose the chance of a lifetime.'

'The stars can be notorious liars.'

'They've never lied to me.' You opened the passenger door of the Golf; it took some wrenching, I noticed, before it yielded with an infernal squeak.

'Do you mind turning on the Beethoven again?' I said. '*Les Adieux,* I think it was.'

Your eyes became almost phosphorescent with delight. 'You like it too?'

'One of my favourites.'

That, I think, did it. We drove to the garage – I couldn't help noticing, with some atavistic patronising approval, I presume, with what easy and deft self-assurance you handled the little blue Golf. I bought a litre of distilled water and a set of jump leads, and we returned to my car. But it made no difference; the cells must have been damaged beyond repair. Even after the jump-start the car just shuddered to a halt again.

'I cannot possibly impose on you any more,' I said. 'I'll call a cab from the supermarket and take it from there.'

'What about my chance of a lifetime?' you mocked. 'I can't just leave you to your fate. Get in.'

'This is really the wrong way round,' I said. 'The damsel on the blue pony saving the decrepit knight in distress.'

'Suits me. Let's go. After *Les Adieux* there's still the *Appassionata.*'

In a manner of speaking, I thought. But it's usually the other way round.

We went back to the garage, but they could not supply me with a new battery. They did direct me to another place, though, not too far from there, where I might be helped. No luck. In the end it took the better part of an hour before we arrived back at my car. We were halfway through the *Hammerklavier* and the supermarket staff was already preparing to lock up for the festive night ahead. Together we started doing battle with tight bolts corroded by old battery acid. It was you who thought of Coca-Cola; and just before the supermarket doors were bolted, you skipped inside to buy a bottle from the none-too-friendly manager. Between the two of us we finally got the better of the job, but by that time we were both looking the worse for wear. A smudge on your left cheek made you look irresistible; but I felt less happy about a large black stain on your long red dress.

'I don't know how to thank you,' I said. There were some sugges-tions I could make, but in my position I could not possibly push it. And I knew better than to try some of my old lines on today's youth. Not that you were all that callow. Early thirties, I should guess. (But no rings, as I'd noticed when I had first, approvingly, checked your hands.)

'You look a sight,' you said matter-of-factly. 'Why don't you come home with me first and get yourself cleaned up? I live just round the corner.'

'Can you spare the time?'

You glanced at your watch: a big, rather cheap, but practical, no-nonsense affair.

'I won't keep you long,' I promised, guiltily. 'Then I must be on my way. I'm late already. You too, I should imagine.'

You shrugged. Then you drove off; I followed. Your house, small and surprisingly old-fashioned, was tucked away at the end of a cul-de-sac, high up on the slope, with a spectacular view.

After some cursory ablutions, as I was reversing in your small back-yard, preparing to leave, you suddenly said, 'What about a quick drink?'

I said, 'Yes.'

And so our night began.

The ceramic sculptures are the first I notice. Not that one can miss them: they are everywhere. Most of them quite small, no more than fifteen or twenty centimetres tall, but there are a few larger pieces in the studio that overlooks the bay. They seem to constitute a fantastic world of their own, spilling into the living spaces of the house: figures that might have stepped straight from Bosch's *Garden of Earthly Delights,* but with a strong African flavour. As if on one of his journeys to hell the old Flemish master has made a detour through Benin, Mali, Mozambique. It is evident that no one has bothered to tidy the place in weeks, perhaps months. But it is a friendly chaos, a smiling and human chaos. (I cannot help reaching for Nietzsche's great line, *One must have chaos inside oneself to give birth to a dancing star.*)

'Who did these?'

'All my fault.'

'The detail is amazing. You must have spent a lifetime on them.'

'Five years. I've lived with them in my mind all my life, but I never had the guts to start doing something about it.'

'I can't believe it.'

A brief pause. Your eyes seem to become even darker. 'My father died eight years ago, you see.'

'What did that have to do with it?'

'Would you like some wine?' you interrupt.

'I'd love some, but —'

'Red or white?'

'Red.'

Without giving me any further opening you go out. I bend over the nearest small sculpture. The detail and precision are indeed astounding. There is even something Egyptian about it: all those gods with the faces of birds and animals. But so perfectly done as if everything has been taken straight from life.

You come back so quietly on your bare feet that I don't hear you, and am startled when you put the tray with the bottle and two huge glasses on the table.

'Will you open for us?'

As I cautiously pull out the cork and sniff it I say, casually and without looking at you, 'You were going to tell me about your father.'

'You don't let go, do you?' Suddenly your mood seems to clear. 'It's not a special story at all. Just the old one of a man who wanted to turn his only daughter into the son he never had. He was a mathematician, and so I had to become one too.'

'That's pretty daunting.'

'I loved him, that's all,' you say, very simply. 'I couldn't let him down. You see, my mother went off with someone else when I was quite small, so there were only him and me.' And then, as the wine stands breathing silently between us, you tell me of how you've dreamed of making sculptures all your life, ever since as a little girl you spent a holiday with him on the Free State farm of some relative, where you played in the muddy trickle of the river with all the farm boys and learned to make clay oxen. Your love of textures, your love of shapes. Your dreams at night of strange enchanting — or enchanted — forms that came to life. But always there were the figures and equations of your father's world to return to. Throughout your school years, and through university. And you must have been brilliant, although now you downplay the whole thing very much and seem embarrassed to talk about it. Then you got a junior lectureship at Wits, and completed your Ph.D., and were promoted to lecturer. But still the dreams were there. And then he died, a stroke, and six months later you gave up your academic career and took the plunge to become a sculptor.

'You certainly had guts,' I comment.

'Plain chutzpah. Fortunately I wasn't exactly destitute. He'd left me some money. Not much, but enough to keep me off the streets. And so here I am.'

That is when you pour the wine, and I do my little number about mocha and vanilla and chocolate.

When much later we return to the subject – by that time we've given up our party plans for the night, and opened another bottle, and had something to eat, and you are more forthcoming – you pull a face and blow out smoke and say, 'Actually it was hell to get started. Okay, I'd always, when I had a bit of spare time, which was never much, made little things, sometimes when I was studying, just to feel something between my fingers, little figurines of plasticine or whatever. But suddenly it was my *life*, you see, and I was terrified. There were many days when I thought I'd done the dumbest, craziest thing ever, giving up a secure job – for this. And all my friends agreed.' A slow, illuminating smile. 'But in the end I knew there was nothing else I could have done. I just *had* to. I don't think anyone will ever really understand.'

'You're wrong,' I say. Outside looms the night – the French doors are open and from far away the deep, reassuring bass boom of the sea goes on and on – and inside are the two of us, alone in all that space. 'I do understand very well. I had to make much the same journey. My father was a lawyer, so I had to be one too, never any doubt about that. That is just the way our society works, isn't it? But unlike you, I didn't wait for him to die. I just kept on writing, secretly, for myself, mainly at night. And then, around the time of Sharpeville, I was in such a state of rage about what was happening in the country, I wrote a novel about it, it seemed to come out in one painful spurt, and Marlene, the woman I was with just then, said I should do something about it. No hope of ever getting it published in Afrikaans, so the two of us worked together on translating it. She was English. I was rather dubious about my chances, but she had a ferocious belief in the manuscript. So she sent it off to London, where she had a friend with some kind of connection in the publishing world, and before I knew what was happening the book came out and suddenly I was the flavour of the month. That gave me the kick in the backside which I needed. I turned my back on my father and all his projects and expectations, and gave up my career as a lawyer and took the plunge.'

'What happened to Marlene?' you ask.

I shrug. 'I'm not sure. It just ran its course. Once the book came out, she started feeling jealous about it. Terrible irony it was: she said it took me away from her.'

'We do need someone to believe in us, don't we?' you ask. By this time we are settled on the somewhat dilapidated old sofa from which the stuffing is coming out, you are lying prone on your back, an arm under your head, one hand holding a cigarette; one knee drawn up, the other foot balanced on it.

'Do you have such a someone?' I ask with some caution; I'm not sure that I really want to know.

'I've been incredibly lucky,' you say. 'Just a few months after I started on my own I had two or three little things on exhibition at a big art-fair thing at the Waterfront. That's where I met George. He simply bought them all, and we started talking, and that was that. I had just popped in to check, in my oldest clothes, looking like something the cat had dragged in, and he had all his cameras draped around his neck, like a big bear in a circus, and we had a coffee, and sat talking until the place closed down for the night, and he took me back to his house, which is this one, and we only woke up again about a week later.'

'So you're still with him?' I ask, in as neutral a voice as I can muster.

'Of course,' you say. 'We're married. We lived together for two years, and then we said I do, I do, and now it's another four years later.'

'I haven't noticed any rings.'

'I lost mine in a lump of clay and we haven't had time to replace it. Anyway, that is supposed to be unlucky, isn't it? But it hasn't made any difference.'

Without meaning to, I heave a sigh.

'What's wrong?' you ask with a small frown of concern.

'I think I've just missed the last bus home,' I say.

You cast a quizzical look at me, but say nothing. A slow question mark of smoke moves thinly from your cigarette up into the air, unfurls, disappears.

'If you are married, why are you interested in a new chance?' I ask suddenly, perhaps more provocatively than I meant to.

'Who says I'm looking for a new chance?' You sound offended.

'That's what you told me the astrologer said.'

You burst out laughing. 'Yes, of course. I went there this morning. I was with a friend, we saw the ad and just impulsively went for a consultation.' You pull a face. 'A seedy little hole in Sea Point. And a funny little woman, like a praying mantis with big bulging eyes and misshapen hands. I don't think she was very good. But she did say a few things that really were close to the bone. She told me I was very sad because my husband wouldn't be with me over New Year's Day, that he was somewhere in the wilderness . . .'

'Is he?'

'Yes, in the Congo.' You interrupt your story to tell me about George's travels, then return to your astrologer. 'She said I hadn't been working as well as I should, because I was feeling lonely and my mind was distracted, and why didn't I give my house a spring-cleaning? It would help to sort out my mind. And you know what? She said I was planning to go out on New Year's Eve, but in the end I wouldn't go, because the new person who was going to turn up in my life might help me sort things out.'

I prefer not to comment. You lean over to find and light a new cigarette. The way you cup your hand around the flame suddenly seems very familiar, but for a moment I cannot place the gesture.

'I think I can do with some sorting out myself,' I reflect. 'For the last number of years I've always had someone coming over to keep my papers in order. Sometimes I placed an ad in the paper, more often than not it was a friend, or a friend's daughter, or niece, or acquaintance, whatever. A kind of Girl Friday. To type my letters, the odd article, sort my papers. I have an old major-domo, Frederik Baadjies, who's more or less taken over the house, but he won't touch my papers. I don't like strangers around, but I really can't cope with all that stuff on my own. Just too bloody lazy, if you ask me.'

'Why don't you have anybody at the moment?'

'The latest one left to get married.'

Lindiwe. I am aware of smiling fondly at the memory, but I suppose there is something wistful in it. I didn't want to see her go. Especially not to get married. Still, I had probably given her a useful induction into matrimony. Not just the secretarial work and a bit of housekeeping with Frederik's reluctant consent. But the conversations. And, I may as well admit it, something of a sentimental education. Surprisingly mature for a girl her age, twenty-three. A beautiful woman, she could have been a model, a thoroughly modern miss. I was fascinated by her hair, plaited in intricate geometrical patterns close to her head, from where a curtain of thin braids reached down to her shoulders. Her body was a dark, lustrous brown, smooth and groomed and radiant, with large and perfectly spherical breasts and lovely feet. With all the energy and inventiveness of youth, but with patience and understanding as well. Over the last few years my forays into love have suffered some let-downs. I am no longer the man I was. I used to take courage from the widely held belief that the longer you remain active sexually the longer you can keep it up. But it is not true. Not true. And Lindiwe had the patience and understanding not to be put off by temporary incapacity. The almost adoring expression in her eyes, the quiet and humorous understanding, with which she would coax the recalcitrant member back into life, the skill of her long, pale brown fingers with the rosy tips. And even if my own performance might occasionally fail, there had never been anything amiss with my tongue. And then she had to go and get married. Very properly, in the Catholic church in Gugulethu; her father was dead, and I was asked as a very special favour to give her away to the bridegroom. Lionel. A handsome coloured man, an up-and-coming young executive. He looked so proud, so tall and erect in his new suit. When I lifted her misty white veil and kissed her farewell, our eyes met in a final smile of complicity. No one would ever know. Gone now, like so many others. Married. Like you, Rachel. What a loss.

I straighten up on the old lived-in sofa, keeping my eyes on your hands, your long strong hands shaped by working with clay, the no-nonsense yet sensitive fingers, the dominant thumbs.

'Were you in love with her?' you interrupt my wandering thoughts.

'With whom?'

'The woman you spoke about. Lindiwe, your Girl Friday.'

I shrug. But the frankness with which you are observing me makes me hesitate. It is a night for confidences; under any other circumstances I may not have opened up so unreservedly, but now I do. 'Yes, I was. I very much need to be in love.'

'You were in love with every Girl Friday you had?'

'I suppose so. Just as I fell in love with every one of the heroines in my books.'

'Even the bad ones?'

'Especially the bad ones. They were in need of redemption. And so was I.'

'Aren't we all?'

'We certainly all need love.'

'You must have loved a lot in your life.'

'But not enough. Never enough.' And after a moment I take the obvious risk: 'What about you?'

'Never enough,' you retort with a straight face, but with what I think may be an impish glint in your eyes.

'You still have time to catch up.'

You refuse to take the bait, and deftly change the subject: 'I can come and work for you,' you say without any warning. 'Two mornings a week.'

'You're a sculptor.'

'I was a mathematician too.'

'That doesn't mean you can type and file.'

'You can always fire me.'

'What I meant was that your sculpture is a full-time occupation. Look at the things you make. It would be criminal to spend all that time on Girl Fridaying.'

'Not all my time. I said two mornings a week. In fact, I have been discussing it with George: finding something to do part-time, just to get out of the house sometimes, a complete change of scene. I need the stimulation.'

'I can't offer much stimulation.'

'You can talk to me. I miss people to talk to in the daytime. In the evenings, when George is away, I can go out to see friends. But the days can be long.'

'Discuss it with your husband first. When he's around again. When will he be back?'

'I never know for sure. A week, perhaps two.' An almost imperceptible narrowing of your eyes; it's the kind of thing I do not miss. 'There's one condition.'

'And that is?'

'If I'm your Girl Friday you're not allowed to interfere with my work. And I won't interrupt yours.'

'Agreed. But I have nothing to interrupt anyway. I've had a block for years now, six, seven, eight.'

'We must work on that.'

'There's always the possibility that you may inspire me to get going again.'

You think it over for a while, then nod. 'I think I'd like that.'

'And occasionally we may break for tea.'

'I'll have coffee.'

'Agreed then.'

'I'll discuss it with George.'

'You sure he won't mind?'

'My husband isn't the jealous type. And he certainly won't be jealous of *you*.'

'Whatever that may mean.'

'All I mean is that he will know that I'm safe with you.'

'Like Father Christmas?'

'Like a creative person.'

A quick change of direction: 'When did you first know you'd be a writer?'

'I told you I started very late. I was already well into my thirties when *A Time to Weep* was published. But I'd always known I would write, and throughout my teens I did, as I told you. But my father nipped it in the bud. Said it wasn't a decent occupation for a self-respecting man.'

'Or woman?'

'I'm afraid his world allowed no space for women. Except for . . .' I shrugged. 'You know.'

'What about your mother?'

'She was the one who always believed in me. Still does, at over a hundred. In her lucid moments, which are becoming more and more rare.'

I withdraw into my thoughts; and sensing, perhaps, that you shouldn't intrude, you wait patiently, smoking. After a while I say, 'I think it began when we had our first English lesson in school. Where I grew up, in Graaff Reinet, it was something of a foreign language. Thanks to my beloved old nanny I knew some Xhosa. But not English. My father couldn't stand the English. The Boer War, you see, in which his own father had fought and died. He himself had barely survived the English concentration camp in which he spent two years with his mother. As a lawyer he had to be bilingual of course, and he had an impressive command of the language. But he left English at the office. At home there was only Afrikaans. So I was brought up with all those prejudices. And then we had that first lesson at school. The teacher read us a poem in English, without trying to explain anything. All we had to do was close our eyes and listen. And that afternoon when I came home, I wandered about in our garden with the English reader the teacher had handed out, and I tried to read from it, aloud. I had no idea of the correct pronunciation, I literally didn't understand a word of it. But I was caught in the strangeness of that other language, its rhythms and cadences, the whole sense of otherness it brought with it. I started doing it every day. And after a week or so I suddenly made the discovery that my own language, Afrikaans, was also made of sounds and rhythms and cadences. As I spoke it out loud to myself I was entranced by how extraordinary everything sounded that had previously been so familiar that I never took a step back to look at it, to listen to it, from a distance. I think that was when I became a writer. Thirty years before I ventured into print.'

'I love that,' you say. 'I love listening to you. You're making the language foreign for me too. It's beautiful.'

A long, easy silence full of thoughts. Then I ask, 'And your sculpture? How did that begin?'

'On that farm I went to with my father.'

'The clay oxen?'

'No, before that.' You stretch out both your legs into the air. The long dark silky dress falls back to your hips. You do not even seem aware of it. You begin to rotate your neat ankles, wiggling your toes. 'It started with my feet.'

'But how . . . ?'

You smile without looking at me, still twirling your ankles very slowly, pensively. 'It was down at the river, one late afternoon. The boys all had farmwork to do, bringing home the cattle, milking, securing the kraals, watering the vegetables and the herb garden, whatever. I was all by myself. I had a swim.' I fleetingly think of Driekie. 'And after I came out of the water I sat on a big smooth rock to dry. My feet were in the water. And as I moved them, they sank into the soft mud at the edge. I could feel it squishing through my toes. Squishing and squiggling. It was one of the most extraordinary sensations I have ever had. Ever. I suppose I was too small for a thing like that, but you know, I think now it was the first orgasm I had in my life. The sheer sensuality of that mud through my toes. I lifted my feet and looked at the thin little snakes wriggling down back into the water. I was totally fascinated. Later, I climbed down from the rock and squatted at the edge of the water to repeat with my hands what I'd just done with my feet. And I knew, I just *knew*, that this was what I would like to do with my life. To work with clay. For a few years I experimented with all kinds of material. But every time I come back to clay, to ceramics. I need material I can shape and bend and twist and form into something new.' You chuckle at a memory. 'In the beginning, when I just started sculpting, I rather liked working with iron, melting it until it was soft and pliable. But I burnt my hands so much, and once even singed off most of my hair. And then, for some time, I tried marble. Which has a special kind of excitement. I seem to think that it was no less a sculptor than Michelangelo who said, "Marble is easy. Suppose you want to make a horse. You just take the block and chip away everything that is not a horse." But that wasn't my line. I don't want to find something that is hidden but already there. I want to make something that has never been before.'

I do not answer, there is no need. In silence I watch you finish your cigarette and reach out for another. You are really smoking too much. It is something that often repels me in others. But for the moment I am fixated on the movement of your hand, the way you hold the cigarette between forefinger and thumb, like a joint. And I can imagine the taste of the tip of your tongue, the smoky smell of your hair in the morning. Which right now I would give my kingdom for. I have known only one other woman whose smoking has so captivated me, and that was Nicolette. Closing my eyes I can indeed smell her hair and taste her tongue. Yours.

And so the night grows very old around us, and very young again. I remember that at one stage you reached for another cigarette, and how upset you were to find the packet empty. But I recalled my stop at the supermarket before you'd come to rescue me, and told you not to worry, and went outside — the wonderful freshness of the early-morning air outside, the first streaks of colour coming over the mountains at the back, the peculiar rustling of silver trees in the stirring of the breeze — and took the unopened packet from the cubbyhole.

When I came back, you were asleep, your hair spilling in a dark blonde pool around your head on the old sofa, your legs now folded, but the dress still rucked up to your hips. I bent over and carefully straightened it down over your knees. Your eyes half opened and you mumbled something. A thin trail of saliva ran from the corner of your mouth. I wanted to kneel beside you and recover it with my tongue, but wouldn't run the risk of waking you.

THERE WAS ONE woman about whom I never had such qualms. She just loved being woken up with caresses, or even with me inside her; usually she was already wet with anticipation. Whether it was ten or eleven in the morning (how she loved sleeping late), or two, or three, or four at night. Her warm voice moist in my ear. No one else I have ever known had so many contradictions poured into one small, perfect body. ('Poured', for with her everything was liquid.) What she loved above all was for me to pour champagne on her nipples and watch it form delicate foaming patterns down her ribcage and her stomach; and I would lick it from her navel, and nuzzle down to her very smoothly shaven sex. The woman who was, without any doubt at all, the most turbulent, the most exhausting, the most incredible love affair of my life; I still wake up shuddering at night when I dream of her. Not for anything in the world – and I really mean that – would I have missed a day of it; yet it drained me and shattered me, and irrevocably broke down much I had previously thought of as vital to me, and added immeasurably to whatever I might today bring to anything as inadequate as a definition of what 'woman' means to me. The kind of woman, I have often thought, who makes one believe that life before death is actually possible.

Even before I met her, I'd heard about her – who hadn't? All the gossip: the scarlet woman, the shameless bitch, living under the protective hand of a well-meaning older man who devoted his life to her. She sucked him dry in every imaginable sense of the word. A lost woman, a mad woman, a witch, a chancer, an unscrupulous social climber, an incorrigible cock-teaser, someone no decent person would allow their daughters to be seen with in public. At the same time, as even other women had to concede, her looks were simply incomparable. 'With such beauty,' I once heard one of them say, 'one can turn the world upside down.' Which was exactly what she did. At least *my* world: and I was only one of many.

The first time I met her, I was expecting someone older, given her reputation, and yet she couldn't have been more than nineteen, at most twenty. (But then, as several men had warned me – nudge nudge, wink wink – she'd been no more than seven when the sugar daddy first took her under his dubious wing.) Yet at first sight there was absolutely nothing disreputable about her. In fact, she made an immaculate impression, in a black dress of an extremely simple and elegant cut; her hair, which appeared to be dark brown, was done up in a simple, homely style; her eyes were dark and deep-set, her forehead was pensive; her expression was passionate and somewhat haughty. She was rather thin in the face, and pale.

But there wasn't much time for leisurely scrutiny. Almost immediately some kind of squabble broke out among several of the men at the reception (a very posh affair, of the kind I wouldn't normally attend alive or dead; but a very good friend was receiving a rather special award, I had been urged to be there for him, and I couldn't very well let him down; glory to God in the highest). I didn't quite catch what the argument was about, but I did become aware of a most unpleasant tone in the altercation: right there in her presence, and knowing that she could hear every word, this group of fine gentlemen were making the most offensive and obscene remarks about her. She didn't bat an eyelid, and that probably encouraged them to become more and more insulting; it was no excuse that they had been to another party just before the reception, where they had got thoroughly sozzled. It was all so noisy, and so distasteful, that I still have no idea of the exact sequence of events. All I know, and all that matters now, is that in some confusing way the two of us were thrown together in the throng, and managed to make our escape through the drunken mob, and suddenly found ourselves outside in the very dark, moonless night. And only came to our senses again when the sunrise dazzled us the next morning among the crown pines on the slope of Table Mountain, somewhere above the Rhodes Memorial. What I remembered was with what primitive relish she had rubbed my semen all over her breasts and stomach and the smoothness of her mound, and how starkly white and wet her thighs were as we got up from where we had spent the night under the dangerously careening flourish of the Milky Way, and she bent over to retrieve the crumpled black dress and put it on, and the grass and twigs in her hair, the lipstick smudged across her face, her carefree laugh, and her taste and stickiness all over my body.

I knew, all the time, that I was courting disaster. Quite early on during our affair good and well-meaning friends had gone out of their way to inform me of everything that was disreputable about her. I refused to listen. Invariably it ended with:

'Don't say I didn't warn you.'

'I promise you I won't. I tell you I *love* this woman.'

Which must also explain my pig-headedness at yet another unbelievable party, this time on her birthday. We had made plans for a quiet and passionate celebration for just the two of us, but in the end she succumbed to the lure of lights and laughter and wine and vodka and something which I'm afraid I can only call madness. That was it, really. She had always lived on the brink, on the very edge of an abyss too dark and terrifying to acknowledge. But that night she went further than on any other occasion I'd been with her. Were there drugs involved too? The constant shifts of mood, from one extreme to the other, seemed to suggest something like that: in the course of one party she could swing from black despair and bouts of uncontrollable sobbing to the shrieking laughter of a child on a merry-go-round. And yet I doubt the explanation of drugs: it is simply too obvious, too easy, too pat. There were darker and more powerful forces swirling in her mind. And certainly in her outrageously articulate and seductive body.

On the night of her birthday – which fifty or more years later I still find terribly difficult to talk about (also because now I know what came later) – everybody went into a kind of collective madness. As if, knowing her all too well, we were all bent on turning it into an extreme experience. Yes, I think that is the only word for it: extreme. We were all – and none more than she – hell-bent on testing the very limits of behaviour, of the body, of the mind and feelings. To see, as a French writer once put it, how far we could go too far.

From the muddle of memories I clung to through the fumes of alcohol and cigarettes and dagga and God knows what else that still cloud the recollection of that night, I remember a kind of auction that took place, with several of the men trying to outbid each other for a night with her. (A night? There were moments when she got carried away so fantastically that she offered herself up for sale for the rest of her life.) Eighteen thousand – eighty thousand – a hundred thousand. One poor bastard, let's call him R, and God have mercy on his soul, actually stormed out into the night and came back, can you believe it?, with a hundred thousand in notes. Everybody went totally over-board, she more than anyone else. I was trying to speak to her, to shout to her, to drag her away, but she just shook me off, laughing hysterically. Until the inevitable happened: she grabbed the bundle of notes and threw them into the fire – it was a bitterly cold August night with Cape rain beating against the windows and a spectral wind howling through the black trees outside – and dared one pitiful young man whom she had rejected a few months earlier (I shall just call him G) to pluck them out of the flames. 'If you do that, I'll marry you,' she promised recklessly, completely ignoring the poor fool who had brought the money.

At some stage I grabbed hold of her. 'Shut up!' I pleaded, 'just shut the fuck up. Why don't you marry *me*? For Christ's sake, I love you. Don't you know that?'

It was before Helena, and the first time I'd ever proposed marriage to a woman; I had persuaded myself that I would never give up my freedom. But in the raging abandon of that night I was prepared to make an idiot of myself. Publicly.

She paid no attention to me, only to G. And he was simply too flabbergasted, I think, to believe her. In the end we all just stared, transfixed, as that whole thick bundle of notes was consumed by the fire.

And after all that, still laughing, but with an ever more ominous undertone to her gaiety, she suddenly turned away from G and went back to R, the one who had brought the money, and caught hold of him, entangling him in her bare arms, like poison ivy, and started whispering in his ear; and the two of them staggered out into the night together. There was little any of us could do to stop them, to stop her.

What I remember after that, is the end. About a year later, if my memory can be trusted. It was Rogozhin after all, I may as well admit to his name now, who 'got' her. Got her in every terrible sense of the word. On the very day that was supposed to be our wedding day. Because, yes, after too many other more or less unbearable turns in our story she did, as suddenly as any of her other decisions, announce that she would marry me. But then did not turn up, literally leaving me waiting at the church door. I had a good idea of where to look for her. But it was only the next morning that Rogozhin opened to my hammering on the door of his flat. When I'd gone there the night before, there was nobody home; or that was how it had seemed to me. All that matters now, is that he was there to let me in the following morning – following what was to have been our wedding night.

The flat was deadly quiet. We both knew why I had come, but it was a long time before I dared to ask him whether she was there.

He nodded.

I got up. 'Where?' I asked.

'There.'

'Asleep?' I whispered.

'Come and see for yourself.'

'It is dark in here,' I said when we came into the bedroom. I realised that I was trembling all over.

'It's light enough to see,' muttered Rogozhin.

'I can just see – the bed.'

'Go nearer.'

We both stood beside the bed. By now my eyes had already become used to the dark, and I could make out the bed; someone lay on it in a completely motionless sleep. I didn't have to ask him what had happened, nor how he'd done it. *Put out the light, and then put out the light.*

At this point Dostoevsky chooses two tiny details to make the event one of the most unforgettable moments in the literature of the world. No one who has read it can remain unaffected by the death scene of Nastasya Filippovna Barashkova. He describes a fly which, awakened from its sleep, started buzzing, and after flying over the bed, settled at the head of it. And he describes (something which reassures me that he shared at least one of my sweeter fixations), amid the bedclothes and a crumpled heap of lace, the tip of a bare foot protruding, as though it were carved out of marble, and dreadfully still. A small foot which I know I have seen and kissed innumerable times in my life. A foot like yours, that early New Year's morning under the multicoloured spread, or that morning in the hospital, protruding from the sheet that covered your lifeless body.

DURING THAT NIGHT when I had my first meal with you and George, the *Don Giovanni* night, the matter of my Girl Friday vacancy was again discussed. It was, in fact, George who brought it up.

'Rachel tells me you have offered her a job.'

I couldn't help feeling a little bit embarrassed. But since he'd raised it in such a straightforward way, it was easy to respond in kind. 'I really need somebody, yes. But I told Rachel I couldn't possibly take her away from her work. It's a rather lowly job, after all. Not really suitable at all for a sculptor who has a Ph.D. in mathematics.'

'I know she's been eager to find something. Just to take her mind off all this –' he gestured towards the little figures all around us, a reinvented and phantasmagoric Lilliput – 'because she needs to get rid of the cobwebs from time to time. And it will make *me* happy too, as I'm away so often and I don't want her to be alone all the time.'

I turned to you. 'It's for you to say.'

'You make it sound like a solemn vow,' you laughed. 'But yes, the answer is yes. With all my heart.'

'Perhaps it is predestined,' George concluded. 'I firmly believe that if something is meant to happen, it will happen.' I had reason to remember his words much later; like much else besides.

And on the first Monday morning after that George brings you round to my house. No special reason, he says, like an embarrassed boy; he just thought he'd like to see me again. Which adds a seal to the friendship – if anything like that is still required. His only worry is that he has an engagement at lunchtime, but I assure him there is no need: I have to drive past Camps Bay to an appointment just after two (which is, strictly speaking, not true) and can drop you off.

After he has turned on the ignition he still lingers behind the wheel for a while to talk. You wait in the background, a hint of amusement on your face. He is clearly reluctant to leave, although he turns down my invitation to tea. We arrange to meet over the weekend, go to Newlands for a cricket match, come home for a braai together.

We turn to go up the red steps to the stoep. You are soberly, casually dressed in a brief white T-shirt which leaves your navel exposed, and jeans and newly cleaned sneakers. I approve of the flexing and unflexing of the tight muscles of your bottom as you move up ahead of me. The steps are steep. Already I can foresee a time when I will have to move out of this place which has been a protective shell to me for thirteen years. Perhaps I should move in with Mam in her old-age home. We might even share a room, complete the circle. She's good for another century.

'George has taken a real liking to you,' you remark when we reach the top. Your breath comes deeply, smoothly. It has a sweetness in it, muskily masked with smoke.

'It's too early to tell.'

'I can tell.'

'Well, it's mutual.' From the front stoep we look out over the city bowl towards the clutter of the harbour, and beyond, past the innocent-looking brown blob of Robben Island across the leaden-blue Atlantic where cargo ships and a few tugboats and yachts and trawlers lie awaiting their turn to come or go. 'Shall we go inside and have a look around? There is still time to change your mind.'

At the front door we are met by my major-domo, Frederik Baadjies, a small and mournful man of uncertain age who has lived with me ever since I moved into this house sometime before the first free elections. Frederik comes from Lamberts Bay on the west coast, from an old fishing family, but his demeanour is that of a butler in a stately mansion. Originally he was hired as a gardener, but it soon became evident that he was destined for higher things: somewhere along the winding road of his long life he had learned to cook, and although his ambition sometimes outstripped his ability, he was clearly to the manner born. As the house is much too big for me, most of it taken up by the books and paintings and sculptures I have accumulated over a peripatetic lifetime, I invited him to settle into a couple of the spare rooms. But plagued by what appeared to be an uncomfortable class consciousness he firmly refused, and moved into the staff quarters. Seven years ago, when Mam chose to move out of the comfortable garden cottage at the back to the old-age home (she, too, had declined to share the house, as she had no wish, she said in so many words, to cramp my style in the matter of dealings with young ladies of various descriptions and inclinations on the premises), I prevailed on Frederik to occupy the flat. From there he rules the household with an unobtrusive yet iron hand, doing the cleaning, the washing, most of the cooking, and expressing largely unsolicited opinions on the acceptability or otherwise of what he discreetly refers to as 'house guests'. The only part of the house he refuses to take any responsibility for is my library, my study and my bedroom. Those spaces are, by his own choice, not only off-limits but non-existent.

Frederik condescends to take the hand you offer him, and offers a brief nod of the head. No smile. I have never seen him smile; he might as well be an undertaker. But the nod is already a sign of approval.

'So will it be tea or coffee?' he asks.

'I'd be happy to make it,' you say.

'Breakfast, Earl Grey or rooibos?' enquires Frederik, pointedly ignoring the offer.

With a touch of contrariness you say, 'I prefer coffee, if it isn't too much trouble.'

I was sure it would faze him (in Frederik's book, coffee is taken in the afternoon, in the morning it is tea), but with the merest inclination of his head he indicates amused approval, before withdrawing to the kitchen.

'I don't know how you managed it,' I tell you gravely, 'but you have just been weighed, counted and accepted. Not everybody is so fortunate.'

'I shall mind my step,' you assure me.

After I have shown you the study and the library and explained what has to be done, you give me a wry smile. 'When did your last Girl Friday leave?'

'Four, five months ago.'

'This is criminal negligence, Chris.'

'I know. That's why you're here, isn't it? But I won't blame you if you decide to leave well enough alone and get the hell out.'

'No, I'll do it.' You sweep another critical glance across the mess. 'But I want you to get a new computer. This one probably came over with the first British settlers. Unless the Khoisan people used it as a totem.'

'But my old one still serves my purpose perfectly.'

'Then God have mercy on your purpose.'

'We can talk about it later.'

'When I was small my father used to say that. Meaning it would never happen.'

'Try me.'

'I will.' You promptly sit down in the middle of the floor and start undoing the laces of your sneakers. Looking up at me you ask, 'I hope you don't mind my taking off these. I can't work unless I'm barefoot.'

'I prefer that too. I mean for you.'

'Oh dear. I hope you're not a fetishist?'

'Just short of.'

Leaving the sneakers right there, you reach out for a hand; I pull you to your feet.

'So where do I start?'

'Let us have our tea and coffee first. My guess is that it will be served in the dining room today.'

'Won't it be cosier in your kitchen?'

'It will. But Frederik will insist on the dining room. If you are allowed in the kitchen at a later stage, you will know that you have become a member of the family.'

'So today it's the full treatment, right?'

'Just because it's the first time. From now on you'll be manacled to the desk from nine to one.'

You heave an exaggerated sigh. 'Don't tell me you're into bondage too?'

At the dining table, washed bright by the morning sunlight falling without any subtlety or compromise through the large sash windows, as we have our tea, the banter easily glides into more substantial talk.

'Isn't this light beautiful?' I ask.

'It's more than beautiful. Without it we would simply not be here,' you say pensively, staring at the window.

'This cup is very much here,' I counter, holding my large white teacup up to the exuberance from outside.

'Not without the light,' you insist. 'It's the most perfect sculptor in the world. And the most enthusiastic. What would this be without the light?'

'A blind person can still feel its shape and weight,' I object.

You nod slowly. 'All right, I'll grant you that. But without the space surrounding it – and space is light, isn't it? – it cannot exist. Sometimes I think it's the in-between spaces that are more important than the objects, the things. I read a story once – you probably know it too?

it's by Abraham de Vries – about a man who didn't care about trees and buildings and stuff, all the clutter that fill up the world around us. To him, all that mattered were the spaces that reach down from above, in between: like tree trunks of light, stems to carry all that space above. Everybody thought he was mad. But they just didn't know how to look.' You finish a scone. 'That's why I prefer making small sculptures: they make the space around them seem larger. And I think the really important things in life, the things that make the rest live-able, the good moments which you can never forget, are like those surrounding or in-between spaces, the delicate stems of light. The moments we think of as "happy". The moments when we discover something, become aware of something else, something more. Eating an apple. A good glass of wine. Love.'

'I prefer to think of love as something more substantial than that.'

'Really?' You almost sound commiserating. 'But love isn't something heavy and solid, is it? If it's worthwhile, it brings space, air, light. And then the solid chunks of dreariness and ordinariness, the blocks of wood and glass and concrete that make up our buildings, become bear-able again.'

'But love is not all ethereal and airy-fairy, Rachel!' I protest. 'It's not just *agape*. What about Eros? If that is what you think, then get thee to a nunnery. Where does the body come in?'

'What I don't like about your way of arguing is the either/or,' you say quietly. 'If I think of the relationship between George and me: it's not a matter of his body there and mine here: what I'm interested in is the in between, where there is neither a solid *him* or a solid *me*, but an *us* that dissolves in light.'

'And if one makes love?' I challenge you.

Your eyes do not flinch. 'The same. Even more so. Surely it's not all the heaving and sweating and heavy grunting that you remember – I don't deny that it can be fun, and good in its own way – but that's not where it ends. Perhaps that is only the beginning. What matters is the closeness, the sharing, the being-together, don't you think? The quiet moments that you can feel and see and sense and know and believe in, *behind* all the thrashing about.'

'And the moment of coming? Is that not defined by the body?'

'Only if it's a very poor orgasm,' you counter very firmly. 'Don't tell me you're one of those orgasm collectors, Chris. Some men, I have heard, collect the knickers of the women they fuck, or curls of pubic hair, or whatever. Some collect orgasms. I would have thought you were beyond that.'

'Don't underestimate the lowly orgasm,' I insist.

'Of course not. Not ever.' There is defiance in your dark eyes. 'But what *is* that moment? Surely not just a series of contractions. Don't ask me to describe it. To me it's precisely what you can *not* describe, *not* put into words, that matters. But of course you're a writer, for you I suppose words are necessary?' Before I can answer, you go on: 'Even so! I told you that for me a sculpture in itself is just the body-thing, the physical, substantial thing, that makes space happen. It acti-vates and electrifies space. Don't you think it's the same with the words you write? Isn't each one of them just put on the page in order to make the reader aware of what can *not* be said – all those blanks that surround them and curl right into them . . . ? That's how I think about love too. The moment of coming, when you dissolve, when you lose all solidity, you become air, you become nothing, you expand into space without end . . .' Then you abruptly check yourself. 'Sorry.' But you don't seem sorry at all. 'Sometimes I just get going.'

'Into pure space.'

A slow and radiant smile. 'You do understand, after all.'

For a long time we sit in silence. The cups have gone cold, but we are not interested in drinking any more. And at last I push back my chair and say, 'Let's get some words on to paper.'

'Let's first clear some space.'

AT NIGHT THE TV screen keeps opening up to the black space that lies beyond: the endless desert in which the American advance through southern Iraq seems to have become irrevocably bogged down. There is no longer just a monotony but an endlessness about it which is petri-fying. As if the real, specific war has become a metaphor of itself – the darkness and endlessness of violence, in which everything else – we, our histories and stories, our loves and memories and hopes – is mired. It is not a sequence of events, but a fate of deadly monotony. Recently, they have been showing what was reportedly the crossing of the Euphrates at Nasiriyah – but the same bridge has now been crossed eleven times, and will undoubtedly be crossed again.

What keeps me awake is thinking about George. Where would he be at the moment? In Kuwait or Syria? I doubt it. He has never been one for the sidelines, witness those photographs he has shown us of Rwanda, the Congo, or – earlier – Somalia and Afghanistan. I have little doubt that he is somewhere in Iraq itself: stubbornly on his own, not 'embedded'. He wouldn't even know that you are dead. Perhaps that is not a bad thing, for either of you. After all that has happened. You used to be so proud of him, Rachel. So much of your own dreams you lived through him. Although, significantly, that never prevented you from giving shape and substance to your own life.

Time to put off the light. They have just crossed that bloody bridge again. Won't they ever get it right?

So MANY BRIDGES I have crossed in my life, so many burnt behind me. This one came in 1952, the year the whites in the country, more particularly the Afrikaners, 'my people', celebrated the tercentenary of the first Dutch settlement at the Cape. To most of them this was the beginning of history – no matter that Khoisan peoples had lived there for hundreds or even thousands of years.

God did not seem to approve of the celebrations, as the climax of the festival in Cape Town was nearly washed out by torrential rains. But that could be, and was, of course also interpreted as a sign of divine approval – showers, showers of blessings. I attended some of the festivities, but not in much of a celebratory spirit, and mainly to keep Father happy. I was then in my late twenties, but within the family he was still the patriarch, the representative of God Almighty. Over the previous few years, ever since I completed my law studies at Stellenbosch, I'd worked for my father's small firm of attorneys. At the time it was flourishing in Somerset West, where we'd moved from

Graaff-Reinet. From the outset his authoritarian style had bothered me; before long, it was rankling in my mind like a burr in a sock. He ran the firm like a personal fief, which was the direct cause of some of the most able members of staff, including Father's partner of many years, Oom Hennie Faure, moving out. I had already been designated as Father's successor, but at sixty-two he was still in robust health and clearly had many years of intractable patriarchal rule ahead of him. So I suppose the groundswell towards some kind of blow-up was beginning to take shape.

I know from long observation, and now from personal experience, that a man's sixties are a dangerous decade. In many respects one is at the height of one's powers. Some physical decline may have begun to set in, sure, but if the body has been properly taken care of this should be negligible. Father never frequented a gym as I used to until fairly recently, but those interminable vigorous daily walks and the pride he took in pushing his body to physical extremes (carrying heavy bags of manure for his garden, digging and shovelling to keep his vegetables and his rose garden in prime condition, moving boulders from one rockery to the other, outdoing Sisyphus) kept him fearsomely fit. What does happen at this age, however, is that intimations of mortality begin to manifest themselves. More often than not, and again I speak from experience, one goes out of one's way to demonstrate one's sexual prowess. That can change everything one does; and the way one sees the world. Everything is touched with the awareness of an ending. A certain desperation sets in. And the conquest of women is a way of showing death the finger.

I was lucky: I could demonstrate my defiant virility in any way I wished. There was nothing to stop or inhibit me. But in Father's generation there was little occasion for an outlet (unless one had perfected the routine, as he had); so poor Mam had to bear the brunt of it, as I realised only much later from the occasional hint she would drop in her hindsight years. Which was all the more reason why that particular turning point came as such a devastating revelation.

At twenty-seven, I certainly had no idea of what he was having to deal with, otherwise I might have been more understanding. But we had never been close: if anything, I was inhibited by his unreasonable and selfish expectations of me. The only thing we shared was chess.

From my early childhood it was an activity he imposed on me – but for once it was something I really liked. It was not just a matter of 'achieving' anything or 'proving' something to him. And he, too, enjoyed it. Make no mistake: he always wanted to win! I can still remember him saying, 'If you ever manage to beat me three times in a row, I'll quit.' The curious thing is that by the time I discovered I *could* do it, I refrained, resorting to the most intricate moves to avoid a win without allowing him to catch on. Or perhaps he did? In later years I started wondering whether this was not the most touching thing about it: that we both knew, but pretended not to. For if we did, there would have been nothing left for us to share.

But in that blessed year of 1952 all this was very deep below the surface. I was just becoming more and more resentful of the way in which he tried to plan my life for me. I was fast approaching the point where so many years of rancour just had to explode. Looking back now, I can see that the van Riebeeck Festival sounded an early warning; but at that stage it was still possible to contain it. The catalyst was Bonnie Pieterse. She was not the only coloured person in the office, but she was the only one held in sufficient regard to have her surname acknowledged; Gerald and Solly, the messengers, were known only by their Christian names.

Bonnie had been working in Father's office for at least five years then. Fresh out of school, she had been hired as a 'tea girl', but because it was soon evident that she had considerable skills as a typist and a stenographer, and in due course as a secretary, she was rapidly promoted. It was also, of course, cheaper than hiring a white woman. Father liked showing her off (it was a time when rather few young coloured women were employed in that kind of position in a white firm): she reflected well on his generosity as a good Christian and an enlightened businessman. Some of the party faithful might have frowned on it, especially in those years, if Bonnie had been a mousey or frumpy little 'Hotnot girl'; but the key to her story was that she was beautiful. Quite unbelievably beautiful. Even though she 'knew her place', as Father would put it, she had a quiet, radiant self-assurance which most of the men coming into the office found almost irresistible. All the more so as she personified the forbidden fruit. Remember that the party had been in power for only four years, and there was all the zeal and sweeping powers of the new broom in the process of adding the insult of numerous new laws to the injury of the old in order to write the country's long-standing sense of racial divisions into the formidably formalised legal system it was now in the process of becoming.

So there was a constant influx of portly white gentlemen in suits and ties and blunt-nosed black shoes who suddenly found it necessary to come and discuss 'business' with Father, and stopping to say a little patronising word or two to Bonnie at the reception desk. I have no doubt that most were tempted to add a fleeting caress to arm or shoulder in passing, but they did not quite have the courage to sink so low. Certainly, the firm flourished, and Father's bow ties grew ever more audacious.

On the day the festival reached its climax with a series of historical presentations and tableaux, Father took the bold step of giving the whole office staff, including Bonnie and the two ever-smiling messengers, the day off so that they could also watch the pretentious spectacle – from well-separated vantage points of course – and 'pick up some edifying lessons from history', as he put it. (They had been duly warned that he would question them about the event the next day, so there was no chance of staying away.) As it happened, when our family wended our way towards the good seats Father had arranged for us in advance, we came past the enclosure where Bonnie, Gerald and Solly stood in their Sunday best with the rest of 'their people'. Father strode straight ahead, Mam smiled vaguely left and right without recognising anyone; I saw the three of them and mumbled an awkward greeting. And as the long pageant unfolded, I couldn't help wondering what they made of the blatant display of how the chosen people of God had, by divine providence, come to rule this land. What I found most offensive was the re-enactment of van Riebeeck's arrival at the Cape of Good Hope and the first encounter between his handful of colonisers in their resplendent finery straight from Rembrandt's *Night Watch* and the sorry band of cringing, beaming Hottentots, soon to be lured into abject submission by the fumes of arrack and tobacco.

I couldn't bear it any longer. I got up and walked away, aware of the consternation with which Father and Mam were looking at me.

It was easy enough, afterwards, to feign a nosebleed. But Father was not to be fooled. And I had seen him in action often enough in magistrates' courts, mercilessly pursuing a point in cross-examination, to know that he wouldn't let go.

'Show me your handkerchief, Chris.'

'What?'

'Show me your handkerchief.'

'Why?'

'Just show me.'

I took it out of my pocket.

'I don't see any sign of blood.'

'This is not the one I had with me at the performance.'

'Then will you please bring me the one you took there.'

'I don't have it any more.'

'Where is it?'

'I think I threw it away. It was filthy.'

A pause.

'Your nose didn't bleed, did it, Chris?'

'No.' I lost my temper. 'There's no need to interrogate me like this, Father. I'm twenty-seven years old, for God's sake.'

'Do not take the Lord's name in vain, my son. Why did you walk out?'

'I was bored, if you really want to know.'

'I found it a riveting spectacle.'

'Then I'm glad for you, Father. But I was getting fed up.'

'With the history of your own people?'

I took a deep breath. Seeing the hue of his face deepen from scarlet to purple, I tried to tone it down a bit. 'Not the history. The performance.'

'Is that the truth, the whole truth, and nothing but the truth?'

I tried to control myself, but frankly, I'd had enough. Why should I continue to humour him? 'No, it isn't,' I said, livid but still controlled.

'Then what is the truth?'

'I'll tell you. I was ashamed.'

He clearly hadn't expected this. For a moment all he could do was open his mouth and shut it again. At last he asked in a strangled voice, 'Ashamed of what, if I may ask?'

'On our way to our seats,' I told him, 'we came past Bonnie and Gerald and Solly. There with the other coloured people.'

'I didn't see them. What about them?'

'I'm sure you saw them. But that makes no difference. The point is, when van Riebeeck's landing was staged, I suddenly thought of how it must look to them to see their ancestors portrayed like that. Like mangy dogs crawling on their stomachs, begging for a crust of bread or a chicken bone.'

'What that lazy, wretched lot wanted was brandy and tobacco.'

I could only shake my head. 'You don't understand anything, do you?' I asked.

'Not when you're talking nonsense like this. Now it is my turn to be ashamed. That a son of mine should say such things. And on a day like this. A day of celebration. A day of thanking God for having brought us through three hundred years of strife and turmoil to such a glorious conclusion.'

'I think we are very far from a conclusion.'

'I won't be spoken to like this!'

'Am I going to get a hiding for this?' I snarled. 'Shall I take off my pants?'

'Chris, I warn you . . . !'

I glowered at him for another moment, then turned and walked out; my car was outside at the gate. I got in and drove to the cottage I had been renting for the past few years. (The mere fact that I'd decided to live on my own had nearly given him an apoplexy. But I had completed my studies, I was old enough to fend for myself, and I had to ensure that in matters amorous my space would be left uncluttered. Above all, I wanted to escape from the increasingly stifling atmosphere at home.) For a couple of days I did not go back to the office; I was seriously considering resigning. On the second evening Mam came to see me. She didn't talk about the confrontation at all, just chatted about the ordinary little things of her day. And brought me a bowl of my favourite malva pudding, with an excessively generous helping of custard.

When I went back, Father didn't say another word about what had happened. And I was too much of a coward to bring it up. So in due course everything slowly subsided into normality again. On the surface at least.

But down below all the unresolved anger was still seething. And every time I saw Bonnie the original rage returned like a cramp in the guts. For a while I couldn't bear to talk to her at all, but slowly that, too, simmered down. And I became aware of something new in my reaction to her. I had always found her beautiful; I knew, consciously, that if she were white I would have fallen in love with her. But as this was totally out of the question – the new Immorality Act was being enforced with such rigour and enthusiasm that the very idea of consorting with a coloured girl was dangerous – I tried to sublimate what I must have felt just by showing an interest in her work. I knew she was studying in the evenings, a secretarial course, and I did my best to encourage her, to assure her how I admired what she was doing. Intolerably patronising, I realised afterwards; but at the time there really was nothing else I could think of doing. I *wanted* to talk to her, I *wanted* her to know I cared. Whatever that might mean. (I really didn't dare to probe it.) Which presumably only exasperated her, made her despise me. She probably felt more respect for Father, I sometimes thought bitterly, because however kindly he might treat her, he certainly always kept her 'in her place'. And perhaps, ironically, even perversely, she responded to something fatherly in his attitude. Her own father, who had been a carpenter, had died when she was seven. One Friday, in an alcoholic stupor, he had staggered in front of a car; so who knows . . . ?

And then it all blew up. In a way I'm sure not one of us could ever have expected.

I had begun to notice, over the first few months following the festival, that Bonnie was becoming more temperamental, more unstable in her emotions. She had always been withdrawn and introverted, preferring to keep her own company, but she'd been even-tempered, reliable, pleasant, efficient. Now she was often moody, ready to snap when she felt affronted; and more than once I'd noticed her crying quietly, or hurrying off to the toilet Father had reserved for coloured staff (male and female). There was no set pattern to it, so it didn't seem to have anything to do with menstruation. 'Perhaps she has a boyfriend who *donners* her. You know what these coloureds are like,' suggested a colleague from another firm who used to look in regularly, when I mentioned it to him. The comment made me unreasonably angry; I cut him short with such vehemence that he could only stare at me uncomprehendingly before he stomped off. As it happened, it was later the same day that Bonnie emerged from my father's office, crying. I was coming from my own office as she rushed past. For once, she wasn't just quietly trying to brush away tears; she was sobbing. I could only presume that he'd berated her for something; her work had not been up to standard either, lately. I was so upset that I immediately headed towards Father's door, prepared to confront him.

'No!' It was Bonnie's voice behind me. She tried to stop me. 'Please don't go in there. He's – he's . . .'

'What has he done to you?' I demanded.

'Please, Chris.'

We both froze. She had never called me by my name before; even though it had been perfectly natural for me to call her 'Bonnie'. To her, I'd always been 'Mr Minnaar.'

'Oh, I'm sorry, I didn't mean, oh please . . .' she stammered.

'What happened?' I asked. 'Tell me, please.'

Without any warning she was in my arms, sobbing against my shoulder. All I could do was hold her, making small, meaningless sounds of soothing and comforting, while I really felt quite over-whelmed, not knowing what to do with my arms.

Across her shoulder I could see my father's office door opening. He came out, and stopped dead in the passage. I shall never forget the expression on his face, which went ghostly white. I saw him mouthing a word, but couldn't make out what it was. To him it must have been a scene worse than his own death. And I later thought: Yes, perhaps that was what it was: not just his own death, but the death of his whole tribe, of everything he'd lived for and believed in.

How little did I know.

He never said a word to me about it. Even our chess dried up. It was all beyond speech. For days, indeed, he never spoke to me at all, not even when I went home for dinner on Sunday. And I know he didn't mention it to Mam either, because one evening she drove to my cottage to ask me what had happened to him, whether I had any idea. She was in a state, and there was nothing I could do or say to help her.

It was very soon after that morning that things came to a head. And the direct cause was the National Party's attempts to remove coloured people from the common voters' roll. Ever since 1948, when the party had scraped to victory with a majority of five seats but a minority of votes, the Nats had been obsessed with the mission to 'get rid of the Hotnots' (who had tended to vote almost en masse for the United Party of General Smuts). In 1951 they had actually passed the Separate Registration of Voters Act in parliament. But as it violated an entrenched clause in the constitution, which required a two-thirds majority to be amended, a veritable crusade was launched to reach that majority, even if in the end it meant enlarging the senate and instituting a 'High Court of Parliament' to oversee the change and block any legal challenge.

In 1952 the Appeal Court turned down the legislation because it was unconstitutional. For a moment it seemed as if justice would prevail – but of course it was only the red rag to the Nationalist bull. In the late afternoon of the day of the verdict the news was plastered all over the *Cape Argus*. (We would have to wait until the next morning to read what Father regarded as 'the proper version' in Afrikaans, in *Die Burger*.) After the morning's court session I had been out to lunch and bought the paper on the way back to the office. Father had gone home, as he'd started making a habit of working mornings only. And it must have been a Friday, for both Gerald and Solly, who were Muslims, were missing. (Knowing that Father would not come back, they had quietly begun to take the afternoon off after mosque.) In fact, only Bonnie and I were in the office when I came back with the paper.

I was trembling with excitement when I threw it down on her small desk. The whole sordid business about the coloured vote had been unsettling me more than anything else the government had been doing lately. (And that is saying something: in the recent past, following the '48 elections, the whole redoubtable foundation for apartheid had been laid, with the Prohibition of Mixed Marriages Act; the Immorality Act, which outlawed sexual relations between people of different races; the Group Areas Act, which forced us all into separate neighbourhoods;

the Population Registration Act, which enabled authorities to determine the race of a person by checking fingernails or crinkly hair rolled
over a pencil or drawn through a comb; the Reservation of Separate
Amenities Act; legislation to control the influx of blacks into white
areas, and God knows what else: the list seemed endless.) I can only
guess that the difficult feelings I had been battling with lately, about
Bonnie, and her position in the office, and the impossibility of her
position in my world, must have helped to complicate it all. Even more
so as I couldn't even try to confront them or do anything about them.
This sudden reversal, as it briefly seemed to me, came as an emotional
train-smash to me, plucking me from the very edge of despair to a
state of uncontrollable ecstasy.

And so, yes, it happened.

One moment we were standing on either side of the silly little desk,
both trembling, looking down at the blaring headline. The next we
were embracing. And then we were on the floor, in a frenzy of lovemaking. It was ecstasy, yes, but also rage, naked rage. There was a
whole world of evil we wanted to get at, but each of us had only the
other to vent it on. How much she, especially, had to avenge! – a lifetime of disregard and second-handedness, the humiliation of being
patronised in the office, our revolting white festival, our laws, our
superiority, Father, everything.

And at the same time it was the very essence of passion too, a ferocious attempt to say *I love you* in the most annihilating way we could
find.

We fought like felines; and yes, yes, yes, we loved. Every single
sense was involved, touch and smell and taste and sight and hearing.
It was unbearable, and it was wonderful. Above all, it was impossible.
And when at long last, slowly, wordlessly, we gathered our clothes that
lay scattered over the desk and chair and shelves and floor, and put
them on in a slow-motion ritual of almost religious intensity, we must
both have known that in that beginning was also our ending.

It was, however, not the end of our story; or of that day. The twist
that followed could not have been contrived by anyone, not even by
a skewed mind. My father made his appearance. He had forgotten some
files and came to collect them. No, he didn't catch us *in flagrante delicto*.

Not at all. We were fully clothed, we had tidied up everything, there was no sign in the office that anything untoward had happened. We were not even close together but, once again, on either side of the desk, as if we'd been discussing business.

He came in, and stopped, then went through to his office without addressing a word to either of us. When he came back, he had the files under his arm. As he came to the desk – we were still standing like two soldiers at attention – he stopped again, and frowned. And suddenly slapped down his bunch of files on the newspaper that by now lay neatly folded between us, and said in the most stinging tone he could muster, 'An *English* paper?'

What was there to say to that?

After a long silence he picked up his files again and prepared to go. Then, very briefly, his self-control wavered. 'The two of you . . .' He shook his head and said no more.

'Chris was just . . .' began Bonnie.

It was as if he'd been stung by a bee. 'Chris?' he snarled. 'Was that what you called him? *Chris?*'

She didn't flinch. What she said, very quietly, almost in a whisper, was, 'Yes, Hendrik. That was what I said.'

I AM WITH Mam again. I had no intention of returning to the old-age home so soon, but coming from the cremation in Maitland I couldn't bear facing Frederik's mournful gaze in my empty house where, I knew, all the disarranged books and unsorted papers would stare at me in unbearable silent accusation. So for you, at least for the mortal flesh, this has been the end. There was a scattering of friends, mainly people whose names you sometimes mentioned and which I could find in your little telephone book in your studio, on one of the rare occasions I ventured back there. You had no relatives.

Most conspicuously absent, of course, was George. After what had happened, no one even considered contacting him; and he must be pretty well out of reach in Iraq right now. A scary business, but I can imagine him happy, the adrenalin flowing, the old trusted Leica – dented by many wars, the film compartment secured with black masking tape – clicking away. From our special correspondent. If he had known, would he have come? So much has happened since those early days when the three of us were together. The musketeers, he used to joke. *One for all and all for one.*

The first time I went to the empty Camps Bay house, just a few days after your 'accident' as for some reason everybody continued to call it, to sort through your things in search of the papers the hospital required, there was a feeling of sacrilege about it. Your absence lay like an unbearable weight on the house, on your studio. It was an invasion of the most private nature, a kind of rape. I felt like a man stealing into his lover's home in her absence in search of incriminating evidence, telltale letters, items of clothing, used condoms, a lipstick message on a mirror.

However well I knew you, it was like encountering a stranger: during your mornings at my house there was such thoroughness about the way you sorted and classified everything; but your own drawers and cupboards were an unholy mess. Most of the underwear seemed to have been thrust randomly into any available space; the clean and the soiled or crumpled were lumped together, shoes and sandals were stuck in just anywhere, dresses were bundled up rather than draped on hangers. Your dressing table looked like a battlefield, with the toy soldiers of lipstick, tampons, small bottles of perfume, mascara brushes, powder compacts, moisturising liquids, all strewn haphazardly across the surface; on the bathroom floor discarded clothes and used towels littered floor and bath and basin. (Admittedly, when you'd prepared for your birthday dinner that evening you had no idea that you were never going to come back; you were not, like Mam, always ready to meet your Maker in the night.) I had to rummage through your most intimate possessions (I never knew you took multivitamin tablets, or used vaginal jelly; and I felt I had no right to know), even through your handbag, where I found your Medical Aid card. As soon as I'd located your ID (on the top shelf in the fridge) I stopped searching; I couldn't bear the intrusion any longer.

The last time I went there, the day before your death, was no easier, although I'd thought I would be inured by then. Why did I go at all?

A kind of leave-taking, I suppose. The small hard fact of your impending death had changed everything. It had not happened yet, but I knew it was coming. There was no hope, and no escape. I opened your cupboard without even meaning to, I felt I should take something, something intimate, not to remember you by as I would remember you anyway, but to keep you close. Perhaps, indeed, a small piece of underwear which I could keep in my pocket. A moon-cloth. I even opened the laundry box in the bathroom. But immediately replaced the lid again. Not because it was too intimate, but because it was too banal. I felt physically sick.

At a loss, irritable, dejected, I went to your studio. As if bent on stirring up guilt in myself, I took one of your small sculptures. It must have been the last one you had worked on. Before – whatever. I needed something I could hold on to, something which had been exceptionally close to you. It wasn't finished yet, lacking the extreme finesse you brought to your completed work, the smoothness, the sheen. But I found something haunting in the incompleteness of it. Two little figurines united in a sexual embrace, no more than fifteen centimetres tall. Your work was often erotic, but seldom as blatant as this; though even in its frankness there was an endearing gentleness about it, a distancing, as if the sex were only incidental to what was really happening between the two. A small female with enormous eyes, like some of those ancient Sumerian statues, her perfect little breasts formed by bright glass marbles stuck into the clay torso. She stood bent over, steadying her knees with her hands; and the male was leaning over her from behind, but resting his elbows on her back as if in meditation, as his elongated penis was thrust almost absent-mindedly into her from the rear. She had the head of a duiker, he was crested like a rooster. What struck me was that strange impression of distance between them: however closely they were joined together, the eloquent spaces that separated his body and hers, obtruded somehow, drawing attention to their separateness, injecting a feeling of ineffable poignancy into the whole relationship. (Of course I am now reading into it what you probably never intended. But you *had been* obsessed by space, hadn't you?)

I went home and placed the piece in a drawer of my desk; it did not feel right to exhibit it openly. And the next morning – well, then you died. And this morning you were cremated. The hospital had raised some objections about the uncompleted formalities, the need for consent from a relative. But in the end I had the impression that they, too, were relieved to be rid of you. I signed to grant them indemnity, and they agreed to release the body. That was what you had been reduced to. A body.

The cremation itself I would have preferred to skip, but there was some unspoken sense of obligation, a need for closure, a send-off to the underworld. Among the small gathering of friends there were only five or six I could remember having met briefly when you and George were still together; we nodded to each other, mumbled something, sat stiffly through the uninspiring mumbo-jumbo spoken by some functionary of the cremation service. (You would have shrieked with laughter; I'm afraid I didn't find it funny at all.) Some of the mourners, if that is what they were, had brought flowers. So had I, but I'd left the bunch in the car. There was some canned music, and then the coffin was rolled away, through a small imitation of theatre curtains. We have our exits and our entrances. We stood around, tried to find something to say, in the end just wandered off.

I remembered, most inappropriately, the dissolute gathering following the disappearance of the quite remarkable young German woman Grethe who had come out to Cape Town – how many years ago? twenty? thirty? more – as a leave replacement for a lecturer in the German Department at UCT. She'd been here for six months. I had met her at some party, although normally I shun parties, and there had been a spark; and we became lovers. Then I received a telephone message on my machine in her deep Dietrich voice, in her clipped and correct English, each word enunciated separately, inviting me to come over on the Saturday night. 'You *must* be there, Chris, I need you to be there, it is very important. Will you promise to come? You, of all people, will not regret it.' There was something so seductive and velvety about the voice that I couldn't possibly resist. I tried a few times to call her back, but there was never any answer. *You, of all people, won't regret it*. Often over the years I have wondered about it. Why me? Because I'm a writer? Because of our special closeness? Some of our more memorable lovemakings? Grethe had been in a class of her own, no doubt about that.

So I'd gone. But her flat was deserted when I got there. Admittedly it was a little early. (Perhaps, I'd thought, there might just be time for a quickie? She had been exceptionally good at these kinds of little surprises.) The lights were on, though. And the door was not locked. I went inside. There were snacks on the dining table, and a number of bottles of wine, some opened and breathing. Had she called in caterers, or arranged something with a friend? I have never been able to find out. I wandered around, through the living room, to the bedroom where we had spent some nights of blessed memory, and back. Poured myself a drink. Went to the record player and put on one of our favourites. Reclined in an easy chair, checking my watch from time to time. She was sure to come back within minutes.

After some time another man wandered in. I knew him vaguely, he was also at UCT, anthropology or something, with a reputation as a stud. And then another. After an hour there were about a dozen of us, all rather uncomfortable, eyeing and circling each other suspiciously, like dogs, becoming more fidgety as time went on.

'I've always known Grethe to be punctual,' someone said at some stage. 'I do hope she's all right.'

'Perhaps I could try to find her,' one of the others said after another five minutes had elapsed.

'But where will you go?'

'I know some of her haunts,' he said awkwardly, but somehow knowingly.

'You knew her well?' I asked.

He hesitated. 'Well, yes.' Then he seemed to make up his mind. 'Well, actually, I may as well say it. Grethe and I have been in a rather special relationship.'

There was a very profound silence. And then, bit by bit, but gathering momentum both in volume and urgency, it came out that all twelve or thirteen of us had been in a 'rather special relationship' with the absent Grethe. Each of us had believed himself to be unique; each had been separately and conspiratorially sworn to secrecy.

The mood was complicated, to say the least. Some were spoiling for a fight. One or two uttered fulminations against our absent hostess. Others were becoming morbid and withdrawn. Two or three of us started finding it excruciatingly funny and began to titter, to laugh, at last to guffaw. But there was an undertone of gloom to it, like laughing in a graveyard. And in a way, I now realise, that was exactly what it was.

For later in the evening, the landlady of the building arrived at the door with a message from Grethe. Who, we learned, had telephoned from Germany to say that she had left by plane for Frankfurt the night before, and wished us all a pleasant party. She hoped we would get to know each other better, after all we had something quite important in common. And about a month after that we heard that Grethe had died of cancer; which she must have known to be in an advanced stage by the time she'd left.

I thought afterwards that if I'd been Agatha Christie, I would have had a murder committed on one of the lovers, and it would be quite a challenge to find the perpetrator. In a good murder story you need guilt.

That was the kind of mood we were in, the guests at your cremation, after the coffin had begun its descent into hell – but was it Orpheus? or Eurydice embarking on a quest of her own? – and we were left to our own devices in this gloomy morning. A day that had seemed unpleasant from the beginning, a lived-in day, a shop-soiled day, second-hand and down at heel.

How could I go home from there? Everything was so unfinished, incomplete. And when I got to my car and saw the useless bouquet still on the back seat, I decided to come here, to Mam. She wouldn't know, I thought, that they were funeral flowers.

'Chris!' she beams when she sees me on the threshold. 'After all these years. I have missed you so much, Boetie.' (That irksome term again.)

With a small sigh of resignation I go to her, crumpled in the chair that is so much too big for her wasted little flour bag of wishbones. I lean over and kiss her, smell her old breath, put my hand on one of hers. It is withered and prematurely cold.

'Sit right here where I can see you,' she says.

But it strikes me that I have once again forgotten the bloody flowers, and excuse myself. 'I'll be back in a minute,' I promise. 'I've got something for you.'

Five minutes later I am back, smiling brightly at her from the doorstep.

Mam looks up, her dull old eyes quickening. 'Chris!' she exclaims in her little insect voice. 'After all these years. I have missed you so much, Boetie.'

'I've missed you too, Mam,' I assure her.

'You're a bad liar,' she says disapprovingly.

I decide not to respond. 'I brought you some flowers,' I announce, trying to sound cheerful.

'You never bring me flowers. Why now? Am I going to die?'

'I'll ask one of the nurses to find a vase for you.' I approach and press the bell beside her bed. A nurse appears, takes the bunch with a look of severe distaste, and goes out.

'Why are you dressed in those awful clothes?' asks Mam. 'You never wear a tie.'

Why have I come here? I grit my teeth and say with infinite patience, 'I told you, a friend of mine died. Rachel.'

'Is she still dead?'

'I think she will be dead for a long time, Mam.'

'I'd give anything to be dead,' she says. And after a moment, 'Why didn't you bring your father with you?'

'He's dead too, Mam.'

'There are people dying these days who never lived.'

'We're all heading the same way. I'm not getting any younger either.'

'As long as you don't leave me in the lurch.' Without changing her tone of voice, she continues, 'Still, I wish you would bring your father along sometime. I know he's feeling guilty. But that's no reason to stay away.'

'What has he got to feel guilty for?'

'Everything. All those women. And coloured ones too.'

'Mam!'

'And he's still after them, I know. That's not nice, is it?'

'What do you know about that?' I ask her, with sudden urgency.

'About what?'

'The women, Mam.'

The nurse returns with a hideous green vase in which she seems to have thrust the flowers with some force. She slams it down on the bedside table, straightens her uniform and stalks out.

'My, what a temper she has,' says Mam. 'I think she doesn't get enough.'

'Of what?' I ask, not sure that I could have understood her correctly.

'Of what she needs,' she says slyly.

'That's not a nice thing to say, Mam.'

'It's not a nice thing to go without.' She straightens the wrap over her knees, turning a poker face at me. 'Why are you staring at me like that?'

'Do you know what you just said?'

'You can't expect me to remember everything.' She adds without any reason, 'A real gentleman always sleeps on the damp spot, you know. And he cuts his toenails straight.'

I briefly shut my eyes to compose myself. Then I try to get her back on track, although I have little hope. 'You were talking about those women,' I say with feigned innocence.

'Why do you think your father was so keen on golf?' she asks.

I have no idea of what she has in mind, but I grimly try to humour her. 'Good for business,' I suggest.

'The golf course is right next to the location, isn't it?' she asks cheerfully.

'You don't mean . . . ?'

'I don't mean anything,' she says in a whining tone. 'But what bothers me is this: when I die . . .' Her voice trails off. It takes a while before she resumes. '*If* I ever die, and God asks me about it, what am I supposed to say? I can't betray my own husband, can I?'

'Just tell the truth,' I advise her solemnly. 'Will you?'

'Of course I will.' She looks at me in sudden consternation. 'But how will I remember what the truth was?' A few tears run down her cheeks, losing themselves in the deep wrinkles. 'But there's one thing I do remember,' she says hopefully.

'What is that?'

'How we used to play marbles, you and I.'

'And you always cheated.'

Two small red spots of indignation inflame her cheeks. 'Chris! I never cheated. I would never do a thing like that.'

'Oh but you did.'

Now she is crying, sobbing most desperately. 'I was the one who always kept you on the straight and narrow. Only yesterday, when you tried to cheat poor Aunt Mary out of her gem squashes. I was so ashamed of you, Boetie.'

'Mam.' Why am I still trying to reason with her, for heaven's sake? Why is it so important to score a cheap point off the poor old creature who doesn't even know what she is saying? Yet I press on: 'That was seventy years ago. I was eight years old, I remember very well. You sent me to Aunt Mary's with four gem squashes from Father's vegetable garden.'

'Exactly,' she says eagerly. 'And she sent you back with three tomatoes. And you were ranting and raving about how she was cheating us.'

'I didn't rant and rave. I just pointed out that I didn't think it was fair.'

'So I said, all right, don't make such a fuss. If you don't agree, just go back to Aunt Mary and ask for one squash back. It was a joke. For heaven's sake, Boetie, it was a joke. I never thought you'd take it seriously.'

'I thought you meant it. And I agreed. But when I came back with the squash, you nearly killed me. Forced me to take the damn squash back once again, and then locked me up in my room until Father came home and you told him to give me a beating.'

'Good for him. That little bum of yours needed a tanning.'

'Most of the time it was quite undeserved. Not that you ever tried to stop him.'

'You had the sweetest little bum,' she says, pointedly ignoring my reproach.

'That was a very long time ago.'

'Sometimes I still think of you as my baby.'

'I wish you wouldn't. I'm an old man now.'

'You know what upset me?' she blunders on. 'It was old Aia who looked after you when I couldn't. Whenever you were fidgety, she would take that little thingy of yours between her lips until it stood straight up like a lady's pinkie when she's having tea from a porcelain cup. Most improper, a black woman and all. But what could I do? I was sick most of the time.' She sighs. 'And now the harm has been done. A man just like your father, if you ask me.'

'I am *not* like him, Mam!'

'You've certainly tried your damnedest. All those girls, all these years.'

'Do you remember a girl called Bonnie?' I launch a frontal attack.

'No. Should I?'

'She worked in Father's office.'

'Many girls worked in your father's office. Every time I found out he got a new one.'

'But I think Bonnie was special to him.'

'Most of them were.'

'She was a coloured girl.'

'That makes sense. But I don't remember.'

'Try to think, Mam.'

'Thinking makes me tired, Boetie. It's been over a century now, you know. And where has it got me?'

'It was soon after the Nats' victory,' I press on.

'When was that?'

I cannot suppress a sigh. 'In '48. Not so long after the war.'

'Yes, your father and the war. Many a day I thought he was going to land us all in jail. Those men he hid away in the attic so the police couldn't get them. Do you remember? Thank God the war is over now, we can breathe again.'

'There's another war on now.'

'Where?'

'America is attacking Iraq.'

'Why?'

'Nobody knows.'

She nods wisely. 'At least that will keep them busy for a while, won't it?' She chuckles. 'Little boys, all of them. If you don't keep them busy they start fighting and it can become very rowdy and unpleasant. Thank heavens, you were never the fighting kind.'

'I was asking about Bonnie, Mam.'

'Yes, the one who died. Poor thing. How thoughtful of you to go
to the funeral and bring me the flowers from her grave. I know your
father would have wanted to go, but he was too heartbroken. He really
loved that girl. Called her his little liqueur chocolate. He could never
get enough of chocolates. Especially the brownies I made. Did I ever
give you the recipe?'

'Many times, Mam. Thank you. But I have to go now.'

'I know. Don't forget to take the flowers. They make me come out
in spots.'

I CANNOT LET go of Bonnie. Of what happened that day, that signal
day. And Mam's rambling has brought it back more acutely, more
disconcertingly than when I first wrote my notes about it. I find it
necessary to revisit it, to tease and worry it more, to see if I can make
it release the secret it seems to hold, or some of it. The shock of
discovering Father's involvement was, initially at least, a major part of
it. Not so much the personal angle, the fact that he had been sleeping
with her for God knows how long, however unnerving that was. But
that his involvement with Bonnie – and for all I knew, other coloured
girls (Mam's reference to the 'location' next to the golf course made
me feel sick) – came *at that time*. He was such a staunch member of
the very party that was going out of its way to make 'sex across the
colour bar' not just a transgression but a sin, a crime against God. I
was both repelled and fascinated by the attempt to figure out the
mechanics of the affair. How would he with his dour correctness and
his innate sense of superiority have set about it? '*Now take off your panties
for the baas. Open up. There's a good girl . . .*' When I was a child, there
was little difference, in my mind, between him and God. The long line
of punishments that marked my trajectory from childhood to adoles-
cence and beyond, still burns in my mind. The religious prelude, the
shameful baring of my nether parts, followed by the thrashing itself,
with Mam forced to look on. (He never knew about her surreptitious
visits to my room afterwards, to apply ointment to the bleeding welts.)

All of it to equip me for service to the nation and to Father, Son and Holy bloody Ghost. While in the meantime he . . .

He never discussed Bonnie with me again. To tell the truth, I didn't give him any opportunity either. The following month I found a position with another firm of lawyers, and in due course moved from Somerset West to Cape Town; until, after Sharpeville and the success of *A Time to Weep*, I gave up legal practice altogether and began to write full-time.

During the few weeks before I left the firm, I tried everything I could to discover Bonnie's whereabouts, but without any luck; she never even came back for her last month's pay. And Solly and Gerald could not, or would not, help. For days I wandered the streets of District Six, braving the inquisitive or suspicious stares to enquire at every shop and hairdresser and fishmonger, but to no avail whatsoever.

It was hard enough to reconcile myself to what had happened. But worst of all was simply the struggle to understand the elements of the event itself. To Father, for all I knew, her disappearance might have meant no more than the loss of a good fuck. (And lately I have been wondering whether this was not doing even him a disservice; I post-poned for too long any attempt to get closer to him. In our chess games I caught glimpses of a different, more generous person hiding inside him. But these were too few and far between. Which I suppose was one of the many reasons that drove me to the futile interrogation I attempted with Mam earlier today.) But what had that afternoon with her really meant to *me*? I know I suffer from the Hamlet complaint: thinking too brainsickly on things. But this is something I cannot let go – because it will not let *me* go. It seems to me now that the day of the pageant during the van Riebeeck Festival had really been a first premonition. Why had the tableau about the arrival of the Dutch colonists disturbed me so? It was more than the humiliation of the Khoi people, or the discomfort it caused me to know that Bonnie and her colleagues and a sprinkling of other coloured spectators were witness to it at the same time. It was, I think, the realisation that they were not merely watching the spectacle, but watching us watching the spectacle. *We* were the real spectacle. *I* was. Their eyes watching me watching the show added yet another pair of eyes to the already unset-tling perspective: in my mind I was watching them watching us watching the show. That was it. My awareness of their presence made me conscious of myself in a way I could not otherwise have been. My whiteness became a product and a consequence of their brownness observing me. It brought a disturbing convolution: for the first time I had an intimation (for at that stage that was all it was, no comprehension or 'insight' yet) of what it meant to be coloured, of living inside a coloured skin, behind and within coloured eyes, and perceiving through them what it meant to be white.

What had been, that wretched day, a mere dawning of a new way of seeing, became, the Friday afternoon in Father's office, an understanding of truly shattering impact. I have tried, since then, many times, to relive, as I am trying at this moment of writing, what had taken place on that floor. Only afterwards could I try to disentangle the − literally − amazing simultaneity of sensations and perceptions. The colour of her skin. Yes. Very much that. The delicate cinnamon colour of the inside of her thighs, paler than the rest. The softness of that skin. Was it so soft by itself, or was it my perception that made it so? Or my perception of her perception of my perception . . . ?

It becomes too ludicrously convoluted. And yet I must persist. I am trying to *understand*, trying to *see*, after all these years. And it is important. Because just as on that day of the festival, only infinitely more acutely, I was not living the moment as a straightforward experience but as an incredibly complicated and many-layered one: while living it, joyously and terrifyingly and ecstatically, as *me*, I was also living it as *me lived by her*. Once again, but more painfully this time, I lived my whiteness as perceived by her brownness. Suddenly (but beyond words, beyond understanding; it was only *there*) I knew, from the inside of her, what it meant to be her, Bonnie Pieterse; to be her, woman; coloured woman. And that brought me a new shocking understanding of who *I* was: a knowledge which would never again forsake me. This *I* could only be I because it was lived through her. Through my imagining her as she was imagining me. Not my white buttocks bobbing and thrusting between her brown thighs. But my whiteness itself, as an abstraction, yet expressed in the most intensely concrete manner conceivable. Yes, I think in that afternoon I understood something of what has so often puzzled and fascinated me: what it must be like to be a woman, to be entered, to be quickened inside.

But even that was only the beginning. For it also made me understand something about being a man: being a man as experienced by the woman he enters. Without this, I now believe, I would never have become a writer.

I'm still not sure that I can adequately explain it. All I know is that that afternoon, with that woman, has for ever changed something inside myself. Without it, I could never have stood before you, Rachel, as I stood beside your bed on the morning of your death.

MOST OF MY nights are now completely blank. If I do fall asleep, it is not before six or seven in the morning. It is as if my accumulating memories of love compulsively require the accompaniment of violence. More and more I am stripped naked in the face of war. Those endless bridges burning endlessly. Houses, buildings, towns going up in flames. The same ones, over and over again.

A day or two ago (I find it difficult to keep up with atrocities) fifteen Iraqi civilians were blown up in a Baghdad residential street. So much for the vaunted 'lethal precision' of American weaponry. Pressed about civilian deaths, Big Chief Rumsfeld comments, 'Stuff happens.' Years ago our Minister of Justice, Jimmy Kruger, responded to the news of Steve Biko's death in detention, 'It leaves me cold.' Today that is all he is still remembered for. Mr Rumsfeld may be heading for a great legacy too. Stuff happens.

There may be much more behind the whole war than even oil. Perhaps macho America is finally finding a way to break out of the terrible depression brought on by women's liberation and by the crushing blow inflicted by 9 / 1 1 on the two phallic towers that embodied the national male ego. A Bush in hand is worth two birds.

Even if it no longer induces sleep, at least it eases the vigil. As good an occasion as any to comment on the birds and the little bushes of one's life.

*   *   *

IT IS SAID that everything in one's love life is determined by the first thirty years. After that, we can only repeat our earlier loves. I cannot disagree more. At most, there is an air of prelude, of foreplay, about the early years, the allegedly 'formative' ones. But the newness really begins to open up and fan out and unfurl after that – not merely as variations, however virtuoso, on the established themes, but as new discoveries. How could anything about *you* have been 'anticipated' or 'prepared' by an earlier love in my life? In a way, I realise, of course, that everything I had ever lived before you made it possible for you to happen; but that is different. You are not déjà vu; nor does your appearance in my life turn all my earlier loves into mere rehearsals. They are all linked, I know that, and am happy about it as I sort fondly through the album of my mind; but there is no easy sameness, and certainly no boredom, in the parallels or intersections I discover or rediscover. The very acknowledgement of 'patterns', if there is ever anything as definite as a pattern, confirms for me the uniqueness of each moment in it. If each moment is inevitably amplified by all the others, it is still not a mere rehashing of what has been. From the interaction itself can come something that has not been before.

And so there is you. Or rather you-and-George, the couple, the inseparables. (At least until it was all shattered.) In no other relationship in my life, I believe, has my image and experience of a woman been so conditioned by her involvement with another man – the one she really loved.

We went to the cricket match together, George and I. He went purely for the pleasure, but even so he couldn't help taking a camera with him. When I asked him about it, he smiled. 'Leaving my camera behind would be like walking about naked in public. Perhaps one day when I'm old enough . . .'

'You think you will ever retire?'

'Not really. I think I'll follow the example of the famous photographer – was it Cartier-Bresson? – who said, when he was asked in his old age whether he had stopped taking pictures, "Oh no, I'm still taking them, I just don't need a camera any more."'

Twice George phoned you on his cell: once to tell you how the match was going; once from the Forrester's pub on Newlands Avenue where we went afterwards to warn you that we would be late.

'She isn't missing us,' he told me with a smile. 'She'll probably be working through the night. She's firing the kiln. The next time she does it, you must come over and share it with us. It's an experience not to be missed. Like a photograph emerging from the white paper in the developer: except that for her the stakes are so much higher, there's so much more work involved, and so much more that can go wrong. Patience. Which she doesn't have. And a sense of wonder, which she does.'

You were still at it when we returned, half dozing in an old rattan chair drawn close to the solid kiln in a small outroom at the back of the garage. Your hair covered with a faded red scarf tied tightly over it, a very big, striped, frayed-collar shirt, undoubtedly one of George's, hanging loosely over the skimpy T-shirt. Cut-off jeans, revealing your sharply angled knees, which were drawn up, so that both your narrow bare feet were perched on the edge of the chair.

He bent over to kiss you. You unashamedly offered him your tongue.

'What about some coffee?' he suggested.

I preferred tea; for me, over the last few years, coffee rules out all hope of sleep. You sided with George and he went to boil the water. When he returned with a tray, on which he'd also placed glasses and a bottle of vintage port, he had one of his cameras with him; and while we sat splayed on our chairs, you never letting the kiln out of sight, he kept on taking quick shots of us, but mainly of you, reclining, sometimes with your arms stretched out above your head, or drooping like a faded but still beautiful flower. It was fascinating how, even when you seemed not to pay any attention at all, you flirted with the camera.

'How did you get hooked on photography?' I asked him.

'Like everybody else, I suppose. Getting a small box for my twelfth birthday.'

'And taking photos of all his little girlfriends,' you interposed slyly. 'In the buff.'

'They just happened to be swimming or something,' he objected quickly.

'Of course,' you said demurely, an inscrutable light gleaming in the depths of your eyes – those eyes that keep reminding me of something, of someone, I cannot grasp.

'It was my only defence, damn it,' he said, perhaps too energetically. 'I was the fat boy at school, remember. The butt of everybody's jokes. This was one way of holding my own. Even getting back at them.'

'You just knew how to ingratiate yourself,' you said lightly. 'The same way you did with me. And still do.'

He turned to me and winked. 'Wouldn't you say the prize was worth it?'

'You must have taken thousands of photos of Rachel,' I said quietly, hoping he would take the bait.

And he did. He got up. 'I have a treasure of them.' He started towards the door. 'I must show you.'

But you caught his hand as he came past and said very quietly, 'No, George, don't.'

There was the briefest moment of tension. He pulled a face and pleaded like a boy wanting a favour, 'Ag please?'

You shook your head quietly. 'Rather not.'

'All right.' He returned to his chair, stopping to fill our glasses. The night continued for some time, relaxed as earlier. But I had become aware, as during the previous evening we'd spent together, of a subtle shift which excluded me from your alliance – even though after the brief exchange about the photos, I detected a suggestion of distancing between you, as between your sculpted figures, the merest hint of a reproachful edge. But it might have been my imagination.

Soon after that I left, and the two of you remained behind, together.

With that, a foundation had been established. We regularly had meals together, at your place or mine, or in a restaurant; you both prized good gastronomy as I did. Like music. We often went out to concerts, preferably to the City Hall. Or we went for long walks, usually along the mountain path from the lower cable station at Kloof Nek, along the folds of the mountain above Camps Bay. George had a hard time keeping up with us, but he insisted on going all the way. 'I need it even more than you do,' he would explain, even though we were forced to make several halts and he would huff and puff like a steam engine.

Making love, I thought more than once, must take him to the edge of a heart attack. But there, as on our walks, I was convinced that he would never give up. How could he, with you there, with your long limbs, your athletic stride, your impossibly alluring body, your navel a small indentation in the slight swell of your belly bared to the caress of the high winds, your cheeks glowing, your dark eyes shining, and the light sheen of sweat on your forehead and the darkening moist patches under your armpits and between your sharp shoulder blades?

Often I accompanied him to the two Wendy houses in Khayelitsha where he ran, with two assistants, workshops on photography for township kids. The enterprise was sponsored by a newspaper, and kept going largely through grants from a Scandinavian NGO. On several occasions they were on the point of withdrawing, as they were convinced that aid was more urgently needed in the fields of primary health care or education or poverty relief. But so far, every crisis had been resolved by a trip to the north, where George's eloquence, backed by his tremendous international reputation, swayed the most hard-nosed sponsors.

It was heart-warming to watch him at work: the endless patience with which he helped the handful of youngsters chosen for his courses; but even more than that, the enthusiasm with which, after the more formal sessions, he would play around with a whole swarm of smaller boys and girls who had gathered purely from curiosity. He would teach them games, joining in the fun like a huge, overgrown schoolboy, laughing with more joyous abandon than any of the children, catching them or allowing himself to be caught by them – while in between, with all the easy grace his Falstaffian hill of flesh was capable of, he would allow them to take turns with his cameras, to take snaps or be snapped, the products of which he would faithfully bring back to distribute among them the next time he returned to the township. It struck me only after several visits how remarkable it was that his Wendy houses, without any protection of burglar bars, remained untouched by criminals and vandals in an area where every commercial concern, formal or informal, from scrapyards to spaza shops to rickety stalls, was barricaded like a fortress; when I asked him about it, he merely smiled. Later, one of his assistants told me that the premises were under the protection of two of the most notorious gangs in the township.

What a father he would make, I thought so many times. There was a line from Dostoevsky's *Idiot* which kept on trailing through my head like a slogan on TV: *It is through children that the soul is cured.* But if that were so, how could he ever have consented to a vasectomy? I'd never, after that first wordless but eloquent gesture in response to my query, brought it up again; but I could only surmise that he had either plunged in much too rashly, or that there must have been medical reasons into which it would be too indelicate to enquire.

But I did bring it up, with you, one morning when you were working at my house in your melodious and efficient way, systematising all my documents, transferring everything to the new computer you had made me buy.

'I was at George's workshop again yesterday,' I told you. 'Every time I see him I'm amazed by his sheer energy.'

'You're not the only one to be amazed,' you said with your enigmatic little smile.

And again, as often before, as always before, I imagined the two of you in bed, or on the floor, engaged in a whole *Kama Sutra* of contortions.

'There's no end to those kids,' I said quickly, to dispel my more lurid fantasies. 'They're enough to sap the energy of an Olympic athlete.'

'He wouldn't do it if he didn't love it.'

'I'm sure of that.' I paused very briefly, then for some reason decided it was the right moment to plunge in. 'He really should make the most wonderful father. I wish he hadn't been in such a hurry with the vasectomy.'

You went on typing.

'It must have been well before he met you,' I said.

You finished a long paragraph. Suddenly you dropped your hands; those long fingers. 'George never had a vasectomy,' you said.

'What?! But he . . .'

'*I* am the dud,' you said very quietly. 'A year after we got married, when nothing happened, we had ourselves tested. They said I could never have children. It's . . . something with the tubes.'

'Oh no.' I didn't know what to say. I felt such a fool. More than a fool: I felt I'd ventured into a space where I had no right to be. As on that day, a year later, when I had to look for your ID for the hospital and had to go through your cupboards and drawers. 'This is terrible, Rachel. I'm so sorry.'

'It's not your fault,' you said with what sounded almost like a tinge of humour.

'I mean . . . Fuck it, Rachel. How do you manage?'

'If it's inevitable, one learns to manage.'

'But why did George say . . . ?' I couldn't complete the question.

'Because in the beginning I was so devastated, I just cried all the time. I thought I should leave him, set him free. I knew how much he'd set his heart on children. Much more than I ever did. But he was so incredibly patient with me. And whenever it comes up, he covers for me. Pretends it's all his fault, makes a joke out of it. Just to make it easier for me.' There was a sudden choking sound in your voice. 'But I know. I *know* what it does to him. Oh God, Chris, I love that man.'

I took your face between my hands to look at you. You stared straight back, unflinching. But there were tears in your eyes. You suddenly put your hands on mine. 'Don't,' you whispered. 'Please don't.' Then you quickly got up. 'I need some coffee. And I'm sure you can do with tea.'

'Let me.'

'No. I need it more than you.'

I thought you would completely shy away from the subject when you came back; pretend the words had never been spoken. But instead, after you had put the tray down, and allowed a decent time for my tea to draw, and poured for us, you said brightly, 'You know, actually, that blow brought us closer together. I can tell you one thing: it has made our lovemaking more passionate and more wonderful than ever before.'

'Unbelievable.'

'It wasn't easy in the beginning. Especially for George. But we worked it out. And since then . . .' The frankness of the smile said everything.

'Then I'm happy for you both.' It could have been an unbearably feeble remark, but what I said was what I really meant; and you seemed to understand.

You took one of my hands in both of yours. I looked down at them. The smoothness and youth of yours, the unevenness in the fingers making them more fascinating. And mine: it was as if I was discovering them for the first time. Not as part of me, but as an object divorced from me, a crab or lobster, unsightly and gawky, the joints knobbled and knotted, the nails horny, the skin blotched.

'My dear, dear, old friend,' you said raising my hand to your lips and kissing it. I closed my eyes in revulsion. How could you? And in my mind I heard those words over and over again.

My dear, dear, old friend.

That was it: that was why you felt so completely at ease with me, why you could confide in me like this, tell me such intimate things about yourself.

I was old, old. Harmless, safe.

An old confessor, ensconced in a cubicle of the mind, offering absolution, posing no threat. You could take off all your clothes before me, and I would not flinch, let alone sprout an erection; there would not be a frisson, nothing at all. That must be what you would think, wasn't it?

Poor old dodderer. Dear, dear old friend.

I went out. I blundered into a doorpost. I couldn't let you see that I was crying, could I? I loved you. Your dear, dear old friend loved you, you see.

And that was what made it so unbearable when only a few days later the three of us went out to a restaurant to celebrate your birthday. How could any of us foresee that exactly a year later the atrocious thing would happen which would end in your stillness, lying there under the sheet with only a foot protruding; and in me here, writing in the notebook I had bought especially for the purpose; writing for the first time in God knows how many years?

There were times in the past, the distant past, when I would come out of a love affair, aching and bruised inside and out, and try to console myself by thinking: *At least I can get a book out of this.* How threadbare, how appalling that now sounds to me.

Every book I have ever written, every book I have ever read, cannot measure up to the sound of your laughter, the movement of your breath, a look in your eye, or even, my God, your voice saying, *My dear, dear, old friend.*

But let me not wander. What was I trying to say? The evening of your birthday. Yes. The three of us in La Colombe. The best restaurant in town. My treat, I had warned you in advance. It was not what I would have chosen, had I been free to choose, to give you. (What then? Something very fine, the finest gold, feather-like and exquisite and exorbitantly expensive, but understated, quiet and happy and beautiful. And, yes – allow me the momentary lapse – the sweetest and daintiest little thong I could find, spending hours and hours over the choice, amid the disapproving stares of shop assistants, particularly the more mature among them. *Dirty old man. Who does he think he is?* All of that fading away in the moment of giving. And then, oh certainly, the moment when you would try it on and spontaneously come to show me. *Look! What do you think?*)

All right, then. The evening of your birthday, 28 February. And after the toast (the moment of contemplation and meditation, in due reverence: the characteristic 'farmyard' presence of a Pinot Noir, in perfect balance with the oak and spice and vanilla, the *soupçon* of coffee, of chocolate, the palate a vibrant cherry and youngberry, steeped in velvety tannins), midway through the unbelievably succulent Karoo lamb in its crust of herbs, George's sudden announcement:

'Chris, we have a favour to ask of you.'

'It can wait,' you whispered with some disapproval.

'No, it can't. Chris, I'm off again on a trip next week. Japan. We've had two burglaries in our street this week, and I'm not happy about leaving Rachel on her own. Could I prevail on you to keep an eye on her?'

My heart jumped. But I kept my calm. 'I cannot possibly take on such a responsibility,' I said without batting an eyelid.

It was quite something to see his face fall. But you caught on immediately and burst out laughing.

'To say it will be a pleasure would be an unforgivable understatement.'

'Even if it involves prising you from your own comfortable shell to come and sleep over in Camps Bay?'

'I'll have to think about that. You know I am an old man. I need my familiar space.'

'I really don't want to . . .'

'Of course I'll come. It will give me such pleasure.'

'I don't know how to thank you.'

'We can work out something,' I said mockingly.

'You're a dear, dear friend.'

Don't forget the *old*, I thought. Oh, it rankled. It still did.

THERE WAS A sequel to that encounter with Driekie in the fig tree, following her distressing story about the boy David who had spied on the swimming sisters and was so mercilessly thrashed for it. Most of the events of that summer holiday were framed by the family's involvement in the centenary of the Great Trek, that blessed year of 1938. Uncle Johnny refused to have any part in it, even though that was regarded by most of his relatives and friends as a betrayal of the Afrikaner cause. Everybody else was drawn into the vortex of celebrations, which had begun months before with the departure of several ox-wagons from Cape Town, heading to the far north, zigzagging through the country, whipping up patriotic emotions to a state of frenzy; it was, people realised much later, the rebirth of a national consciousness which was to culminate, a decade later, in the National Party's victory at the polls in 1948. On 16 December that year, the day traditionally celebrated to commemorate the triumph of the Voortrekkers over the pride of Dingane's Zulu warriors in Natal, the arrival of the wagons in Pretoria sent waves of near hysteria throughout Afrikanerdom. (That no one else in the country, neither the English-speaking whites nor the vast majority of blacks, had anything to celebrate, was easily ignored.)

A single small turbulence disturbed the even flow of the days leading up to the great celebration. One evening there was an argument between Father and Mam on the stoep, to which I was the only witness. I couldn't make out what it was about, except that the name of one of the coloured womenfolk in the kitchen came up several times. Eva. And that this seemed to upset him most violently. Throughout the next day, from morning till evening, he never emerged from their bedroom. All my anxious queries were met by a single terse response: 'Your father is thinking.' I was never told the reason, and not one of the grown-ups ever mentioned it. (When, later, I dared to broach it to Uncle Johnny, all he said was, 'Sometimes wine should just be left to ferment on its own, so all the stuff can sink to the bottom.' That word. *Stuff*.) But in an inexplicable way the weight of that day kept pressing down on most of my youth, the sum and summary of a man I would never be able to understand. (A man I'd have *wanted* so much to understand? For what was really behind it? Not just anger. Much rather, if you asked me, something like sorrow. But why?)

When the hallowed day arrived at last, we all – Aunt Bella, her five pretty daughters, Mam and Father and I, but not Uncle Johnny – set out from the Franschhoek farm to the huge gathering in Cape Town. It was, if I remember correctly, some three days after Driekie had celebrated the rites of womanhood in the fig tree (even if what all the womenfolk had bewailed and celebrated as the first sign of blood turned out to have been no more than the juice of squashed purple Adam figs). It was a memorable day, in which religious fervour and patriotic passions combined in the kinds of scenes normally associated with being possessed by spirits. Time seemed to uncoil and turn back upon itself.

The Parade in Cape Town was transformed into a laager of ox-wagons. All the men, their faces obscured by beards that had been tended for many months (in several cases assisted by the liberal application of foul-smelling potions, including chicken shit), were dressed in corduroys and moleskins, with crudely made veldskoens and wide-brimmed hats; all of them smoked pipes, and many carried ancient rifles or newly plaited sjamboks. The women strutted about, bedecked with full-length Voortrekker dresses worn over innumerable petti-coats, with finely embroidered kerchiefs and huge pointed kappies, looking like occult birds with outsized beaks. I could not stop staring at Mam, Aunt Bella and the girls, the latter of whom, though copi-ously covered from head to toe, I somehow found particularly alluring (for I now knew, and how, of the *filimandorus* hidden under each of those billowing skirts); and Father, with his trimmed beard and twirled moustache – once more, after his brief mysterious withdrawal, the undisputed lord and master of our clan – and his shiny heirloom pocket watch on a silver chain draped across his ample belly, was a godlike stranger arrived from another space and another time.

The speeches, and the prayers, were many, and boring. But for me there was something heady about the spectacle as a whole. Unlike fourteen years later, at the van Riebeeck Festival, I was not put off by all the chauvinistic pretence. On my thirteen-year-old mind the propaganda was still working. The *volkspele* made me dizzy. I couldn't keep my eyes off my cousins, whose ages, as I now try to recall, ranged from Wilmien (seventeen), down to Trienke (ten), past Fransie (sixteen), Alet (fourteen), and of course Driekie (twelve). Whenever the *tiekiedraai*, of which there was a lot, caused those long skirts to swirl and billow up, there were glimpses of slim ankles to be had (and even encased in veldskoens and socks those were still a privilege to the eye of the beholder, young or old); in fact, even slender or plump calves and the odd proverbial dimpled knee was in evidence if you knew how to anticipate the moves. In the course of the dances I took my turn with all five cousins, and that was enough, by the time we set out for Franschhoek again in the late afternoon, to make my head spin. Theirs too, I presume, judging by what happened in the night.

We were so tired that it was all we could do to sit through the interminable prayers (said by Father in the stubborn absence of Uncle Johnny) that followed the evening meal of soup and home-made bread and *bokkems*. And after that we all headed straight to bed. Mine was up in the attic, as all the available space downstairs was occupied. In spite of the fatigue I couldn't sleep. My head was still reeling with images of my cousins hopping and skipping with their flushed faces and bright eyes. I was in a state of unbearable excitement, trying to think up daring schemes to lure Driekie from the room she shared below with some of her sisters; wondering how she would respond to an invitation to return to our wise fig tree. As it happened, the moon was nearly full, and there was something particularly stimulating about the idea of a repeat performance in the night. But the only remedy was to wriggle out of my pyjama trousers and reach down to my groin.

I felt I was on the point of something momentous happening when there was a sound at the door, which opened on to a small wooden landing from where a steep ladder descended to the ground below. In a panic I scrambled back into my pyjamas, just in time to sit up and recognise, in the moonlight slanting in from the door, Driekie's silhouette. This was too good to be true.

But it turned out to be not quite what I had for one wild moment believed: she hadn't come to join me, but to call me outside, giggling and fidgeting so much that I had difficulty making out what she wanted. Trying my best to conceal the pointed pyramid in my trousers, I sidled after Driekie, down the ladder.

'Where are we going?' I whispered.

But she just shook her head, put a finger to her pomegranate lips, and led the way, round the house to the back, across the moonlit backyard, and into the barn. Once inside, without warning, we were surrounded by a number of very black shadows that interposed themselves between the two of us and the wide, open doors. It took a few moments for my eyes to get used to the treacherous light inside: the moonlight made a dazzling white pool stretching from the door to about midway into the barn, but the rest was pitch dark. I was suddenly getting scared. But when I turned to go, the way was blocked. And then I heard a ripple of giggles, and realised that my captors – if such they were – were only my cousins, all five of them, as Driekie had by now joined their ranks.

Because of the moonlight (as ghostly and deceptive as that night, so many years later, when Daphne was to dance for me), everything seemed totally unreal. I would prefer to think that it was a hallucination, or a dream that had overwhelmed me just as I was ready to climax on the narrow little bed up in the attic. Because surely the whole thing was too perverse, too far-fetched to be true? Five staunch young girls from a God-fearing family . . . ? No way. And yet I should perhaps have been forewarned by Driekie's games in the fig tree; and even more so by the shocking story she had told me there with such unsettling, dark glee to draw me into her spell: about David, and their sinful Sunday swimming, and the punishment they had watched with such mixed and deeply troubled feelings.

Had they conceived of this night, in fact, as some very strange and very twisted response to David? Or was it their collective retribution for what Driekie and I had been up to in the tree where, I know now, I had my first taste of the forbidden fig and acquired, for the rest of my life, what the French call *le goût du Paradis*, the taste of Paradise? Or was it simply an irrational outgrowth of the collective excitement of our day?

Whatever it was, there was something terrifying about that place in the night, with its very stark contrasts between pool of light and surrounding darkness.

I was still trying to escape. But by now they were holding hands in a very tight circle around me. And they were all still wearing their festive clothes, the long-beaked kappies, the full-length skirts that swept the dusty floor, sending up small puffs of very white dust; but they were barefoot now.

'Oh come on,' I tried to reason with them when it became clear that they were not going to let me through. 'We're all tired. I want to go to bed.'

A small, high-pitched wavelet of laughter rippled through them. The circle was still very tightly drawn.

Then I tried to plead. 'Please, just let me go. What do you think you're doing anyway?'

No go.

I was getting angry. 'Stop it, this is enough. You're being very silly.'

Another little spasm of laughter.

'If you don't let me go, I'll have to use force,' I threatened, hoping that might intimidate them. I was much stronger than any of them. But of course there were five of them, and they knew it. More importantly, it had been inculcated in me from the time I could walk, and they must all have known it, that a boy dared not lay hands on a girl. God would shrivel up your hand or smite you with some other form of dire punishment.

Every time I tried to make a dash at what seemed to me a potential weak link in the chain of arms, the circle would draw closer. I could feel their hot breaths on my face. I tried to grab some of the small hands surrounding me, to tear them apart. That merely increased their glee. In desperation I grabbed a forearm between both of my hands and gave it the feared 'donkey-twist'. There was a single high-pitched cry, immediately muffled in a sound of sobbing. But the girl, whoever it was, did not let go. And this turned out to be a turning point. Now I really *was* the enemy, to be stalked, to be enclosed, suffocated, attacked, wounded.

The circle of dancers became a tight huddle of vengeful young girl-bodies, pouncing on me from all sides, jumping on me, bringing me down, pinning me down. They were all over me, like a swarm of rats with sharp little teeth and pinching hands and raking nails and pointed knees and elbows. I had to smother my moans of rage and fear and pain: how could I possibly give in to a coven of demented girls?

Since I couldn't very well shout out aloud and run the risk of attracting the grown-ups to the scene, which would make my humiliation incomparably more terrible, I tried to hiss at them the most wicked of insults and curses. 'Fuck you!' I snarled.

Somehow that merely added to their merriment.

I was driven to such an extreme that suddenly the most taboo of words broke from my lips: 'Cunt! Cunt! Cunt!'

The viciousness of the attack increased. So did their suppressed laughter. And in the process, the nature of the attack changed. They were no longer trying just to pin me down, to suffocate me with the accumulated weight of their wriggling and twisting bodies: they were trying to strip my clothes off me. I held on for dear life, but both my pyjama top and trousers were so loosely fastened that it was hopeless to hold on. I heard and felt the buttons of the top being wrenched from their buttonholes. There was a tearing sound as one of the sleeves was ripped off. Then they tackled the cord of the trousers. By now, regardless of every rule, I was kicking and hitting out, grabbing at anything soft, twisting, even biting. Several of them were gasping and moaning with pain. But it only made them more reckless. The trousers were stripped down to my ankles. I was dragged by my feet into the white pool of moonlight, where I tried to sit up, to huddle in a ball, to protect my privates from their vicious hands and peering eyes. But they kept on unfolding me, rolling me over, stretching me out. And laughing at me, taunting me, prodding me with their feet. Then one of them spat on me. The gob hit me on the chest and trickled down to my stomach. The rest of them followed her example.

And something awful happened. In spite of my rage and humiliation, I could feel a hard-on growing in my groin. My God, not this, not in front of all those taunting, peering eyes. Once again I tried to roll myself out of reach; once again they grabbed hold of my hands and feet and stretched me out as on a medieval rack.

What were they really avenging? Something that had been done to them, or to one of them? Something of which they had learned, somewhere, somehow? Something they could not even articulate but which they sensed darkly, looking ahead into a future of which as yet they knew nothing? I don't know. I don't know.

At some stage I got to my feet again. Immediately the circle reformed around me. I began to charge at them, head lowered, aiming at the thin but deceptively strong arms that were trying to contain me; then going straight for them, crashing headlong into them, trying to wind them, to break them down. All I could remember, for a long time afterwards, was the madness of their dance continuing, the inarticulate, primitive chant with which they mocked me and insulted me and jeered at me. The swinging and flaring of their wide long dresses, the bare feet dancing or kicking out. And at last, somehow, perhaps because they'd had enough, or were too tired to go on, or took pity on me, or just got bored, they allowed me to drop down in a wretched little heap, off centre in the barn, in the darkness away from the relentless spotlight of the moon; and all of a sudden they were gone, melted like shadows into the endless shadow of the night.

Somewhere in the dark I found what was left of my pyjamas and tried to cover my body with the tatters. Up in the attic, panting, dazed, I flopped down on the rustling mattress. And fell asleep, assaulted by an erratic succession of dreams, and half woke up at the first light of day, and discovered from the sticky mess about my crotch that I'd just had the first wet dream of my life. I had just become a man, as Driekie had so recently eased into womanhood in the fig tree.

*   *   *

IRAQ MAY WELL be Bush's big wet dream, his passage into his own warped notion of manhood. It is sickening to behold. Yet I cannot stop watching, night after night. A kind of paralysis seems to have settled in. There is, they say, a drastic need for reinforcements. Right now it would appear that the war may in fact continue for many months. I'm beginning to think that even if the campaign may totally overrun Iraq, even if all the military objectives were realised, that would still be no more than the beginning. The real war may go on for years, for a lifetime. In a certain sense it may never stop again. Is this – this violence without end – what underlies our efforts and achievements, even our loves? For as long as we believe we must 'prove' ourselves. For as long as we have the need to define our maleness, perhaps our very humanity, in terms of our ability to conquer and to destroy.

THE MACHO THING. I think the first time I really saw it naked, and regrettably I *mean* naked, was while I was at university, in my final year. There was a party in one of the men's residences. Must have been the end of the year, just before swot week and the final examinations. It began unremarkably enough. Dancing in the dining hall, which had been stripped of its usual furniture and 'decorated' by a merry invasion of girls. The theme had something to do with 'our ancestors', and those in charge had decided to revert to the era of Cro-Magnon. Men with clubs and Tarzan loincloths, long-haired girls in skimpy skins strategically draped and safety-pinned. A boisterous lot, but that was par for the course. Very soon we were all totally, hopelessly pissed. And that went for the girls too. (In those days they were all, still, girls. Not 'women'.) After midnight, when the official festivities had to stop as the Sabbath was nigh, groups of inebriated males and females spilled into bedrooms. All highly irregular, but that was 'tradition', and tradition at Stellenbosch was, as I believe it still is, revered above rules and regulations.

The girl I was involved with at the time was a Wagnerian beauty, and her name, fittingly enough, was Isolde. Thinking back now, I am pretty sure that this was not her real name, but that because of her stunning Nordic looks I had designated her as Isolde in my mind; and this is the name that has stuck. I was, as usual, and unavoidably, star-struck, and head over heels in lust with her. But she was like a blank wall. A solid ice wall in some inhospitable northern clime. An iceberg, a glacier. I tried and tried, but she would only smile condescendingly, or at the rarest of moments, literally offer me her little finger to suck. And I took it. God, how I took it. It was not that she was a tease, or in any way misled me: she was always utterly frank in the intonation of her *No*. (Just hearing her voice saying *No* was enough to make me come in my pants. I'd never masturbated so much in my life; and that is saying something. Even in my wettest dreams I could, at most, behold a stalactite of pure ice slowly thawing, causing drops of crystalline moisture to run chillingly down the beautiful, frigid sides.)

Isolde found herself in a peculiar position on campus. Most of the girls seemed suspicious of her because of her stunning looks, but once they realised that she was not really interested in men and unlikely to become anyone's rival, they were more prepared to accept her, even if they remained somewhat wary of her. (Was she a lesbian? The thought struck me only years later. Those were the forties, to most of us the thought would not even occur. I can remember once having a long conversation with a close friend, Johann Koch, when we'd heard for the first time about a phenomenon called homosexuality. We found it highly improbable; the mechanics baffled us. As for something comparable among women, we laughed it off: sex meant penetration, did it not?, so the question could not even be posed. And at that stage, with little more than some basic and rudimentary fumblings to rely on, we did not even know about the existence of the clitoris. As for the use of the tongue, Johann found the very thought disgusting, while I preferred to keep to myself my little dangerous knowledge as it seemed to me a purely personal predilection.) Most of the men were drawn to Isolde; she was the subject of much foul-mouthed male spec-ulation at teatimes, and undoubtedly of a welter of male fantasies. Many tried to approach her, but were unceremoniously rebuffed. The fact that I seemed to be the only one vaguely acceptable to her, even though it was common knowledge that I'd made as little inroad on her redoubtable aloofness as any of the others, caused them either to envy me in secret or sneer at me in the open.

What both men and women held against her, and used more and more jeeringly against her, was that her family were Sappe, members of the South African Party, the governing party of Field Marshal Smuts. At an overwhelmingly Afrikaner institution like our university, this was tantamount to treason: how could any self-respecting person support Britain in the war against Germany when the collective memory still nursed the suppurating wounds inflicted by the Anglo-Boer? Not only was Isolde's family on the side of Smuts and England, her father was actually in North Africa fighting the Germans. All this while Afrikaner extremists, most of whom were not necessarily pro-German but ferociously anti-British, were revered as national heroes, and a fair number of activist leaders of the so-called New Order were indeed interned in concentration camps at remote places like Koffiefontein because of their enthusiastic promotion of the Nazi cause. So it was easy to revile Isolde as a traitor to the Afrikaner Struggle, a useful smokescreen for the grudge at having one's amorous advances rejected.

I tried to keep politics out of it, but that was hardly feasible. When I asked permission to bring her home with me for a weekend, Father first made some not-so-discreet enquiries and then summarily vetoed it. Instead, I was summoned home forthwith. He told me in no uncertain terms what he thought of the latest avatar of 'joiners', descendants of the vile breed of Boers who had betrayed their own people by siding with the British a half-century before; and then, changing tactics, confided in me the truth behind a small trickle of strange and mostly bearded men who, over the previous six months or so, had regularly turned up at our house after dark to be lodged, in the utmost secrecy, in the recently refurbished attic for anything between one night and several weeks. Those men, he told me in a conspiratorial whisper, were all members of the New Order, in hiding from the government's police, either before or after the perpetration of heroic acts of sabotage on railway lines, post offices and the like. When I cautiously expressed a measure of doubt, he became nearly apoplectic; then managed to control his fury in order to plead, in his most eloquent courtroom manner, for understanding. These were the real heroes of our time, he impressed upon me, the true descendants of the intrepid patriots who had left behind, a century ago, the land of milk and honey the English had established at the Cape, to open up the barren interior and spread the gospel among the heathen; and of the handful of Boers who, fifty years later, had taken on the full might of the greatest military power in the West and nearly brought it to its knees; and of those God-fearing men and women who, ever since, had borne the cross of poverty and humiliation in anticipation of an opportunity to rise again, with the help of God Almighty, against the imperial enemy who was still trampling us underfoot in the country of our birth. Et cetera, et fucking cetera. If I had any regard for the greying hair of my devoted parents, I would never again mention the mere name of the traitor-woman Isolde who was sullying a noble Nordic name with the godforsaken actions of her despicable father. Et cetera once again.

After that, I tried to circumvent the increasingly thorny issue by taking her for a few days of the September vacation to the farm of Aunt Bella and Uncle Johnny. To my great joy, he immediately warmed to her and they struck up a surprisingly hearty relationship marked by a good deal of wine drinking and uninhibited laughter. I hadn't seen Uncle Johnny quite so jolly before; and as for Isolde, I read in her carefree demeanour the signs of a thawing which could only be to my advantage once we were back on campus. But I had reckoned without the way in which politics were beginning to infiltrate our family relationships. Whether the move was initiated from home or, more likely, by Aunt Bella becoming more and more uptight about the signs of sinful imbibing that marked Uncle Johnny's reception of the immaculate Isolde, I was called to the telephone on the third or fourth day of our stay. Father was on the line. I had to get 'that scarlet woman' off the farm and present myself to my parents before the setting of the sun on that unholy day.

She wanted to go with me, but I could not take the risk. Just as well, because when I arrived home that night the message from my father was stark and simple: if I were to have any contact with Isolde ever again, I would be disinherited; already the shame I was threatening to bring upon my parents' heads was almost irreparable. Did I want to send them straight to a premature death? If not, I should defer to the Fifth Commandment. Not only the future of our family, as far as I could gather, but the survival of our nation was at stake. I had to choose, here and now, before God.

What could I do?

From then on I shunned Isolde. But I had a shrewd suspicion that even if I hadn't, she would not have had anything further to do with me anyway. Such was the state of affairs on that witches' sabbath in October in the men's residence when we were all staggering about drunkenly and noisily, in search of something to vent our pent-up energies on. At some stage, it must have been close to three or four in the morning, when few of the revellers were still on their feet, I landed in a bedroom on the top floor. There must have been fifteen or twenty boozy men around. The girls had all gone. (I believe a spoilsport female warden, more intrepid than most, had irrupted into the residence an hour or so earlier and herded her resentful little flock of innocent lambs out of the den of iniquity.) All that remained to be done, it seemed, was deeply serious drinking.

And then, at five minutes past four (I checked), Isolde entered the room. 'Entered' is not the right word. The door was violently kicked open from the outside and she was half carried, half pushed through it. It was she, no doubt about it. But it was not the Isolde I knew. For a start, she was completely drunk. She was also completely naked. The man who was pushing and carrying her, had her underwear draped over his head. He was holding her from behind, his hands under her arms and one knee raised under her buttocks, so that her breasts and hips were thrust forward. I shall never forget the shocking contrast between her ice-white body and the dark mat of pubic hair of her mound which neither I nor anyone else in that room had ever seen. The man was pushing her forward with considerable force, so that she was half sitting on his knee, her legs akimbo and her feet jerking in desperate little kicks to reach the floor.

In the total silence that greeted their entry – only the music was still blaring through the room and the rest of the building – the man dropped her to the floor and said, gasping for breath, 'Here you are, boys. Now's your chance with the fucking Sap bitch.'

It was one of those scenes where you want to close your eyes, and yet you cannot, because they seem to be forced open from inside.

Isolde was making funny giggling sounds, as if she found it all unspeakably funny. But it could have been whimpering.

Some of the men, recovering from their bewilderment, were starting to undo their clothes. A general cheering billowed through the room. And a chanting began, as on a grandstand at an intervarsity rugby match, a rhythmic scanning of 'Cunt! Cunt! Cunt! Cunt!'

I still don't know what possessed me. I can only remember that at some stage – three or four of the men were already naked, prancing about with priapic glee, and others were kneeling beside her to pull her legs apart and hold her down – I pushed through the throng of reeking male bodies and shouted with a voice I myself did not recognise, 'For fuck's sake, boys, stop it! You can't do this!'

'And why not?' someone asked with unmasked aggression. 'We'll never get another chance like this!'

'Stop it!' I yelled again. My voice was breaking. 'Jesus, boys! If it was one of us, we'd have fallen over each other to pick him up and carry him home to sleep it off. Just because she's a girl . . .'

'Sap cunt! Sap cunt! Sap cunt!' they roared.

Anonymous hands were grabbing me from behind, tugging at my clothes. 'Stop moaning, man. You can go first.' They started pushing me forward, towards the spreadeagled Isolde who was still lying there, giggling and whimpering, stark white on the filthy floor, among empty beer bottles and cigarette butts and pools of vomit. I felt my belt go. A cheer went up. Somebody emptied a beer bottle on to Isolde's crotch. Foam bubbles briefly frothed in her dark pubic hair. My pants were tugged down to my knees.

'Fuck you!' I bellowed like a bull being castrated, and stormed forward, flailing my arms and kicking in all directions, lowering my head to butt it into the nearest face.

If they hadn't been so drunk, they could easily have overpowered me. But I was fired on by a rage that seemed completely and utterly to possess me. In some inexplicable way I crawled half under her and hoisted her inert body on my back, and broke through the mass of stinking, sweating, beer-belching bodies, moving into them like a battering ram, trampling whatever and whoever came in my way, aiming my knees and my feet at stomachs and groins and faces. Until we were out on the landing. A number of them, I had no idea of how many, came after me, but I was already on my way down the stairs, more tumbling and falling than walking.

When I was halfway, the ageing house warden came stomping up from below, gaping myopically at me through sleep-tousled hair as he tried to tie up the cord of his baggy gown.

'What the hell . . . ?' he stammered.

But I was already past, and he had no choice but to continue upstairs to face the mob. In a crazy way I had saved them, because I'd carried off the *corpus delicti*. And the poor man, half blind without his spectacles, could never be entirely sure that what he'd seen passing him on the stairs was a naked girl draped across the shoulders of a half-clothed man. (I had by then shed my trousers in order to free my legs.)

At some ungodly hour – the birds were already cavorting in the trees, shrilling and twittering to cleave my throbbing head – I stumbled into my rented room a block or two away, and shed my load of pale femininity on to the narrow bed. She dropped like a bag of wheat. I had the befuddled presence of mind to cover her with a bedspread, before my legs went limp and I flopped down beside her, half over her.

I don't know when I woke up. It must have been in the late afternoon. My head was splitting. In a complete daze I stared around me. Isolde was sitting on the foot of the bed, wrapped in the bedspread, staring at me with mad eyes through matted blonde hair.

The first thing she said, in fact the only thing for a long time, was, 'How could you have done this to me?'

Even the next morning, after I'd somehow forced or coaxed her into sleep again and then spent the night under a tree in the garden (where I got rained upon at dawn, a most unseasonly event), she refused to believe me or even listen to me. She had no recollection, or pretended to have no recollection, of what had happened in the men's residence. I was bitter, and carried a foul taste in my mouth for days; but perhaps I shouldn't have blamed her too much. I couldn't be too sure about my own memories.

Much later in the day – I didn't know exactly when, and frankly I didn't care – Isolde wended her way back home to her own residence, still shrouded in my bedspread like a mummy. I never found out whether she'd run into any trouble, nor did I try to make enquiries. I sometimes saw her on campus again, but we never spoke. Only once, in later years, did I experience something comparable in the aftermath of such a crazy night, and that was the day after Daphne had danced for me. She, too, erased everything after the event. But at least on that occasion I myself had something to remember, secretly, if rather wryly. This time it was a total loss.

The only rather bittersweet consequence was that a small delegation from the house committee of the men's residence came round to my digs several days later to offer me their thanks. They were lavish in their praise for the way I'd risked my life to save them all from a fate worse than death. In their eyes I was, truly, one of the boys.

SOMETHING LIKE THAT — that blanking out — could never have happened to you. You are too unflinchingly honest. I remember so many of our conversations from the time after George's departure, when I stayed over to look after you. That first evening: You are sitting in the middle of the floor in your studio lightly clutching your feet, your chin on your drawn-up knees. 'If something were to happen to me,' you say, staring straight at me, 'what would you do?'

'Nothing will happen to you. I won't allow it.'

You pull a face. 'No, but seriously. *If.*'

'I'll roll over and die very quietly.'

'That's funny. That's what George said too.'

'Then don't ask such questions.'

'I suppose I just got jittery with the burglaries in our little street.'

'It is precisely to make sure it doesn't happen again that I'm here,' I remind you.

'I know. And I am grateful. Also, it makes George feel better. He is always worried about leaving me behind. This time more than ever. Although I told him it is good for me to have time and space on my own.' A gesture towards the work table. 'I have such a lot to do. I'm thinking of an exhibition in the spring, have I told you?'

'You haven't. It's wonderful news.'

'I get very uptight about exhibitions. I love sculpting, but I can't stand the public side of it. Putting all my work on show. It's like taking off one's clothes in front of strangers. Sculpting is such an intimate thing.'

'Yours especially.' I get up and cautiously take one of your figures in my hands: a penguin-like creature with a human face, sitting on a nest filled with small, squirming babies. 'I don't know how you do it. The detail of the feathers. And in these others, the way in which you capture the texture of materials: you can see this is silk, this velvet, this one wool. It's like that sculptor from the eighteenth century, I think, Houdon. But he was more earthbound, restricted by the real.'

'It's much easier for me,' you say. 'I can imprint the real materials on the wet clay and leave it to dry. Houdon had to replicate it in marble.' A reflective pause. 'But in one way or another we are all restricted by whatever we think of as real.' I am aware of your large, searching eyes on me.

'My impression is that the one thing you're always trying to do is to break out of restrictions.'

'You romanticise me. Your whole world is romantic.'

'Not yours?'

'I hope not.'

'What is yours?'

'I'm not sure. That's the point. I just want to learn to *see*. If I can do that, I'll be halfway there.'

'Halfway between here and — what?'

'I don't know yet. Just somewhere else. Everything that's really worthwhile is somewhere else.'

'And you don't think that is romantic?'

'No. Because I don't fantasise about it and I have no illusions. I don't think I'll ever *get* there. In fact, I don't think I'd *want* to.'

'The in-betweenness again?' I ask. You nod quietly, perhaps wistfully. I resume: 'I have a story to tell you about that. A love story.'

'You have a love story for every occasion.' You must have noticed the reproach on my face, because you quickly qualify what you have said: 'I don't mean it in any belittling way, Chris. Please don't think that. If anything, I think I admire you for it. I certainly envy you. If we are together, I always feel that my own life has been so – *narrow*. Even now with George. Don't get me wrong. I love that man. I really love him more than I've ever loved anyone. But I sometimes wonder whether it's good for me.'

'Love is always good for you, even if it leads you to hell.'

'I don't agree. It can limit you. Because you don't want to hurt the person you love, so you hold yourself in check. Every inch of the way there are *other* possibilities, other roads branching off – but if you're in love, you close yourself off to them. You make compromises. That is my greatest fear.'

'Even when I am in love, I've always tried to explore the byways, and I've never regretted it. Or almost never. In fact, that's part of what the story I have for you is about. A byway not taken. And which I've regretted ever since. So I was stuck in between.'

'When did it happen?'

'It was in France, when I went there after the country here went mad in '76. I was away for seven years. First in London, then mostly in Paris, as I'm sure you know. It must have been about halfway through my stay that on a visit to Amsterdam I met a girl. She was a sculptor, actually, like you, and she lived on a riverboat on the Amstel. Maike. The dirtiest hands I've ever seen on a human being, probably because she worked with iron and scrap metal and stuff, collected old car parts which she stripped and gave a new lease on life, did a lot of welding. But Maike is not the story, just a kind of background to it. We spent a week together inside her boat, pretending we were sailing through foreign lands and places of the imagination, our own Amazon, our own Lake Titicaca, our own Ganges, our own Yangtze Kiang. I was, as usual, convinced that this was the beginning of something that might last for ever and a day, and kept on asking her to come and join me in Paris afterwards. But Maike was not a tomorrow person, she hated thinking about the future. The past was already a no-no place, but the future was worse. All that mattered to her was now, this moment in the heart of the flame, as she put it. The sex was so good that I couldn't bear to think of not going on, not repeating it in the future. It's like travelling. Any new place I come to, and I used to travel a lot, I look at as if I might return to it one day, imagining what it may look like from the future. This used to drive Maike up the wall. Up swaying sides of her long fish-shaped boat, where we lived like Pinocchio in the belly of the whale.'

'So after you went back to Paris . . . ?' you gently nudge me back on track.

'Maike had no telephone, so I had to rely on letters. I wrote to her every day. Trying to persuade her to come. In the beginning I thought of it as a whole life together. Then, slowly, I began to cut my expectations down to size. A month. Three weeks. Two. What about a weekend . . . ? I was just beginning to give up all hope and bury all my dreams when quite unexpectedly she wrote to say: All right, she'd come over the following weekend. Arriving at the Gare du Nord at six on the Friday afternoon. I spent the whole week tidying up the little garret in which I lived at the time, off the place de la République. Which was ridiculous, because she wouldn't even notice. But to *me* it mattered.' I fall silent for a minute.

'Here,' you say, 'have a cigarette.'

'You know I don't smoke any more.'

'You're starting again tonight.'

'It's a filthy habit.'

'Then please be filthy with me.'

I hesitate, shrug, take the cigarette you offer, and watch you closely as you lean over to light it for me. The smoke smell of your hair, the brief bright flare of the match against your cheekbone.

You lean back. 'And on the Friday she came?'

'Yes, but that's not the story. The real story, the in-between story, the story about the lost love, only started on the platform at the Gare du Nord. Where I arrived more than an hour early, to make sure I'd be there, waiting, when her train pulled in. I'd visualised it like one of those Monet scenes. But of course there were no steam trains around any more. Not that it mattered. I was there. Soon Maike would be there. And the future would begin.'

I draw the smoke in deeply, too deeply, and begin to cough. You watch me, giggling like a little girl at a circus. It takes a minute before I am able to take the next pull, more cautiously this time.

'As I was waiting for the Amsterdam train to arrive, another train was preparing to leave from the same platform. There were little knots of people all along the platform, to see off friends and relatives. Passengers were arriving in twos and threes. It wasn't very full. And then I saw the woman. I just noticed her skirt flaring briefly around her legs as she mounted the two or three steps into the coach. French legs, slim and tanned and beautifully shaped.'

'Of course,' you say, your eyes shining with suppressed laughter.

'That was that. One of the myriad little things one notices in the course of a day. But then, the next moment, she appeared at the window right opposite the spot where I was standing. She stretched up to put a small case on the luggage rack.'

'And you saw her outstretched arms. And her breasts. And possibly a wisp of underarm hair. If it was summer.'

'It was midsummer. How did you know?'

'Just guessed. I'm slowly getting to know you.'

'And then she sat down, straightened her dress –'

'Her rather flimsy summer dress?'

'Indeed. Straightened it on her thighs. And looked out.'

'Right into your eyes.'

'Right into my eyes. And did not bother to look away again.'

'You must have been very beautiful.'

'*She* was very beautiful. Very black hair.'

'Of course.'

'And so she looked at me, and I looked at her. One of those moments when you feel, quite irrationally, perhaps insanely, that suddenly your whole life is at stake. I began to move towards the window. She sat without moving, looking at me. And gave a slow, easy smile. As if she knew I was on my way. I mean, really, *on my way*. Not just towards the train, but towards her. My whole life. Her whole life. And then I stopped. I had to make a decision. A few seconds, and the train would begin to move. She was leaning closer to the window. Pressing her forehead against it. I could see her breath misting up a small patch. She looked, I looked. And yes, then the train began to move. You know how those trains in Europe start moving. There is no sound, no jerk, just an almost imperceptible gliding. Her mouth – perhaps I am imagining it now, so long afterwards, but I could swear her mouth was half open. Breathing. And I was right there. Outside. Only the window in between. An invisible barrier, except for the small, erotic patch of mist on the pane. There was still time, a few seconds, no more, then she would be gone for ever. I was thinking frantically about Maike who was due in another half-hour, about everything we had been waiting for and dreaming about. And the train was gliding faster. Another moment. There was nothing I wanted more than to get on that train. But for once in my life I was being reasonable. I tried to calculate, in a single instant, all the possibilities for the future. The train was gathering speed. I was running outside on the platform. She was inside, waiting. All I could do was to put out my hand as I ran, and press it against the small patch of condensating moisture on the cold glass. And in that instant, only for that instant, she pressed her forehead against my hand from the inside. And then she was gone.' I stop speaking. I cannot go on. 'You know,' I say after a while, with an effort, 'I have sometimes thought that perhaps it was the single most perfect love affair of my life. You would say: because of the glass in between. I would say: in spite of the glass.'

'And obviously you never saw her again?'

'No. But not for lack of trying. After that weekend, I returned to the Gare du Nord every single day for three weeks, at the same time. Just in case she was making the journey every day. But she never came back. I had missed my only chance.'

After a long silence, almost grudgingly, you ask, 'And the weekend with Maike?'

'A mess, a total fuck-up. For both of us.'

You nod quietly, wisely. 'What else did you expect?' you say.

'What about you?' I ask. 'What was the most perfect love of your life?'

You ponder this for a while, frowning with concentration. 'I think it happened when I was three years old. A little dog, his name was Pixie. He got run over by a car. From that moment I knew that one couldn't rely on love. It ends when you least expect it. There's nothing you can do, nothing at all. It's *got* to end. That is what love is about.'

'How can you be so defeatist?'

'There is nothing defeatist about it,' you protest. 'If we lived for ever, or for two hundred years, or a hundred and fifty, then love – certainly sex – would lose all its urgency, its whole meaning. It would become a purely repeatable thing. But now, because of time, and because of death, because that is what gives time its meaning, repetition is informed by the need to affirm, to make sure, to set up something in the face of an ending. The notion, the very possibility, of the erotic, is shaped by time. Don't you agree?'

'In one way I believe you're right,' I admit. 'I think of love as a train, on an endless journey. It runs its course, whether we are there or not. For a certain distance I am on it. At every stop – and there are very many – people get on and off. Every now and then a woman comes in and shares my compartment for a while. But sooner or later we get to a station where she has to get off. And someone else comes in. And at some stage I, too, will have to get off.' I bring my face very close to yours, with an urgency that surprises myself. 'But when you're on the inside of love, there *is* no time. It may be an illusion, but at least it is an illusion of infinity. The train is there. It goes on. Is that not what you feel when you are with George?'

'It's possible,' you concede. 'But at the same time I know, I know all the time, that it will end.'

'When I asked you about your most perfect love, I was rather expecting you to say that it was George.'

'And you may not be altogether wrong. It's certainly better than anything I had before. But "perfect" is too big a word. There are all kinds of things in it: happiness, fulfilment, wonderful sex, care, affection, friendship, you name it. But there's fear in it too. And a fair deal of guilt.'

'Fear of what?'

'Of death, since you mention it. I wake up at night and touch George's face, or I tense up to listen with every fibre of my being, to make sure he is still breathing. Knowing that one day it will stop. There is nothing as sure as breath. Because our whole life depends on it. And because it's mortal.'

'And where does the guilt come in?'

'I'm not sure that I can talk about it.'

'Fair enough,' I say. I get up and put out my hand to help you up too. 'I didn't mean to intrude. It *is* very private.'

You stand opposite me. 'I think if there's one person I *can* talk to, it is you,' you say quietly. 'In a strange way I even owe it to you. You have come so close to us.'

'I have no wish to pry, Rachel.'

'This isn't about prying. Perhaps it's about a need to confess.'

'I'm very much a heathen, not a priest.'

'So much the better.' You come past me towards the large, open French doors and step out on the balcony. It is a quiet night. One can hear the sea far below, breaking against the boulders. The tide must be coming in. 'Come to me,' you say.

I follow you outside and remain standing behind you. I can smell your hair again. Mingled with an indefinite, subtle, extremely complex aroma that says *you*. A touch of perfume, a touch of sweat, a touch of sadness, a touch of you, woman, a human smell.

'Where does the guilt come from?' I ask again.

'Being alive, I suppose.' You say it lightly. Then half turn towards me, your face in darkness. 'Perhaps it's just about the children,' you say. 'You see, I knew before we were married that I couldn't have children. But I couldn't bear to tell George. I thought . . . What does it matter anyway? It is too late.' You take a small step back to lean your head against my chest. I lay my hands on the smooth roundness of your shoulders. There is no sensuality in it, just a closeness, an involuntary response to your need for closeness and confession.

'Why didn't you?'

'I was afraid he would reject me. I couldn't bear it.' This time the silence lasts for a very long time, before quite suddenly, unexpectedly, you say, speaking into the night, 'Did you know I was married before?'

'I never suspected that.'

'It didn't last for long. Two years. We were much too young. I wasn't even out of university yet. He was very jealous.' A pause. 'And very violent. When he heard that I was pregnant he was convinced it was another man's child. He wouldn't believe me.'

'Did he have any reason for thinking that?'

I feel you tense against me. For a while I expect you to cut off the conversation. Then you say very softly, 'I suppose he had. I was . . . No, I'm not trying to defend myself. I was wrong. But I was unbearably lonely. And he preferred the company of his old friends. But I *knew* the child was his. No doubt about that, not at all. I assure you. A woman knows.'

'I don't need any assurances.'

'But he refused to believe me. He started hitting me. He was drinking more and more, and when he came home he'd take it out on me. I was actually feeling sorry for him, can you believe it? He became more and more violent. Once he broke my arm. He'd get quite beside himself. And I lost the – the little thing inside me. Then he got scared, he didn't want me to go to hospital, he was afraid they'd find out. There were complications. I nearly died: not that I cared much at that stage. And that put paid to children.' Your shoulders move in a shrug. There is nothing I can say. For minutes on end there is only the sea, coming in, far below.

MUCH LATER WE went inside and I retired to my bedroom. I could still hear you moving about in your studio. There was such a desire in me to go back to you, but I knew you needed to be alone; and perhaps I did too. I couldn't sleep. Everything we had talked about turned over and over in my mind. I thought of the nameless girl who had left from the Gare du Nord that long-ago late Friday afternoon. Her face came back to me, the way she had leaned against the train window to press her forehead against the imprint of my hand on the cold glass. Her eyes were open. Very dark eyes, bitter-chocolate eyes. Like yours. And suddenly it dawned on me that, yes, she was the one you kept reminding me of. That girl I'd never known. The same eyes, the forehead, the wide mouth. Even the little mole like a beauty spot high up on her left cheekbone. Only the hair was different. How vividly she came back, as if the many years – a quarter of a century – in between had quietly faded away. The same face. I was sure of it. Not a shadow of a doubt.

I'd allowed that one to escape. And you? I shook my head on the pillow. You had already got away. And George had, in his quiet way, made sure of it. I couldn't tell if he'd done it by design, or in total innocence. All that mattered was that, by asking me to look after you, by making you my responsibility, as it were, he had guaranteed that I could never lay a finger on you. I was in a position of absolute trust. I could never think of betraying it.

I kept the light on. I did not feel like reading. I simply lay awake, between the fresh-smelling crisp sheets, listening to the dull sounds coming from your studio.

Were you working, or just fiddling about?

Later I heard you going to your bedroom. The conjugal bedroom. Water running. I could hear the rush of it from the geyser in the ceiling above my head.

You were taking your bath. No sounds to betray your movements now, but I could imagine you, reclining in the warm water. Your curls getting damp. Your face glistening, your eyes closed. Your breasts in repose. (What would they look like? One can never guess with any certainty beforehand. Until that instant when a woman uncovers them for you. That first moment of risk, when she turns to face you: *Here I am, unarmed, available, for you, what do you think of me, of this, of these?*) Your knees protruding from the water. Your toes.

I leaned over to take a book from the bedside table, but could not concentrate. I was all ears, trying to catch whatever shadow of a sound might come from your bathroom. My whole body was tense with listening.

The water was let out; I heard it gurgling into the drain outside. You moved to the kitchen. I could hear the kettle being switched on, the hiss of the water. And then, quite unexpectedly, your footsteps down the passage. The light sensual suction of your damp bare feet on the floor. You were listening at my door. You probably saw the chink of light below it, because after a while there was a very cautious knock.

'Chris? You still awake?'

'Of course. Come in.'

You came in with a cup of rooibos tea and a mug of coffee on a tray. You were wearing a short, light housecoat, barely reaching down to your knees.

'This will help you sleep.'

'How did you guess that I couldn't?'

'Just took a chance.'

You gave me my cup and settled easily on the foot of the bed, cross-legged, the tray with your own mug balanced on your knees.

'I didn't mean to upset you,' you said. Not contrite; perhaps concerned.

'No. It just takes a while to settle into a strange room.'

'I hope it won't be strange for long.'

'Thank you for telling me what you did.'

'I didn't mean to burden you with it. I don't normally go about looking for shoulders to cry on. But I felt a bit defenceless with George gone. And I had a feeling I could trust you.'

'With anything.' I felt like saying, *With your life*, but didn't.

'Why did you never remarry after your wife died?' you ask.

'It was hard enough to get married the first time. But I loved Helena very much. And she'd made it very clear that she would not sleep with a man unless she was married to him.'

'You got married to have sex?'

'It was not as crude as that. I wanted *her*. All of her.'

'You think one can ever "have" anyone? All of anyone?'

'No. If there is one thing I know now, that is it. But I suppose at the time I still thought something like that possible. I thought I'd sown my wild oats and should try to commit.'

'Would you have married her if she hadn't said no?'

'It's impossible to tell now. Women who say no have always held a special attraction for me. Not just to sex: to anything. To the world. To what everybody expects of them.'

I thought of all the days and nights of arguing with Helena. The reasoning, the pleading, the rage, the banter, the supplication. Once, after a whole night of passionate imploring, I tried to change my approach. 'For goodness' sake, Helena,' I said. 'This is really blowing it up out of all proportion. Why can't you just say yes and let us make love? It's not such a big deal, is it?'

'Yes, it is,' she said in her quiet, decisive way. And that was that.

'So in the end you succumbed,' you said, looking particularly satisfied, as if you'd scored a personal victory.

'I did. I even thought of it as a new stage of my life. Even though I was scared.' I felt an urge to tell you about how it happened; but in the end I still held back.

'Why were you scared?' you asked.

I shrugged. 'It's not so easy to find a reason. All I know is that I *was* scared. Remember, I was already past forty. Settled in my bachelor ways. Perhaps it was because of my parents' marriage. Because of my father. What he did to my mother. She never really spoke about it, but I knew, I could see. Before their marriage she'd dreamed of becoming a teacher. But he didn't believe in a married woman working. Her place was at home. You know the set-up. What made it worse, the way I see it now, is that she believed it too. One thing she did was to keep on reading, though even large-print books have become too much for her. Voraciously. Making notes all the way, something I no doubt inherited from her. For no clear reason, just to have something to hold on to. She still has hundreds of notebooks. The sign of a wasted life. While he . . . Anyway, I just couldn't face for myself the prospect of following in their footsteps. Until Helena came into my life.'

It was getting late. I had a feeling that we both would have liked to go on talking, the way we had that New Year's Eve when we first met. But it seemed prudent to wind it up. You took my empty cup, put it on the tray and got up from the bed. There was a brief hesitation, and then you offered me a small vestal kiss on my forehead. *Dear, dear, old friend.*

'Shall I put off the light?'

'Not yet,' I said.

You closed the door behind you. I still had the image of your long legs moving under the skimpy little housecoat. I could hear you putting off the lights as you went down the passage to the kitchen, and then to your bedroom. The quiet, final closing of the bedroom door. Then the night settled in.

I tried to think of you. Your peaceful breathing, your body in repose. Superimposed on your face was the remembered face of my lost stranger, all those years ago.

Perhaps the whole episode had been so touching because of everything that was happening around it. Those years in Paris. My political involvement with the ANC, the urgent meetings, the planning for a future that, even as we planned and plotted, seemed no more than a preposterous dream. And all the compulsive fucking that went on, as if that were the only way in which we could cling to a sense of reality.

Then Maike filtered back, like a warmth insinuating itself into my bloodstream. I yielded to the luxury of the memories I could summon. Every part of her body a piece of a jigsaw to be fitted together. The texture of her hair, the angle of her elbows, the curve of her spine, the dimples of her lower back, her large, magnificent breasts in which I could bury my whole face. And the most tousled, tangled pubic patch through which I have ever had to find my way. A near impenetrable little forest, a small private Amazon to get lost in. But when one finally got down to the river, slipping and sliding through reeds and weeds and rushes and undergrowth, one could slither through the mud and dive in, wholly immerse oneself, stay down for an impossibly long, long time, nearly drowning, before coming up again, panting and heaving and covered in purple prose.

No one could have been less like Maike than Vanessa. She was Lindiwe's predecessor as my Girl Friday. In fact, she was the one who'd introduced Lindiwe to me. She was coloured. Very light-skinned, with a heightened flush in her cheeks, and sparkling eyes, and an unusually wide, generous mouth. It was that vivacity, that air of irrepressible fun, that caused most of her problems, and determined the whole course of our relationship.

When she first came to me, in reply to an advertisement I had placed in the papers following a few rather disastrous assistants in my employ, recommended by friends and acquaintances, she was newly divorced. Which came as a surprise to me: I couldn't believe that there was any man in his right mind who would let her go. But, of course, she soon made it clear what a shit he had been. Not that he'd abused her in any way. Unless indifference could rank as abuse; which I suppose it can. 'I think we just knew each other too well,' she told me. (I learned at a very early stage that the relationship between a

Girl Friday and her employer, especially when it is linked to a serious difference in age, prompts confidences which may be unheard of in many other situations. And to Vanessa, because of her particular circumstances, it seemed to come quite naturally.) 'We literally grew up together, we were like brother and sister. And also, I'm sure we got married too young. I was only twenty-two, and he a year younger.' Once they had come to accept the inevitable – although to me, looking in from outside, it seemed everything but inevitable, damn it – they managed to coast along more or less comfortably and evenly. Until he met somebody else and asked for a divorce. She had just turned twenty-eight. That was some six months before she came to me, and her troubles had already begun.

It is a phenomenon which, up to a point, I can understand: the way in which a young and attractive woman, newly divorced, or newly widowed, becomes a target to every man in sight. A hind to the hunters. Not only the 'available' unmarried ones, but the married ones too. In fact, she seems even more alluring to the married brigade. There may actually be something comical about the way in which they fall over their own feet to make an approach. But very soon there is nothing funny about it any more. It becomes revolting, nauseating, infuriating. The more she tries to protest that she is not interested, the less they believe her. Just a matter of finding the right one, they assure her. Come on, babes, give it a chance. You won't regret it.

It's like an ailing animal set upon by others of its kind. Perhaps the vulnerability of the individual brings on a panic about mortality in the others: of course they have no understanding of it (as little, it would seem, as their human equivalents), they just sense it, instinctively, murderously. They cannot rest before they have turned the victim into a bloody mess of torn skin and flesh. This is how these men appear to me, I'm afraid. The scent of vulnerability, of possible weakness, is overwhelming: it makes it so much easier to demonstrate their frantic macho image of themselves. And the slightest sign of resistance makes it worse: now the challenge is that much greater, it lends so much more excitement to any blood sport. The first sign of a bull faltering in the arena makes the crowd go mad.

There are the never-ending assaults on her resistance: Come on, baby (or sweetie, or lovey, or pussy, all the diminutives), I know you're dying for it, you need it, you want it, I'm really doing this for *you*. And when she turns them down, all those highly sophisticated, successful, highly educated men (like those exemplary young leaders of the future in the university residence, waving the signs of their manhood at Isolde), they respond with the vilest and most filthy abuse: then *she* is the one who has teased and provoked them and now betrays them, the frigid bitch.

I have transcribed all of this (as if there was any need to refresh my memory) from old notes, from many different periods in my life, but most pertinently from what Vanessa told me at the time. She'd had to give up her lucrative job as a highly paid secretary in one of the city's top firms of accountants, because she could not take the harassment any more. (And when in desperation she went to the manager to complain, *he* took her out to console her, and afterwards forced his way into her flat and nearly raped her.) She was obliged to take up a few part-time, private jobs, like mine; even that did not put an end to the approaches of the sex-crazed pack. When she went out with girlfriends at night, members of the pack (the faces changed, as did the lines of approach, but the lust and the arrogance never did) would materialise from nowhere to try their luck.

There were times when I found her in tears; mostly she was so livid that it took hours, and many cups of tea, to calm her down sufficiently to resume her work. Between us, there was never 'anything' at all. Not because abstinence had been forced on the relationship from the outside, or by her, as had happened with Daphne, or Isolde, or for such a long time by Helena, or some others I can think of, but because her distress ruled out any possibility of a move from my side at all. I was up in arms with her, against the world of men deranged by testosterone. I *wanted* to protect her, I *had* to protect her; and for once the very fact that she was beautiful, and vulnerable, ensured that I would never dream of taking advantage of her. (As, in a different context, George's trust guaranteed your safety in my household; and, for that matter, in your own.)

In the end we thought up a remedy together. It was very simple and very obvious, but we congratulated ourselves on our ingenuity.

And it worked. I gave her an engagement ring, quite an expensive one in fact, and we started going out together whenever she, or I, wanted to go to a concert, or a film, or a meal. It was astounding to notice how soon the news spread. Vanessa could begin to relax; she was safe. There were still a few chancers who caused us moments of anger, but usually they were quite easy to handle. And it even brought us some comedy – when she was harassed in a restaurant, for instance, and excused herself for a minute to go to the Ladies from where she would call me on her cell, and I would turn up soon afterwards to claim my 'fiancée'.

On at least one occasion it didn't turn out well. The man in question, a very important executive as it happened, felt so insulted that he threw a tantrum in front of all the patrons of the Green Point restaurant, treating Vanessa like a whore and me as her pimp.

'You fucking decrepit old fart!' he shouted at me. 'Won't miss an occasion of screwing a *halfnaatjie*, will you? Well, I won't stand for this. I'm going to teach both of you a fucking lesson you won't fucking well ever forget.'

I made the mistake of telling him to mind his language.

'I will fucking well say what I fucking well please,' he retorted, pushing me against the counter.

'I'm not talking about the expletives, sonny,' I said, trying to keep my cool. 'I'm concerned about the paucity of your vocabulary.'

'You fucking *what* . . . ?' For a moment he stared at me, then struck me a blow to the side of my face that made me reel.

At which point the manager came out from behind the counter and, assisted by two of his waiters, shoved both of us outside. Vanessa followed hard on our heels. The moment we landed on the pavement outside, she let fly with her handbag, hitting our assailant at the back of his head. The unexpectedness of the blow sent him staggering against me, which provoked him into a flurry of blows to my chest and shoulders and head.

'Will you please call the police to take this thug away?' I asked the manager in as dignified a way as possible, which in the circumstances could not have been very impressive.

'Thug?' screamed the man. 'You call me a fucking thug?'

'Just an ordinary one,' I said.

His next blow landed me on all fours on the pavement. It could have become very nasty indeed, but fortunately the two waiters, assisted by several of their colleagues, intervened and managed to pin the aggressor's arms to his sides. I did not respond, mainly because I was too busy spitting out blood. Vanessa was kneeling beside me, cradling my head in her arm and uttering soothing words which I wished afterwards I could remember.

A few minutes later the police arrived and we were all taken to the Three Anchor Bay station. The restaurant manager followed in his car. It took a while for things to calm down sufficiently for statements to be taken. But thanks mainly to the manager intervening on our behalf, it was sorted out in due course; and as it happened Vanessa's attacker recognised my name while the constable behind the counter was painstakingly writing down my statement, and began to gawk at me in shock. 'Oh my God,' he muttered, 'are you the writer? Oh fuck, oh holy shit.' He thrust his hand at me. 'Look, I never realised . . . I'm so sorry. . . Whatever you do, please don't go to the newspapers with this . . . Just tell me what you want. Anything, I swear to God, I promise I'll . . .'

'That is for me to decide,' I said with as much haughtiness as I could muster through my badly swollen lips. 'For a start, you can apologise to Ms Booyse.'

'I'm not interested,' said Vanessa and stalked out.

It still went on for some time – the constable trying desperately to get everything on paper, the manager interrupting after each phrase to correct or add something, the executive pleading non-stop, and I trying to stop the blood. But at some stage we left in the restaurant manager's car, leaving the fucking champ on the cold pavement addressing his imprecations and supplications to the distant stars.

This was not yet the end. When we came home, Vanessa insisted on first attending to my mouth – which wasn't too badly hurt after all: just a tooth which had cut into my cheek – and then leaving me on the couch in my study with a tot of neat whiskey while she went to the kitchen to make me some tea with several heaped teaspoons of sugar. It was only much later, after the surge of adrenalin had dissipated, that she started crying.

She was trembling all over, still too upset to speak. All she could say, several times over, was, 'I thought we'd put all that behind us.'

'What do you mean, Vanessa?'

'He called me a *halfnaatjie*. That was all he could think of. After everything that has happened in the country we're still trapped in black and white and coloured and all the rest. Isn't this supposed to be the new South Africa?'

'He's just a single idiot,' I tried to soothe her. 'We're not all like that.'

She shook her head violently. 'He's not a single idiot, Chris. Didn't you look at him? He's supposed to be one of the upper crust. If that is the way he thinks – it was the first thing he said, the first thing that came to his mind – then what about the rest?'

She started sobbing again, now more in anger than in hurt.

I held her for the better part of an hour, speaking softly to her, trying to exorcise her rage and pain. And when at last she seemed calmer I insisted on running her a very deep, very hot bath, and left her in the bathroom while I returned to the study and poured myself another whiskey.

I was in the kitchen, rinsing the glasses, when she came back, so softly that I didn't hear her. She was wrapped in a big white towel, the ends of her hair were still wet. It seemed inevitable, natural, that I should put my arms around her, hug her. She responded with unexpected passion. It would have been so easy simply to go on. I think we both needed the sheer relief. But something incomprehensible in myself reached out to stop me. Don't ask me to explain. In most similar situations in my long life I would have taken the plunge. If there is one thing about relationships I believe in it is Zorba's dire warning: *There is one sin God will not forgive: if a woman calls a man to her bed and he will not go.* But this once I desisted. For a moment I continued to hold her, then I let her go.

She stared at me uncomprehendingly. There were tears in the corners of her eyes.

'We cannot, Vanessa,' I said, half choking on the words. 'We're both too upset. We cannot do it to each other. We shall never forgive ourselves. If we want to make love tomorrow, or next week, or a month or a year from now, yes, it will be wonderful. But not now. Do you understand?'

And half an hour later I took her home.

We never spoke about it again. It wasn't necessary. And we continued as before, as if that night had never happened. Which, in a way, was absolutely true. She continued to be my Girl Friday. We continued to go out together and pretend that we were lovers, to keep away the raptors. But never again was there another moment of weakness. If weakness it had been. (I am not suggesting that I lived an entirely monastic life for the two years Vanessa was with me. There were a few inconsequential flings, nothing memorable – either for me or, I dare say, for the women. During a week of workshopping in Pietermaritzburg there was Charmaine, an eager but bland, run-of-the-mill Colombard; at a festival in Stavanger there was Astrid, a pleasant Tinta das Barrocas, down-to-earth, ready for drinking on the spot; in Cologne, where I had to collect a prize, which at my age becomes something of a bore, there was Gertrud, a rather thin, metallic Zinfandel, with little prospect for ageing – and I was a flop.)

The arrangement worked perfectly. It was not just a form of protection for her: it brought both of us a feeling of security. I had, by then, had a few disheartening experiences with women, when unexpectedly, at the decisive moment, I was unable to 'perform'. The long-trusted old body was no longer up to it; not every time, and not predictably. That night with Vanessa, I have no doubt, it would have 'worked'; but it was no longer an option, and barely a memory.

And yet the relationship came to an end. Not because of anything that happened, or did not happen, between us; but because of something entirely different. Politics, to give it its shortest, dirtiest name. And even that may not be quite just.

Her family had been, for a very long time, divided by politics. They lived in Athlone, where her father was a school principal. A gentle, God-fearing man, he supported the government's disingenuous new tricameral parliamentary system, because he saw it as a step forward; her two brothers violently opposed it. One of them was detained for months, the other one emigrated. The tensions broke their mother's health. One day, after a quarrel, she ran out of the house. In a back street she was set upon by a band of skollies and gang-raped. She survived, but her mind was damaged and she was committed to Valkenberg. When Vanessa was eighteen her father died when he tried to squeeze into an already overfull train and was thrown out by an irate white conductor and died under the wheels. So from the very beginning Vanessa was conditioned by anger and political resistance. The problem was that all she really wanted was to lead a normal life – whatever that might be. But trying to be normal in an abnormal society – going to UWC, preparing herself for a career – turned out to be more difficult than many other choices available to her.

For some time after the beginning of the transition in the early nineties a rewarding future seemed possible.

The first few years were a blur of celebrations, expectations, euphoria. Then the disillusionment began to settle in. For Vanessa the final straw was when the ANC entered into an alliance with the old (but allegedly reborn) National Party which had denied her people the vote, then uprooted thousands of coloureds from District Six and else-where, relegating the Hotnots to second-class citizens. She could not understand how so many of these rejected people preferred to vote for this alliance.

'When the whites were in power,' she told me with flaming eyes, 'we were too black for them. They threw us out into the sand of the Cape Flats. Like meerkats. So we started working for the ANC. We thought Mandela would give us back the dignity we once had. But we didn't realise that he would not be allowed to have the final word. And now we're too white for the new fat cats, and we're still out in the wind. I can't stand it any more, Chris. When there's an election coming, they travel up and down the place to woo us for our votes. And then they just turn round and kick sand in our faces. I've had enough.'

'But what can you possibly do?'

'I'm going away. I told you my older brother is already in Canada. The other one was killed in crossfire between two gangs. Now I'm going to Canada too.'

I said the stupidest thing I could possibly have said: 'What am I going to do?'

Without warning, she put her arms around me and kissed me. 'Come with me, Chris,' she said.

It was such a temptation. But Canada is too cold for my old bones. I've been to Calgary and Edmonton and Vancouver for conferences, and several times to Harbourfront in Toronto. Met wonderful people. Wonderful writers. But I wouldn't last through the first winter.

She went on for some time. But I know her heart wasn't really in it. What would she have done if I'd accepted? It would have been the end for both of us.

Vanessa went, but not before she had brought me Lindiwe as a replacement. I stayed behind. And not too long after that you came. I felt vindicated after all.

Now I just don't know any more.

THE LITTLE DARK one, is how after all these years I still think of her. In a sense she paved the way for Vanessa, because with her, too, I was never involved sexually. Not for lack of trying, but right from the outset she'd made it clear that the last thing she wanted to be concerned with was the body and its needs. And unlike the relationship with Helena so long ago, this one offered no prospect of solving the problem through marriage. But I found her so fascinating as a person, and her dedication to what she believed in – her feminine intransigence – so obsessive, that it was unthinkable to opt out of it. For years, I think, she influenced my choice of women; and although she made it clear that she found this a weakness in my make-up she never tried to interfere, to make me desist, to change my mind. It was the passion she brought to everything she truly believed in that hooked me. And in one way or another, I am convinced, the slightest hint of that kind of absolute dedication, the fierceness of that passion, in any other woman I ever encountered, provoked an immediate reaction in me, like the needle of a compass which unfailingly points North.

Thinking back now, I realise that I did not know all that much about her: her life, I mean, her background, her story. What I do know is that she was very young when she'd lost her father (she was barely twenty when I met her, by which time he'd been dead for years). But he had remained the major influence in her life; there was something almost incestuous in her feelings for him. She often took me along on Sundays to put flowers on his grave: very simple flowers, arum lilies or marigolds or heather; and then I had to help her tend the grave. She used to take a little spade with her, the kind a child would use at the beach, to dig up the weeds and spread the soil smoothly across the surface, almost like making a bed, or covering a body with a shroud. She would scrape it down with her hands, and her fingernails used to be black with dirt by the time we went home.

At some stage I met her sister too, who was a few years older. A pretty but somewhat vacuous girl. She never spoke much and seemed mostly to defer to her younger sibling whenever there were decisions to be made about a restaurant to go to, a film to see, friends to visit. There had been two brothers as well, who had both died in the border war: and for her this was the catastrophe that determined the rest of her life.

Since the death of their father they had been in the care of an uncle. I never met him personally, but from all accounts he was a strict and rather dogmatic kind of man. Discipline, discipline all the way. Much like my father. And this was where the trouble started, because it would seem that there had never been any love lost between the father and the uncle – an old family quarrel that went all the way back to their parents. Her father, as far as I could make out, had been a likeable but stubborn man who had charted the course of his life – in politics, in the choice of a career, in everything – without any regard for the wishes of the family. The uncle, a stickler for propriety and correctness, intractable and downright mean under an exterior of piousness and conformity, soon made them understand that they were a deplorable lot who should be eternally grateful for his benevolence after the death of the no-good head of their own family. And this, fired as she was by her fierce feminine independence, she simply couldn't stomach. A disastrous clash became unavoidable. She would not be dictated to by a man, least of all by such a shit.

The aunt, I gathered, was quite sweet and caring; the older sister seemed to get along with her quite well. But not my little dark one.

In that relationship my only role really was that of father confessor. Because of the age difference, I presume, she was inclined to come to me with whatever bothered her. There was, for example, an episode with a young man who was head over heels in love with her and wanted to marry her. In the beginning she resisted, she was too young, she did not yet feel ready for marriage; but he was really very serious and seemed to care a lot for her. I believe she turned to him mainly because she saw him as a possible ally against the uncle. So they did get engaged, which was shortly before she came into my life. And then the problems began.

High-minded and caring he might have been, but he was also a young man of flesh and blood. That was when she started confiding in me. He was always at her, couldn't keep his hands off her. She became quite embarrassingly frank. Kissing she could accept. Even, although initially with some reluctance, the fondling of her breasts. When he proceeded his explorations into her knickers, she found it alarming. But for his sake – she couldn't help feeling sorry for him, he was so very eager – she allowed it; even had to admit in the long run that it was no longer so terribly distasteful. (At this stage of her confessions to me I started wondering about the priesthood: all the occasions for vicarious fulfilment; and for such a good cause.) But when he started expecting her to bring him to climax too and even – just once, oh please, oh please – to take him in her mouth, she felt she had to put an end to it. No so much because of guilt feelings or remorse or anger, but simply because she felt there were many more useful things they could do together. ('Don't do anything you feel you may regret later,' I piously advised her; it was not *my* loss anyway, and it might even get rid of a youngster I'd come to detest because he was being allowed access and privilege of a kind denied to me.) So she dumped him. 'That takes care of him,' was all she said about it. Now she could turn her mind to more worthy preoccupations: mapping a future in which she wouldn't always have to be dependent on a man.

This aggravated the relationship with the uncle. Again I was the one she turned to for advice, as if I were the father she'd lost. Or not even a father but a grandfather, which I did not exactly relish. But I had to play my part. For her it was very serious indeed, and she needed me.

The end, I believe now, had really been unavoidable from the very beginning. A matter of two unrelenting wills, the immovable object and the irresistible force, the rock and the hard place.

The first time she told me about it, I did not take it very seriously. So much so, that I cannot even recall exactly what triggered it. Something to do with her dead brothers. She had religiously clung to an annual commemoration of their death, putting flowers on the graves; and that year, for some reason, the uncle was otherwise occupied and could not take them to the graveyard. Whereupon she threatened to hitch-hike her way there on her own. A very banal situation, but it soon escalated out of all control. What it came down to was that he'd laid down the law, and she had refused to comply. Not surreptitiously at all, but quite openly, as if confrontation was what she *wanted*. The outcome, no doubt, of a lifetime of conflict, starting at the time when her father had still been alive. This, she resolved, was the day of reckoning.

'This time he went too far,' she told me. 'I've always tried to be reasonable, but now he's being deliberately perverse. This is something that concerns me alone, not him. And I won't let him take decisions for me.'

'He can make life pretty miserable for you if you resist,' I warned her.

'So what? It's miserable enough as it is.'

'Perhaps he, too, is just trying to be reasonable. Can't you sit down and talk to him? Perhaps you can come to an understanding.'

'I don't *want* to understand,' she flared up. 'I just want to say No.'

'That won't bring you very far. Whether we like it or not, our only hope is to compromise.'

'I'm sorry. I want all or nothing.'

'I'm just trying to help you find a solution.'

'Nothing that is based on compromise can ever be a solution to me.'

'There's no sense in demanding the impossible.'

'You've got it wrong.' There was something like madness in her now. 'Don't you understand, Chris? Only the impossible is worth demanding.'

'Please, please. You're making a very big mountain out of a very small molehill.'

'If you think it's just a molehill, there's no point in talking to you any more.'

'Try to take a step back. Look at it. Think about it. It's a matter of your will against your uncle's, not life or death.'

'If life means always giving way to that man, then I'd rather take death any time.'

How sickeningly did I remember those words afterwards. At the time I took them to be a mere show of bravado. After all, really, what *was* at stake? All right, she might have had reason to feel upset, angry, frustrated. But all that was needed was a little perspective.

No way. I remember that during one of our arguments at the time she melodramatically pulled out a white paper flower she must have hidden in her shirt. It was pretty crumpled, and limp with sweat. But almost triumphantly she threw it in my face. She was breathing deeply, almost too perturbed to speak. All she could say was, 'What about *this*? Does this mean nothing to you?'

'What is it supposed to mean?' I asked cautiously, not wanting to upset her even more.

'This was my brother's,' she said. She was crying now. 'When I was ten, the two of them went out one night. They only came back at dawn. I hadn't slept all night, I was too worried. Then, when they came back, my younger brother, the one I really cared about, saw me hiding under the stairs. And he kissed me and gave me this flower. It was just a playful, almost teasing way of bonding with me. But it touched me so deeply that I've kept the flower all these years. This is the flower I wanted to put on the grave. And now that miscreant wants to stop me.'

'Now, now, that's no way to talk about the man who's done his best to give you and your sister something in life.'

'He can stuff his life up his backside!' she cried. 'I told you I'd rather die!'

'This is madness, you know,' I pleaded as gently as I could.

'Then just leave me alone with my madness,' she declared histrionically.

Was it really worth it? How *could* it have been worth it? Twenty years old, her whole life before her. The little dark one: with all the makings of a real beauty-to-be. And then to take her own life like that. Nobody expected it: we all thought her threats were teenage bravado, nothing really serious. And in such a melodramatic way. A rope from a beam in an outroom.

Antigone, Antigone, all these years the enigma of your death has haunted me. The ferocity of that *No* you have been hurling at the world, indefatigably, unremittingly. Not just at your uncle Creon, but all of us, all the men, even those of us who loved you, but who have failed to understand. And my relationship with you – as with Nastasya Filippovna, or Dulcinea del Toboso, or Lucy of Lammermoor, or Anna Karenina, any of a host of other women from books – has hardly been less passionate, and less formative, than those with Anna, or Tania, or Nicolette, or Jenny or any of the other women who have shared my bed and the history of my time.

MY NIGHTLY INCURSIONS into Iraq have become more hectic again, after the suggestion of a lull a week ago. The invaders appear to have changed their minds and there is a new urgency about the attack, which makes one think that they are once again calculating in terms of weeks, not months. The US Third Infantry Division is now fighting on the outskirts of the holy city of Najaf, while in the north another holy city, Karbala, is being targeted. This one, they say, is where Mohammed's grandson Hussein lies buried. No holy stone will be left unturned. The whole enterprise reminds one of nothing so much as an unscrupulous man intent, by hook or by crook, on 'getting' a particular woman. When he finally overpowers her and is pounding away in the dark, he discovers that he has made a mistake: it is the wrong woman. The choice before him is to go through with it, or pull out. A murky situation. All one knows for certain is that somebody is getting fucked.

As MY 'WIFE-SITTING' continues, our relationship has settled into an easy rhythm. The electricity of the first night has dissipated and we are indeed behaving like good friends (like an old married couple?). In the mornings whoever wakes first makes breakfast: never an elaborate affair, but at least I have succeeded in weaning you from the three or four cups of very strong coffee which you told me used to be your staple diet. Now you are happy with one. How you have managed to remain so healthy, and so beautiful, with your pernicious lifestyle is beyond me; you must have an exceptional constitution, or a special cohort of angels taking care of you.

After breakfast the one who hasn't prepared it, washes the dishes. And then you go to your studio while I return home (except for the two days a week you accompany me to do your Girl Friday stint, to which Frederik appears to be looking forward as much as I). Towards evening I drive back to Camps Bay and we go for a meal, or cook up something for ourselves; much later I retire to bed, or settle into a big armchair in the studio to read or occupy myself with my notes while you work on your sculptures. When there is a firing to be done, we stay up the whole night. I find it enthralling to watch through the peephole every hour, every half-hour, towards the end every ten minutes or so, for the small white cones to start wilting and bending over. Then follows the twelve-hour wait before the door can be opened to reveal the transformation the sculpted figures have undergone. Pure alchemy.

'One wouldn't think you were – what did you say? – seventy-eight years old when you peep through that hole,' you say, watching me in open amusement. 'You look a small boy.'

'That's what it makes me feel like.'

'Now you *must* go to bed,' you order me very sternly, very motherly.

'Not if you're not going too.'

'I'm not sleepy.'

'Nor am I.'

'Then let's talk.'

And we do. What you often come back to is my marriage, which seems to hold a special fascination for you.

'There is nothing more to tell,' I object. 'You must know it all by now.'

'Not everything.'

'*Must* you know everything?'

'Unless I do, there will always be something about you that escapes me.'

'Thank God.'

'What was the best thing about your marriage?' you ask.

It is a question that comes up many times, and the answer is not always the same. This time I say, 'I think it was when Helena was pregnant. To see her growing bigger, her navel turning inside out, her breasts swelling. To have her hold my open hand against her belly, or to press my ear against it, and feel the baby moving inside and responding. It was hers, it was mine, it was ours. I never had such a feeling of sharing with anyone again. Sometimes we played music for it. We didn't know whether it was going to be a boy or a girl –'

'What did *you* want?'

'A girl, of course.'

'The possessive male. Just as well it turned out to be a boy. You would have smothered a girl.'

'I've always smothered the women I loved most.'

'But this one you played music to.'

I smile at the memory. 'It was incredible to see the different ways the baby reacted to different kinds of music. Beethoven set him jumping with joy, kicking and churning about . . .'

'Perhaps he hated Beethoven.'

'Chopin caused a kind of gentle, rocking motion. I always had the impression he found it amusing and was chortling with laughter. And Mozart made him serene and sleepy.'

'And once he was born?'

'A very strange feeling. While he was inside Helena he felt so much part of us. Now, suddenly he was a stranger, someone neither of us knew, with his own wants and needs and comforts and – very strongly – discomforts. It seems an awful thing to say, but he was something of an intruder.'

'A difficult child?'

'Not more difficult than others. Actually, he was usually very good. But he was – strange. And suddenly his needs were more urgent and immediate than mine. The old story.'

'You were jealous?'

'Yes, I was. Unashamedly. It was just something I couldn't come to grips with.'

'But you saw it through. You stayed with Helena, you were faithful to her. For how many years . . . ?'

'We were married for six years.' I sit looking down at my hands. Why am I so obsessed with them nowadays, so horrified? I move my fingers, studying, as so often in recent years, the gnarled joints, the blotches on the skin. How much joy have they not caused and known over the years? What is left of all that?

To my surprise you put one of your hands on mine. 'Don't look at your hands with such disgust, Chris. They are so wise, they know so much.'

'They have forgotten much.'

'Hands do not forget,' you reprimand me. 'Bodies don't forget.' Your fingers still move across mine, caressing them like a touch of butterfly wings. 'All the women you have ever loved are here.' A pause. 'Helena is here.'

'I wasn't fair to her, or perhaps to anyone.'

'You're too hard on yourself.'

'How can you say that? You don't know, Rachel.' I sigh and shake my head. 'You don't know.' I look you in the eyes, the full mystery of those dark, almost-black eyes. 'Least of all about Helena.'

'But you stayed married to her for six years. That must count for something.'

'I'll mention that to St Peter at the gate.' I enfold your hand in mine. The smoothness of the skin, the firmness of bone underneath, the nails cut very short. 'He won't absolve me, Rachel. I was not faithful to Helena.'

'What happened?'

In the dark – we are at the dining table among the remains of our long meal, there is only a single candle burning, the rest of the house is in darkness; from outside, through the open French doors, comes a glimmer of light, and the sound of the restless sea – in the dark I yield easily to the temptation of confession. *Amplius lava me ab iniquitate mea.*

'The first time was just a few months after Pieter was born,' I say. It all comes back to me, a tide coming in. There was a writers' conference in Durban. A hectic turmoil of days and nights. At the end of the closing session on the last day, we were besieged by a mob of autograph hunters, eager students, groupies. It took the best part of an hour to work through all of them. Among the last stragglers – the inevitable and ubiquitous old ladies, bespectacled young men, matrons with an ingrained look of frustration, pale bluestockings, chatty youngsters, all of them eager to score a final point or garner a final word of everlasting wisdom – was a striking blonde girl with a single thick plait down her back, standing somewhat apart as if annoyed by the presence of the others, but embarrassed about coming forward too boldly. I had already noticed her in the audience, crammed in among the rest of them, yet somehow strangely set apart. How could I not notice her? During my intervention in the panel discussion our eyes had met a few times. It was as if silent messages were being passed to and fro. And at last, as the remaining bunch began to unravel, I blatantly forced a passage through them, turning a deaf ear to last-minute comments and questions, and went right up to her, fired by adrenalin, but also conscious of the reaction setting in: weariness, resentment, a need now to be left alone, for God's sake.

'You've been waiting long enough,' I said, making sure no one else could hear. 'Come, let's go.'

She did not even seem surprised, as if she had been expecting just that all along. Together, we went off into the balmy star-mad night.

And then I couldn't find my car. I remembered exactly where I had parked it, but it was gone. For what seemed like most of the night, we wandered up and down several blocks in the parking lot, into side streets and back.

At long last she asked in a patient, serene voice, 'What does the car look like?'

'A red Peugeot.'

'Number?'

I told her.

'Did you drive up all the way from Cape Town?' she asked.

'Of course not, I . . .' And then it struck me that, of course, I'd rented a car at the airport. We went to the exact spot where I'd parked it, and found it, and I opened the door for her.

Only when I turned the ignition did she burst out laughing, with such merry abandon that I couldn't help collapsing too. It felt, suddenly, as if we'd known each other for years.

I didn't know Durban very well, but drove in the general direction of the sea. Somewhere, in the wee hours, we found a deserted stretch of beach. When we got out we kicked off our shoes and left them in the car. I put out my hand and she took it. We walked into the dark, fragrant with invisible tropical flowers and stars and ozone. Neither of us spoke. Far away from everything we stopped and kissed, and took off our clothes, and made love on the sand. She was still a virgin, and it hurt. But when I wanted to pause, she put her hands on my buttocks and drew me back into her. 'Don't stop, don't stop, please don't stop,' she said.

We lay there, together, for a long time, reluctant to return to the world. By the time we went back naked to the car, the first hint of daylight was gleaming dully on the sea and the stars were fading.

'Thank you,' she said with almost amusing formality. 'I've been waiting for a long time for this to happen.'

'What is your name?' I asked.

'It doesn't really matter,' she said.

She directed me to the sprawling house where she lived, stuck in a wilderness of purple bougainvillea and red hibiscus in a remote suburb I would never be able to find again. Before I could get out to open the door for her, she was already out. She blew a kiss at me.

With an acute awareness of loss I looked after her. She was carrying her green sandals and her knickers in her hand.

'AND THAT WAS that?' you ask after a long silence.

'I wish it was. It should have been.'

'But . . . ?'

I have no choice but to tell you the rest. A month, two months, later I had a letter from her, sent to my publishers and forwarded by them. There was no address at the top and no name signed at the bottom, but the three pages in impeccable calligraphy gave a surprisingly humorous report on the aftermath of our escapade. Little details, startling yet quite endearing, of the painful discovery of grains of sand inside her, and the excruciating effect of sea salt on the mucous membranes. Followed by a rather more unnerving account of how, the morning after, her father had come upon her while she was soaking her blood stained underwear in the bathroom, and how she'd brazenly, in open defiance, responded to his furious interrogation by announcing that she'd slept with Chris Minnaar, and what about it? And how he'd threatened to take a plane down to Cape Town to beat the shit out of me, and then toned it down to a resolve simply to write to my wife and inform her of the event, until at last he'd been prevailed upon to give it up, and settled for a week of moping. At the end of all this there was a quiet moment of reflection: *Now when the hurly-burly's done, and the battle lost and won, I know it was worth it and I'd do it again any time. In fact, I wish we could.*

It was maddening to leave it at that. But there was nothing I could possibly do. I felt some trepidation at the thought that an irate parent might yet materialise on our doorstep; but as time passed, the prospect faded. And life returned to what passed for normal. Even though I would still wake up some nights with a throbbing erection, but also with an inexplicable feeling of dread, and a much more explicable feeling of guilt.

And then a second letter came, about a month after the first. And this time there was a name. Marion de Villiers. Which did not suit her at all, not at all. How could that night-girl, that salt-water-girl, that first-blood-girl bear a name like Marion de Villiers? My first thought was: I don't want to know this. It changes everything and spoils everything. What was more, this time there was an address on the back of the envelope.

From that moment, precisely because I did not want to, not under any circumstances, I knew I would go back. I fought valiantly against the idea: it was preposterous, it was ludicrous, it could only end in disillusionment. But I *had* to go back.

For a few humiliating weeks there was a toing and froing of letters; and then I found a reason to go to Durban (the major complication was that Helena decided that she'd like to go with me, which necessitated a lot of scurrying with new arrangements and explanations, all of which banalised and sullied an already unsavoury endeavour). And I went, alone.

Marion picked me up at the airport. This time I was to stay with her; the parents were away on holiday. What she hadn't foreseen was that her older, married sister would unexpectedly break up with her husband and move into the parental home as well, broken-hearted and irremediably furious with the male of the species. There was still time to check into a hotel. But Marion, more and more scheming, less and less like the nymph from the sea I had miraculously known – once, oh in another lifetime, in a foreign land – had set her mind on the family home. The sister, she assured me, was too shattered to put in an appearance and would probably remain locked up in her room.

It turned out differently. The sister, whose name is still a blank in my memory, bluntly refused to allow us to share a room ('The man is bloody well *married*, Marion!' I heard her scream). For most of the evening, after we'd come home from a restaurant, she and Maid Marion fought in the dining room, while I sat sulking in Marion's little bedroom at the back of the house. I was tempted to call it a night and clear out, but every time the sister went to the bathroom or the kitchen, Marion would slip out to plead with me – oh please, please! – to stay: it could only be a few more minutes, an hour at most, and then she would be back in my arms. But some time after midnight she presented herself at my door, her face bloated with crying, to announce that she was going to spend the night in her parents' bedroom. For some time I still went on hoping that during the night she might come tiptoeing, and naked as on the beach, to my bed; but when I ventured into the passage once or twice the light in the dining room, where the sister kept her bitter vigil, was still resolutely burning; and in the end, from sheer weariness, I fell asleep on Marion's virginal bed. At least, I thought nastily, she wouldn't have sand in her pussy this time.

As I came from the bathroom in the morning it was just in time to overhear a conversation between the two siblings. I could make out that the sister had received a telephone call to summon her to her lawyer's office for an immediate interview. As she rushed out, slamming the heavy front door behind her, she viciously shouted back at Marion, 'So now you can have the whole fucking house to yourselves!'

What followed was even worse. Wrapping herself around me like a clinging, bloodsucking forest creeper, Marion started urging me to go to the main bedroom where we could do the two-backed beast in the matrimonial bed. But I baulked at the idea. Not that I was scared about not being able to perform under pressure – in those days, I regret to say, there was no coordination between my mind and my prick. It went – or came – as it wished, irrespective of whether I approved or disapproved. But somehow the whole business had just become too complicated, too sordid. Guilt about Helena was gnawing at me like the fox at the boy's heart in the old fable. As soon as I could extricate myself I telephoned for a taxi and left. Marion remained moping in her room and did not even come out to see me off.

'DID THAT TEACH you a lesson?' you ask, in a tone of sympathy, yet unable to repress a chuckle.

'It certainly did. Never to make love with a sister in the house.'

'But did it cure the urge to stray?'

This time I find it hard to answer. But how can I lie to you? 'No,' I say. 'It was only the beginning.'

'But *why*?'

'What makes you think I know?'

'I'm sorry, Chris, I don't buy that. You're not one of the lower forms of life that act purely on instinct. I want to know.' A pause. 'And I think it's time for *you* to know.'

I cannot help smiling. 'Fair enough. But I cannot promise it will get us far. I agree that trying to find answers or reasons cannot be avoided, it is part of the package. But surely it is not the only thing that defines us. Especially when we are talking about love. Perhaps love only begins where language ends. Which is why we talk about "making love": the body enters into it to make something exist which was not there before. We literally *make* it, we bring it into being.'

A challenging little smile. 'Aren't you now reducing the body to its sexual organs?'

For a moment the word shocks me out of my line of reasoning; but then I recover. 'No, Rachel, I mean a hell of a lot more. There are also eyes, and hands, and feet.' For a moment I hesitate, then raise my hand with a show of audacity that surprises myself. 'And even a little mole on the cheekbone.' I dare to touch it with my finger.

'Now you're idealising and romanticising again,' you scold me.

'No. Because I accept the body with all its faults and foibles and failings, its bad smells and its weaknesses. But just as I cannot think of the body as only beautiful and seductive, I cannot think of it as exclusively ugly and repulsive. It is all of this, and also more. Always more. Isn't that what it really is about? That *moreness* that makes us human.'

'You've wandered very far away from my question, Chris.'

'I don't think I have. Look, I was with Helena: I think I can say I was happy with her, although *happy* is another of those words we use too glibly. At least we were not *unhappy*, we had a child, we had a reasonably good life, on the whole we functioned well together. I did not go in search of adventures because I felt unfulfilled at home, or because my wife didn't understand me, or whichever of the old excuses one can think of. I had what I needed – if anything is ever as easy as that. What *does* a man really "need"? All I'm trying to say is that something in me wanted *more*, and still does. And I honestly don't think it is something peculiar about *me*, but that it is something human.'

Your eyes are uncompromising and defiant. 'Isn't that the real problem, Chris? That you kept on desperately, compulsively trying to find that *something* somewhere else, always somewhere else, in other people, in women, rather than accepting that the only place you could possibly find it was inside yourself?'

'What about paradise?' I persist. 'I've always thought that paradise is the only true fulfilment we can dream of – I mean something that literally fills us, completes us – but surely the point about paradise is that it can never be here, only ever somewhere else.'

'That kind of paradise can never be real, only a dream, an illusion.'

'You don't think that dreams are relevant or indispensable?'

'It still depends upon whether we are looking for them outside ourselves, or inside.'

'I'm not sure that the distinction is so important. As long as we agree that paradise is *necessary*. As neccessary as the fact that it can never be attained. Every time we think for a moment – because it can never be for more than a moment – it slips away. Was I in paradise with Driekie in the fig tree? Absolutely not. It seemed so. For a moment. But I cannot think of Driekie without thinking of that horrible prelude with David or the terrifying aftermath when she and her sisters humiliated me. Just as I cannot think of Marion on the beach that night without remembering the visit to her parents' home afterwards. And even the girl on the train. She had no consequence. But I lost her without even speaking to her.'

You do not answer immediately. But in the end you shake your head. 'She could only have been a moment of paradise inasmuch as she became part of yourself. And then we're back with what I first said.'

'But don't you understand? Even if she is inside me, she still drives me out to look for other moments and manifestations of paradise.'

'Only if you're looking for an excuse to go on philandering. If you keep on looking for paradise somewhere out there, breaking your legs after every new cunt you get a whiff of. In the long run it just isn't worth it, because all that matters about them is what is already inside you. You only have to acknowledge it.'

'How can I deny the impulse that makes us human?'

'That is shit. Who are you to tell me what is "human"? Is the urge to fuck more important than the urge to share, or simply to be together?'

'Can they not be expressions of the same urge? Is anybody ever totally and completely self-sufficient? What about the Hegelian *You are, therefore I am*?'

'A wish to share with others is different from either making your whole life dependent on somebody else – or, worse, the need to make somebody else dependent on *you*.'

'Those can be individual aberrations. They do not invalidate the urge.'

'Don Giovanni's need to fuck,' you say, 'is the urge to run away. He cannot face his loneliness, so he needs to impose himself. There is an imbalance of power. In the urge to share there is a recognition of equality. That makes it totally different.'

'It is still an urge to go beyond yourself.'

'The problem I have with your argument, Chris, is that you make your concept of what is "human" totally dependent on it. Doesn't "human" *also* leave us a choice? To commit or not to commit?' You lean forward. 'Do you think *I* never feel tempted by another man? However much I love George? But I would never, ever, betray him. Because I chose, with open eyes, to stay with him.'

'And if *he* had a fling?'

'I would respect him for exercising his freedom of choice, and then I would tell him to fuck off.'

'You wouldn't really.'

'I would.'

'And if he comes to you to confess and asks to be forgiven?'

'The need for absolution cannot cancel what happened. It would still have been an act of betrayal.'

'Don't you think "betrayal" is putting it rather strongly?'

'That is what it is. I can't think of anything worse than the betrayal of trust.'

And then another memory breaks through whatever barrier has kept it from me for so long, the only one from my whole life which I would wish to obliterate. That last day we were together, Helena and I. The final quarrel in the car, little Pieter crying on the back seat. The wipers dumbly swishing to and fro, to and fro in the steady rain. It was about another woman. Ironically, one of the most insignificant of my little affairs. Inconsequential, as I would have thought of it – except that this time there *were* consequences. For how long Helena had known about my straying, I still don't know. But on this day her long-suffering patience ran out. Her lovely face was ugly with anger. And what she said was scorched into my mind for ever – not just because of the accident that happened mere minutes later, but because of the words themselves. 'It's not that you slept with her, Chris,' she said. 'That is bad enough, but I think I could learn to live with it. But that you slept with her and now try to deny it. *That* is the betrayal. That you thought so little of me that you cannot even be honest with me. This I cannot forgive.' She grabbed my arm in rage. I fiercely, blindly, tried to free myself from her grip. And skidded off the wet road in the rain.

'What are you thinking about?' you ask quietly.

I shake my head and look at you in some bewilderment. It takes a moment to return to what we have been talking about. Then, somewhat to my own surprise, I tell you about the memory.

You also take a while before you respond. Then you ask very quietly, 'Have you forgiven yourself for it?'

'Can *you* forgive me?'

'It's not *my* forgiveness you need,' you say, more gravely than I would have expected.

For a long time it feels as if we have reached the end of our conversation. Then, with an urgency that almost shames me, I ask, 'Don't you think an act of infidelity can add something to one? Surely it may widen one's experience, make one a more complete person, with more to share with one's partner. You know, that was actually what I often felt, coming back to Helena.'

'Chris! That is the most banal of all excuses.'

'That needn't make it any less true.'

'I'm sorry. I fail to understand that.'

'Sometimes it is the very things we can *not* understand which make life worth while, don't you agree? To Creon, Antigone was mad. All that interested her was the impossible. And how can we ever "explain" Nastasya Filippovna? Challenging Rogozhin to get the money – and then burning it – and then going off into the night with him after all?'

'And getting murdered for it.'

'I'm sure she knew that was the risk she took. And she was willing to do so.'

'Is this a plea for madness?'

'A certain kind of madness, I suppose, yes. Unless you have a problem with freedom.'

'Not with the concept. But if freedom is something you measure only in terms of yourself, your own needs and wants, I do find it problematic. And that affects your view of love too, doesn't it? The moment you expand it to include another person besides yourself, it is impossible to express anything at all purely in terms of *I want – I want – I want*. Surely we should be more mature than just to think of our own pleasure.'

'Do you really think my whole life has been a waste, based on illusions and false premises?'

'Not at all. It is *your* life and I get the impression that you have always lived it as it has suited *yourself*, because you have never allowed anyone else into it. So for you it could work. And obviously has. For me it cannot. Not ever.'

'Are you blaming me now?'

'The very fact that you should think that, tells me that you are not as free as you hoped you were.'

'How do you get there?'

'Because it seems to trouble you that I think what I do. So my opinion matters to you. And that imposes limits on you.'

'Your opinion does indeed matter to me. Because I care about you.'

'But not enough to make you think of changing your life.'

'You can't teach an old dog new tricks.'

'You can, if the dog cooperates.'

'Not this one.'

'Then it's just too bad.' Your eyes seem to be challenging me and pitying me and mocking me all at the same time.

SHARING, YOU SAID. Simply being together. How much of it did you say from conviction, how much purely for the challenge of argument? For there were few things, I came to realise, you enjoyed as much as arguing. You certainly sent me back to my marriage with Helena. And the manner in which it was framed by my encounters with Melanie: the misty night on the rocks just before our wedding; the day on the beach after the accident, when Melanie came to me with all our unfinished business, and suddenly began to cry. Between these two brackets, Helena offered security, predictability, companionship: precisely the things I needed – precisely the things I needed to get away from. Later in life I came to miss, dearly, the sense of a 'home' to come back to, as Odysseus had, haunted by Penelope's moon-cloth. On more than one occasion I seriously considered getting married again, but the risk seemed too great; and I was getting too used to having my own space and keeping my own hours (even though most of these were devoted to writing). You would call it selfish, self-centred. Undoubtedly. But it was also preventing others from getting drawn into my life and being hurt. At the same time it meant forfeiting the dimension of stability which, with Helena, had so ironically, perhaps even perversely, helped to make sense of my wanderings and rovings.

It all goes back so far. I have noted the groping beginnings, the first tastes of paradise. But there was a specific crossing of a threshold, my own rites of passage, where, for once, I was indebted to an older woman. Not that much older – she was thirty-five, I twelve years younger – but enough to make a difference. Anna coincided with a turning point in our history, the electoral victory of the National Party in 1948. There was only one other election in my life that marked me in such a personal way and that was in 1994, the country's first free election, which I celebrated with Jenny. But I'll come to that later.

For black South Africans, 1948 marked a descent into darkness; for Afrikaners, a first step towards the light of political emancipation; for me, it celebrated an inner, very personal liberation. Until then, the joys of sex had tended to be involved with darker feelings of guilt and fear of damnation: Katrien brought the dire warnings about sin and punishment linked to the happy discovery of the *filimandorus*; Driekie in the fig tree was followed by the hellish orgy of the teenage Bacchae; the memory of the ice queen Isolde was overshadowed by the night in the men's residence. But Anna was unadulterated pleasure.

Anna van der Watt was a secretary in the party office in our constituency, in the same building where my father ran his practice. In more enlightened times she would have been an organiser, but at that time the position of secretary was about the highest a woman could aspire to. A most able person, with people skills I have seldom seen matched by others, and with drive, ambition and enthusiasm which in the end must have made a decisive contribution to the result in that constituency. Anna was recently widowed. Her husband, a big-game hunter of some repute, had been shot by one of his colleagues on a trip into what was then South-West Africa – a tragic accident, the official version had it; a diabolically well-planned action by a man who'd had his eye on Anna for some time, said some insiders. If the latter was true, the two lovers were handling it with seasoned skill by having, as far as anyone could establish, absolutely no contact with each other after the mishap. (That is, until they unexpectedly got married eighteen months later, but that might have been another story.) Depending on the version one subscribed to, she was known either as the Merry Widow or the Black Widow. Certainly not the kind of woman a fresh-faced young man, newly out of university with an LL B (*cum laude*) to show for it, should get involved with. And I had no aspirations to do so either.

During the last hectic weeks before the elections, when any available body was roped in to work for the party and keep the Sappe (and the coloureds) out, I came to know her better. Even began to find her attractive, with her rippling light brown hair and green eyes and full breasts and the feline grace of her body. But that was that. She was too old for me; she would never give me a second look. And anyway, I was much too timid and inexperienced even to contemplate a move of my own, especially since several of the more senior party workers had made no bones about the fact that they were interested.

During the day following the elections, as one result after the other was proclaimed over radios in every house and shop and office in town, an atmosphere of muted hysteria was building up. And by nightfall on the second day, when the improbable news of a Nationalist victory was a fait accompli, madness took over. There were huge festivities in the town hall, which spilled outside into streets and squares and vacant lots, with bonfires, fireworks, dancing and carousing into the small hours. All of which remained no more than a distant backdrop of noise to my own celebration.

What happened, was that Father had charged me with the chore of locking up the party offices in the late afternoon, after all the organisers and helpers had filtered out to join the revelry; but I had got so caught up in it all that I quite forgot about the matter. It was only when, some time after eight, I jostled my way into the town hall to listen to the speeches (it was, after all, still the party of my own choice, and I was sharing in the collective flush of triumph) that from a distance I saw my father on the platform with the dignitaries and realised that the offices had not been locked. There was no need for alarm, in those days crime was not really an issue, and almost everybody was in the town centre for the celebrations; but I knew how fastidious he was about the right way of doing things. So I fought my way back through the crowd again and walked into the cool but bracing late-May night.

The offices were dark, and my first impulse was simply to lock up from outside and wend my way back to the town hall. But for some reason I decided to go inside first and make sure that everything in the building was in order, all the windows closed, the furniture in place, just as I knew my father wanted it. When I opened the door to his office – the very door through which he would emerge four years later to confront Bonnie and me – there was a sound. I froze. A burglar? A vagrant? A marauding cat? I switched on the light at the door.

Anna was behind his desk, her body crumpled over it, her hair dishevelled. There were telltale signs that she had been crying. She looked up when the light went on. Which of us was the most startled was difficult to tell. She uttered a small cry, and I mumbled a confused apology: 'I'm sorry . . . I didn't know . . . I wasn't expecting to find anybody here . . . I just . . .'

By that time she was on her feet, straightening her hair, wiping her face with the back of her hand. 'No, it's my fault, I didn't mean to be here, I . . .'

'Why are you not at the town hall?' I asked.

'I didn't feel like being in a crowd. It's . . . ag, *sommer* . . .' She took a deep breath and became more composed. 'I suppose I was just tired after these last few days, the last few weeks.' It was only some time afterwards that I learned how, after all her tireless work for the party, Father had forgotten to invite her to the celebration, and much later before I came to the obvious conclusion that she had secretly been in love with him all along, perhaps even since before her involvement with the hunters.

'But you *belong* there, Anna. After all you've done.'

'I don't belong anywhere,' she said in a tone of self-pity. 'Nobody cares about what I've done anyway.'

I looked hard at her. This did not tally with the impression I'd had of her during the time we had been working together: the ever-competent, ever-smiling, indefatigable secretary who could joke with the men, expertly ward off all the predictable attempts at sexing up to her without making the offender feel a fool, do whatever she was asked to do and then come back for more; and who often brought plates of home-made *beskuit* or meringues or milk-tarts to the office to liven up our tea and coffee breaks.

'I caught you at a bad moment,' I said. 'Do you want me to go?'

'No, stay. I was just tired. All the pressure was getting a bit much. I think I've had enough of people for a while, especially of *some* people . . .' She left the sentence trailing.

'Like my father?'

'I didn't say that.'

'It wasn't necessary. I know him well enough.'

'You don't know half of him.'

'Top half or bottom half?' I joked.

She smiled. The tension was broken.

'Shall we go for a walk?' I proposed.

'As long as it isn't downtown.'

'We'll go where there's nobody else.'

'I'd like that,' said Anna. There was a kind of molten fire in her eyes I hadn't noticed before. There was actually a lot about her, I realised, with a tingling warmth spreading through me, which I hadn't noticed before.

I put off the light. We went to the front door together. I let her out and locked it behind me. When we came outside she took my hand, an easy, spontaneous gesture. My face felt warm, and the light autumn breeze was chilly against it. I'm not sure how far we walked. I tried afterwards to find the place again, but could never be quite sure that it was the right spot: there was a vacant plot overgrown with long grass and a clump of trees. There we kissed. And then she took off my jacket (I was still formally dressed for the celebrations), skilfully removed my tie, and with slow precision, obviously knowing exactly what she wanted to do, undid the buttons of my shirt. I took off her blouse, and she helped me with her bra. There was some light from a street lamp on the corner and I remember the yellowish sheen of it on her breasts, and the small dark shadows of her nipples, puckered and taut in the cool night air.

Far away, downhill, there were fireworks going off, rockets streaking through the air in multicoloured arcs and parabolas, exploding in showers of fire; but we were engrossed in our own fireworks. There was no need for me to initiate or direct anything; Anna took over. It was like diving into a churning millstream.

But I was too overwhelmed by it all, in too much of a hurry, and when I came I heard her moaning against my neck, 'Too soon, too soon.' But she smothered it in her own wet kisses as her body continued urgently, demandingly to undulate against mine, while high above us the dizzying spectacle of lights continued, and I slowly became conscious of the perspiration on my back turning cold in the light wind.

We got dressed again and she took me home to the rather ugly new building where she lived, not far from there. There were people coming home from the festivities and we didn't want to be seen; so she whispered her flat number in my ear, 303, and went up first, and I followed five minutes later.

This time I did not come too soon. I stayed the night. Both of us had heavy, snotty colds in the morning (which, mercifully, was Saturday), and that wasn't romantic at all. But our lovemaking amply made up for it. Anna was a wine that had gathered in its body all the generosity of deep earth and a Cape climate, years of maturing in wood and darkness, with all the munificence of sun and summer and cleansing wind, and the deep secret growth of rainy winters.

It was the beginning of a few exceptional months in my life. Anna taught me more than all my previous eager or laborious but rather impetuous explorations in the past. First of all, she brought home to me the virtue of patience. And I learned about a woman's needs and delights – *her* needs and delights – and about possibilities that would never have occurred to me on my own. She was a woman of baffling contradictions: always correct, even conservative, at work (although her imperturbable good mood and her gift of laughter prevented it from ever becoming staid); she even taught at Sunday school; but in bed she was a virtuoso, her resources and inventiveness a constant source of marvel and discovery. She showed me little tricks to revive passion within minutes of the most depleting orgasm; and she brought a sense of fun to it which caused us, many times, to collapse in laughter even at the moment of coming. Together, we would try out every imaginable variation of the *Kama Sutra* or the *Ars Amatoria* and a selection of more obscure, and more titillating, manuals she had stowed away in a navy-blue suitcase under her bed. One Sunday, after she'd come back from church, she spread a towel on her bed and we shaved her mound and every little fold and curve and crinkle between her legs. In the winter months she let the black hair under her arms grow, because she discovered that it gave me a kick. (The combination of shaven sex and tufted armpits was particularly exhilarating.)

On Anna's instigation, we even introduced some experiments with violence into our lovemaking. Nothing really heavy, that never turned me on. But she soon proved to me that paddling her bottom with a wooden spoon was invigorating to both. And she could be taken to extremes of pleasure by kneeling on the bed, head buried in the pillow, legs spread wide, encouraging me to flagellate, at first very lightly, but with increasing vigour, the thick-lipped length of her sex, sometimes with the same wooden spoon, a few times with a broad belt, while she would moan and cry out and thrust her buttocks higher and higher to receive the blows and her wetness trickled down her thighs. Or she would lie on her back, her knees planted on either side of her head, raising her tantalising sex to receive my blows, until neither of us could bear it any longer and I would plunge into her from above like a diver in search of abalone.

It was not only Anna's body I came to worship during the time we were together: she taught me, to my own amazement, more about my own than I had ever suspected. And she was always eager to discover more, to probe further, to explore beyond custom and tradition and myth and taboo. Love really only began on the other side of all that, she insisted. The starting point was not to hold on any more, but to let go – of all inhibitions and prohibitions and blocks and brakes, to go beyond frontiers and boundaries. And I suppose the very fact that in her everyday life she was such a model citizen and secretary made it that much more exhilarating.

When we were not making love in her flat, we would drive to secluded places where we were not likely to be discovered or recognised (we were both obsessive about keeping it secret): small farm roads and tracks in the mountains and valleys around Stellenbosch, Franschhoek, Paarl; or to stretches of the coast which, in those days, were still largely unspoilt – Macassar, Steenbras, Kogel Bay, Rooi Els and beyond. It was idyllic, Edenic.

We spoke about everything under the sun and moon. Even about politics. To my surprise she was not such a staunch supporter of the party as I had thought. In fact, as time went on and the party revealed more and more of its real intentions, she lost all faith in the official line. My own gradual drift away from the safe and trusted world in which I had been brought up, undoubtedly dated from that time. It was all the more decisive for the intense personal life she shared with me. In the beginning, at least, I would probably have swallowed hook, line and sinker whatever she said, simply to make the good sex last; but slowly it filtered in more deeply than that. I was discovering, in every way, that there were more things in heaven and earth than I had dreamed of in my severely circumscribed little philosophy. And those things were never theoretical, abstract, distant: in the miraculous reality of her body it all became flesh. It came to define my life and then to set me free.

It had to end. Not just because of the intensity, or the ever-present need to keep it secret from Father and our colleagues, but quite simply because Anna had to move on. I could never expect her to find her be-all and end-all in what was then still a callow youth. (It was time, too, for her to prepare a return to the hunter-lover who was by now ready to make a comeback from the obscurity into which he had faded after the 'accident'.) After a year she told me, with what I can only call compassion and generosity, but very firmly, that it was time for me to leave. I had graduated from her school of love. It had to happen before I became irrevocably hooked on her; what I now needed, she made clear, was to stand on my own feet and meet the world on my own terms. It was devastating. And yet she'd managed to explain it all with such warm, even humorous, understanding, that I could not feel bitter or rejected. I know now that much of what I wrote in my novels, later, after Sharpeville, really grew from the first stirrings of insight provoked by my relationship with her – its beginning, its tumultuous middle, and its end.

She was, I now think, my Scheherazade. I do not say it lightly, or with any narrow understanding. The more I reread the *Thousand and One Nights*, the more I believe that it is perhaps the greatest Art-of-Love the world has produced: much more extensive, profound and subtle than anything formulated by Ovid or the authors of the *Kama Sutra*. And it is even more remarkable because its focus is not the production of male pleasure, or even communal pleasure, but the role of the woman. (It is pretty practical too: *How to get your man and keep him*.) That young girl, seventeen or eighteen years old (assisted, indeed, by a little sister wise beyond her years), knew how to tame a king bent on violence and revenge, and a hater of women, and transform him, not into a slave of love, but into a creative and fully human *man*. How to expand his experience and his knowledge of his world, by exposing him to diversity. And all of that through inventing and telling stories, for hundreds of nights, for weeks and months and years, for a lifetime. Stories about kings and queens and magicians and merchants, about sailors and beggars and fishermen and peasants, about voyages by land and sea and into the depths of the spirit and its desires: in order to extend the boundaries of the known, the familiar, the everyday, to explore realms of mystery and delight and danger and magic and passion. And so it becomes a gigantic, multifarious, astounding allegory of love and lovemaking, all of it embodied in the largely untold but continually present story of the love between Shahriyar and Scheherazade. Through them, lovemaking and narrative become interchangeable. For is not lovemaking a form of storytelling? – our bodies telling each other the most intimate stories about themselves. Each of the individual nocturnal tales can be read as a commentary, even as a manual, on the unfolding relationship between this man and this woman; and what they learn about love is all rooted in the wisdom she – a young virgin to start with! – imparts through her stories.

Scheherazade does not simply postpone death by enthralling the king in her storytelling: she *engages* with death. After the first few nights it no longer matters if a story is left unfinished at the coming of dawn: it is through the intricacy of the story (all those embeddings: Scheherazade telling about a fisherman telling about another fisherman telling about yet another . . .), and the processes of its telling, that she ensnares Shahriyar. Some of the tales are images of – or refutations of, or challenges to – his own relationships with women: but it is seldom simple or straight-forward. What Scheherazade does is to show him an infinite variety of possibilities: a thousand and one different ways to rule, a thousand and one different ways to negotiate absence, or to deal with others, or to face the self, a thousand and one different ways to make love. In this way she releases him from the trap of narrow or absolute definitions about life and love, about right and wrong, about transgression and punishment and revenge and forgiveness. Her stories – her love – teach him how to be wise. If he is wise as a king, he will be a good lover; if he is a good lover, he will rule wisely, over others as well as himself. And this, I realise in retrospect, is what Anna van der Watt set in motion in me.

I continued to see her over the following years: in the party office where she stayed on as a secretary, and later as the wife of Ockert Grobler, the hunter-murderer. They had children. She became a matron. We never spoke about the 'old days'. But she would sometimes, when we met at this or that social occasion, give me a very secretive smile from which I knew that the more she appeared to be a model citizen, the wilder and more magnificent she must be in her dreams, and in bed. I could only hope that Ockert Grobler could do her justice. In my own bed, when I masturbated, or in moments of pleasure with other women over the years, I would continue to render homage to the Scheherazade I had known.

* * *

I MENTIONED THAT other watershed election of my life, in 1994, after Mandela had come out of prison and for four years the country had gone through the convulsions of transition and negotiations. As the date of 27 April approached, we were all struck by apprehension: there were explosions all over the place, right up to the morning of election day. Among white conservatives there was a sense of doomsday approaching. Cellars were stocked with tinned food and candles, paraffin and petrol, many women sewed black clothing for their families in case they would be called upon to flee under cover of darkness from the forces of evil, while the ANC was toyi-toying in the streets of towns and cities and along rural roads. As it happened, the day turned the whole country into a carnival of celebration in which, briefly but miraculously, three and a half centuries of colonisation on the palimpsest of history were suddenly obliterated by a new layer of joyous meaning.

I was with Andrea at the time; she was coloured, and we'd been together since before Mandela strode from prison in February 1990. (I shall return to her later. As she'd become more and more involved in the ANC structures preparing for the coming dispensation, we'd had less and less time to spend together – although we'd kept promising each other that things would soon be different: after the next meeting, the next demonstration, the next conference; certainly after election day . . .)

We woke up very early, before five; in fact, we'd hardly slept at all. For Andrea, it would be the first time in her life she could vote in her own country; for me, the first time I was prepared to do so since 1948. We were going to separate polling stations – she was part of a monitoring team of the ANC who would be travelling all over the Western Cape to keep track of what was happening; I had just started working on a book, *Return to Sunrise*, and had selfishly decided to go to a station where the queues were not expected to be too long. After checking on the radio, I chose Mowbray. A mistake, as it turned out: busloads of voters from elsewhere, Khayelitsha in particular, had just been disgorged at the station when I arrived, and the queue at the gym hall that had been converted for the occasion must have been almost a kilometre long. And the rain was coming down in grey sheets that almost wholly obscured the mountain. It was going to be a long day. I was seriously tempted to go home, to tune in to the radio again and choose another polling station.

Just then a few informal entrepreneurs turned up alongside the queue with bundles of black plastic refuse bags which we could transform into raincoats. Almost immediately this led to a loosening of the tongues. Soon we were all bantering and joking and laughing together. The man beside me turned out to be a black municipal cleaner from Khayelitsha. Behind us were a law student from UCT and a large, jovial woman, a domestic worker from Rondebosch; in front of us a white medical doctor from Groote Schuur and a coloured vagrant who, it transpired, lived under a nearby bridge. In our stylish black plastic raincoats we all looked much the same; more importantly, we were joined together by a common purpose – the making of that portentous little cross at the end of the long wait.

Not even in a rugby queue have I encountered so much humour, such sharp wit, and such a sense of camaraderie. To stretch our legs, we took turns to wander up and down the queue, encountering everywhere strangers bubbling with eagerness to talk, to share with us their expectations for the day, their reminiscences of the previous months, or years, or lifetimes. For a few hours we escaped from the singularity of our lives to discover how much we actually had in common. The rain, the cold, the hunger, the memories of the past, the hopes for the future, erased all the customary awareness of difference – in a country where, for centuries, *everything* had been predicated on difference. Some individuals opened sandwiches or chocolates they had brought along for themselves, happy to share with all the bystanders; it was a partaking of loaves and fishes. One man, some distance back, who turned out to be a plumber, left in his bakkie while his new friends kept his place in the queue, and came back with a whole load of hotdogs and sandwiches and cool drinks from a café in Durban Road. The husband of a queueing woman arrived with a shoebox of food for her, assessed what was happening, and promptly returned home to stock up with new supplies for twenty or thirty more people. And a few shrewd street vendors who had got wind of the marketing possibilities, began to ply their trade up and down the constantly lengthening line. A water tower at the edge of the Liesbeek River provided shelter for those in need of toilet facilities, and soon a roster was estab-lished, for ladies and gentlemen in turn. Not a single person was complaining or grumpy; laughter rippled up and down the queue, like vocal Mexican waves.

It was after about three hours that I met Jenny, who had been standing some distance behind me. She had begun to feel nauseous and had broken from the queue to sit down for a while, her head between her knees. Impossible to miss her. Pretty and fair-haired, slight, with big eyes, and a sharp, intelligent face which in the circumstances seemed alarmingly pale. It turned out that she had been working all night finishing a paper for some conference, and had gone without break-fast that morning, so it was nothing serious, just unpleasant. As it happened, I had just been offered a sandwich and a small carton of fruit juice by the plumber, and I persuaded her to share it with me. Afterwards, for safety's sake, I brought her the doctor who had been standing in front of me. Soon the colour returned to Jenny's cheeks, although there was still something feverish glowing in her eyes, which were a very deep luminous blue, almost violet.

We started talking. I learned to my delight that she was recently divorced; she was an anthropologist (later that night, back at home, listening to the rain outside, she told me about her research into the phenomenon of the moon-cloth; but there in the queue we had other things to discuss). It turned out that we had much in common. Her father ran a bookshop in town, specialising in second-hand and anti-quarian books. After a messy divorce from her mother he had brought her up in their cramped and rather mouldy little flat upstairs from the shop. Some of her best memories involved tiptoeing downstairs at night in her long nightdress to pick a book from the shelves and snuggle up in bed with it. Her father did not mind; in fact, he encouraged it, with the sole provision that the book should be restored to its place afterwards in the same condition in which she'd found it.

Only once had such a nocturnal mission gone wrong, in an entirely unforeseen way. She was thirteen or fourteen. It was midwinter and she'd just run a bath when she realised that she'd forgotten to choose a book for the night; knowing her way by heart, she promptly tripped down-stairs, naked, to find something. On nimble bare feet in the half-dark she nipped up the tall ladder to reach the top shelf under the high ceiling where she had recently discovered her father's collection of erotica. She was perched on the top rung of the ladder when the light was turned on and a strange man appeared at the end of the narrow aisle: she had forgotten that her father sometimes arranged with out-of-town customers to come in for a browse after hours. All she could do was to huddle with her head pressed against the ceiling and hope that the visitor would go past without looking up. But he was taking his time, and she was beginning to shiver and turn blue with cold. And then he started climbing the ladder too, heading quite obviously for the same destination. The ladder was not very steady. When the stranger reached up and accidentally touched her knee, he uttered a smothered sound of shock, looked up, saw a live naked girl where he had expected a book of erotic drawings, lost his footing and tumbled down. The ladder toppled over, Jenny landed sprawling on top of the visitor, and scrambled off on all fours, leaving it to the embarrassed stranger to explain to the incredulous shop owner what had happened. By the time her father came upstairs to ask for her version of the story, she was already thawing in her brimfull bath, assuring him with an angel-face through clouds of steam that she had no idea of what he was talking about.

It was that look of innocence which hooked me – precisely because I soon discovered how deceptive it was. For as I was to discover before the end of that long day, there was no end to Jenny's capacity for pleasure, which often reminded me of Tania in France, with her over-the-top approach to sex. But I'll get to that later.

As we followed the random lines of our excited conversation, the queue kept inching forward, sometimes coming to a dead stop for half an hour or more while the election officials in the gym hall frantically replaced their stocks of ballot papers, pencils, indelible ink and other materials; then there would be a brief surge forward, before we settled once again into a barely perceptible shuffle.

We were hardly conscious of the delays, as our conversation grew more and more eager. It was as if we'd spent lifetimes together and after a long separation now had to cram all the catching-up into a single day. From time to time she would grab my hand to lend urgency to what she was saying; in sudden spasms of cold, we would huddle together for warmth – while all around us the exuberant conversations and newly established comradeships among the hundreds of other people flourished and flared despite the wind and rain. It was as if with every tentative step forward we were also moving closer together, Jenny and I, feeling the current of electricity between us running ever more strongly, until it was almost unbearable. Even if we never saw each other again, her luminous eyes would be burned into my memory for ever. But we no longer even considered as a possibility that after the voting we might go our different ways. History had thrown us together, no man would put us asunder.

After nearly seven hours, we entered the polling station in a tight embrace, and reluctantly parted to go to separate booths to make our crosses; then, like schoolchildren on the last day of term, ran to my car hand in hand, as if it had all been agreed in advance, and drove home on what felt like automatic pilot, and burst into the house like two pieces of flotsam washed up by a tide. I am sure we might have made love right there on the front stoep, in the rain, had Frederik not opened the door for us and stood back in his imperturbable manner to let us in.

He mumbled something about coffee and crumpets (having left with Andrea at daybreak, he must have come back from his own voting long before us; I wasn't expecting her before midnight or later). Right then, it was the funniest and most inopportune thing we could possibly think of. We both collapsed in laughter. Poor Frederik must have been deeply offended, but true to form he did not show anything. He merely withdrew to the back of the house, presumably to put as much distance between himself and us as possible while we took off our muddy shoes and charged upstairs, littering every step of the way with items of clothing. Our teeth were chattering with cold, but even that could not restrain us. The elation of the day had charged us with too much energy to think of anything else.

I ran a luxuriously deep bath for us as we stood on the dark red mat, shaking with the extremes of cold and passion. And then we plunged in. It was like the night, she said later, when she'd sought refuge in the hot water after scaring the stranger in the bookshop out of his wits. We very nearly drowned ourselves in the process. When once I quite literally came up for air, I discovered that the water on the bathroom floor had flooded into the bedroom, leaving a dark stain on the sisal carpet for weeks to come, which re-emerged after every spell of bad weather for many months as an eloquent reminder, like arthritic pains.

Only after we had eased the first wave of desire, we noticed that the water was discoloured. It started as a faint, delicate pink; but slowly darkened as a small whorl of red unravelled from between her thighs like an exotic flower blooming. Her period had started. There was something incredibly beautiful and moving about it. That was when I had my first lesson in the tradition of the moon-cloth. And Jenny was still holding me in its thrall, hours later, when we finally decamped to the kitchen for some copious late-night eating and drinking, Jenny wrapped in a royal-blue dressing gown from my cupboard, her long blonde hair plastered to her glowing cheeks

Andrea came home well after midnight, by which time we were more or less ready to retire. For a moment her arrival startled me. But there was no occasion for alarm. She showed all the signs of immoderate celebration herself and was accompanied by a tall young black man she had met at the last of the polling stations she had monitored during her long day. It had occasionally happened in the past that one of us would bring someone home: after the first year together, our relationship had become very open-ended. But this was the first time both of us had a companion for the same night; and somehow it was exactly as it should be. With a brief wave in my direction, she led her own election prize past the kitchen to the spare bedroom. For both of us it was an end and a beginning; and Jenny and I remained together for a year.

THE FINAL DRIVE towards Baghdad is underway, sooner than expected. The US, Sky News showed last night, have seized a bridge over the Tigris thirty kilometres from the capital. (Another bridge, or the same one again?) The Third Infantry Division has now encircled Karbala and is moving north. They're showing continuous spectacular shots – more spectacular than the fireworks exploding over us that first night Anna and I made love – of the bombing of elite units in Baghdad. It is now estimated that within four to eight weeks the city will fall. The expectation is that at any moment an invisible 'red line' may be crossed by the invaders, which may invite retaliation with the much vaunted weapons of mass destruction. From sheer perversity I cannot wait for that invisible line to be reached. On the other hand, from the Iraqi television comes a self-assured statement that the crossing of the Euphrates is an illusion; nothing of it is true, and the Americans are not advancing. Perhaps this whole war is an illusion, it is not really happening, except on TV. Perhaps I have never loved you. Perhaps my mother is a camel.

GEORGE BROUGHT HOME a funny little clay camel for you. Why on earth he should have thought a camel an appropriate gift to bring from Japan, I don't know. He loved surprising you with his presents, and you loved receiving them. It was like a birthday. And of course there was much more besides the camel (which from then on you proudly exhibited among your own sculptures, and in due course even copied and incorporated, in weird and fantastical ways, in your work). There must have been a whole suitcase full of presents when he came back. He even brought me something: a very beautiful little lacquer box, hand-painted with wonderfully stylised erotic pictures. They matched the small collection of netsuke which he brought you, very old, in exquisite smooth ivory turning yellow like mellowed piano keys, representing loving couples, human and animal, in a variety of almost-impossible positions.

The pride of the presents was a new wedding ring to replace the one you'd lost: an intricate Oriental design in white and yellow and red gold. You were unexpectedly subdued as you held out your finger for him to put it on – a perfect fit; he must have taken the measurement before he left – but that must have been because you were so overwhelmed by its strange and intriguing beauty.

While we are all admiring the array of presents in the studio the day after his return (you had invited me to go to the airport with you to meet him, but although my first reaction had been to accept, I'd decided that the two of you deserved to be alone for a while), you caress the smooth patina of the intricately carved little couple of a woman and a monkey. 'I think we should try out all these positions,' you suggest, looking up at George with an impish glint in your eyes. It is exactly what Anna would have said, all those years ago.

'Is there anything you haven't tried out yet?' I tease.

'I wouldn't do it with a monkey,' you laugh.

'I often feel like a big uncouth ape next to you. A gorilla or something,' mocks George.

'I'll always make an exception for you,' you say. 'You taught me to love the jungle.'

Through the open buttons at the top of his shirt I can see the luxuriant ground cover of black, curly hair on his chest. And like often before, in spite of my efforts to suppress the thought, I imagine the two of you together: the smoothness of your limbs, his heavy, hirsute body. I can see your nipples entangled in the dense undergrowth of his chest. The image is deeply perturbing. But it is soon overlaid by our conversation; and then we go out for a meal at the Japanese restaurant in Hout Bay, so that George can compare his recent experience of the real thing with the local approximation.

Over the next few weeks he is working almost day and night in his darkroom, a surprisingly cramped little pimple at the side of the house, to follow up on the photographs he has taken in Japan. I am invited to lend a hand, which pleases me immensely. Not only because it gives the two of us time to spend together, but because it means a return to an activity which was once a quite serious pastime. It was in the late seventies, when I was working on a book on the '76 riots with the driven, passionate, young activist photographer, Aviva. The project was her idea; I wrote the text, she took the pictures. The rather obvious title, *Black and White*, we chose together.

Aviva was a small, slight person, with more passion than one would have expected her frail frame to contain; but there was no end to her dedication and her anger. The nature of her work had prompted a number of run-ins with the Security Police and we always went to bed expecting to be awakened by the ominous knock on the door at three in the morning – the sort of fear that was to be repeated, after my return from Europe in the eighties, when I was with Abbie. That time it did not end so well; but although with Aviva there was always an awareness of danger, we also knew that there was an invisible, thin, red line protecting her – because some years earlier a close friend of hers, a coloured girl, Claudie, had had a brief and ill-advised clandestine fling with a man who soon afterwards became the secretary of a deputy minister in the Nationalist hierarchy. On a few occasions the couple had used Aviva's cottage as a hideout, so she knew about the affair. She had been sworn to secrecy, and even though the political implications of the relationship pained her, she would not betray her friend. It ended very dramatically, soon after the man had been appointed secretary, when Claudie died in an inexplicable car accident. No one was ever indicted, and no names were mentioned; but Aviva had her own suspicions, and she began to make enquiries.

Very late one night, she had a visit from a stranger who said he was a colleague of the new secretary. It was a very friendly, almost unctuous, man who just wanted to tell her of his deep sympathy about the sudden death of her dear friend Claudie, and to reassure her that she herself had absolutely nothing to worry about. Why should she worry? Aviva asked. Unless there had been something fishy about Claudie's death . . . ? No, no, no, he told her. It was just one of those things, wasn't it? She should try to relax and get on with her life. It was in Claudie's interest, and in her own, to let the whole unfortunate matter rest. Didn't she agree? She was terrified, so she agreed. But from that moment her dedication to the anti-apartheid cause was absolute.

As the man prepared to leave, she managed to summon enough courage to issue a quiet warning of her own: Since Claudie's death, she told him, she had been living in fear of something happening to her too. And so she had been forced to take precautions. He should tell his friend the secretary, as well as his boss the deputy minister, that she had written a full statement including not just her suspicions, and all the details she knew about the relationship, but everything that had come to light during her enquiries into the accident; and this statement had been lodged with a lawyer, who had instructions to divulge it all if ever anything untoward were to happen to her. They parted on the best of terms, but the man did appear somewhat pale as he went out into the dark.

It procured for Aviva some space to manoeuvre and to work on the photographs for our book. This was the tenuous, invisible line drawn around her: it was impossible to tell when she might overstep it and unleash all the regime's weapons of mass destruction against her; but at the same time it was a line they dared not readily overstep from the outside. In the meantime we could continue working together, on Aviva's field trips and in her darkroom. I picked up as much about photography as I needed to know for the novel *In the Dark* which I wrote once I was safely in London. At the same time it drew me into the processes of an art form I'd long been fascinated by but knew little about. And, perhaps most importantly, it was at the heart of one of the most meaningful love affairs of my life, with enough of Durrell's plumbing, and enough metaphysical enquiry, to last me for a very long time.

I told George about all this as we worked together, he handling the cropping and lighting and printing, while I performed the more menial but ever-spellbinding tasks of developing and fixing the prints.

'Actually,' he said, 'Aviva Scholnik was one of my role models. I remember seeing one of her exhibitions here in Cape Town before she left the country. I must have been in my early twenties. And then that book came out. It was immediately banned here, of course, but I had some contacts in London and someone smuggled me a copy. That woman had a technique without peer. Above all, she had the *eye*. You can have all the technique in the world, but unless you have the eye you may just as well become a bookkeeper.'

'She certainly changed my life. She taught me to write in a different key. A more visual key. Apart from the fact that if it hadn't been for her I would not have left the country just then.'

'What a pity she never came back,' said George. 'We need more photographers like her.'

'For many years she couldn't risk it. And then she met her German, and got married, and that was that.'

'It must have been tough for you?'

'Not really. We'd broken up before she met him.' I pulled a wry face. 'That's the way it goes with love, isn't it?'

'I hope not,' he said with a quiet smile.

'I suppose I was talking about *my* loves,' I qualified. 'You and Rachel are something else. You know, you're about the only couple I've met in years who make me feel that there may be something to be said for marriage after all.'

'I still can't quite believe it,' he said disarmingly. 'Rachel is the most incredible thing that has ever happened to me. I've always been rather awkward with women, especially with beautiful women.'

'Yet you've worked with lots of them in your life.'

'I know.' A boyish grin, the kind which made me understand why you fell in love with him. 'And it's not as if I came to Rachel with a clean slate. But I could never really believe it would happen. Every time someone showed interest in me I got quite weak in the knees with sheer gratitude.'

'And I'm sure every time they took advantage of your naivety – if that is what it was.'

'I never thought of it that way. I just counted each lovely little blessing as it came. And not one of those was a match for Rachel.'

At some stage during our hours of work, every day, there would be a knock on the closely sealed and blacked-out door, and you would call from outside. And five or ten or sometimes forty minutes later, depending on our work, we would join you in the studio to inspect what you had been doing in the meantime, and have tea (coffee for you, while you smoked like the most reckless and desirable of chimneys), and plunge into one of our breathless, dizzying, endless conversations. They were, you used to say, like one of those descriptions which George had once read to you, of a sentence in a novel by Thomas Mann, where you dive in at one end of the Atlantic and finally emerge at the other with the verb in your mouth. Except, I think, we often skipped the verbs, and just continued our explorations in the hinterland on the other side of the sea.

The three of us went out together quite often. Mostly films, occasionally a concert at the City Hall (there was one really memorable Beethoven recital), once an unexpectedly moving production of *Tosca* in the Artscape. Which was followed, predictably, by a discussion that lasted for so long that in the end I was invited to sleep over. Since my wife-sitting stint this had happened more than once, a quite natural extension of many a long evening of argument and discussion. On this occasion it began with a comparison between the evening's perform-ance and, inevitably, the great performances we knew on disc: the purity of Caballé, the passion of Leontyne Price, the controlled fire of Renata Tebaldi, the dulcet tones of Kiri Te Kanawa – and then, in a separate category altogether, the divine Callas, with di Stefano and Gobbi. From Callas we moved into the role of Tosca herself.

'A bit overdone,' muses George. 'Romantic melodrama is all very well, but it can so easily lose itself in muddy feelings. The "Vissi d'arte, vissi d'amore" is probably the best thing Puccini has done for a soprano, and every time I see Tosca laying out Scarpia's body and lighting the candles, I am moved to tears. But apart from that . . . I think the different dimensions of the story become confused. There's no balance between the private and the political. That's what all three of us are struggling with all the time, isn't it? – you in your writing, this one in her sculpture. I in my photography. And in *Tosca* it doesn't work. Unless it is exceptionally well done, it's just too much of a ten-cents-a-dozen emotion.'

'How dare you say that?' you storm – a reaction which, judged from his laugh, is exactly what George has tried to provoke. 'In our time, in this country, what we have is a *lack* of feeling. Everybody knows everything about things like democracy, transparency, accountability. Been there, got the T-shirt. But damn it, that isn't all that matters. We've become ashamed to admit that we have a private life and personal feelings. We don't seem to trust them enough any more, we don't believe in them. Don't you agree, Chris?'

'There are feelings and feelings,' I try to avoid taking sides.

'I don't mistrust feeling,' George persists. 'Only *false* feeling, *ersatz* feeling, cheap emotions. Even Tosca and Cavaradossi have their share of it. The kind of feelings Don Giovanni professes to have for all his women, only until he has bedded them. Then it all goes out of the window.'

'The problem with Don Giovanni,' you say (it is a topic about which you can always be relied on to have a comment), 'is that he never grows up. He wants everything, and he wants it now.'

'Is that so different from Antigone?' I object, more vehemently than I may have meant to. 'All those exceptional individuals who refuse to toe the line, to accept mediocrity, the eternally young ones who keep the world from growing staid and grey, the Peter Pans who keep magic alive?'

'You are not just hopelessly romantic, Chris, you are incorrigibly sentimental. And that is unforgivable in a man your age.'

'Anything should be forgiven in a man my age,' I say. 'I'm entering my second childhood, remember.'

'All I can tell you is that you've got Don Giovanni totally wrong.'

'It's easy to judge from the outside,' I caution. 'Can we ever be sure about what drives Don Giovanni? Do you think *he* was ever sure? Perhaps he really believed in what he was doing, every time. He may have had a much more profound conviction than you accuse him of.'

This is where you squarely turn against me. 'No, Chris! He most certainly didn't! Look at how he behaved to Donna Anna, to Donna Elvira. No, damn it, that was shit. You can't compare it to Tosca. She *feels*. She feels enough to murder the hateful Scarpia and kill herself.'

'But Mozart's music is better,' I try to trump you.

'That's not the question. Mozart's music itself condemns Don Giovanni. As far as I remember, he has two rather precipitate arias and a charming but very short canzonetta. Even Leporello gets a better deal than his master, musically. And the most beautiful arias are given to the women, including the little peasant Zerlina. Mozart sides with them because what they feel is genuine.'

'Because women are better equipped to deal with feeling?' George says defiantly.

And thus begins a whole new argument, to be continued the following morning.

In one way or another, this returned in many of our conversations, always coming to rest, eventually, in the comfort you and George found in your relationship, the brightness and humour with which everything could eventually be resolved. *That,* I thought, like the story of Scheherazade and Shahriyar behind the tales told during their nights, was what it really was about. And it was in evidence again during one of the best experiences we ever shared. You had nagged us for a long time about going to the Cedarberg; most of the time there was other, more urgent, business to occupy us. But this time, in mid-April, you simply went ahead and booked a hut, and blithely confronted us with the fact of it.

It meant taking a risk with the weather, but it turned out to be perfect: the warmth of late summer still lasting, but somewhat attenuated, the days becoming gentle and vulnerable around the edges, with a lucent tranquillity in the heart of it, the merest quiver of approaching winter. Above all, an awareness of endless space opening up to all sides, as in a Rilke poem – an autumn sonnet or one of the *Duino Elegies*. The vineyards that surrounded us for the first half-hour were turning from green to the deepest shades of Cabernet, bringing back a distant harvesting summer in the vineyards of Bordeaux, at Saint-Émilion. (Tania covered in sticky red grape juice from her deep navel to her pretty toes.) Then came the gentle billowing of the Naples yellow and burnt sienna and terracotta wheatlands as, to the right, the acetylene flames of the mountains on the horizon deepened in colour from almost transparent blue to deepest purple. After the wheat followed the dark green of the citrus orchards, teeming with early oranges like a swarm of little suns nesting in them. And then we turned off towards the mountains, which seemed to open to welcome us, closing again behind in wall upon wall of dun-coloured slopes and high red cliffs.

We drove past the Algeria forestry station towards the camp at Krom River where you had booked the hut. It was comfortable enough, but because the weather was so splendid, even in spite of the slender hint of a chill, we unanimously decided to move outside and spread our sleeping bags under some tall trees beside a very shallow, very clear stream of rapid water. George and I made a fire and he prepared supper: in his hands even something as straightforward as a braai became a gourmet experience, thanks to an assortment of home-made condiments and sauces which he'd brought along. As it was midweek, there were no other campers at the picnic spot. We had the mountains and the stars to ourselves.

Again, our talk ranged over everything in heaven above, and in the earth beneath, and in the water under the earth. George had previously told us a lot about his visit to Japan; but this time he really explored it in depth, probing everything that appeared mysterious to Westerners like us: the mindset behind the sand patterns in the Zen gardens of Kyoto, the ritual of the tea ceremony, the love hotels, the profound philosophies informing the relations between men and women. The two of you must have discussed much of this at times when I was not present, because you could fill in a surprising number of links between what he had to say and features of your work: the absences, the silences, the beyondness, the in-betweenness. And from there our minds returned to these mountains: the San drawings not far from our camp, the sculptures made by wind and sun and rain along the cliffs and outcrops and deep kloofs.

Sometime during the detours of the conversation I simply drifted off. When I woke up, the stars very white above me and almost within reach, and a deep silence on all sides, your two sleeping bags had disappeared. I was still too dazed with sleep to grasp the obvious, and suddenly gripped by a kind of primitive terror about being abandoned, I dragged myself from my own sleeping bag and stumbled off in search of what I myself could not explain. First this way, then that. After a while I came more clearly to my senses and retraced my steps towards the picnic spot beside the stream which was still rustling along, unperturbed and lyrical.

Amid the silence I thought I could hear something else, something human, and wandered in that direction. Now the sounds were clearer. It was your voice, moaning softly, in half-smothered tones, but slowly going higher, becoming more expressive. For a moment I thought you were singing to George in the dark, it was so melodious, but then I heard the deeper groaning of his voice as a rhythmic accompaniment to yours; and I knew what was going on. It is something I normally cannot listen to – an association of foreign hotels and unfamiliar rooms in distant places, sounds unpleasantly reminding me of others threatening to invade my space, obtruding into the privacy of my own dreams or thoughts, my own enforced solitude in a strange place – but this time it was different. Not because I knew you (in different circumstances such knowledge might have been even more embarrassing), but because there was something so unabashed, so affirmative, so free and happy about it, that there was nothing to feel ashamed or self-conscious of. I may well be romanticising again, but I felt that this was what lovemaking ought to be like.

I knew I ought to leave you to your shared and mumbled music; but I could not move. Not until your voice rose from the low, joint rhythms into a single clarity, like the warble of a nightbird, clear as a flute, so haunting that it brought a shiver to my spine. Only then could I tear myself away, and cautiously return to our spot, realising too late how soft and vulnerable my bare feet were on the uneven ground strewn with branches and rocks and smaller stones. Emptied of thought, but not of feeling, I crawled back into my cold sleeping bag. After a long, long lifetime of sharing my loneliness with others, other bodies, women, at the end of it all, here I was on my own, forsaken it seemed even by memory.

When I woke up from the sun in my eyes, your bags were back in place, close together, and you were both fast asleep. Your left arm was outside the sleeping bag, George's right; your hands were clasped. In the thin sunlight the new wedding ring glinted almost too bright on your finger. I went down to the stream to wash, brushed my teeth, and then made a fire on the still glowing embers from the night before. By the time I had breakfast ready, you were awake too. And afterwards, in the thrilling cool of the early morning, we set out on the route you had planned for us, up to the Wolfberg Arch, apparently some three or four hours away.

Five, as it turned out, because we were not all as fit as you. But it was worth every cautious step and painful breath of the way. It was like a journey into the heart of the craggy mountains, a quest for origins, for innocent beginnings. Past huge rock formations like vast ragged sculptures, orange and red and grey and black, mottled with lichen, pock-marked and gnarled, ageless: monoliths like solitary figures abandoned by their tribe; others like small crowds or congregations turned to stone by an unknown malignant passing god who did not approve of trespassers; and some of them like couples, groping towards each other or welded together by age and wind – mountains resembling another tribe and state of being, and yet replicating ours, with the same silences, the same staring, the same attempts at understanding, the same agonies, and always the same urge, the same desire. To be together, to be joined at the hip, never to be left alone.

The arch itself, where we spent a leisurely hour for lunch, was magnificent. One could imagine dinosaurs waddling through it, thousands or millions of years ago, incomparably bigger and stronger than us, their puny successors. Yet they were all gone now. And we, too, would be gone one day. All our inventions and achievements and dreams and wars gone, our music and our writings and our paintings gone, lost beyond memory. All our loves gone. On this ancient earth only these motionless rocks would remain as testimony to what had been or might have been. Not even as testimony, because there would be no one and nothing left to read them, interpret them, understand the first thing about them.

Somewhere in the distance, behind rocks and brittle bushes and a small cluster of gnarled cedar trees on an outcrop, there was movement. A little buck scurried away, darting this way and that, then disappearing like a shadow, as if it had never been there at all. A few small stones were still clattering downhill, then even that was gone. Far overhead a lone bateleur eagle made a single loop, uttering its forlorn cry – like your cry of love in the night – and then sailed away over the cliffs and was eclipsed. It, too, might never have been there. Like us in due course, all too soon.

It must have been from staring too hard at the cliffs and rocks, imagining too much, that about three-quarters of the way down, on a steep incline littered with the stones and pebbles of an ancient rockfall, I lost my footing and stumbled, and fell. It wasn't dangerous, I only rolled a few metres, but I grazed my hands and knees rather painfully. More seriously, I twisted my right ankle. Both of you were immediately at my side to help me up, but the leg was too painful to stand on. You made me sit and wrenched off the boot. Already the ankle was beginning to swell.

There was a thin little stream cascading down the steep slope only a hundred metres or so to the left, and you accompanied me to it, and helped me to bathe my foot in the water. Cold as icicles it pierced up into my leg. But it numbed the pain, and after a few minutes the swelling seemed to stabilise. Even so, I could not readily step on it with my full weight. Which meant that I had to be supported by both of you, dangling between you like an oversized, clumsy marionette (from a Noh play, George joked), the rest of the way back. Our progress was painfully slow, and very soon we realised that night would fall long before we had any hope of getting back to the camp. I wanted you to leave me there and return on your own; from the camp you could drive to Algeria and get some help. But that would still mean attempting a rescue, and a hazardous descent, in the dark; so you wouldn't hear of it. In the end we agreed on the only practical, if not very pleasant, solution: making a halt for the night right there.

The weather was still perfect, except that it was much colder than the previous night. But then, thanks to your vile smoking habit (to which I had, by now, become a happy convert), we had lighters, and so could make a fire. There wasn't much time before dark to collect wood, but at least we could protect ourselves against the cold for most of the night. After having wolfed down all the provisions we had brought along for lunch, there was no food left to stave off the hunger; there was only the little stream to drink from. We huddled tightly together, this time with you in the middle, and roasting our fronts and freezing our backs, we sat through the night.

To help us forget about the cold George tried to entertain us with a story about a fall he'd once had on the slopes of the Rigi in Switzerland. He hadn't gone there to ski, he quickly assured us – 'that would have been a short cut to hell' – only to take a walk along the sleigh track. But engrossed in taking photographs, he didn't look where he was going, and to make it worse he was wearing leather-soled shoes. Within a few metres he slipped and started falling. 'I fell,' said George, his face a caricature of suffering at the memory, 'and I fell, and I fell, until I thought it was impossible to fall any further, and then I fell some more. I lost my cameras. And still I went on falling. After some time I saw my arse coming wheeling past my head, but still I fell and fell. It just wouldn't stop. I tell you, if I'd brought a book along I could have read it from cover to cover before I got to the end of my fall.'

'And when you did,' I asked, 'were there any unbroken bones left in your body?'

'Quite a few,' he said with a sly grin. 'Because I'm pear-shaped I have a fair amount of built-in protection. And I realised that in future my best safeguard would be to put on more weight. So I've been working on it. What I did . . .' His voice trailed off. It was getting too cold to go on talking. Silence was insinuated into us with the cold, as our wood ran out and the last few flames died down. And sleep was impossible. But there was more than enough time to think.

Through the biting cold I remained conscious of the shadow of warmth coming from your body on my left. If I hadn't hurt my leg, I thought, the two of you would have been together again now, lying in each other's arms, sharing the warmth you were now sharing with me. You might be making love. You with your warbling call. Last night you were a couple, I was the outsider. Now we were all together. I had taken up some of your space. I had come to belong. I was being acknowledged, drawn into your generosity. Meagre as this warmth was, we were all sharing it, a primitive osmosis, a fusion, body to body.

I grimly reminded myself of a story that used to warm me through much of my childhood: the sad and heroic tale from some time after the Great Trek, when a twelve-year-old girl, Rachie de Beer, a little Snow White of the veld, had wandered about with her small brother in search of a strayed calf and got lost in a snowstorm, and saved the little boy's life by pushing him into a hollowed-out anthill and curling herself up in front of the hole to keep out the snow and the wind; and as it got colder, she took off all her clothes, bit by bit, dress and petticoat and small woollen vest and broekie, to keep him warm. In the end she was wearing only her little veldskoens, which must have made her nakedness appear even starker. When they were found the next day, the little boy was still alive, if only barely; but she had frozen to death. To my eternal shame I used to derive during much of my boyhood a guilty thrill from the idea of the thin naked girl curled up in the snow, and imagined myself in a weird act of heroism, approaching in the blinding storm, also stripped of my clothes, and lying down behind her, putting my arms tightly around her, tucking up my bare legs into hers from behind, my knees under her cold thin thighs, and feeling the darkness of death enveloping us together. There was something shameful about the memory. But I could not ward off the lurid imaginings that chilling story set alight inside me.

On this occasion, at least, you had George on one side and me on the other, all of us wrapped in many layers of clothing, to save you from a lingering white death. This was probably the closest I would ever be to you, I thought. For one night our separateness was suspended. We were part of a single formation in the mountains, returning to our own elemental beginnings. I was aware of tears that stung my eyes, a vast reservoir of gratitude welling up in me to you, woman, merging for a few shining black hours with all the women I have been with in my life, all of you together saving my life, redeeming me. And then even the thoughts seemed to go numb inside me.

We were close to frozen by the time the first grey dawn came filtering down the mountainside and we could unbend our seized-up joints to go in search of more wood to rekindle the fire and revive our bodies before we set out again on the last stretch to the camp. My ankle was swollen to a monstrous size. I could not put my boot on again and had to stuff it into the rucksack in which I'd carried my share of food and water up the mountain.

It took three more hours to get back to the camp. But it felt like returning home to Ithaca after years of wandering in the wilderness. We gulped down several glasses of neat whiskey (good, Irish) before we even thought of making breakfast. Then we devoured all the food that remained, and which had been meant to last for three more days, washed down with a bottle of red wine. A rich full-bodied Merlot which I shall never forget. An intense aroma of cherries and ripe strawberries, a liberal dash of cinnamon and vanilla, a wealth of ripe plums and mulberries on the palate (even after the whiskey), with generous mocha tones and firm, supple tannins. And an aftertaste that lasts for ever.

It was afternoon before we finally packed up and left. I felt guilty as hell for cutting short what had been meant to be a long and adventurous excursion full of walks and climbs and discoveries. And yet the atmosphere in the car on the way back was unrestrainedly jolly. We sang silly and bawdy songs, and laughed, and told filthy stories, all the way to the Cape, where in spite of my protestations you took me to Vincent Pallotti Hospital to have the ankle X-rayed. To my relief it turned out to have been, indeed, only a sprain. Even so, both of you refused to take me home and leave me there on my own (even though I assured you that

Frederik could cope). I was forcibly taken to Camps Bay with you and put to bed in the room that was by now generally designated as mine. My only compensation was some of the most lurid dreams I'd had for many months, and I woke up with a morning glory still staggering in spasms of uncontrollable delight, which is not something that happens to me very often these days. I couldn't remember the details of the dreams, but they were all about you; and at some stage all of us were involved in a threesome in a single sleeping bag, with stars raining down and shimmering on us like quicksilver. After that, in the vain hope of being granted a repeat of the dream – which, if not unequivocally 'wet' as in my days of full potency, at least could qualify as 'damp' – I accepted to stay in your home until the ankle was fully recovered.

IT WAS AFTER the scorched earth that followed in the wake of the Soweto uprising in '76, and after the murder of Steve Biko the following year, that I met Aviva at an exhibition of her photographs in Johannesburg, where I had gone to the launch of my book *Intimate Lightning*. Not even a launch. After some unpleasant previous experiences the local representative of my London publisher had merely arranged a small private function in the bookshop of a friend in Braamfontein. Even so, the SB turned up in full force. A phalanx of very polite, very broad-shouldered, very shallow-eyed gentlemen in sports jackets and ties and flannels, who confiscated all the copies of *Intimate Lightning* imported for the occasion, and wrote down meticulously the names of everybody in the bookshop. Not a word was said about the book. They were merely acting on a complaint, they explained with smiles like knife wounds cutting across their Aryan faces, that the shop had not asked permission to be open after hours; and that it was a mixed gathering; and that liquor was being served.

I was supposed to leave for London the following day for the official launch of the book. But I was already seated in the plane when a very apologetic gentleman – whom I immediately recognised as one of our visitors in the bookshop the night before – came on board,

approached me in my aisle seat, leaned over and invited me to accompany him. It wouldn't take a minute, he said.

He was right. It didn't. In the airport building I was ushered into
a small room behind a panel which didn't look like a door and where
no one would ever have expected an office. Several of the other sporty
men from the previous evening were already assembled around a low
table of imitation sapele mahogany on which sat the black Samsonite
suitcase which I had checked in an hour before.

I was invited – that word again – to list on a sheet of paper all the
contents of the suitcase. Afterwards, without bothering to look at the
list, the *primus inter pares* opened the case. They all stood back in silence
as if expecting a detonation. When nothing happened, they opened up
a narrow gangway for me to approach the suspect piece of baggage,
and I was – yes – invited to unpack it. Each item brought to light –
every shirt and handkerchief, every pair of pants and underpants, every
jersey, every book, every condom, every little box or bottle of medicat-
ion – was passed from one investigator to the next, inspected from
several sides, probed, sniffed at and finally, with what seemed like
sincere regret, put down on the unencumbered end of the low table.
This took almost an hour. Then I was – so help me God – invited to
repack the suitcase, while the surrogate Inspector Clouseau left, holding
between a thumb and a forefinger, with obvious distaste, as if someone
had ejaculated over it, the list I had compiled. We waited. From time
to time I looked at my watch. Whenever I caught someone's eye, my
look would be met with a smile of deep understanding, but clearly
also of satisfaction. Long after the scheduled departure time of my
plane Inspector Clouseau returned, nodding at me with an expression
of real contentment, as if he had just concluded a very successful
quickie with a colleague, presumably female, somewhere in the entrails
of the sprawling building.

'It is all right,' he said. 'You may go now.'

I clenched my teeth in a very tight imitation of a smile. 'Thank you,'
I said frostily, then stopped. 'Would you mind telling me just what all
this was about?'

All of them, as if by prearrangement, looked at one another, and
the spokesman said, 'We have been tipped off.'

'I see. Tipped off about what?'

'That you might be trying to smuggle copies of your book out of the country.'

'But the book is being published in London,' I pointed out. 'Why would I smuggle copies *to* London?'

'One never knows,' he said, unfazed.

'You're right,' I said, still trying to meet their deadpan stares with one of my own. 'Well, I must commend you on your thoroughness.'

I went out, carrying my neatly repacked black Samsonite suitcase, found my way to the rent-a-car section and returned to the hotel from which I had already checked out. Not having anything else to do for the night, I went down to the lobby, flipped through a newspaper and came across an advertisement for an exhibition of photographs by Aviva Scholnik which was to be opened that night. I had seen some of her work in newspapers before, but never in the flesh. And that was how I turned up in the Carlton Centre an hour later.

The first person I recognised in the throng inside was one of my charming friends from the SB, who had been at my gathering the previous evening, but not at the airport that afternoon. One cannot attend every single cultural event in town. Not expecting him there, I actually greeted him before I realised who he was, and then quickly lost myself in the crowd. There were so many people that it was difficult to get to the photographs on the walls, but I jostled my way through. And the exhibition was more than worth the effort. This was an artist who could capture the fleeting, revealing moment, poignant or shocking as the case might be, but in such a way that something lasting was burned into the mind of the spectator. Most of the photographs had been taken in the wake of the Soweto upheavals, and it was a miracle that they had actually been allowed to go on show: it was only later that I heard about the link between Aviva and her friend Claudie who'd had the liaison with the secretary-to-be. They were either under constraint to allow her some scope, or – more likely – they were giving her rope and waiting for the moment to pounce.

It was some time before I came across Aviva Scholnik herself, in a back room close to the toilets, where she was having a quiet cigarette on her own, out of the crowd. The place was rank with dense blue smoke. I'd had to ask several people before I found her; but having seen the work, I felt the need to speak to her personally.

My first impression was of a half-developed photograph: a few stark blacks (hair, eyes), the rest a Rorschach assortment of greys still undecided about which way to go. An incredibly small person, even more incredibly thin, a mere wisp of a girl. Not exactly a girl either, she must have been thirty-four or thirty-five then. I, of course, was in my early fifties.

'You have some unexpected visitors here,' I said.

'People just gatecrash.'

'I was referring to the SB.'

A quick shadow flitted across her eyes. 'Are you sure?'

'I just recognised one of them. They came to my book launch last night.' I told her about the event, and its sequel.

'Well, good for them. Perhaps some of the culture will rub off on them,' she tried to quip, but it was clear that she was extremely nervous, smoking through an oversized cigarette holder, like Audrey Hepburn in *Breakfast at Tiffany's*. She did remind me somewhat of Hepburn, the eyes especially. But also of a Filippo Lippi madonna: one of those naughty girls he was reputed to pick up in the back streets at night when he slipped out of the monastery, and whom he would paint, after they had disported themselves, as the Holy Virgin.

She knew about me and my books in the same way as I knew about her and her photographs; so it was easy to get talking. And the pressure – the crowd, the police lurking – inspired a closeness which might not have been there under more normal circumstances. I have no doubt that the air of vulnerability surrounding her (although I soon found out how tough she could really be) was an added attraction. So it was not only as an artist, but as a woman, that she held my soon quite passionate interest. This was compounded when after barely half an hour of talking in the thick cloud of smoke that seemed to swirl in a slow, deadly whorl through the small room, a stranger made a rather brusque entry, grabbed her by the arm and said in a snarling whisper, 'For God's sake, woman, you're not hiding away again, are you? Come with me!' He was young; younger, it seemed, than she. With shoulder-length hair, not recently washed, and a pale ascetic face that seemed permanently fixed in a dissatisfied scowl. Rather beautiful long hands, and he clearly was aware of that. He tugged at her arm. 'Come *on*, sweetie!' The possessive endearment offended me more than anything else.

She pulled back. 'I'm talking to someone, Wayne.' (As it happens, no male name pisses me off more than Wayne; so the hostility in the thick air must have been as tangible as the smoke.)

He looked at me as if she had just scraped me from her pointed shoe. 'And who might this be?'

I did a very rude thing, which I hope is not in my repertoire of customary reactions. I said, 'None of your business, sonny. Buzz off.'

To my surprise and delight she burst out laughing. That, as far as young Wayne was concerned, was the last straw. He seemed to consider lunging at me, but must have suddenly decided to take the dignified way out – presumably because he did not have the build of a pugilist – and strutted off like a young rooster with a long white thorn stuck up his arse.

That guaranteed us another half-hour of talk, before she decided of her own accord that she owed it to her guests to make a reappearance. I remained behind for another few minutes to finish the glass I hadn't touched during our eager conversation, before I followed her into the exhibition space, which was by now less congested than before.

Just inside the door I could see the SB man still hovering, and for a moment I was tempted to go over and engage him in some heavy cultural conversation, but then decided against it and made another, less pressurised, turn through the hall. I was quite prepared to see her go soon, although I was resolved to get her number before she did; but Waynie-boy did us an unexpected good turn by coming over just at the moment when she was writing her number on the back of an empty cigarette packet for me. He must have seen what she was doing (he was the kind of vulture that never missed anything; he should have joined the SB), for he went a shade paler than before, raised himself to his not very considerable height, and hissed, 'I see you are otherwise engaged. So I'll just fuck off.'

'Good idea,' I said.

This time I was sure he was going to hit me. But as several other guests chose that moment to come and say their goodbyes, Wayne had to make a most unimpressive exit on his own.

This put me in a generous mood. I even asked her, 'Are you sure you shouldn't go with him?'

'He can go to hell,' she said. But the next moment, looking round with a frown of worry on her forehead, she added, 'Now what am I going to do?' She turned to me. 'Do you think you could call me a taxi?'

'No,' I said firmly. 'I'll take you home myself. I rented a car at the airport.'

'But you . . .'

'I promise I won't place your virtue at risk,' I said with mock solemnity.

She laughed, and I took her all the way to Greenside, where she lived in a somewhat ramshackle old house. Sadly not on her own, I deduced from some items of male clothing lying about.

Aviva was clearly exhausted, so I did not accept her invitation to a good-night drink, and drove back to my hotel. I knew already that I would not be taking the next plane to London the following day after all (I would phone the publisher in the morning, using the SB as an excuse), nor would I return home to Cape Town. Instead, I phoned her late in the morning and proposed meeting for dinner.

She had already accepted, when she suddenly said, 'Oh, but Wayne . . .'

'If you already have a date with him,' I said smoothly, 'please don't let me stop you. Or else you could bring him along.'

'No, no, I don't think that will work.'

'Well, perhaps I should just say goodbye then. I'll probably be going back to Cape Town tonight.' Which I had absolutely no intention of doing.

'No, please don't. I can always see Wayne later. At what time would you like to come round?'

That was the beginning. Not that it was smooth sailing. If my intuition, or my experience, was anything to go by, she was as eager as I was to start something. But she was held back. By Wayne (to whom,

I discovered that evening, she was in fact engaged, with a wedding date already set), or by some scruples of her own, or simply by the confusion she was in, surrounding the exhibition and the knowledge that the SB was on the prowl. Whatever the cause, I could feel that it was serious. I could also feel – or at least hope – that it was temporary. So we had a few nights and days of talking, of dining at her place or in restaurants, of sauntering around Zoo Lake, of making trips to the Hartebeespoort Dam or the Magaliesberg. After that, I returned to Cape Town, safe in the knowledge that I had to come back in a fortnight for a lecture at Wits.

The whole story took longer than I had anticipated. Considering how eager we were, it was amazing that we could hold out for so long. But we did – because, I should hope, we both sensed that it would be worth our while. It was three months before Wayne finally cleared out, under the impression that he was the one who'd put an end to it. And then another four weeks before we could find a watertight reason for her to come to Cape Town. (It is always smoother on one's own turf; although the challenge may be greater away from the stamping ground.) But when finally we came together, in a manner of speaking, all those months fell away from us like old skins.

Without her clothes Aviva was even smaller, slighter, than I'd expected. She almost seemed anorexic. But not in a sick or appalling way at all: it just confirmed the waif-like appearance she made, her Madonna-like beauty. With those huge dark eyes. And no breasts at all, barely a swelling, just two very prominent nipples perched on her chest like large death beetles. The unbelievable frailty of her arms and legs, her ribcage like a little bird's, her jutting hip bones. It seemed as if all the flesh on her frame was concentrated on the mound of her sex, which was disproportionately – but beautifully – high and rounded, overgrown with a luxuriant mop of long black pubic hair, not crinkly at all, but soft and feathery; and the vulva itself, the little inside lobes as well as the more naturally fleshy, ovoid outer ones, was of an unusual plumpness, almost spherical, like a large exotic mushroom in the fork of a tree, a little pleasure dome if ever I've seen one, where Alph the sacred river ran down to a tideless sea. No, not tideless. Her tides were convulsive, an ebb and flow that could take you very far, far back, before hurling you out, wildly and triumphantly, on a ribbed and windswept beach without end. (I have transcribed this verbatim from the notes I made after our first night; I know it is about as purple as it gets, but nothing but the most royal purple can do justice to Aviva.)

It was serious, for both of us. I'd had a few brief flings after losing Helena and Pieter in the accident, but this was the first real relationship. I gave up the house I'd been renting in Gardens since the accident, and moved to Johannesburg; Aviva's ramshackle old place was big enough for both of us. I'd seldom worked so hard, so focused, in my life. We were planning our book together, our *Black and White*, with her photographs, my text. We were driven by a lot of anger, but it was a good, inspirational anger that kept us on a permanent high.

Even so, it was also a tough time. Ever since the conflagration of '76 the country seemed to be going into a spin-dive of violence and rage and disaster. My hopes of being published locally had finally dried up with *Intimate Lightning*: in my own country I had become a writer without a word, and there was something more and more futile about embarking on new books – including our photographic book in progress – without any hope of seeing it published here. Censorship controlled everything. And in the background hovered the ever more sinister figures of the SB. The awareness of being under surveillance, day and night, was beginning to gnaw at our resources and rack our nerves. A few nasty things happened to Aviva: her little Mini was blown up in her garage two minutes after she'd made an unplanned stop at home to collect some films; and one night a firebomb was hurled into the bedroom where we normally slept but which, by pure coincidence, we had vacated for the night because her cat had pissed on the bed. There was considerable damage, but at least we'd escaped with our lives. All the signs were there that the thin red line around her had finally been overstepped: the weapons of mass destruction, all those sinister invisible forces of poison fumes and gas and infernal bacteria were being mustered against us.

The relationship itself kept us going. The sex was still explosive. We were both, in one way or another, making up for lost time. But the pressure was becoming too much to bear.

Aviva was the first to broach what both of us could feel building up for months: 'It's not worth it any more, Chris. We've got to move on.'

I knew she was right, but I found it almost unbearable to admit it and pull up our roots. 'If we go now, we admit defeat. How can we possibly play into their hands like that?'

'It's only your pride, your pigheadedness. There's nothing shameful about moving away to fight from elsewhere, attack from a different angle.'

'Think of how they'll gloat.'

'Let them gloat. You're a writer, I'm a photographer. We shall have the last word.'

'Not if neither of us can publish or say anything.'

'We can still hit them from there.'

'Just being here, staying here, hits them harder than anything we can do from elsewhere. Can't you see that? That's why they are turning on the screws: they're getting desperate. They know we may be losing battle after battle but we're winning the war.'

It was the morning after the bomb. We were cleaning up the debris in the bedroom. She pointed at the half-charred remains of curtains and bedding and carpets around us, and asked, 'Does this really look like winning, Chris?'

'A temporary setback.'

'If they kill us, we can't do *anything* any more. And that is what is going to happen if we stay here.'

'They won't dare to go so far. They're counting on intimidating us.'

'This was not intimidation.' She gestured again at the rubble in the room. 'When they threw this bomb, they counted on us being inside.'

'What about your threat to tell the truth about that secretary's involvement with your friend Claudie?'

'I believe they have weighed up the odds and decided they don't care any more. The old rules don't hold any longer. This is life or death for them now. And so it is for us too.'

'Please, Aviva! Don't let them win.'

'That is precisely why we must leave now.' And then she said the one thing she knew I had no defence against: 'My mind is made up. I'm going anyway. If you want to stay, then stay.'

Trying to attract as little attention as possible, we left instructions with some close friends of hers, and left within days, on separate flights: Aviva to Zurich, I to Frankfurt; and met a week later in London. Most of our possessions were forwarded in due course by the friends. It was a tense time, but all went smoothly. I can only presume that the SB were so relieved to be rid of us that it suited them not to make any fuss.

We found a dingy little place to stay in Acton, and immediately set to work on preparing *Black and White* for publication: it was imperative, mainly for my dented sense of dignity, to make our statement as soon as possible. Within a few months the book was out, and because the press was eager to exploit the whiff of sensation which surrounded our 'flight' from South Africa, it became something of a cause célèbre, not only in the UK but in America and several European countries. Believing that our bridges were now irrevocably burned behind us, we set to work to carve out a new life.

What followed was one of the most hectic times I have known. The turmoil was good, at least initially, because it prevented us from dwelling too much on the past; but after nine months or so I began to feel trapped, with no or little time to write: there were too many other things happening all the time – conferences, discussions, interviews, festivals, in the US, all over Europe, and of course in Britain. We moved house a few times, and regularly changed our telephone number, in our attempts to find a more private space; but nothing really worked. We were caught in a net which in many respects we welcomed and sometimes needed, but which also ensnared us. In the beginning it affected me more than Aviva, who seemed to thrive on the stimulation of challenges and new projects, but in the long run the impact was corrosive.

We travelled a lot, both separately and together; and the joy and excitement of meeting up afterwards and catching up with each other's lives added a dimension to our relationship, but it was exhausting too, and the lack of time and energy brought us to the end of our tethers more readily than would otherwise have happened. In that whirlpool we began to lose sight of each other. Our love became an old, hollowed-out pumpkin, the flesh and seeds scooped out, leaving no inner core from which we could set out on our foragings into the world, or to which at the end of a day, or a week, or a meeting, or a trip, we could come back to replenish ourselves. We kept on assuring each other that it was only temporary – another few weeks, another month or, at most, another year, and all would fall into place and our life and love would become manageable again. But it only got worse.

And there was something else gnawing at Aviva. It took me a long time to realise, but when I tried to mention it, she would close up and refuse to discuss it or deny that there was anything wrong. It was this: in my writing, as I slowly learned to withdraw from pressing demands and carry on working, battling with *In the Dark*, my new book, in a tiny room I had rented as a study near our latest flat, in Stockwell, I had a ready pool of memories to draw on; and should that ever become depleted, which didn't seem very likely, I could find an endless supply of new material in the community of exiles we had entered – a locust swarm of South Africans of all kinds, black and white, old and young, miserable or enterprising and ambitious; but also from elsewhere in Africa, from South America, from the Middle East or Central Europe, all of them converging on London. But for Aviva it was different. For some time she could return to her old negatives and make new prints, but memory in itself was not enough; as a photographer, she needed a here-and-now to engage with. She had no interest in taking nice studio portraits, or recording weddings or social events from Buckingham Palace to Ascot. Her art, and her reputation, had been shaped by the struggle back home, her most memorable work had been determined by oppression and resistance; she had a deep need to believe that what she was doing was having some effect, or making some change to people's perceptions about their real world, about South Africa. And for that, she needed to be *there*, not *here*.

I tried to steer her towards the world of exiles, and for a while she became charged up with it. But soon she found it counterproductive. Depressing images about exile, she argued more and more passionately, did nothing to encourage or galvanise people back home: in fact, they were working *against* the struggle by disheartening the oppressed. She no longer felt needed, a vital cog in the great machine of resistance. She was just another exile – better known than most, but no longer really effective. The machine, the batteries that charged her, were elsewhere, no longer lodged inside herself any more. And instead of bolstering and helping her, I was becoming an obstacle to her. My writing became, for her, a way of withdrawing from the world and, particularly, from her; it was an opting-out, not a plunging-into. She may have been right.

All that really mattered was that we were running out of steam. She started accepting commissions to faraway places (Chile, Peru, Iran, Turkey, Sri Lanka), and when she came back she often spoke about new friends or contacts she had encountered, or travelled with on the tour. Returning from the Chile trip, there was an American name that came up with noticeable regularity, Raymond Cook. In the beginning, when I asked about him, she would shrug it off. But after a month or so it all came out. Yes, there had been an affair. Nothing serious, she'd been feeling very down, and he had been so helpful and understanding, and one late evening after they'd had too much to drink, et cetera. It upset me less than I would have expected, and it was the absence of outrage which alerted me to just how far we had drifted apart. Also, to be fair, I had had a diversion of my own in her absence, with a provocative young journalist from Ghana. So we had a session of mutual *mea culpas*, which led to a springtide of making up lasting for a night and a day, and a few months of rediscovered bliss. But the end had already signalled its presence, in the undertow of our shared tides. I had encounters with Uschi from Uppsala, and Ghislaine from Grenoble, and Hannelore from Hanover, while Aviva spent time with a Richard and an Amos and one or two others never more specifically identified; and then we broke up, by mutual consent, although there were tears and recriminations and despondency as well, seasoned by relief on both sides.

TWO YEARS AFTER Aviva and I had arrived in London I packed up and left. I had strongly considered going back to South Africa, but not much seemed to have changed there — and if so, then only for the worse. In London both Aviva and I had become drawn quite deeply into the ever-changing community of ANC exiles — it was a way of staying in touch, I suppose, although it also kept the wounds open – and dreaming together of 'going home' and of that ever more improbable day when the old order would have passed, was a way of keeping one going. There were also, since '76, more and more younger people around, although most of them were just passing through on their way to the training camps in Angola, or to Berlin, or Prague, or Moscow, and this lent greater urgency and purpose to being there.

Our involvement with the ANC became more and more overtly political, but it remained rooted in the personal, thanks to the community of exceptional individuals we met, whether artists or officials, academics or cadres: enthusiastic and passionate and sensitive and determined women and men, committed people, people with wide-ranging interests, people who could laugh and cry and plan and talk through long nights and who never stopped dreaming. It offered us an intensity of living unequalled by anything either Aviva or I had ever experienced before or since. (I do not want to sound ridiculously romantic. Not everybody in the crowd was exemplary! The group had its share of misfits, of chancers and cheats, of layabouts and parasites, of drunks and junkies, of mean schemers and – yes – sell-outs and traitors. But among those we worked with there were, I think, more individuals memorable for their special qualities than in any other comparable community I have yet encountered.)

But deep down, even among the best of them, despondency was growing, as the Vorster regime darkened into the Botha years: on the surface there seemed to be signs of thawing, of changing course ever so slightly, of taking the most obvious edge off oppression, but below that there was a hardening and increasingly bitter polarisation to deal with.

So when I left, it was for France. There were programmes set up for preparing people for the day-to-day practicalities of managing change, however far away that still seemed to be. And although most of these were designed for young recruits and I was already approaching sixty, my books and my increasing international profile seemed to guarantee my credentials. In March or April 1981 I arrived in Paris, and was immediately drawn into one of the programmes for running a viable underground alternative to the regime back home. In the end I stayed for five years and became something of a fixture. I know that a number of the younger comrades were cynical about my presence, but the fact that I'd passed muster with members of the older guard, like Tambo and Slovo and Wolpe, broke down some of the resistance or suspicion; and on the whole I was always made to feel welcome. At the very least I was tolerated, and perhaps indulged. I was allowed to become something of an honorary member of a new fledgling group with the rather disingenuous name of 'Amandla', that replaced the misbegotten Okhela. This turned out to be a mixture of a writer-in-residence (in between stints which I continued to do in that capacity at universities in the US, Canada and Australia, and even once or twice at Patrice Lumumba in Moscow or in Leipzig), and what Lenin had designated a useful idiot. It meant that I was given access to all the 'facilities', such as they were. Most memorably, but in the long run also most perniciously, I was drawn into the most dizzying fuck fest of my life.

Siviwe Mfundisi, the man in charge of Amandla, was the most accomplished womaniser I had ever come across, and he hand-picked quite brazenly from the casting couch all the female recruits for the organisation, mainly on the basis of age and looks. During those few years, I regret to say, it was mostly a matter of quantity rather than quality, and there must have been few countries in the world which were not in due course represented. The common denominator was mainly a kind of upfront beauty: it was all there at first sight, what you saw was what you got; no secrets or surprises, nothing of the romantic notion of 'mystery' which has been the driving force in my lifelong addiction to women.

But there were a few exceptions who stood out, and still do. And the test is probably this: the notes I made on those women who shared moments of my life at the time were all destroyed when I came home at last – they were too precarious to keep; I had to bear in mind the possibility that they might be confiscated by the SB on my return, and so I had to get rid of them, not without regret, even distress. But the memory of a handful, no more than two or three, survive without any aide-memoire. And so, if any number of them are now no more than names from a lost album, there are these few I can never let go of, as they will never let go of me. Because, precisely, they did not 'belong', they were different, the rare exceptions, each unsettling in her own right, a disturbing and illuminating presence among so many almost-not-theres or just-about-theres.

I did meet Nicolette through Amandla, that much is true. But in no way was she ever one of 'them'. For one thing, she would never have come near Siviwe's casting couch. For another, she was much older than the rest. They were all in their twenties or very early thirties (a few still in their teens), whereas she must have been on the darker side of fifty: it was difficult to guess, and *she* would most certainly never tell. There was a curious vanity about her, she was obsessed with her 'dignity'. And yet I remember early mornings when she would bring me coffee and sit cross-legged on the foot of my bed, naked, with none of her usually rather overdone make-up on, as if she couldn't care about the ravages of time. A lived-in body. The lines on her face especially. Her neck which was threatening to become scrawny. Her small but sagging breasts. Her drooping buttocks. White stretch marks on her belly. Too-bony knees and feet. And yet! It was not just that there were moments when I could see how beautiful she must have been once, twenty years ago perhaps – the sharp features, high cheek-bones, striking nose, the long blonde hair, the cat-body with its languid, undulating movements, her kind of boyish grace – but that, in a way that had little to do with what could be itemised, she was beautiful *now*. She is one of the few women in my life I find impossible to trans-late into words, even though that is supposed to be my *métier*. I feel like a painter trying to paint a model who refuses to sit still, she is always moving about, pulling faces, frowning, pouting, putting out her tongue, eating an apple, smirking. Often she had the utterly vulner-able look of a little girl lost; then, in a moment she could become hard and cynical and aggressive, even offensive. Her eyes could be piercing and frank and direct; but often she would gaze about vaguely, with a myopic absence in her attitude, an almost professorial detach-ment. Her voice could be deep and sexy and seductive; but it might also be simply hoarse from too many years of too much smoking, too much drinking, too much everything.

I met her at a do the exiles had arranged in the suburb of Aubervilliers one evening. Drab surroundings, modern concrete apartment buildings covered in graffiti, swarms of dirty little Third World kids cavorting about. She turned up late, escorted by someone I'd vaguely met but did not really know, Bongani-somebody, a large, loose-limbed man, pleasant enough when he was sober, but notorious for his aggressive behaviour when he got drunk, which was most of the time. That night, too, it did not take long for him to lose it. He said he was tired and feeling shit and wanted to go home (he'd just come back from a month-long trip to Moscow, Leningrad and Kiev); Nicolette wanted to party. They argued in a corner for a while, in low voices. Then he started to shout obscenities at her. Somewhat to my surprise, she responded in kind. Some of the people were amused and egged them on, laughing. But that was the wrong thing to do. He went right over the top and hit her a straight right to the jaw which would have done any lock on a rugby field proud. She staggered back. A trickle of blood came from her mouth. A couple of men grabbed Bongani from behind to drag him off (but they were laughing, as if it were all a huge joke). That was when she lunged forward and let fly with an almighty kick – she was wearing tall black boots – that hit him in the groin and made him fold double, retching.

'You fucking bitch, I'm going to kill you!' he gasped.

She spat blood into his face.

Then he was dragged out by his comrades and, as I learned later, deposited in a taxi and sent back to wherever he had come from. Instinctively, I took her by the shoulders and steered her to a corner.

'Let me go, dammit!' she said, but without much conviction. And when I complied, she did not move away. I found a glass of whiskey and put it in her hand. Neither of us said a word. Her eyes, the colour of smoke, were inscrutable.

The party resumed like a stream that encounters a boulder in its way, churns for a moment in a white-water rapid, then whirls around it and ripples on as if there has been no interruption. At some stage, still without saying anything, she left my side and melded into the dancing. I watched almost absently, but soon found myself spellbound. She danced with the kind of demonstrative abandon that makes it impossible not to look. But in the end she drifted out of it again. All I know is that while the rest went on eating and drinking and making merry, the two of us landed on the floor in a corner and talked.

'Thank you for rescuing me,' she said through the blue smoke of her Gitane.

'I didn't. I just brought you to a neutral corner.'

'I'll do better in the next round.'

'What on earth brought you to the party in the first place?' I wanted to know, because she was so obviously not one of us; at that stage I still thought she was French.

'Bongani,' she said matter-of-factly.

'Don't tell me you're attracted to South Africans?'

'Why not?' she asked. 'I was born in that shithole.'

Perhaps it was a mistake to enquire further, for she launched into a rambling story of which it was hard to make out head or tail. I can recall that a job with Dior featured in it, and a nightclub in Montmartre, and a father figure from the Old Testament, and a man who committed suicide because of her, and a pilgrimage to Chartres (before or after the suicide?) where she slept with a stranger whose face she never saw and whose name she never heard and whom in the raptures of love she begged to strangle her. 'I thought that would be the best kind of death that could ever happen to me,' she said. On some of those events she elaborated during the time we spent together afterwards. Once she got going she was such a hypnotising, enthralling teller of tales that days and nights simply flowed together – but nothing was ever really clarified; she repeated many of her stories several times but no two versions were quite the same. But there was one event to which she returned compulsively and of which the details never varied, at least not much.

'I slept with an ambassador,' she confided in me, with a strange mixture of shyness and arrogance, as if that were her real – her only? – claim to fame in a rather confusing world. And after a brief pause (for deliberate effect?) she added in a stage whisper, 'A *South African* ambassador.'

'My God!' was all I could say. 'How could you? What on earth . . . ? I mean, for God's sake . . .'

She gave a mysterious smile: supercilious? defiant? mischievous? ashamed? serenely confident?

'Oh, it was long ago,' she said with a shrug, but only after finishing her glass of neat whiskey. 'Before things turned sour down there. Or just at the beginning. The time of that Sharpeville thing. Strange to think of it now, but you know, it didn't really seem to matter.'

'But how could you have got involved with someone like that?' I repeated.

'I think I loved him,' she said simply. Her smile made her seem much younger, almost childlike. 'Do you find that so strange?'

I had to shake my head very slowly, but I did glance around to make sure nobody was listening. 'No. I suppose if you really loved him, it is not so strange.'

'Why would that make a difference?' she challenged me sharply.

'Because love is something else. Isn't it?'

'No it isn't. Love is shit.'

'Meaning?'

'Meaning nothing. I want some more whiskey.' A pause. 'Please.'

I took her glass, and went to refill it, and came back to her. Many of the guests were already seeping out into the night.

'I didn't mean that,' she said after taking a good mouthful.

'Mean what?'

'That love is shit. I just didn't like you saying it is "something else". For God's sake. What's your name?'

'Chris. Chris Minnaar.'

She gave no sign of recognising it, which I found singularly comforting.

'For God's sake, Chris Minnaar. Whatever love may be, it is *never* "something else". It's where we belong. Like the sky. I mean, if we were birds.' Another of her pauses. 'I wish we were. I've always wanted to fly. Sometimes I do, when I make love.'

'Like with your ambassador?'

'Why do you ask?' There was a harsh tone of suspicion, perhaps accusation, in her voice.

'You were the one who started about him.'

'But I said nothing about making love with him. For all you know we never did.'

'You did say you slept with an ambassador.'

'Did I?' She took another swallow. 'Well, then I suppose I did.'

'Did he love you too?'

'He treated me like his dirty little secret.'

'And you revolted against that?'

A shrug. Her smoky eyes narrowed briefly, but that was all.

'Or did you meekly accept it?'

She sneered. Then in a crude gesture wiped her mouth with the back of her hand, smudging lipstick across her cheek. By now she looked much older again.

'I cost him his job,' she said. 'I made sure he was fired. For sleeping with the enemy.'

'Poor man,' I said with a straight face, but this time she did not take the bait.

Most of the guests had gone by now; it was time for us to leave too.

When we reached the door, she grasped me by the arm, as if in a sudden panic. 'Can you take me home?'

'Where do you live?'

'No, I mean: can I go home with you? Bongani will kill me if I went back to him now.'

'Oh, but . . .'

'I'm not asking you to fuck me, Chris.' An ugly laugh. 'Just to let me sleep at your place – a bed, a couch, a floor, anything. I can even sleep in a bath. I love baths. Until I've sorted out things back there.'

I wasn't sure whether to smile or frown, to be sympathetic or reluctant, to cold-shoulder her or be the gentleman. In the end, rather diffidently, if I remember correctly, I agreed. I asked Siviwe, our host, to telephone for a taxi. Aware of his sardonic look, I escorted Nicolette to the door and we went to the small apartment I rented at the time, behind the Gare Montparnasse. She did not speak on the way back.

When we got home she asked for something more to drink.

'Are you sure?' I asked.

'You think I've had enough?' With that unpleasant, provocative look in her eyes she said, 'You're right. I've had enough. But I still want more.'

An hour later, when I tentatively suggested that it was time to turn in, she suddenly became surprisingly docile. I showed her to the bathroom, and while she was inside remade my bed for her, and spread sheets and blankets over the couch in the small lounge for me, something I'd often done when I'd had guests before.

She spent a full hour in the bathroom. When she came out, with an old blue dressing gown of mine draped over her, all her make-up had been removed and her face was naked. In some ways it looked older now, every line and wrinkle showed; but there was also a freshness about her, a complete vulnerability. Perhaps that is not the right word either. It was more like a complete honesty: *Here I am, this is what I look like, I don't care. Do you?*

I didn't either. And she shook off the voluminous dressing gown, which suddenly made her look much smaller, thinner than before – not as skinny as Aviva, but slight nevertheless – and with an unusual mixture of defencelessness and quiet assurance. She knew her own body and was comfortable with it; and she could share it without giving herself away, but also without withholding anything.

One notices small things about a new body. A little birthmark high up on her left thigh. A single, prominent curl disturbing the straight top line of the small triangle of her pubic hair; much later, as she lay in my arms with her naked back against my naked belly (Rachie de Beer?), the way she twirled and twirled a small lock of her blonde hair (dyed, but blonde) until she fell asleep and lightly snored. She even farted once, which I found an amusing and endearing show of trust.

Sometime in the morning, not early, she folded herself out of the bed and wandered about with her vague, vacant gaze as if she'd forgotten where the bathroom was, although she had spent so much time there the night before. I followed her with my eyes, with an intense curiosity as if I were a discoverer looking at a new landscape. I took in the awkward grace of her body, no longer young, yet with a persistent, fluid youthfulness about it. The cellulite on her thighs below the flat buttocks which must once have been small and tight and round, the delicate web of blue and red varicose veins behind her knees, her too-often dyed hair tousled on her shoulders. I also noticed the bruises on her body, some old enough to fade into a yellowish green, others darker, angrier, recent. On her back and buttocks, her thighs, her breasts. Was that Bongani's way of staking out his territory? Or had she been passed on from one lover to another? And yet it did not repel me. It was as if in spite of all the signs of having been used and abused, nothing had really touched her or harmed her, not where it mattered. And the marks of fading youth achingly brought home to me the awareness of my own ageing body. She did not close the bathroom door when she went in. I heard her pee. When she re-emerged, I smiled and put out my arms towards her. Come, I wanted to say, let us be old together, let us be young together.

But she wandered away again, towards the kitchen, and came back with an apple. Then stopped, and went back for another, which she offered me. Sitting cross-legged on the bed facing me, every wrinkle in her belly above her small mat of pubic thatch visible, she took her time finishing her apple, crisply biting into it, sending a fine spray of juice over the blanket, some of it clinging to her chin, her shoulders, her pendant breasts. It was an almost unbearably erotic experience.

When she got up to throw the tiny core that remained into the waste-paper basket in the corner, she stopped in front of the bed and looked down at me.

'Do you think I'm old?' she asked, cupping her hands under her breasts to push them up.

'I think you're very lovely.'

'You should have seen me when I was with my ambassador,' she said. 'I was beautiful *then*. And of course very young.'

'It is enough for me to see you now. Come to me. I want you.'

'You cannot have me.' But she came to kneel in front of the bed and threw back the blankets and took me in her mouth, her long, damaged hair falling over her damaged, beautiful face.

IT WAS SUNDAY, and we spent most of it in bed. In between we dragged ourselves from the stained and crumpled sheets to prepare something to eat, and then crept back, and made love once more, and talked with passion.

Like the night before, she kept returning to the man she called 'my ambassador'.

'What happened to him in the end?' I asked, my interest stirred.

'I lied to you last night,' she said, as if that was an answer. 'It wasn't I who brought him in trouble. I mean, it was *because* of me, but I didn't want to harm him. I tried everything I could to save him, but what was there I could really do? There was such a huge, powerful machine behind him.'

'So he was recalled?'

'Yes. But after that I wasn't sure. I kept trying to find out, asking people. There was an old concierge or something at the embassy, Lebon his name was — it was still in the Avenue Hoche in those days, not that awful Fort Knox fortress on the Quai d'Orsay — and Lebon was a great gossip, so he kept me up to date. But of course there was no way of knowing for sure, the old *salaud* would turn anything into a good story. Anyway, it was from him that I heard my ambassador died. Of a stroke, Lebon said. Not so long after he left.' I am surprised to see her eyes fill with tears. 'You know, when I heard that, I just wanted to die too. In fact, I was so desperate, I jumped into the Seine, right behind Notre-Dame. It was something I'd often thought of doing, but I never had the guts before. But this time I did.'

'But you didn't die,' I said soberly.

'No, the bloody *flics* and the *pompiers* were there too quickly. Treated me like scum. Just dumped me in a hospital. It was terrible. I thought, when I got out of there, I'd go straight back to the Seine. Only, I couldn't face it going wrong again. So as soon as I was discharged I went to Notre-Dame, and bought a candle, a really long one, and lit it for him. It wasn't much, but I thought, oh well, we can all do with a candle.'

'I'm so glad you didn't die.'

She pulled a face. 'I'm not so sure that it's anything to be glad about. All I know is that I'll now wait for the real thing. Unless I find someone like that man, when I joined the pilgrimage to Chartres for Easter, I told you about it . . . ?'

'The one you asked to strangle you?'

'Yes. I still think that would be the best death of all. To go while you're coming.' A bright smile, but only for a moment. 'But where will I find a lover prepared to do a thing like that?'

'Don't look at me,' I said with mock seriousness.

'Why wouldn't you do a thing like that?' Nicolette insisted. 'If someone you really, really loved asked you to?"

'Please,' I said, feeling a shiver caress my spine like a caterpillar moving all the way down. 'Don't even talk of such things. The mere thought gives me the creeps. We're here now. Death is very far away.'

'Death is never far away when you make love.' As with everything she said, I couldn't make out whether she'd really uttered something profound, or whether she was simply spilling whatever came to mind. And so we made love again, and for the time being at least kept death at bay.

What I knew, then and during the time that followed, was that this was a dangerous liaison, and I was on dangerous ground. It would not be difficult to fall in love with Nicolette. And then I would be lost. It would be love, not because I could see in her the girl she might once have been, but because of what she was at that moment. *Because* she was no longer young, *because* of the beauty of time in her, and *because*, precisely, she made me aware of the death we both carried in our blood and bones.

That was why I could not let her go. I remember how, even on that first day, when we came back to gasp for air once, I lay tracing with a fingertip an angry bruise across her left nipple. She put her hand on mine.

'Bongani?' I asked.

She nodded.

'You're not ever going back to that man,' I said.

She nodded again, then asked, 'But what shall I do?'

'Stay with me.'

'But . . .'

She did not go on, and for the moment we left it at that. In the days that followed she took me on long walking tours through Paris, showing me quarters and streets and sights I had never dreamed of, even though after two years in the city I had come to think that I knew it. We did not speak again about whatever might happen later. There was a strange feeling of permanence in the way she took possession of the place: she still had a key to Bongani's apartment and went back there a few times in our early days together to retrieve her things when he was out. From then on she squatted, rather than settled, in my place, littering it with her clothes and shoes and fake jewellery and make-up and hairpieces and creams and lotions. If it did have to end sometime, it was not yet in sight.

And that was why I was caught so completely unawares when, coming home from a conference one late afternoon, she was not there. A few empty bottles, an odd shoe, a torn pair of jeans, a few thumbed and tatty fashion magazines and a battered-looking black-and-red vibrator with broken batteries (I checked) were all that remained. Enough to show that she had been there. Enough to confirm that she was gone. I suppose I could have started asking around among the ANC cadres; I might even have gone in search of Bongani and confronted him directly. But I couldn't. Even if I were to find her, she would not come back. This was the end, and had to be. To respect the dignity of a relationship also implies accepting the end when it comes. Except in my mind, except in my dreams, where the aftertaste of her still lingers. Even in you, Rachel, she continues to lurk. Absent and forever present.

BAGHDAD, THE TV showed last night, has been plunged into darkness by the continuing bombardments as the US tries to take the main airport. The end now seems much closer than anybody had expected. On the very outskirts of the capital there seems to be almost no resistance. What could have happened to the 70,000-strong Republican Guard? What has happened to military intelligence? Where are the hidden weapons?

I have to remind myself why I am watching these nightly shows: to help me sleep, to find perspective on love, and on my women. The ubiquitous image of us, men, fucking up the world – counterbalanced by women who must keep it going, to safeguard sanity. All my life I have been surrounded by violence of one kind or another, it has framed every relationship I have ever had. And when it seemed, with the liberation of Mandela and the dawning of free elections, that we had finally outpaced the nightmares of apartheid, new forms of violence irrupted into my relations with women. Only now, with you gone (and how violently that happened) and a vacuum of events surrounding me, do I feel released into a space where no milestones are left to mark my progress and help me find my bearings. The violence is still there, but somehow I have become inured to it. Like any junkie I need my daily shot. It takes less and less effect, but I cannot kick the habit. And so I turn to Iraq.

AFTER OUR RETURN from the Cedarberg and once I'd gone back to my own home (much to Frederik's relief), most of my daily stimulation came from knowing you and George were there; and twice a week, without fail, you turned up to impose some order on my study. Frederik had become used to your visits, and accepted your presence without question, which was more than he'd done to some of your predecessors. I had the distinct impression that he, too, had a special spring in his step on the days you came.

In the run-up to your exhibition, now fixed for September in the AVA gallery in Church Street, I tried to persuade you to suspend your Girl Friday duties and turn to your own work, but you wouldn't hear of it. You needed the time away from sculpture to clear your mind, you insisted, which I refused to buy; but it was with great relief that I pretended nevertheless to believe you, as I don't know how I could have coped without you. Not because of the work, but because of you. Even if it was only two mornings a week, Tuesdays and Fridays, your presence had subtly transformed the whole place. It was visible in the flowers you brought, the small rearrangements you made in the furniture, without asking, the smells you stirred up in the kitchen (something Frederik wouldn't stand in anyone else); but it was much more evident in the change in atmosphere. It was simply no longer an old man's house: there was hope in it now. I hadn't registered how autumnal the place had become over the past years – even if I could observe it, painfully and rebelliously, in my body. There have been times, recently, when the once so true and trusted old root of evil delight could no longer do its bit on its own and had to be thumbed in on the slack. How humiliating the mere thought would have been even ten years earlier. Now one has to be grateful for fringe benefits. Soon it will be time for the days when the doors shall be shut in the streets, when the sound of the grinding is low, and I shall rise up at the voice of the bird, and all the daughters of musick shall be brought low; also when I shall be afraid of that which is high, and fears shall be in the way, and the almond tree shall flourish, and the grasshopper shall be a burden, and desire shall fail: because man goeth to his long home, and the mourners go about the streets.

Coming home after the Cedarberg, even if by then I had resigned myself to the knowledge that I could not think of you as a sexual possibility, your presence became part of the routine that both kept me going and helped to reconcile me to the failing flickerings of desire in my dry old age. I remember days of actually feeling relieved that nothing could ever happen between you and me, blessed in George's presence, in the closeness and assurance of your love. Because suppose these restrictions had not been there, suppose we were free to love openly: how would I have fared? How could I ever bear the shame of making a pass and then failing you?

We often worked together, you and I – not just on the mornings you came over, but on the many days when George was in the dark-room or off on an assignment and you needed help with stacking your kiln, or firing, or mixing glazes, or preparing the special paints and concoctions you used for your sculptures. And there was never any awkwardness. The framework within which we were allowed to meet and share had been established so surely and unambiguously that I could be happy, even carefree, within it. And when George put in an appearance, we could readily and generously include him – go for a meal, go to a concert, potter around in your garden or mine, buy provisions, attend auctions or exhibitions, be a threesome without an odd one out.

I developed more and more of a closeness with George. You encouraged it, because you were always concerned that he tended to be too absorbed in his photography to realise that he needed friends, so you saw the time he spent with me as a healthy and necessary dimension of his life. As for me, I have never been one of the boys, never had a busy social life. Not that I consciously withdrew from people; and wherever I went, I invariably had one or two good, solid friendships with other men. But I have never known a need of that kind of bonding which defines the contours of so many men's lives.

At school, even at university, I had played rugby, fly-half and sometimes inside centre: not by choice – I was pushed into it by my father who felt the need of a son to be proud of. He made a habit of coming to watch when we played: that was what made it special. He didn't turn up merely to be critical, but – I soon discovered – because he was really quite passionately interested. In his youth, he told me, he'd also played. Eighth man. But then broke a leg which didn't mend properly. And now I was his surrogate on the field. Even more than chess, it was a way to communicate with him. And the mere fact of his presence beside the field made me feel that life was worthwhile after all. Even though I had very little natural talent for the game, I learned to enjoy it for his sake. And there were other, unexpected compensations in the rowdy closeness, the slapstick and competition of the dressing room and the playing field. I remember days when being ground into a muddy spot on the field and nearly drowned in five centimetres of dirty water with three or four or six men sitting on me, twisting my ankles or thrusting knees up my groin or squeezing my balls or biting chunks from my ears or farting in my face, was the badge of a worthwhile existence: this was what being a man was about, this gave sense and substance to it, this was *the life*. And Father was there! In that brotherhood there were discoveries of generosity, of exuberance, of joy, even a willingness to share pain or despondency or anger, which made it all seem worthwhile.

There were those special moments, after a try or a successful line kick or a good sidestep or a well-timed pass, when a high-five, a slap on the back, a hug around the shoulders, a hand ruffling your hair, confirmed a camaraderie and a physical male closeness that gave me a real sense of belonging. More than that, I discovered that being covered in mud, stained by grass and blood and snot, sporting grazes and cuts and, God willing, broken legs or collarbones or arms or ribs, was the surest way of gaining access to some of the most beautiful, and certainly the most willing, girls around. So how could I complain?

But close friendships? Not really. And that was why being with

George was not just good for him, but for me too. I could confide in him some of my most private fears about growing old, even some of the anguish about the likelihood of impending impotence, and my secret rage and despair about drying up as a writer. So many years now . . . Would I *ever* get something down on paper again? All I could show for these years were my notebooks – the many, many notebooks which still surround me here where I keep myself busy filling the void of your absence. I remember how I once thought of Mam's vast collection of notes culled from her years and years of reading as 'the signs of a wasted life'. Is that all my own notes will amount to in the end?

With George I could share memories of my early days of exuberance mixed with misgivings and self-doubt after the publication of that first book, *A Time to Weep*, which so unexpectedly catapulted me to notoriety; of the years between that book and *Radical Fire*, my last (so far). I could discuss with him the uneasy limelight during my years of international success (whatever that might mean) balanced by disapproval from the local hierarchy of power and the constant surveillance of the SB, as well as the suspicion of some more conservative local writers who could not mask their disapproval of me as a political sell-out.

I spoke of the brief fulfilment but also the increasing *dépaysement* of my years in London and Paris after the publication of *Black and White* with Aviva and *In the Dark* on my own.

To him I could talk about my women, the joys I'd known as well as the grief, the sadness of loss or betrayal or – yes – guilt. And, in recent years, more and more, the fear of futility.

We could laugh uproariously together. But there were also moments, fleeting as they may have been – when I told him about losing Helena and little Pieter, or about Nicolette, or about Abbie – when I could shed tears in his presence without feeling ashamed.

And George reciprocated.

From the way he told it, I could hear that with almost no one else, perhaps not even with you, had he been able to speak so frankly about his feelings of shame and inadequacy as 'the fat boy' at school, or his failures with girls before he won acclaim as a photographer. As on previous occasions, he admitted how, even when through his work he began to be sought out by desirable women, he could never get used to the mere idea that a woman might want *him*: every time he'd had a relationship he thought of it as a one-off miracle, never to be repeated, and therefore to be greedily grasped while it was there – a sense of inadequacy, never healed or assuaged. 'Even as I went to bed with a woman for the first time I just *knew* she was going to reject me in the end. How could any woman possibly *choose* to be with me? And so, more often than not, I would be the one to break it up, to spare myself the humiliation of being rejected.'

Until he'd met you, that is.

How often did our conversations come back to this? – 'Chris, do you *really* believe Rachel is happy?'

'She adores you, and she knows you worship her.'

'But is that good? The very words you use: *adore*, *worship* – do they not suggest that there's something wrong? That we're trying too hard to prove something to ourselves?'

'That is crap, George, and you know it. I've told you before: the two of you are the only reason why I believe there may still be something to be said for marriage.'

'I sometimes think I am doing her an injustice by staying with her. She deserves so much better than me. She should be free to choose.'

'She *was* free to choose when she chose you!'

'One day Rachel will discover her mistake. Then she will leave me.'

'How can you say a thing like that?!'

'I cannot fulfil her real needs. Not all of them.'

'Nobody in this world can fulfil all the needs of another person. We're all like intersecting circles. There are simply no two circles that overlap perfectly. There's always a little segment left uncovered. Which is why one keeps going frantically in search of that uncovered bit. At least, that is what *I* have been doing all my life. But some people – and you and Rachel strike me as good examples – are wise enough, or simply mature enough, to accept the circle part and even learn to appreciate it. How boring it would be to find a perfect fit. Nothing left to go in search of, or to long for and pine for, no art, no music, no writing, nothing.'

'I think *you* and Rachel would have been better suited than us.'

His directness startled me. I felt I was going pale. But I tried to remain calm: 'If I were a hundred years younger, perhaps, who knows. But what's the use of wondering?' (I could not help but think of all the nights I'd spent wondering about just that.)

'I'm worried about my work,' he persisted. 'It keeps me away from her too much.'

'You both need your separate space. That is why it is so good when you do come together.' I felt a bit embarrassed about the way it came out. But then decided to match his openness: 'That night in the Cedarberg – I couldn't help it, I'm sorry, but I heard you. And I may as well say it: I envied you.'

He blushed like a big schoolboy. 'We didn't mean to disturb you. Rachel tends to become a bit – vocal.'

'It was very beautiful. And it is a motion of confidence in you. In your relationship.'

'But can it last?'

'How can you ask that? It is good *now*. I see no end in sight.'

'One never sees an end. Do you believe love can last for ever? I mean *for ever*?'

'No. Because we die.'

'That's not what I had in mind.'

'Let's leave that to death, or to life, to decide. I certainly don't believe in thinking about endings before they're there.'

'Rachel believes very firmly that anything that begins, must end. Including, most especially, love.'

'And you?'

'I don't want to. I really don't. But there is always this fear. That with her it will turn out just as with the others.'

This was – when? Perhaps in May, perhaps in June. On a cold rainy day, on our way back from the Cape Flats where I'd attended one of his workshops in Khayelitsha for the kids. On the back seat were a number of brightly coloured empty boxes which had been filled with food and goodies when we drove there earlier: 'Picasso or someone once said that you cannot paint with cold feet,' he'd explained. 'Well, you certainly can't work on an empty stomach. So I first make sure they are fed before we start.'

I remember it all so well, as if each word had been spoken to prepare ourselves for what was to come.

Then came the day in July.

George had gone to Johannesburg for a week, an assignment on the 'new' Soweto. As before, I drove over to Camps Bay to wife-sit you in his absence. You had tried to dismiss the idea when he'd first broached it, but he was adamant. You needed to work, he said, and you couldn't concentrate properly if your nights were sleepless. It just wasn't safe any more for a woman to be on her own at night. And so the arrangement went ahead.

It was easier than the first time. We knew our roles by now. Both of us, and George, had been welded into them by the previous months. And particularly the memory of the Cedarberg trip, prematurely aborted as it had been, had brought a new calm, a new steadiness which made all three of us more confident.

And so that day. One of those immaculate, unbelievable Cape winter mornings, perfect and blue and resplendent with sun, the mountain-side glistening with new streaks of water: preceded and followed by rain and dark masses of cloud, but suddenly opening up into a magic world of light. I had slept late, but had been aware of you pottering about in the house since sunrise. By the time I came into the studio you had already started on a few new figures – you always had three or four taking shape at the same time, your hands working at incred-ible speed, with prescience and precision and passion, as if they were functioning independently of you, as if you could work with your eyes closed.

And you were happy with what you'd done so far, you couldn't help talking about it as you picked up the new figures and thrust them into my hands, and stood back, and laughed, and looked up at me, the deep light of the day falling in through the picture window like a sheet of pure white saturated with all the colours of the rainbow.

'I wish George could be here to see it. I phoned him last night and he said the weather was miserable up there.'

'Don't forget, it was miserable here too, yesterday. But I agree. Today he should have been here.'

'You should see him working on a day like this. It's as if he goes mad with light. I often think that is how Van Gogh must have felt. And whenever we talk about it he always reminds me, "But that is what photography is about, Rachel. It's drawing with light.'"

'I wish he could be here right now: to see your face in the light from the window. And your shoulders. And . . .' I checked myself.

'My breasts?' You smiled and lightly cupped your hands on them, a perfectly natural gesture, as if in a painting, an Annunciation, perhaps.

'You must be the perfect model.'

You turned pensive. 'He *has* taken some rather good shots.'

'I'd love to see them,' I said impetuously, forgetting for a moment what your reaction had been the previous time. But that was so long ago. Perhaps you had forgotten too.

Spontaneously you said, 'Actually, I'd like to show them to you.' I was glowing, suddenly, with a curious light-headedness. It was like the day in the fig tree when Driekie kicked off her little panties down to the ground below; the night when Nicolette dropped her towel. It was like the moment Nastasya Filippovna, having burned all the money in the grate, went out into the unpredictable night with Rogozhin.

You come back from George's darkroom with a large buff envelope, and sit down next to me on the comfortable old couch, leaning against me. You draw a thick wad of photographs from the envelope and put them on your lap. The jeans are frayed, I can see your knees through them.

Without the slightest hint of embarrassment, as if you are showing the snapshots of your last holiday, you pass one after the other to me in silence. They are all nudes. Some are stylised studio studies, with lighting that is sometimes subtle, sometimes dramatic, a dialogue of light and shadow that moulds your body in space; others are more frank, probing, revealing more of who you are, what you may be thinking, what your body can be, can do, what it might like to be. They are disarming and breathtaking. They are beautiful. But they are not comforting, not 'nice'. They have nothing to hide, nothing to be coy about. There are still others, even more daring, more provocative, presenting you in contortions that go beyond light and shadow, that say things about you, and through you, which unnerve me and even shock me with their probing questions and their unavoidable, incontournable truths.

I look at you, at an angle slightly from above, as you lean against my shoulder. I see what I have never noticed before: a small patch of grey hair at the crown. It is like a sign of winter in a summer landscape. And suddenly it exposes you to death and ending, in a way I would never have believed possible before. I look sideways at your face, but your attention is fixed on the photographs in your lap, your eyes light-filled. A blush on your cheeks? But if there is, then not of shame but of something else, an unspoken and perhaps unspeakable excitement, a flush of accomplishment, even of pride. In this moment I understand why, when George wanted to show them to me the previous time, you wouldn't let him. But with a suddenness that disarms me, I also understand why, this time, you want me to look at them, to see you as I have never seen you before and never thought I could. And never might again.

After a long time I arrange the photographs to square them very precisely, and put them beside me on the armrest of the couch.

'You are unbelievably beautiful,' I say, struggling to control my voice.

'George is a fantastic photographer,' you say, almost demurely.

'Yes, the photographs are brilliant,' I admit softly. 'But I'm talking about *you*.'

'I am not beautiful. You still don't know me. You don't know my shadows.'

'I know enough of you.'

I move to face you. You look at me, your eyes focused very directly on me, unflinching. I know that this cannot be avoided or denied. In this light that falls on us, and that seems to come from us, nothing can be hidden.

I remember precisely how I imagined you as a wine the very first time I met you: fresh and bright, with an intense straw-like and green-peppery and lemon-grassy bouquet, and hints of asparagus and gooseberry, a fleeting farmyard presence, and the merest touch of tannin, a complex fruitiness that lingers on the aftertaste, beautifully balanced for ageing. Yes. But I believe now there is so much more. A crispness of tropical fruit, of winter melon with its sweetness gliding into an almost almond-bitter follow-up. The taste of woman, which is beyond the taste of fruit and wine. This is what God warned Adam and Eve about, what He wished to preserve them from, knowing they would not be able to bear it.

Between my hands I hold your face, very lightly, like a precious object that can fall and break very easily. Yes, I think. This is you. This is what is happening. This is the choice to be made. It is now, it is here. It is as it must be. I know what is possible and what is impossible.

And I know, perhaps for the first time in my life, the meaning of the difference between them.

I know now what to choose. And I know what I stand to forfeit. I can feel my hands trembling very lightly. Unless it is a tremor from your face.

I lean over and very gently, almost without touching, press my mouth against your forehead. Like years ago, my hand against a face behind a moving window.

The choice is made. I turn away, to the light that comes from the window.

'Shall I make us some tea?' you ask behind me.

'I'd love some.'

I hear you moving about in the kitchen, hear the water coming to the boil. The light in front of me makes no sound. After some time your footsteps come back. I turn to face you and take my cup from your hands. You sit down in the armchair opposite.

'Why are you not having coffee?' I ask.

With a slow smile you say, 'I thought I'd like to have a cup of tea with you today.'

'It's the first time I've ever seen you drinking tea.'

'There's always a first time, isn't there?'

'Not always,' I say, almost primly.

Then we sit facing each other, and drink in silence.

When it is over, you take our two cups back to the kitchen. You come back. I look up at you. I take the pile of photographs from the armrest and without looking at them again, slide them back into

the large buff envelope. I close it very meticulously, almost cere-
monially.

I say, 'Thank you.'

You take the envelope from me. You also take my hand. You raise it
to your lips and press a chaste little kiss on the knuckles.

'Thank *you*,' you say.

The description of the wine, it seems to me now, did not work. You
have never been a mere list of attributes. It sounds almost vulgar now.
You are, I think, as unattainable as a Romanée Conti.

The light is still there, outside, falling in through the window, serene
and confident, like an accomplishment in its own right.

ON THE WAY here to the old-age care centre I bought Mam a small
cup of ice cream, which she is scooping out with the little spoon,
relishing every lick like a small child. Today she is not propped up in
her too-big easy chair, but stretched out in her high white bed.

'I wish you'd bring me this more often,' she says, as she starts scraping
out the last bits with a crooked finger. 'But I know it's bad for the
figure.'

'Nothing wrong with your figure, Mam,' I assure her.

'Perhaps not. I can still turn a few heads, don't you think, Boetie?'

'No doubt about that, Mam. You're still in great form.'

'But you mustn't tell your father,' she says, with a hint of anxiety.
'He won't like it. He always thinks he's the only one.' She chuckles
with malicious glee, peering at me through the thick glasses which
make her eyes look like fish swimming in an aquarium.

'He's dead, Mam.'

'Is he now? He never told me.'

'A good fifty years ago,' I assure her patiently. 'It was after I left the
firm. A heart attack.'

'Serves him right. Who was the woman?'

'What woman?' I feign innocence, hoping to find out more.

'There was a woman involved, I seem to recall.'

'Don't worry about that now.'

'Trust you to cover up for him.'

'I'm not trying anything of the sort. And you know the truth well enough. He died right on top of a woman. His secretary.'

'Now what would he be doing there?'

'Looking for gold,' I snap, irked.

'Aren't we all?' she asks, and screws up her cornflower-blue eyes, the only youthful thing about her.

'I wouldn't know, Mam,' I say primly.

'You should know. You've been around with so many women too, haven't you now?' A nasty little smirk: 'You see? There's nothing about you I don't know.'

'Must be something in the genes.'

'I've never approved of women wearing jeans,' she declares emphatically. 'They put lewd thoughts in men's minds.'

'In women's too, I fancy.'

'I've never nursed a lewd thought in my life, Boetie.'

'You weren't exactly beyond reproach after Father died, Mam.' Seeing her stubbornly purse her thin dry lips, I am tempted to provoke her further, but decide against it.

'If anything happened, it was because of him. Or you. Probably both.'

'That was not what people said. You even had an affair with the dominee, didn't you? Soon after Father's death.'

'People say many things, especially if they're jealous.'

'Did they have reason to be jealous of the dominee?'

'It would have been very short-sighted of them. He was such a harmless man. Wouldn't cast a leering look at a fly. If he's the one I'm thinking about.'

'Mam, please. Let's try to be decent.'

'I was forced to be decent all my life. First my father, then Hendrik, now you. I also wanted a life, you know. Now I think I'm old enough to let go. How old am I?'

'You'll be a hundred and three, come August. In three months. We were born in the same month, you and I.'

'Fancy that. So you'll be a hundred and three too?'

'The same month, Mam. Not the same year. I'll be seventy-eight.'

'Someone must have got it wrong. It wasn't fair to a young girl like me.'

'Were you and Father ever happy together?' I ask.

'How must I know?' She sounds coy. 'Men look at these things differently, don't they?'

I persist: 'But when you got married? Right in the beginning?'

'I was only a child when my father made me marry Hendrik. Seventeen or eighteen, just when I wanted to start living. Because my ma was sickly and he couldn't handle a girl-child on his own. Remember?'

'I don't know, Mam. I wasn't there.'

'You were never there when I needed you. But *he* was there. Dearie me, what a terrible man. At it, all the time. "I *must* have a son. I *must* have a son." But I was too small for him. All those miscarriages. How many were there? Must have been hundreds. At least three. And then the still-born boy. The doctor said never again, I won't make it. But your father wouldn't take no for an answer. And so there you were. Puny little brat, and I couldn't even feed you.'

'Lucky you found Nannie to pull me through.'

'Who's Nannie?'

'I was told she was the girl who nursed me.'

'Must have been one of your father's little cupcakes.' She chuckles.

Is that a clue? I suddenly wonder, a sickening feeling. If Nannie had really been involved with him, the child she gave up for adoption could have been the brother I'd been looking for all my life. I want to find out more. I must. But I know it will be time wasted. And even if she did say something, how can she be trusted?

'At least I survived,' I say after a long pause.

'Don't talk too soon. You have death written all over you.'

'Perhaps it's somebody else's death.'

'Could it be your wife's?'

'Helena died many years ago, Mam.'

'Good for her.'

'You never approved of her.'

'Why should I? She never took care of you properly. No-good little twit.'

'Helena was a wonderful wife and a wonderful mother.'

'Then why don't you ever speak of her?'

'Because she's dead.'

'When did she die?'

'In 1972.'

'Wasn't that when they killed Verwoerd?'

'No, Mam. It was actually his death that brought us together, six years before that.'

'Very considerate of him. Always such a gentleman, your father used to say.'

She sinks away into her hit-or-miss memories, I withdraw into mine. All those months of arguing and pleading with Helena; but she stood firm: no wedding, no sex. But I was so scared of taking the plunge. Forty-one years old, time to make a move, but how could I commit myself after seeing what marriage had brought the two of them? And then that day in September. I was in a café in Green Point, buying bread and milk, when the news came over the radio. Some of the customers dropped their purchases. A young boy took his chance, grabbed a handful of sweets from an open jar and ran for it; no one even thought of pursuing him. And outside on the streets, the silence. People standing in little groups, staring. Waiting for the apocalypse. Even after the previous attempt — what was the man's name? Pratt — people thought of Verwoerd as immortal. But this time he was brought down in parliament by a messenger with a knife, the radio had said. I stood there on the pavement, among the others, waiting for the news to sink in. I thought back, all the way to 1948, to everything that had started there. The tightening of the steel frame around us, the laws and prohibitions, the growing hate, the growing fear. Bonnie, that morning at the van Riebeeck Festival. And the day on the office floor. Sharpeville. Daphne dancing in the night. Our journey into darkness, like a runaway train gathering speed. All of it focused on that one name: Hendrik Frensch Verwoerd. That avuncular, smiling face. That one can smile and smile and be a damned villain.

Then, at last, it hit me. The man was dead. A mad elation grabbed hold of me. Tucking the parcel under my arm as in my rugby days, going for the line, I forgot completely about my car parked in front of the café and started running. It must have been instinct that drove me to Helena's cosy little flat in Gardens rather than my own house: at a moment like that I could not be alone. I ran and ran. It must have been three kilometres, but I wasn't aware of anything but the urge to get to her. There was once an intervarsity match against Ikeys when I got the ball just inside our own half. Two minutes to go to full-time, and three points behind. I never saw anything on the way. There were bodies between me and the line, but by some miracle I got past them, around them, through them. I could have passed, but never even thought of that. There were two or three Ikeys hanging on to me as I barged over. The finest moment of my rugby-playing years. I could see Father jumping madly up and down on the side-line. The only time I ever saw him lose his formidable composure in joy. He didn't realise that I had seen him, and when he came to congratulate me afterwards, he was as collected as ever. But that didn't matter. I *knew*. On this day of the murder it was the same thing. I drew back my ears and sprinted through the streets. Helena's building. Two flights of stairs up. Her door. It wasn't locked. I just threw it open and burst inside, panting, dropping my parcel on the floor. The milk bottle broke.

'Chris, what has happened? What's the matter?'

Her white, scared face against mine, her arms trying to hold me.

'Helena, Helena, my darling . . . !' I could barely speak. 'Verwoerd . . . It's Verwoerd . . . Somebody stabbed him, he is dead . . . !' My weight pulled her down and we both landed on the floor, in the pool of milk, among the shards of broken glass. It was a miracle that neither of us was cut.

'Please calm down and tell me,' she begged.

'I told you, they killed him.' And suddenly the words burst from me: 'I'm going to marry you. Let's do it. Now.'

For once, there was nothing she could do to stop me. I myself didn't know what was happening. But it happened. Then *she* was the one who was crying, but whether it was from joy or shock I couldn't tell. Only much later did it dawn on me exactly what I had said. Now nothing could be retracted any more. We *had* to get married. And we did.

'Is that what you came to tell me?' asks Mam in a bewildered little voice. 'That Verwoerd is dead? But I knew that. It was on the radio.'

I take a deep breath to keep my composure. 'Nobody is dead, Mam. Except Rachel. I told you last time.'

'I don't even know her, why should that upset you?'

'Because I loved her.'

'You fall in love too easily. You always have.' A twisted smile. 'But so did I when I was young and beautiful. We just never get what we want, do we?'

'Rachel was special.'

'Why? Who was she?'

'A friend. Don't you remember?'

'I can't keep track of all your little friends. I can't even keep track of my own. We have outlived them all. It's a lonely life, Boetie.'

'I am here with you.'

'I still have such a lot of catching up to do,' she says. 'Soon it will be too late.'

'What are you talking about?'

'You're too young to understand.'

For her, that clinches it. It is a line she has used so many times, infuriating me, but to no avail. I remember when I was fifteen or sixteen, I found her chuckling in a corner of the kitchen when I came home from school. I wanted to know the reason.

She shook her head, still laughing. 'It's a terribly rude story Aunt Myra told me this morning.'

'Tell me.'

'You're too young for it.'

'Please, Mam!'

'I'll tell you when you're eighteen.'

'Promise?'

'Cross my heart and strike me dead.'

She thought I would forget, but I didn't. On the morning of my eighteenth birthday I reminded her. She frowned for a moment, then burst out laughing. 'I know I promised, Boetie,' she said, 'but it really is still too rude for your young ears. Tell you what: you ask me again when you're twenty-one.'

'That's not fair, Mum.'

'Who ever said the world was a fair place?'

I did not forget. On my twenty-first birthday I demanded to hear the story. This time she postponed it to my thirtieth. And when at last, on that day of days, I cornered her to hear the truth, the whole, and nothing but, she gazed at me in bright surprise, shook her head, and said, 'I'm sorry, Boetie, I have no idea what you're talking about.'

And now it certainly is too late, for both of us.

I lean over and pat one of the small crooked claws on the sheet. Like so many times before I gaze at her: the tiny little creature, crumpled like a piece of paper thrown away because the wrong words have been written on it (that is the problem: we have no chance to revise). How often, since my childhood, have we been at loggerheads. I could never satisfy her that I was working hard enough, and then I would be locked up in my room until Father came home; and he had only one way of dealing with malingering or recalcitrance. But afterwards, when he was working in his study, she would tiptoe into my room and gently rub ointment into the welts and cuts and bruises. It doesn't matter that she no longer understands. She has her moments of illumination. And even when her mind wanders, she is here for me.

I lean over and say in her ear, 'I love you, Mam.'

'I suppose I love you too,' she says, and closes her eyes behind the monstrous glasses, and dozes off peacefully. But it lasts barely a minute. Then she wakes up and looks around her in bewilderment, almost in fear. 'Where am I? What place is this?'

'This is where you live, Mam.'

'Where is Gerhard?' she asks.

'Who is Gerhard, Mam?'

'Don't you remember Gerhard?'

'No. What about him?'

'And Jeremy?'

'Who was Jeremy?'

'And – what was his name again? Michael or Michiel or something?'

'Mam, I don't know. Who were these people?'

'Which people?'

We go round and round. Every now and then there is a glimmer of possibility, I feel myself approaching a likelihood of revelation, of discovery, but then it fades away again. Is this where I am heading also? Will I, too, one day, wonder: Who was Helena? Who was Daphne? Who Nicolette? Bonnie? Freckled Frances? Tania? Who in God's name was Rachel? I must get on with these notes. Before I forget. Before it all gets lost.

THERE IS ANOTHER woman from my years in Paris I must mention here. I took her home with me, and she spent a night in my apartment: but I do not know her name. All I know is that my notes will be incomplete without her.

I was coming back from a tryst in one of the narrow side streets just off the place de la République. (It was some time after Nicolette had left me and I was living in the rue des Filles du Calvaire at the time.) It must have been two or three in the morning, and this bundle of rags was lying in the gutter. It was raining lightly. As I sidestepped the bundle, it moved. I stopped. It sat up. It was an old woman. She stank to high heaven; and alcohol was the least part of it. Sometime during the night I tried to pin an age to her: seventy, eighty? But one cannot be too sure. She might have been forty, going on ninety.

Why did I stop? Surely I should have known better. Perhaps I was simply immobilised by the smell.

Whatever it was, having stopped I couldn't just stride off.

'Do you need help, Madame?' I asked.

She responded with an obscenity; with it came a blast of breath that nearly felled me.

No, she didn't need help, she was perfectly happy to die right there. What could I do?

I painfully levered the old crone into a standing position, offered her what support I could, passing my left arm behind her back and thrusting the hand under her left arm. It came to rest on a sagging breast, like an old calabash in a crumpled bag. She suddenly giggled coquettishly: there is no other way to describe it. I held my breath and grimly staggered on. It must have taken us half an hour to reach my place, and almost as long to mount the worn stairs to my garret.

Once home, I thought I should offer her something to eat first, but the stench was too overpowering. I opened all the windows, although the January air was freezing. Then, leaving her on the couch in the lounge, I went to the bathroom to run a bath as hot as a human body could bear, and half dragged, half marched her over the threshold, showed her the bath, nearly shoved her head right into it, and ordered her to clean herself up while I went in search of something she could wear. There were various pieces of female clothing in the vast armoire that dominated my bedroom – shirts and skimpy tops, a variety of filmy underwear, a jersey or two, narrow skirts, fishnet stockings, that kind of thing – but few of them seemed of much use in the circumstances. After a long search I did manage to assemble a weird-looking outfit which would just have to do.

When I knocked on the bathroom door there was no answer. For a moment I was seized by panic: suppose she'd died on me? I pushed open the door. She was lying on the floor, half undressed, snoring, fast asleep. I shook her awake, but it was clear that there was no other way: I would have to put her in the bath and watch over her to make sure she didn't drown.

She was like a chicken rejected by a supermarket – a chicken as they are sold in France, with the beaked, closed-eyed head still attached to the long floppy neck with its spare stubble of feathers. I washed her. She gave her silly giggle again when I went between her legs, between her scrawny buttocks. I thought of Mam: but that was twenty years ago, and compared to where she is today she was still a hale and hearty eighty-something. Yet it was not revolting. It was like coming face to face with – what? It sounds too easy, even insulting, to say *woman*. But that was what it was. I thought of all the girls' and women's bodies I had caressed over the years of my life, all the way from the giggling little Katrien in the dark, and Driekie among the fig leaves, to those nameless ever-ready ones in London and Paris, and it was as if, somehow, they were all subsumed in this little bundle of bones with its claws for hands and feet, and its sagging head, and the grey crow's nest between her stick legs which made her look like a rag doll with her stuffing coming out. Poor naked wretch.

I washed her with infinite care, and tried to hold her up while I dried her in a huge spongy towel. The whole place would have to be disinfected afterwards; but I did not think of it then. All that was important for the moment was to get this unbelievable, yet all-too-believable emblem of humanity dried, and dressed, with my own dressing gown to cover up; and then to get some food into her. As she kept dropping off to sleep, I had to spoon-feed her. Much of it dribbled down her chin, and some was splattered on her shrunken chest. But in the end it was done, and then I lay her down on the bed, covered her with every blanket in the place, and withdrew to my lounge-cum-study to read, and make some notes, and to keep my vigil.

It was almost noon when she woke up. She seemed stronger now, and ate a surprisingly hearty breakfast. And then she became hurried and spoke about going. I tried to find out where she might go to, but that made her angry. I had no right to probe into her private affairs, she squeaked at me in a high little voice like a wet rubber glove moving across a polished surface.

Only when she had already opened the door to go, did she stop. A thought appeared to have struck her. Her face contorted in a rictus, she cupped both hands over her groin and with feverish, glittering eyes – as if she was the one who was doing *me* a favour – asked, '*Tu veux? You want?*'

No, Madame, I did not want.

And then she left. She would not allow me to accompany her. I heard her stomping slowly down the six sets of spiralling stairs to the ground floor; and then the loud bang of the front door.

Of course I never saw her again. But she is with me all the time. Whenever I am with a new woman. And whenever I am all by myself.

A FINAL ASSAULT in Baghdad appears to be underway. Suddenly everything is happening at unprecedented speed. My nights are full of sound and fury. The city is now almost completely encircled: the First Brigade holds the airport and the western parts, the Second is in the process of securing the south, the Third holds the north-west and the marines are in the north-east. The blacked-out capital is dominated by the sound of heavy machine-gun fire, rocket launchers and artillery. No one has as yet reported the discovery of the weapons that brought them here.

The Iraqi Minister of Information, Mohammed Saeed al-Sahaf, insists persuasively that the Iraqi forces are still pushing back the invaders. In fact, he affirms, 'there are none of their troops in Baghdad'. We can all sleep peacefully tonight.

And of course, what keeps me awake in front of the small screen in the dark, is knowing that George must also be somewhere there, taking photographs perhaps of the very same events I am looking at. It places me both there and here, a disconcerting simultaneity.

IF I DO think back to that morning with the photographs in your studio, there is a feeling of completeness about it. What had happened, what *could* have happened, was now accomplished, and we could go on. There was a serene inevitability about it. It was George himself who had said, so long ago, in a moment of illumination, 'What must happen, will happen.' And Ecclesiastes: *A time to every purpose under the heaven.* This may seem a shocking analogy, but I think about it, now, the way I think about your death. For so many weeks, ever since the accident, while you were lying in a coma, I lived in fear, in unspeakable terror. Any moment the telephone might ring and someone would say: *She is dead.* In the beginning, that was what I most feared to hear: that you were dead. Later, as the slow dark weeks dragged on, what I dreaded was that you might *not* die. Because it was unbearable and degrading to see you like that, wasting away, going and going, but never gone. I couldn't sleep at night. I could find no rest. Waiting, waiting. Knowing it might go on for weeks, months, even for years. How could I see that happening to you? To *you*?

And then, on that morning of 20 March, at seventeen minutes to ten, you died. At last it was over. I could rest now. The worst had happened, for nothing could be worse than that. I was flooded by a broad, deep, absolute relief, a peace such as I had never known.

This was something like the feeling I had after we had renounced the possibility of making love that morning. No need to concern myself with questions and surmisings and wonderings any more. I know I had accepted, long before that morning, and you had most explicitly confirmed it, that nothing *could* ever 'happen' between us. Not just for George's sake, but for ourselves. In spite of this, there had always been the *possibility*. Even without being conscious of it, there had been the unrealised anxiety: *Was* it, by any chance, still going to happen even if it shouldn't? And if so, when? And how? It was debilitating and exhausting. Humiliating too. But now there was no more to wonder about. This was the real peace that passeth understanding.

It meant that, without ever again having to talk about it, we could go on with our lives. That unnatural tension was gone. You could be you, I could be me; together we could face George, and ourselves, and be a threesome as before, only better equipped and more fully than before.

When he came back to Cape Town, we both went to the airport to meet him. And without the slightest ripple the stream of our friendship flowed on, deep and calm. There was a special celebration on my birthday in the first week of August. (Three weeks later there was a much quieter and more private little celebration for Mam in the old-age home; but I did take her a huge cake with a hundred and two candles, which I had to blow out for her while she looked on mumbling about the unnecessary fuss.) It had been your idea, you told me later, to go completely over the top, with streamers and singing minstrels and a cake from which a naked girl would jump; but sanity had prevailed (with some nudging from George, I'm sure) and it became a very classy affair at your home, with you in a full-length black dress (but barefoot) and your light-brown, curly hair piled high on your head, and George and me in dinner suits; and candles everywhere – from the entrance, down the passage, and all over the studio and the lounge, even on the balcony. The weather cooperated: the rain of the previous days cleared up, the wind died down, and the sun put on a dazzling spectacle over a newborn world.

You overwhelmed me with your gifts: George gave me a photograph he'd taken of me, surreptitiously, on our Cedarberg excursion. Yours was a small sculpture, an exquisite little Madonna, so delicately beautiful that I was almost scared to touch it. And the meal, a joint effort, was a gastronomic hymn. George made pan-fried duck's liver, prepared in raspberry vinegar and served with poached pears; you rounded it off with floating islands. Each of the wines was a master-piece in its own right — Thelema, Meerlust, Haute Cabrière.

But there was something missing from the evening. Instead of the customary, spontaneous warmth there was an almost studied politeness, a distance that upset me all the more because of the obvious efforts both of you were making to appear your usual bril-liant selves.

A disconcerting cooling had already begun. And I knew exactly how and why. The balcony was where it had first surfaced. It had nothing to do with the three of us as individuals, but was imposed on us from outside, which lent an edge of the unnecessary to it. It began, in fact, about a week before the birthday, with a nasty episode two houses down your little street. The owners, with whom you both were quite friendly, had been out to work (he is an architect, she a script person with a film company) when, in broad daylight, at two or three in the afternoon, a couple of strangers had arrived with a huge box on the back of a truck, ostensibly to make a delivery. In spite of the recent burglaries in the area, the housekeeper, Faridah, who had been with the couple for years, suspected nothing amiss and opened the door for them. But the moment they were inside, they overpowered Faridah, tied her up and ransacked the place. The truck was loaded with loot: TVs, recorders, washing machine, the metal gun cabinet, antique furniture, a heavy safe which they removed with angle grinders and blowtorches. And then they returned to rape Faridah. ('They looked such decent people,' she sobbed afterwards, when she was interviewed by the police in hospital.)

Both George and you were in shock when, not suspecting anything, I arrived at your home for a drink that evening. The two previous burglaries in the street had been bad enough, but at least had not been violent, and as several months had elapsed since then, calm had returned to the neighbourhood. Most days, when George was away on assignments or shootings of his own, you left your front door open. But this, George insisted, would now have to stop. One just could not take chances any more. You agreed, and so did I. But a few days later, when George arrived with two men from a security company, you were up in arms. They started taking measurements. Every door and window had to be protected, a daunting gate operated by remote control had to be installed at the top of the driveway, and the large balcony in front of your studio had to be closed in with burglar bars. Sensible measures, all of them, obviously; but the idea of having your wonderful view of the bay obscured by a grille was too much.

'I won't live in a prison,' you said.

'A cat burglar can easily climb up the front, on to the balcony, and come in from there,' George pointed out.

'Then let him. I can't work behind bars.'

'Don't be unreasonable, Rachel,' he pleaded.

'Chris?' You turned to me. 'Help me. Make this man see reason.'

He unexpectedly took offence at that. 'I am not "this man"!' he protested. 'I am your husband. I love you. I want to do this for your own safety.'

'Why didn't you talk to me first? How can you just turn up here with a truckload of men and start putting up bars in front of my studio?'

'It's not a truckload of people, Rachel. It's just the manager and his assistant.'

'Well, they can fuck off. I don't want them here and I won't be a prisoner in my own house.'

The visitors, deeply embarrassed and not knowing what to do, slunk out of the room.

Once again you turned to me: 'Aren't you going to help me?' you asked angrily. 'How can you let George do this to me?'

'I'm sure Chris will understand reason,' said George, an expression of pure misery on his big face.

'Are the men now ganging up against me?' you exploded.

'Look, chaps,' I said awkwardly, 'I don't think I should be drawn into this.'

'But you can see reason, can't you?' you appealed, your cheeks flushed with emotion.

'If Chris can see reason, he will understand my concern for your safety,' said George.

This was unmanageable, and terribly unfair – to our friendship, to me. All I could do was to back out. And leaving everything unresolved, I mumbled my apologies and left. The security man and his assistant were still huddled outside, next to their battered bakkie. They shook their heads at me and shrugged as I came past.

In these circumstances, my birthday only a few days later could not possibly be the celebration we had been looking forward to. Not one of us referred to what had happened, and although I was dying to know the outcome, I dared not ask any questions. Your studied silence made me think – at least hope – that you had begun to resign yourself to the inevitable.

The silence persisted for three weeks. It was just after Mam's birthday on the 23rd, when I went to your house for tea one Sunday morning – a miserable rainy day, as it happened – that I noticed how the balcony had been completely secured with iron bars. An attempt to soften the effect with some ornate curlicues actually made it worse. I could not hide my shock, but when I looked at you, both turned such set faces in my direction that I decided to shut up. Not that this lasted for long: we knew each other well enough not to keep on dissembling.

As I might have expected, it was you who brought it up. You looked most desirable, if I dare say so, in a chunky sweater, corduroys and thick orange woollen socks. But your body language said unambiguously: *Keep off!* In the middle of one of the unusual silences that punctuated our conversation, you made a sweeping gesture towards the balcony. 'What do you think of my new view?' you asked abruptly.

'An awful grey day,' I tried to sidestep it.

'The weather suits me perfectly,' you said bitingly. 'I feel exactly like that.'

'It will clear up, Rachel.'

'*I* won't.'

'Oh, come on, Rachel,' said George in a cajoling tone.

You opened your mouth to snap at him, but then stopped yourself. 'How can anyone expect me to work in a place like this?' you asked after a while, more composed, but with a flat bitterness to your voice that sounded completely unlike the Rachel I'd known.

'We have to make compromises to survive,' I said cautiously.

'Bullshit,' you responded.

'I've also had to put up security bars and top my garden wall with spikes,' I pointed out.

'But you can look at the sea over them. These things hem me in completely. Just look at them . . . !' Your eyes were brimming with tears, one of the saddest sights I'd seen in the eight months I'd known you.

'Please, my love,' said George, slipping off his chair to go on his knees next to yours.

'If only you'd asked me first,' you reproached him. 'But just to confront me with it like this!'

'It is to keep you safe. Because I love you, dammit.'

'Peter, Peter, Pumpkin Eater,' you hissed at him. 'I'm not going to live here any more.'

'We'll need security wherever we go,' he pleaded.

'I really don't care,' you said.

'Let us all try to be reasonable,' I said. 'I'm sure we can find a solution. Right?'

'You mean you want *me* to be reasonable,' you snarled at me. 'Because to you I'm the one who is unreasonable. I am the woman, aren't I?'

'I can't deny that you're a woman,' I said, trying to sound as cheerful as I could. '*Vive la différence* and all that. But this is a dilemma and I'm sure we can face it together.'

'I'm going to cancel my exhibition,' you unexpectedly said with a cold firmness that cut through my guts. 'There's no way I can work in here.'

'What are the alternatives?' I asked. 'Let us start working from there.'

'I prefer to start with this house as it is.' You corrected yourself: 'As it *was*.'

'In the country we live in . . .' George began.

'The country we live in is ruled by shit,' you cut him short.

'Then we have to learn to live with shit,' he said calmly. 'If the choice is between surviving with some dignity, and being killed or raped . . .'

'I'd rather be raped than live with this!' you cried.

'Now you're being . . .' I bit my tongue. I couldn't go on.

'Go on, say it,' you sneered. 'Say it. I'm being childish – or stupid – or a bitch. Underline what is most applicable.'

'You're being grossly unfair to yourself,' I said.

'Then please be so kind as to make me see the light.'

How on earth had we got there? It seemed as if our very friendship was beginning to cave in. And for the time being we were paralysed, trapped in it, unable to find a way out.

'Just a wild idea,' I said at last, in trepidation. I looked into your smouldering eyes. 'Start by taking away these bars. Use them in your hedge, or as a trellis in the garden, or wherever. Grow tomatoes or passion fruit or pumpkins on them. Even donate them to Pollsmoor Prison. Then you design something new. A grille you can live with.'

'I cannot live with a grille.'

'But you can try.' I did my best to turn it into comedy. 'See it as a challenge to your creativity.'

'The monkey decorating the bars of her cage,' you said. But the viciousness was out of it.

'While you're at it, you can start making some sculptures of creatures trapped in little cages. Monkeys, humanoids, toads, reptiles, anything under the sun or the visiting moon.'

Slowly, slowly we returned to a semblance of reason and good-natured mellowness. By the time we decided to prolong the morning into a meal at one of our favourite haunts in Green Point, we could begin to find some fun in the world again.

'I can see why you've been successful with women,' you said, without anything leading up to it, sometime during the afternoon.

'I don't agree with the observation,' I said. 'But I'd like to hear the reason. Is it because I've been so good at putting them behind bars and in cages?'

'No, I think you have a way of taking them out of their cages.'

'I wish it were true. Sometimes, when you get somebody out of a cage, you land her in worse shit than before.'

Why was I thinking, at that moment, of Tania?

SHE WAS, INDEED, one of 'them' – the seemingly infinite liquorice allsorts of girls and women surrounding our Amandla project in Paris, largely hand-picked by Siviwe Mfundisi. But Tania was different. She was not, in Siviwe's terminology, a tissue to blow your nose in and throw away. To begin with, she was not a groupie; she was a dedicated member of the project, and not there just for the fun and the fucking, but because her whole life was tuned in – but gaily, brightly, not gravely – to the idea of going to South Africa one day and being part of the shaping of a new country. What she had in common with the rest of Siviwe's corps de ballet, was that she was beautiful. Dark, delicate, petite, perfectly shaped and surprisingly young, twenty-three, with sloe eyes and a mouth like a pickable plum, long slender hands, toes like pomegranate pips, and a fountain of laughter somewhere inside her, always ready to bubble over.

Siviwe himself presented her to me. That made me wary, as I knew from experience his very smooth habit of disposing of exes by handing them down, with a show of generosity, to his comrades when he needed to clear his bed for the next incumbent. I think Tania had the same apprehension, and when we went home to my place from the bistrot where we'd been introduced, we were still, in a manner of speaking, sniffing at each other like two dogs that had just met on a corner and were not sure which one was going to snarl first. But as she had just been thrown out of her digs, she didn't have anywhere else to go right then; and I had invited her on the explicit under-standing that she could park in the bedroom while I took to the couch – which was how any number of my other affairs had started. It was my last year in Paris (although I did not know it yet), and I had just moved from the rue des Filles du Calvaire into a charming if still somewhat sparsely furnished apartment high up in the rue Vieille du Temple.

On the way there, as we approached the corner of the rue des

Francs-Bourgeois, she suggested that we have another drink on a terrace. It was a hot night in July, and most of Paris was on the streets; there was music pulsing everywhere, the night sky was an impossible shade of inky blue, and one had the impression of sleep-walking, wide awake, a few centimetres above the ground. So her proposal was quite understandable – it seemed like a sin to turn in early. But I had an idea that she wanted to work up some courage first, before facing a strange man in a strange apartment, even if her attitude and the easy flow of her conversation did not betray any tension. My suspicion was confirmed when she started drinking several gin and tonics in quick succession. At any rate, the combination of the alcohol, the free-flowing summer night, the music (a violonist and an accordionist, resembling the cat and the fox in *Pinocchio*, came down the street and played at our table), the carefree talk, the theatrical sky above, all helped her to relax, and by the time we got up and shouldered her bundles and picked up her large suitcase to face the rest of the journey home, we were chatting and laughing like old friends. We had so much fun as we staggered up the scrubbed wooden stairs, waking most of the neighbours along the way, that we both collapsed in a heap on the floor when we arrived. And it was immediately clear that the couch would not be needed for the night.

But what seemed to seal it was when, with half her clothes strewn about us on the floor, I turned my attention to her navel, which was one of the most perfectly shaped, and certainly the deepest, I had ever had the good fortune to come across. I waxed lyrical about it. 'This needs a celebration,' I said. 'I must drink from it.'

Unfortunately there was no appropriate drink available, so I proposed returning to the last bistrot and buying a bottle of champagne. Tania was amused, but tired too, and the whole thing was nearly wrecked when I wanted her to put on at least some of her clothes so that she could go with me. No, she said, that was taking it too far. If I really wanted to go, I could go on my own. I did. But the bistrot was closed, and I had to traverse half of Paris before I found what I wanted. By that time I was pretty exhausted too. And when at last I stumbled back into the apartment, Tania was fast asleep, right there on the floor where I had left her.

For a while I stared down at her sleeping face, very pale against her dark hair, a thumb in her mouth. How could I possibly disturb her? But as I kneeled beside her, she stirred, and mumbled something, and smiled, and I gently pulled away the drape she had drawn across her, and saw that she had taken off the rest of her clothes. She was lying on her back, one leg drawn up sideways, the foot resting against the knee of the other. Well.

I started kissing her navel, probing it with my tongue, very gently. I have had some rather disappointing experiences trying to wake up a sleeping woman to make love. But this time it worked. She thought, she said later, that it was a butterfly fluttering its wings against the gentle swell of her belly. And once she was awake, I poured the champagne over her, the way Nastasya had taught me to do it, just a trickle, which foamed in the deep hollow of her navel and spilled over the sides, and ran down towards the dreaming double fold of her sex. Her mound was smooth and free of pubic hair. In some women the shaven mound seems to expose the sex too obviously, too relentlessly, too brazenly, dare I say too in-your-face. In some, the lips are too busy and overstated, unnecessarily elaborate, like those flesh-eating flowers from foreign jungles. In Tania everything was perfect. It was neat and precise and small, like the slice of a mandarin. Its promise was interiority and fulfilment. It invited the unfolding, the probing, the discovery from which no traveller returns unchanged.

We did not think of sleeping before mid-morning. It was the beginning of six months of honeymoon. Most of the time we spent in Paris, but we also travelled together to Amsterdam, to Geneva, to Rome, and through many regions of France. She was a magnificent travel companion, a born explorer. It was her idea to walk along the Gorges du Tarn. Hers, too, to spend several weeks during the harvesting season in the Bordeaux region, near Saint-Émilion, picking grapes and then treading them in huge vats – divested of our clothes, to prevent them getting stained.

After our stint on the farm, Tania had to go back, while I stayed in the region for a few more weeks to attend a course in tasting and build on the knowledge I'd acquired, so many years before, from Uncle Johnny. But I couldn't wait to return to her. Back in Paris, there was no end to Tania's initiatives, or to the pleasure she took from sex — and brought to it. It was fun, above all: exuberant, frolicking fun. What she loved, was to find unusual, and preferably risky, times and places for making love, where we might be discovered at any moment. In the Bois de Boulogne or even an alley of the Jardin du Luxembourg among the statues of dead poets. On the back seat of a car, with friends in front. In a plush box in the Théâtre des Champs Élysées, listening to a performance by the Berlin Philharmonic (not really her cup of tea, which was why she chose to make love instead). In a telephone booth in the boulevard Montparnasse. Below the grandstand of Roland Garros during a match. Even, once, in a confessional in Saint-Sulpice which had just been vacated by a priest. The most daring, which I'm sure could have landed us in prison, was a quickie on Napoleon's imperial throne in the palace of Fontainebleau. And when we were home, she would find other diversions to spice it up. If I was on the telephone, she would calmly unzip my pants and start fellating me. Or while I was on her, making love, or between her legs probing her folds and depths, she would dial a friend and try to reach orgasm while talking.

'So that I can remember you when you go,' was her laconic response whenever I tried to question her.

'I won't go anywhere without you, Tania.'

'When the time comes you will leave me.'

'How can you say that?'

'I'm not blaming you, Chris. I'm only saying what's true. You must know it too.'

'I don't know it and I don't want to.'

'Then you're a coward, and I don't sleep with cowards.'

'I'm happy with you.'

'I'm happy with you too, but that doesn't mean it will last.' (When so many years later you said almost the same words, it was like Tania's voice speaking through you.) And then she placed her head between my hips, resting her cheek on my temporarily flaccid penis — we were on the kitchen floor, I think — and said, 'One thing you must know: I will never be a burden to you. If you feel you have had enough of me, you must tell me, and I'll go.' There were times, like this, when she sounded incomparably older than her tender years.

'I'll never have enough of you, Tania,' I assured her.

'Don't be silly. Of course you will. You have other things to do in the world besides being with me. One day you must go home to the Struggle. You have your writing. I can never come between you and any of that.'

Which was, I suppose, good reason not to be upset when she left. Yet I had no idea that it would be permanent when it happened. I thought she'd gone to visit friends in the country; she had often talked about them, a farmhouse near Moulins, which she'd wanted to see in spring, among the almond trees in blossom. For a few weeks she had been off-colour, dispirited, lethargic, with dark circles under her eyes. She often threw up. My God, I should have read the signs. But she had always been so conscientious about taking her pill.

She wasn't sure for how long she would be away. 'A few days,' she said when I asked. 'Perhaps a week. Or even two. Depends on how I feel. I shall phone.'

'Stay for as long as you need to,' I assured her. 'I want you back in blooming health.'

But she did not telephone. And when I tried the Moulins number she had scribbled down for me, it was out of order. Even then I did not get unduly worried: I thought she'd made a mistake writing it down.

After a month I realised that something was very wrong. That was when Siviwe phoned. 'Sorry to upset you, comrade,' he said. 'But Tania won't be coming back.'

'What do you mean?' I couldn't believe what he'd just said.

'She is dead.' He explained, with what was, for him, quite unusual sympathy. It was all very basic. Tania had had an abortion. She'd thought she could take it in her stride, but there were complications. By the time she contacted him it was already too late. He'd pleaded with her, but she didn't want to 'impose' on me and had made him promise to convey the message only after the funeral.

It was almost impossible to believe. Worst of all was to come to terms with the fact that she hadn't told me. She should have known that I would never have given her up. Nor the child. I had always had very strong convictions about abortion – probably the atavistic Calvinism with which I'd grown up. The idea was unbearable.

'That is probably why she just went ahead,' said Siviwe. 'That little Tania had her feet on the ground. She certainly knew that a child would be an impossible complication in her circumstances. And in yours. So . . .' There was an eloquent silence. 'Both of you fucked up by that country over there.'

'I loved her.'

'I know she loved you too, Chris. She often spoke to me about it. But for that very reason she could not go on with it. She was that kind of person.'

That kind of person, I thought. My God, I had lived with her, shared almost every day and night with her for six months; yet I did not know what kind of person she was. I did not know enough to have foreseen this. I did not know enough.

What I did know, blindingly, was that my time in Europe had run out. This was the decisive moment. I could no longer stay away from the place that had made me the person *I* was. For better or for worse. I had to go back.

THE DECISIVE MOMENT — certainly the most spectacular of the war so far has been the toppling of a six-metre statue of Saddam in Baghdad. After seeing it happen forty or fifty times (I must confess to having sneaked some looks during the day as well), it does become somewhat déjà vu, but what the hell. A telling observation: the first reaction from the US troops was to hoist the American flag on the statue. Then, presumably, somebody in authority intervened and hastily replaced it with an Iraqi flag. But the Freudian slip had already showed. And it was the stars and stripes. America, America *über alles*. The one thing it has always excelled at is putting on a good show.

TURNING POINTS WE often recognise only in retrospect. But not one of us needed hindsight to realise, at your exhibition in mid-October (the date had to be shifted from September when you decided

to start working almost from scratch, and you were incredibly fortunate that a cancellation had made it possible to change), that this was
a watershed. For your art, without a doubt, and the reviews in the
press – there was even a TV spot on *Carte Blanche* – said as much. But
most significantly for us, the three of us; for you.

You had been driving yourself even harder than before; much too
hard, I believed, and tried to persuade you to hold back, but that only
made you angry. And I laid off very quickly, remembering how mad
it had made me in my youth when Mam always pretended to know
better and tried to push me harder, and I revolted, and it would end
up with me locked in my room, and Father coming home to effect
the predictable closure.

There was a startling change in your work during the two months
between my birthday and the exhibition. What I had tossed out as a
random suggestion, not seriously meant at all, you had unexpectedly
taken up as you set to work on a series of ceramics, both sculptures
and decorated, curiously contorted pots, on the theme of incarceration. Some figures were surrounded, in a stark and straightforward way,
by bars of all shapes and sizes; in others, the figures – human, animal,
vegetable, or a mixture of them all – were attempting to break through
the bars, reaching out as some of the inmates of Dachau or Auschwitz
on old photographs pushed their emaciated arms and faces through
the barbed wire; even more hallucinating were the figures who had
their prison bars embedded inside them, like scarred trees growing
around or through skewers or crowbars lodged in them. There were
even some grotesque Giacometti-like stick figures, in which iron bars
seemed themselves to be metamorphosing into human shapes with
outstretched arms in gestures of beseeching or menace. In the pots,
shards and jagged iron spikes stuck into the clay half melted during
the firing, and the rust formed unpredictable shapes and deep rich
colours created by oxidising. You even returned to some of your earlier,
already finished, pieces and hemmed them in with bars and grilles, or
stuck spikes into their gullets or eyes or ears or arseholes. In three or
four of the sculptures the figures had disappeared completely: all that
was left were the bare cages, shockingly contorted bars, like clusters
of spaghetti cast in rusted iron.

I was drawn into much of the laborious process: the bisque firing followed by the slip glazing, the painting with pigments – I remember those flaming yellows, the vivid reds and greens, the deep cobalt blues – followed by the final glazing. The cages posed endless problems of their own. Much of it, especially in the first week or so, was hit-and-miss. The iron bars would simply melt in the firing and leave a mangled mess, or cause the clay figures to crack. Sometimes these unforeseeable results were in themselves spectacular, haunting. But mostly they were useless.

As time began to run out, even with the date pushed forward, you resorted to making the bars from clay too, and painting them with iron oxide. These were in disquieting contrast to some of the earlier pieces you'd left untouched, of half-human and half-animal children or madonnas (like the one you'd given me), realistically painted, challenging the spectator with an unnerving and deceptive air of innocence and idyllic beauty. In the end you had enough work for what was undoubtedly the most remarkable exhibition of your short career. It took its title from an Alan Paton book: *Ah, But Your Land is Beautiful*.

George contributed a lot to the preparations. He did almost all the welding of the ironwork, spending days and nights on it. Which made it all the more upsetting that he had to miss the exhibition itself after all. Impossible to blame him: an invitation to visit the Palestinian territories right then was something he simply could not turn down, and it arrived only days before the changed date of your opening. But it came as a blow, even though you kept a very brave face.

'*Che sarà sarà*,' you said philosophically. But there was an edge to it which did not escape me.

During the opening there was more than enough distraction to forget about George – particularly as the sales reached something of a frenzy: an American collector bought twelve of the forty pieces on show, and that created a stampede – but afterwards, when we finally managed to extricate ourselves from the crowd and drive off into the night for a quiet dinner *à deux* at our favourite place, La Colombe, your excitement was tempered by melancholy.

'It was amazing,' I say, as the sparkling wine is served – Achim von Arnim's amazing Aurum. With specks of real twenty-four-carat gold leaf glinting through the foam.

You nod absently, twirling the glass between your strong fingers.

I have to do something to lighten the atmosphere. Making a some-what deliberate effort, I tell you about the exhibition a friend of mine, Bridget, a painter, had at one of the top galleries in Johannesburg a few years ago.

'A friend, or a lover?' you ask.

'Something of both.'

'You think that is possible?'

'It has worked for me. At least, we began as lovers. At the time of the exhibition we were friends.'

'Hm.' You don't seem convinced.

'If you *must* know, we slept together again after the opening.'

'Ah, good.' At least I've managed to get your attention. 'How did that come about?'

Carried away by the memory, I plunge into the story. Bridget and I had driven up to Johannesburg together a day or two earlier and conferred with the gallery manager who had invited me to open the exhibition, and who turned out to be an exotically beautiful blonde woman in her early forties, Vera. For both the women there was much at stake: it was not only the opening of the exhibition but also of the gallery, in a prime spot in Rosebank; at the same time a few of the top vintners from the Cape were invited to use the occasion as a show-case for a selection of recent prize wines from an international event in Frankfurt. I immediately felt attracted to Vera, and the feeling appeared to be mutual, which made me very grateful for the friend-ship my relationship with Bridget had eased into.

For the time being there was no opportunity of pursuing the possibilities, as we were simply too busy arranging everything for the exhibition. But there certainly was electricity in the air, an unspoken agreement that after the opening . . . And then, quite unexpectedly, everything very nearly came to a premature end. On the morning of the exhibition Vera phoned in consternation: the pantechnicon that had to transport the paintings from Cape Town had got stuck some-where between Colesberg and Bloemfontein. Vera wanted to cancel. But Bridget was horrified by the idea: we had come all the way from Cape Town, the invitations had been sent out, the wines had arrived, all the delicacies had been ordered, we just *had* to go through with it. I promised to adapt my opening speech to the occasion to ensure that the public would not be antagonised. I would simply present it as a prelude, a whetting of the appetite. But as it turned out, no adaptation was required. That evening the gallery was awash with people, spilling into the open spaces of the mall where it was situated, even into the street. Everybody was drinking – the wines were an exhilarating success – smoking, talking, having a ball. It went on until well after midnight.

All three of us were on a high when the last guests finally oozed out. We repaired to Vera's luxurious mansion in Northcliff (a place she'd acquired as part of a divorce settlement from a millionaire Italian husband whose shady past might or might not have included some involvement with the Mafia) for a more private celebration. And after several more bottles of the best, it turned into a rollicking clinch *à trois* in the course of which we stumbled and tumbled through most of the rooms in the palace, ending up in the illuminated pool at daybreak in a surrealist tangle.

Two days later, the pantechnicon arrived, the paintings were hung and Bridget went to help Vera with the phone calls, to inform all the opening-night guests that the exhibition would now go ahead. But almost without exception the reply from every person they contacted was the same: 'But we've already seen the exhibition, we were there on the opening night.'

'Which undoubtedly gave the three of you reason for another little get-together?' you ask.

'You have a one-track mind, Rachel.'

'Not you?'

'All I can say is that I discovered, in the course of those two encounters, more about the imaginative limits of the human body than I had ever thought possible before. For one thing, it gave me a much more profound understanding of many of Picasso's paintings. So you may say that it was all in the name of aesthetics.'

You laugh with such mirth that everybody in the restaurant looks up. The mood has lightened. The evening, it seems, has been saved. We place our orders. Asparagus in an exquisite orange-flavoured mousseline sauce for you, followed by Norwegian salmon; for me, artichokes, and duck with prunes.

'At least tonight's crowd got value for their money,' I smile.

'George wasn't there,' you reply flatly; and suddenly we are back at square one.

'I'm sure no one regretted it more than he,' I plead.

You shrug, avoiding my eyes.

'You can't blame him, Rachel.' I reach for your hand on the table-cloth, but you pull it out of reach.

'He had a choice.'

'Coming at this moment, with everything that's happening on the West Bank, it was a chance in a lifetime for a photographer like George.'

'I didn't try to stop him.'

'But you didn't approve either, did you?'

'No, of course I didn't. How could I?'

'Your show – his assignment. It's a tough call for anybody.'

'Chris, there's not much point in discussing it now. We'll just have to get used to doing our things separately.'

'He was in this with you all the way. He worked with you every day, every night.'

'And when it mattered most, he went off.' In a shocking change of direction you ask, 'Do you think he has another woman?'

'Rachel, that is preposterous!'

'Did he say anything to you?'

'Of course not. Because I know for a fact that there was nothing to say.'

'Do you *know* that?'

'I know George.'

'I also thought I knew him. Now I am no longer sure.'

'How can you say that?'

You inhale deeply and look me right in the eyes. 'I asked an astrologer and she told me.'

'I don't believe it. This isn't a little game. You're playing with both your lives.'

'It's the same woman who told me last year that on New Year's Eve a broken-down car would bring a stranger into my life.'

'Pure coincidence. Rachel, you can't be serious.'

'I know what I know.' There is a set to your jaw that unnerves me.

'You'll have to get over this. And quickly.'

'Yes, Grandpa.'

That hurts, and I know you know it.

The rest of the meal passes in polite conversation. I wish I could go to my own home afterwards, but I owe it to George, and perhaps to you too, to stay over like the last time.

You clearly have the same misgivings. 'There is really no need for you to stay,' you say when we stop at your house in Camps Bay.

'I'll feel more comfortable if I do.'

'So will George,' you say. 'But is it really for the two of you to decide? Don't I have any say?'

'Now stop this nonsense!' I snap. 'You've done enough harm for one night.'

You gape at me: I have never been so sharp with you before. And rather to my surprise – and your own? – you turn contrite, take a deep breath and say in a small voice, 'I'm sorry. I didn't mean that.'

'It is still for you to say whether I should stay or go.'

A pause. Then you say, 'Please stay.'

Predictably, perhaps, it is a sleepless night, and I get up much earlier than usual – to find you already in the studio, not working, just having a quiet cup of black coffee in an armchair in the far corner.

You look up quickly when I come in, put the cup down and come to me, pressing your head against my shoulder.

'Can you forgive me?' you ask.

'Nothing to forgive.'

'Yes, there is. I was out of line last night.' A wistful smile. 'I think it's hormonal. But I don't want to hide behind easy excuses. What I said about George – do you think you can just pretend I never did? Please. I feel ashamed.'

'You were sad and unhappy and left in the lurch. Now you can make a new beginning.'

'A rather strange feeling.' You gesture towards the work table and the shelves where the sculptures used to be. 'They always kept me company. Suddenly it is very empty.'

'Nothing like starting again.'

Your eyes seem to narrow slightly. Perhaps in understanding? 'You must know a lot about that,' you mock. 'Does one ever get used to it?'

'Not really. But that isn't necessarily a bad thing. Every time there is a new challenge. Knowing that anything could happen.'

'Which could be bad.'

'It could also be wonderful. I keep hoping.'

'Doesn't one ever get too old to hope?'

'No.'

'I wish I could be so sure.'

'It's up to you, Rachel.' I put my hands on your shoulders. Strange, I think: today it is a purely paternal gesture. 'Why don't you start on a new sculpture today?'

'It's too soon. I feel depleted.'

'Try. Just to keep your hands busy.'

'Will that bring George back?' you ask without warning.

'George will come back by himself.'

'Do you think so?'

'I know it.' I press my hands tightly to your shoulders, then let go.

As I prepare to leave, you say behind me: 'You know, I think I discovered an important thing last night.'

'What was that?' I wait for it.

'I no longer need George.'

'Don't say that, Rachel.' I swing round to face you again. 'That is terrible.'

'It's not terrible. I don't mean it to be terrible. It's just — something I realised. I still love him, of course I do. I'll always be here for him, and I hope he will for me. But something has shifted. The *need* is gone, Chris. It's a lonely feeling. But I think I am free now.' However good you made it sound, it was like news of a death in the family.

* * *

THERE WAS AN uneasy awareness of death, too, in my homecoming from Europe in the mid-eighties. Not death in the family, this time, but the convulsions preceding the death of a whole society, an old world drawing to a close. Emotionally, mentally, I knew it was time to come back. But I had no idea of *what* I was coming back to. Initially, it was an unsettling experience of not being part of anything, of being no longer *there* but not yet *here*.

In many respects my life, certainly as a writer, was easier than it had been before I'd left. The weight of censorship which had pressed so crushingly on everyone involved with the arts had begun to ease up (certainly for those of us who were white; to be black remained a sorry fate). Books previously banned, including my own, were being unbanned. It was not so easy to discover the reasoning behind this. Some suggested that a regime headed by the unfortunate lump of flesh named P. W. Botha, whose mind was left uncontaminated as he was reputed not even to read newspapers, had lost its interest in writers and their nefarious preoccupations. Or had the government actually become sophisticated enough to realise at last that simply ignoring the possible subversions of books or their authors instead of drawing attention to them through various forms of persecution, was working to the advantage of the regime? Or was there a more plausible and more practical reason altogether in the fact that there were so many real dangers menacing the regime – from international sanctions and boycotts to resistance in the churches, in the univer- sities, in the new trade unions – that the SB had their bloodstained hands too full with urgent and immediate threats to worry too much about the arts? Whatever the reason, I no longer had to lie awake at night in fear of the infamous knock on the door at three in the morning.

Among Afrikaans writers, I must admit, I did not meet with any warm reception, as they seemed to regard me as something of a traitor for having chosen to write in English. But most others, particularly black writers, readily embraced me as a fellow combatant in the polit- ical struggle; and this made life much more manageable.

However, this was cold comfort. The situation was still dire, perhaps more than ever. It was, above all, chaotic and unpredictable – all the more so because of the erratic behaviour of a state president who seemed to be sinking steadily into dementia.

Inside the UDF, which I joined soon after my return and which had become the front for the still-very-much-banned ANC, there were flickerings of hope, glimpses of a better future already becoming visible through the infernal gloom of one state of emergency after another. Even if that future could be reached only through an apocalyptic blood-bath, which seemed to be the general expectation, it was no longer the utter impossibility it had appeared only a few years earlier. Delegations of business and cultural leaders, many of them Afrikaners, were beating a track to Harare, to Lusaka, to Dakar, to Paris and else-where to meet representatives of the ANC and start planning a shared future; there were rumours of the imprisoned Mandela initiating discus-sions with the regime. But on the surface there was a deepening gloom. There were protests and demonstrations; there were massive arrests, and deaths in detention. At one point the state president had to be almost forcibly prevented by one of his ministers from arresting a group of more than sixty leading Afrikaners on their return from Senegal.

I had no certainty about having made the right choice, coming back. In fact, more often than not, it would seem that I had acted like a bloody fool. And yet I never thought of giving up and going back to Europe. That was the one thing my years in London and Paris, my years of trav-elling in voluntary exile, had made clear to me: that *this* was where I wanted to be, and needed to be: and this was not something that required explanation. The country was like a woman I had to come back to. Not necessarily a woman I could live with, but a woman I could not live *without*: a woman I needed, beyond words, in order to know who I am. A woman like Helena had been, perhaps. With this difference: that this woman could not only be betrayed by me, but was also capable of betraying *me*. Hurting me and wounding me. Deeply. Yet never unforgivably. In fact, a woman who *needed* forgiveness as much as I needed it from her. Ultimately, I suppose, a woman who showed me that we both needed to be forgiven all the time − not just by each other, but above all, perhaps, by ourselves. And that was why I remained in the country. In my heart of hearts I had no choice. South Africa had become the only woman in my life I could not ever, finally, leave, because she would not leave *me*. Till death us do part.

Which does not mean that I'd come back to live happily ever after; or that I did not often doubt whether I was in my right mind, staying with her. There are some women, I am beginning to learn, with whom one stays *because* you are mad. And because you need to live with your own madness. End of message.

Even on the most personal front there were reasons to doubt the wisdom of my decision to come back, and then to stay. I made a few attempts to contact women I had known before. Once or twice it was not too bad. But there was something desperate about it. One should not, I began to think, go back to bodies you had loved, and left. A second wind in love is a rarity. But I refused to give up. Sometimes it would take something very small to swing the scales. I remember, from the very first day I returned, in the arrivals hall of what was then still Jan Smuts Airport, sitting down on a bench to get my bearings (I had deliberately not informed anyone of my return, not knowing what to expect, but also wishing to have some time for myself), and seeing a young woman in tight-fitting jeans and T-shirt stroll past. And from a little thing like that I would draw hope. The world was not yet over. There was life yet. There were still beautiful women around. I was still there. It was a point to start from.

There were some good moments: I remember Petro with the deep blue eyes whom I met with old friends in Sandton, where I remained for a fortnight before going on to Cape Town, and with whom, on the spur of the moment, I subsequently spent a wild weekend on the Wild Coast, a week before she was going to get married to a young tycoon. Only during our weekend did I get a fleeting hint of unresolved fears lurking behind her eyes; only in retrospect did I discover in the excesses of our couplings a desperate uncertainty, not just about her personal future with the young moneyman who was going to convert her into one of his many possessions, but about the future of the country: *Let us fuck and make merry, for tomorrow we die* . . . I recently learned that he is at the moment doing time in jail for embezzlement; at least he brought some members of his provincial government down with him. What has happened to Petro, has not been reported.

I also remember Kathy, whom I met in the wind at Cape Point above the raging sea and wrapped in my jacket against the unexpected cold, and then took back to my hotel where her nimble tapered fingers did wonderful things to my frozen nether parts, and who spent a week with me getting warm again, and only when she left told me she was married. Or the exotic Diana, whom I met in the lounge of a beachfront hotel in Sea Point one evening where she'd been dumped by an angry boyfriend, and who had the most unbelievable green eyes I had ever seen in my life; but who two days later, before she decided to return to the unworthy boyfriend after all, confided in me that she was wearing coloured contact lenses. No need to expand on these and other women of that whirlwind time. They were good moments, yes; but in one way or another, every single time, it was followed by disillusionment, the moment of wry or sad discovery that all was not as it seemed, all was not well, perhaps nothing would ever be well again – for them, for me, for all of us. The small deceits, the small lies, the small treacheries. Nothing important. Lives were not at stake. But the world, like the country, was not quite a good place any more.

Freckled Frances seemed to be an exception. By that time I'd been back for a couple of months. I had found a more permanent place to stay, a flat high up in Tamboers Kloof, not all that far from where I'm living now. I had a few invitations to contemplate – a lecture here, a festival there, a writer-in-residence somewhere else – and the early anxieties about what might await me, politically, socially, had dissipated. The SB seemed to have lost interest in me. And Frances struck me as a possibility of something more wholesome and long-term than the others I'd tried and tested since my return.

I had known her before. But as with Melanie – God, how long before? – there was unfinished business between us. And it seemed we were driven by instinct, if not by pheromones, once I was back in the country, for both of us simultaneously started putting out feelers, each about the other. The reason why, the first time round, our love had never been consummated was both simple and silly: at that time she had acquired a dog, a ridiculous little Maltese poodle, who for some reason couldn't stand me; and whenever we moved in the direction of her bed the creature would go crazy and jump on top of me and try to pull me off her (we could not attempt anything at my place, because she wouldn't leave the little mutt behind). Which was either so funny that we would collapse in laughter and lose whatever passion we had worked up, or I would fly into such a rage that I would try to murder it, whereupon she would start laughing at *me*. And before there was time to find the kind of obvious solution the situation called for, I had met Aviva in Johannesburg, and then I'd left. At the time, Frances had been in radio broadcasting. Now, with her striking looks, she had shifted to television where she was in charge of a quite prestigious programme in Cape Town.

I fondly thought of her as the Little Partridge. She was indeed as speckled as a quail's egg, but in a most alluring way. And I was captivated by her soft sweep of ginger hair, with a gleaming of copper and gold where the light touched it. Where her skin had been sheltered from the sun – her hard, small breasts, her compact, tightly packed bottom, the insides of her thighs – it was the rarest milky white with a hint of pale blue veins, delicate as eggshell. Her pubic hair was ginger too, a very thin, tentative, wispy haze, a mist of reddish down that barely fuzzed the slit of her neat little *filimandorus*.

And she was funny. I can remember how, on the way home from a film or a concert or a walk on the mountain we often had to stop, clutching a wall or a railing to recover from a bout of helpless laughter. She had the most boisterous, vulgar laugh, deep from her very guts, I have ever heard coming from a woman. She could set a whole theatre going once she started. More than once she was so overcome that she wet her pants, which she would then promptly kick off and leave behind.

Her wide, generous mouth was almost always smiling, as if life was a precious, hilarious secret no one else knew about. This was important for the small but emphatic part she played in my life. Because to understand how a woman like Frances could crack in a crisis, one must appreciate the enormity of the pressure.

Our first few months were a festival of unclouded joy. Then the crunch came. From the moment she came home from work that Monday afternoon I could see that there was something very wrong. But for a long time she evaded my questions in a way that just confirmed my suspicion more eloquently than anything else. Only when I had poured her a second generous drink did she say, staring into the depths of the red wine: 'I had a visit today. A rather unexpected one.'

'Who was it?'

'Two men. Sort of middle-aged. In sports jackets and flannels. Grey shoes. You know . . . ? I first thought they were funny, like caricatures of themselves. But then suddenly it was no longer funny.'

I could feel a bunch of very long, very thin fingers touching my scrotum. Not Kathy's kind of touch, with her tapered fingers. This was fear.

'You mean . . . ?'

'Security policemen. A Colonel Retief and a Major Stemmet.'

'And . . . ?' All this time since my return, I had thought that they'd let go of me, turned to other, more urgent business.

'They said they had photographs of us. You and me.'

'What kind of photographs?' My jaws were tight.

'You know.'

'But how . . . ? When . . . ? Where . . . ?'

'They didn't elaborate. Does it matter? It could have been that day on Signal Hill. You know, among the rocks, when we thought there was no one else. Or on the beach at Llandudno, when it was so cold.'

'There wouldn't have been anything to photograph. I must have shrunk to about two millimetres.'

'That didn't put you off.' For a moment she giggled. Then she took a deep breath. 'No, seriously, Chris. If you think of it, there must have been more than enough opportunity.' She fell silent. Bit her lip. Looked up again. 'It could even have been here, right here in your flat. A half-open window. A chink in the curtains. They don't need much, do they?' No hint of a smile any longer.

'But what's the point of it?' I asked. 'What did they want of you? We haven't done anything that could be of any use to them at all. So why . . . ?'

'All they wanted, they said, was for me to confirm that there has been a relationship between us.'

'So what? We haven't tried to keep it a secret.'

'That's what I cannot understand. They just wanted me to make a statement, and sign it, to say that we have been . . . "intimate". That was the word they used. Very discreet.'

'And if you don't?'

'They said they hoped it wouldn't come to that. "Think of the embarrassment," they said, "if something like that landed on the desk of someone high up in the SABC."'

'Blackmail.'

She shrugged impatiently. 'What's the difference? I'd lose my job, for sure.'

'And what would be in it for them?'

'I don't know. They didn't say.'

'It's pure intimidation, nothing else. They cannot get any mileage out of it at all. If either of us were married or something, yes. Not now. They're bluffing, Frances. Just call it. You have nothing to lose.'

'Except my job.'

'But it makes no *sense*! Nothing at all.'

'It seemed to make sense to them.'

'What did you tell them?'

'I said I had to think about it. They were quite understanding. Except they said they couldn't be kept waiting too long.'

'If they really wanted to, they could still use the photos — *if* they have any photos. So what difference would it make to have a state-ment in support?'

'I don't know, I don't know, I don't know.'

Already, I thought, it was beginning to have an effect; already it was beginning to seep in between us. They knew so well how to manage this. They had so much experience.

I asked her to wait. To try, if she felt up to it, to play the staring game. See who blinked first.

She agreed. But that night we did not make love.

A week went by without any move from them. A week without the sound of her laugh. We were just beginning to relax, assuming they'd accepted that they had overplayed their hand, and that would be it. But then they came back. The moment Frances came home that afternoon I knew what had happened. I didn't say anything, just looked at her. She nodded.

'Yes,' she said, clutching her glass of whiskey very tightly; her knuckles showed white through the taut skin. 'Yes, they came round again.'

'Anything new?'

'Not really. Except that I know now, for sure, that they have the photos.'

'How do you know?'

'They showed me. Only one. They took it out of a thick buff envelope. It looked like there could be ten or twenty inside.'

'Easy to pretend.'

'They don't need more than one.'

'What did it show?'

'Us.' The hint of a smile. 'Quite a funny one, actually, but I didn't feel like laughing.'

'Where?'

'Oh Jesus, Chris, does it matter? It showed us. Fucking. No doubt about it.'

'Photos can be faked. Everybody knows it.'

'Please try to sound intelligent. What do these things matter? They've got photos of us, they can do us harm. That's all there is to it. Isn't that enough?'

'Just calm down for a moment and think about it. Suppose all that is true. How can they really harm us?'

'My job, I told you before. They mentioned it again.'

'But why should *you* interest them?' I pulled myself together. 'I'm not trying to be deprecating or anything, Frances. But they are concerned – or supposed to be concerned – with state security. Where do *you* fit into that?'

'I am with you. You matter to them because you're a writer, you're an enemy of their system, they'll do anything to discredit you.'

'They used to be concerned about that. No longer. They've got tougher enemies now.'

'Perhaps they don't think the same about that.'

'So how will they discredit me by telling the world I've slept with you?'

'I've thought about it a lot, Chris. I can come up with at least one reason. They can push you to break up with me, or me to break up with you. It won't incapacitate you. But it would hurt you.' An almost unbearable pause. Then: 'Or wouldn't it?'

'Of course it would, for heaven's sake.'

'So by doing it they might just be applying the first bit of pressure to make you more careful in future. Not to be quite so hard on them and their system. For my sake. And if they carry on long enough, they can start discrediting you enough to pull your teeth. This Chris Minnaar is really just a compulsive womaniser. One cannot take too seriously what he says. Wine, women and song. He can be shrugged off. Even by well-meaning, serious people who have been reading you all these years. Or *especially* by such people.'

We talked deep into the night. There was only one possible outcome: Frances had to consent to their game. Draw up a statement, admit she had been 'intimate' with me. Sign it. And leave it at that. Of course they would hang on to it, keep it for whenever in the future they might find it useful. They might accumulate five, ten, twenty-five of these statements over the next months or years. And then . . . ? It was a chance we had to take. At least we still had each other, didn't we?

Or did we?

She didn't hear anything more from them. For all we knew, it might have been a bluff. But what mattered was that we did not escape unscathed. We could no longer make love, go to a restaurant, climb the mountain, spend a day at the beach, without wondering whether we were being watched by someone, hiding somewhere, someone who had an infinity of time at his disposal, but who might also pounce suddenly, when we least expected it. Pounce how? There was no way of knowing. And that was the point.

Frances, Freckled Frances, with the carefree smile and the indomitable inner joy, Frances was the first to crack. How could I blame her? All I knew was that the way ahead could only become more difficult, though I had no idea, then, of just how difficult that might be.

That was when I knew, for the first time since my return, with quite dazzling clarity: *I am home again.*

FROM THE DAY George returned from Palestine I had the impression that the turbulence at the time of your exhibition was over. As usual, he brought you a whole suitcase full of presents – not the obvious kind of object one picks up at the airport, but each of them clearly selected with great care, with love. (Just as his gifts for me showed the trouble and thought that had gone into the choice: a novel by a young Palestinian writer, Izzat Ghazzawi; a beautiful coarsely woven Bedouin cloth for the couch in my study.)

His account of his visit, of his nightmare experiences in Ramallah and Gaza City and Nazareth, was as dramatic as anything he'd ever told; his eye for the small human facts of everyday life remained extraordinary. Some of his anecdotes about the stratagems employed by Palestinians to avoid the constant Israeli raids or to pass through checkpoints, were reminiscent of stories from our own Struggle, of comrades evading arrest by the Security Police; and like the combatants from our anti-apartheid forces, he managed to clothe his tales in a downbeat humour which had us in stitches. But he could just as readily move us to tears.

He'd been present when the Israeli army moved in to avenge what they regarded as an act of intolerable defiance from an old man living on the edge of a village near Ramallah. Most of the olive groves in the area had already been destroyed by nocturnal raids ('because the soldiers knew that the whole of Palestinian culture and economy depend on the olive,' George explained); but this old man, half blind and in his eighties, still had a few trees in his backyard. So he'd put up a water tank on his flat roof to catch whatever little rain that fell. But he had not asked for permission to install the tank (he hadn't even known that official permission was required to catch rain on his own roof in his own tank for his own trees), and so the mighty army moved in with their mortar bombs and machine guns and reduced his little house to rubble. George showed us the photographs he'd taken of the old man sitting on a stone in front of what had been his home, his bearded face with the eyes half blinded by cataracts turned up to the sun.

'You see why I *had* to go?' he asked in the silence that followed. A rhetorical question, but I realised that it was specifically addressed to you, and guessed that his absence from your exhibition must have come up for discussion.

On the surface, it seemed to me that all was well again. That was until, a few weeks later, I helped him to put up a small exhibition about his visit which the Muslim Council had invited him to mount in the District Six Museum. Afterwards we went for tea. And that was when, without any prelude, he asked, 'Chris, do you think Rachel is okay?'

'Of course,' I said. 'Why?'

He put sugar into his cup and stirred it for a long time. 'I don't know. It's just a feeling.' He went on stirring. 'There's a kind of distance in her these days. As if she's not quite with me. As if she's holding something back.' He put the teaspoon down, but kept staring at it as if deliberately to avoid my eyes. 'Even when we're making love.'

I could feel the blood draining from my face. This was too intimate. 'I cannot judge about that,' I said evasively.

'Ever since I came back, Rachel is not the same,' he persisted.

'I've had the impression that the two of you are as happy as ever. She loved the presents you brought.'

There was an unexpected bitterness in his voice: 'Do you know what she told me afterwards, when we were alone in the bedroom?'

'What?'

'Nothing directly. But she just, without any reason, started telling me about her first trip to Europe, years ago, as a student. About the jolly Dutchman who drove their bus, all the way from Holland, through Belgium and France and Italy. He had the habit of buying presents for his wife in every town they came to. And when the students teased him about it, he used to say that it was his way of keeping her happy. "A present for every time I'm unfaithful to her," he used to joke.'

'She told you this about *your* presents?'

He nodded. 'There were no accusations. But why did she have to tell me that?'

'It could have been pure coincidence. She was probably just embarrassed about being showered with gifts like that. I know she missed you terribly.'

'That's not what I'm talking about,' he said testily.

'She did feel very bad that you couldn't be at the exhibition,' I said as non-committally as I could.

'She couldn't have felt half as bad as I did. But she knew it couldn't be helped.' He started stirring again. 'You think she still blames me?'

'Have you asked her?'

'I have. She ducks the questions. It has never been Rachel's nature to avoid things.'

'It may blow over.'

'You're not being honest with me, Chris,' he said. He spoke very quietly, but it made me cringe.

I still don't know why I came out with it like that, but I decided to meet his challenge and said, 'Is there another woman, George?'

He flushed a deep red, but it might have been from anger.

'What the fuck kind of a question is that?' he asked. He had difficulty controlling his breath.

'Is there?' I asked in desperation. Why had everything suddenly become so unbearably complicated?

'Is that what she says?' he asked. It sounded as if he was ready to burst into tears.

I took a very deep breath, knowing that this might ruin everything between us, for ever. Then I nodded.

'How did she . . . ?' He brought himself up short.

'She went to see an astrologer.'

He stared at me. 'You're not serious?'

I shrugged. 'You know Rachel better than I do.'

He started saying, 'But she . . .' Then stopped, with a helpless gesture. 'So she knows.' This was even worse than his initial show of shock.

'You mean it's true?' I asked.

He said nothing.

I couldn't say anything either.

He sat with his head in his hands. I wanted to put out a hand and touch him, but I couldn't. He was too far away, in a space where I could not reach him. And I felt sick about everything.

'It wasn't meant to happen at all,' he said. This time he made no attempt to hide his tears. 'I suppose it was the unbearable pressure we were working under. We literally didn't know from one day to another whether we were going to get out of there alive. And she was there too. A French photographer. She would go into the most dangerous places with me. No fear at all. Just rage, a rage so pure it was unsettling to see, like a white-hot iron. And afterwards, in Jerusalem, in the King David Hotel, just before I flew out again . . .' He looked at me as if crying for help. 'I didn't mean to, Chris. For God's sake, don't you understand?'

'It's not for me to understand.' I sat in silence, unable to touch my tea. Then I asked, 'Why didn't you tell Rachel?'

He shook his head. After a while he asked, 'Do you think I should?'

'I think it is most unfair of you to ask me, George.'

'I *am* asking you.'

'All I can say is that Rachel is not the kind of person who can live with a lie.'

'You're right.'

'Are you still in touch with . . . the other woman?'

'Danielle?' A long pause. Then he shook his head, but he was still avoiding my eyes.

'Are you serious about her?' I asked.

There was another long pause before he said, 'I was attracted.' Adding hastily, 'But I think it was the circumstances. I love Rachel. I swear I do.'

'It's not I who need your assurances.'

'You condemn me.'

'I don't. I am deeply sorry for you. But even more for Rachel.'

'You love her, don't you?' he asked unexpectedly.

'Yes,' I said, meeting his stare without flinching. 'Like a father.'

'An incestuous father.'

This was getting out of hand.

'That's a despicable thing to say, George.'

'It would be a despicable thing to do, don't you think?'

For some time I really didn't know what to say. I'd already betrayed your confidence by telling him about your visit to the astrologer. I thought of you, that evening when we discussed whether I should come to stay with you while he was in Palestine; and how you'd said, *Is it really for the two of you to decide? Don't I have any say?* I knew it was not so easy to get out of it; but I had taken my decision, for better or for worse.

'My love for Rachel, like my love for you, has never been anything to feel guilty about.'

He remained staring at me for a long time. At last, almost reluctantly, he sighed and said, 'Then I'm sorry for having thought what I did.'

The moment he yielded, I went on the attack. 'You'd rather hoped you would have something to accuse her of, didn't you? That would have made it easier for you, given you an excuse.'

Seeing the unmasked pain in his eyes made me feel lower than the proverbial shark shit on the bottom of the sea. Whatever happened after this, our friendship could never fully recover from what had been said between us. It was like losing a limb from my body.

After that – I have no clear recollection of time or sequence here – I still had to face you. We went for a walk along one of our old routes, the path winding from Kloof Nek above the Atlantic. George was working in his darkroom; he was the one who'd proposed the walk. With a hidden purpose to it? Nothing among the three of us was innocent any more. You were leading the way; from behind I was watching your easy stride, the motion of your body in the skimpy top, the frayed shorts, the sturdy walking boots. Alluring? Of course. Yet it was not as before. It no longer shortened my breath with desire to look at you. Something had indeed shifted, as George had said, and it was affecting not only him, but me too.

It was you, as I might have expected, who opened the conversation in your disarmingly forthright way: 'So you spoke to George?'

I was conscious of my own sharp intake of breath, but I did my best to play it cool. 'He asked. I couldn't avoid it.'

'Exactly what did you tell him?'

'About your astrologer. And your suspicion about another woman.'

'And he confirmed it.'

This was unfair, and I told you so. But you shrugged it off, with a hint of annoyance.

'I'm not trying to wheedle anything out of you. But you spoke to George about things that concern me, intimate things, and I think I have a right to know.'

I repeated what I'd already told you.

'What did you tell him about us?' you suddenly asked. 'You and me.'

'There was nothing to tell.'

You stared very hard at me, but said nothing.

'Was there?' I asked.

'Only you can decide on that.'

Dear God, what had become of us? Where were we heading for?

'I wish everything could be in the open among all three of us, like before,' I said.

'I don't think we can ever go back to that,' you said with quiet determination.

'That morning in your studio . . .' I began.

'There's no need to talk about it, Chris,' you said, your eyes becoming distant. 'Nothing happened.'

'I know nothing really happened, Rachel. Except in our minds. Or at least in mine. I don't know about yours.'

A long silence. The sea an unbelievable, Homeric colour below.

Then you said in a whisper, 'In mine too. And in a way it does complicate things, doesn't it?'

I couldn't think of anything to say.

You sat down on a large grey rock and stared out over the ocean so far below us. 'I agree with what you said,' you remarked at last. 'About how good it would be to go back to how we were. But can we ever, really? There are things one cannot talk about. One just has to live with them.'

'A loss of innocence?'

Her shrug looked like an expression of contempt, and I decided not to argue.

'What has happened, in all three of our lives, has happened,' I said at last. 'Nothing of it can be undone. What we should look at is the future. What to do next.'

'What do you propose?'

'I'm not a counsellor and I have no wish to be drawn into it.'

'You *are* in it, whether you want to admit it or not.'

You were right, of course. I remained silent for some time, then said, 'You and George have to find time to be together. Just the two of you. And not at home. Go away somewhere.'

'You think that will help?'

'I cannot think of anything else. You could of course go and talk to a proper professional counsellor.'

'What a bourgeois thing to do, Chris. Would *you* go for counselling?'

'I'm a writer. I provide my own therapy.'

'You used to be a writer. You are no longer.'

That bit to the quick. But I could see you didn't mean to be cruel. It was a simple truth, and I myself had said it often enough.

'Do you still love George?' I asked, with a suddenness that surprised myself.

'Yes, I do.' The briefest pause. 'But it is a sullied, wounded love.'

'Is there any other kind?'

'We shall have to see.'

We saw. Not immediately, for none of us spoke openly about it for some time. But early in December, when the two of you came over for a meal at my home – I had left the cooking to Frederik, and he'd done a splendid job – George made a low-key, matter-of-fact announcement over dessert: 'Rachel and I have decided to go away for a while over the Terrible Season.'

'Oh?'

'There's a resort in the Drakensberg,' you said. 'Guaranteed to turn old lovers into new ones.'

'I'll drink to that.'

'What will a wine for such an occasion taste like?'

I looked hard at you, forced a little smile, and avoided the challenge: 'Let's each make up our own mind. All I know is that I hope it has the capacity to mature.'

'Chicken.'

'At least this old chicken crossed the road and learned to survive.'

Once you had left, I wandered aimlessly through the house, without bothering to put on lights. Although I did not want to admit it, I was upset by the news of your holiday. For purely selfish reasons: I'd looked forward to a celebration for just the three of us. To recover, perhaps, some of our old camaraderie. And to commemorate, on New Year's Eve, our first meeting. Now I might have to join other friends, and I have less and less of a stomach for such things, especially if everybody is straining to make them seem festive. Then I'd rather stay home by myself. Not my preferred company either.

At least you wouldn't be away for too long: from just before Christmas to just after New Year. And I knew it was indeed the best thing by far you could do. Perhaps the beginning of a new year might restore some of the old hope.

And when you came back and I went to pick you up at the airport, you both seemed so relaxed that I felt convinced it had all been resolved. Over lunch the next day, you confirmed my impression; except that it was not the conclusion I had naively foreseen.

'Well, I know you want to know if the plan worked,' you made the announcement. 'George and I have sorted everything out.'

'I have a bottle of Veuve Clicquot on ice,' I said, pushing back my chair.

'Wait,' you stopped me. 'It may not be quite what you expected.'

'What do you mean?' I could feel my jaws go numb. I knew, from the way you said it.

'This one and I have decided to split up,' said George. I think he was close to tears, but he was smiling. So were you. I was the only one who cried.

MAM, THIS MORNING. I spent just over an hour with her, but she hardly spoke. Most of the time she slept, quite peacefully, it seemed. And I sat gazing at her as I have looked at so many sleeping women in my life. But this was different. All the others have come and gone. Some stayed for a night only, or a few nights, or not even a whole night; some for weeks or months, a few of them stayed for years. But in the end they went. Only Mam has always been there. Soon it will be a hundred and three years, if she lasts until August, which I am now beginning to doubt. Nearly eighty of those she has spent with me. That is an almighty long time. I know she has often wondered about me, sometimes despaired of me; she never thought writing was an acceptable occupation for a self-respecting person. But she has always *been* there. For better or for worse, in sickness and in health. Mam. Today she lay there, so unbelievably small, smaller even than before. From time to time she half woke up, smiled vaguely at me, but showed no sign of recognising me. This had never happened before. And when she spoke – a few random rambling sentences – she once addressed me as Father, and then as the doctor who had treated her for dyspepsia forty years ago, and then again as a woman I couldn't place. Quite, quite undone.

For years I have been expecting this to happen. Yet I still feel wholly unprepared. What distresses me is the prospect of losing touch with much of myself, of my own memories: that part which is invested in her and which will go with her. Most of all it is the simple fact of losing her which I find so hard to grasp. She has always been here: how can she, suddenly, *not* be here?

All the predictable questions and self-recriminations: Why had I not done more for her? Not just these last few years of incapacity, but right from the beginning. I knew how desperately unhappy she had been with Father, his infidelities, his arrogance, his cruelties, his hypocrisy; yet I had never showed much understanding. In the beginning I was too scared of him; later, after Bonnie, too angry. The strange thing is that if she really slips out of reach, I will have lost him too, irrevocably. Was it enough to have played chess with him, or to know he was standing on the sideline of a rugby match? What was he doing that long day on Uncle Johnny's farm when he withdrew into the bedroom to 'think'? Why did I not try to find out? It was easy to blame him for everything. But what have *I* done? Or not done?

There must be things about him I should have known or tried to know. Whence this need for cruelty and domination in him? Where did his insecurities – for that must have been at the root of much of it – come from? Had he really loved Mam? If so, why and how had it spilled out and gone away? And if not, what had really been behind his decision to marry her, this young girl not yet out of her teens, placed in his charge, rebellious, ultimately helpless?

What had driven him to be unfaithful to her?

And after his death, when she was set free, if that is what it was: what had driven *her*? Surely not revenge, a desire to offer tit for tat.

What has driven *me*?

Is there something essentially, constitutionally, wrong with us? Is there something lacking in our make-up as Afrikaners? How far back does it go in history? – this insecurity, this unresolved anger, this wretched need to prove ourselves? Or is it a human failing? Yet not all humans fall victim to it. Where have we failed them – we three as a family, and as a man, a woman, and again a man? Could anything have been repaired in time? Can anything still be repaired, now, at this late hour?

I sat there and sat there, and couldn't move. Partly because I was scared that if I went away it would really turn out to have been the last time. In an utterly illogical way I felt that if that happened, if I forsook her in this extremity, I would be ultimately responsible for her death. How can I possibly take responsibility for another death?

Even her lying there, so quietly that more than once I thought with a sudden onrush of fear that she had already died, became a silent accusation.

Mam. Mam. Mam. I looked at her, willing her to open her eyes, to acknowledge me. Yet if she had, what was there I could say, could do? Even a last sip of water, I thought, to moisten her sunken lips. What was there I could have said? *I love you, Mam*? What would that have meant? What does it mean? Have I ever really known? Have I ever cared enough?

Mam, Mam. I still couldn't move, staring fixedly at her wizened little monkey face which I could no longer recognise, awed by the silent, silent slipping away. Beyond my reach. So much in my own life, I now know, has remained beyond my reach. Starting with her, the first woman of my too-long life. All the others? Have I ever really known anyone? Have I ever understood anything?

'Mam.' She didn't respond, perhaps she hadn't even heard me.

I kept staring at her, willing her eyes to open, but to no avail. It is hard to understand this simplest of events: that a whole life can be reduced to such utter insignificance – everything she has heard, and said, and seen, everything she has tasted or felt, the wonders of the world, the bitterness she has outlived, what love she may have known, the pleasures of the flesh (those long-ago words: *I guess I have been blessed in that regard*), all of it shrunken now to this.

I tried, randomly, to recall moments she had told me about, but they didn't seem to add up to a whole. Her happy early years, happy because she was left alone to wander about on her parents' farm and to dream – about going to university one day, studying abroad perhaps, living life to the full. Frail and small she might have been, but she had will and passion enough for three. And then to find her married off at seventeen, to a man she hardly knew, just because her father couldn't cope with bringing up a girl-child with only a sickly wife to help him. All her dreams shattered in a blow. Instead, there were the demands and desires of a hard man, much older, to deal with. She fought against it; he treated her like a child or a small domestic animal, amusing and pretty, but not to be taken seriously. He'd awakened the passions of the body in her – at times they became so violent that she hid herself in shame; the very enjoyment she derived from love, made it suspect – but he had no regard for her other needs. In all fairness, his own harsh background, with – who knows? – another father straight from the Old Testament, had not prepared him to deal with such. All her bright dreams were turned inward on themselves, and soured, and became bitter and resentful. Her body itself seemed to revolt, in rejecting child after child until, out of sheer desperation perhaps, it brought her the son her husband demanded of her.

But it was not the stout Boer boy he had expected: this son was puny and squeaky, and had to be nursed by another; if he later learned strategies for survival – rugby, athletics, top position in his class, choosing law as a career – it was never quite what the father would have wished. And there was no hope of another chance: Mam's health was too frail to risk another pregnancy. Which meant no more marital relations during her years of precarious fertility. During which he found ample solace elsewhere (having already tasted it well before). But Mam? What recourse was there for her? To lock it all up inside, and feel rebellion surge and rage, but with no way of venting it – except through working for the Church, and feeding the poor, and leading the Women's Auxiliary, and cooking and sewing and knitting like a woman possessed.

Until, mercifully, he suffered his convulsive death on the prone body of his latest secretary. It was then that she turned to feeding – ever so discreetly – the pent-up passions of a lifetime on a few of the available and eager men from their circle. (Even of this I cannot be sure – it is hearsay, gossip, conjecture, perhaps wishful thinking.) I know that she received offers to remarry, but emphatically turned them all down. 'I can never get used to the smell of another man again,' was how she put it. One had been enough; too much. All she got out of it was a reputation. Stern men turning up with pious faces and blunt-nosed black shoes, solemnly to warn her, always in her own best interest, against the temptations of the world. She had to beware of jeopardising the proud Minnaar name, dragging it through the mud. The Church elder, the party stalwart: oh, do be careful, Mrs Minnaar, be careful, Madeleine.

In the beginning she took it all with demure submissiveness (though laughing her head off, with me, as she mimicked them after they'd left). Gradually she became angry. 'Why the hell should I listen to them? I know the lot of them. Most of them have women in the location on the other side of the golf course. Most of them get rich on the money of others, they even steal from the Church. They're like your good father, just a great deal worse. Nobody said a word about his philandering. They all looked up to him, envied him. But if I dare to go out with a man on a Saturday night, even if it is for a meal or a film, all the fingers point at me. Especially those I wouldn't be seen dead with. Or the ones I turned down. They can all go hopping sideways.' Then the unexpected wink accompanying the old line: 'I have a lot of catching up to do.' Both triumphant and sad. Rage, rage against the dying of the light.

And now, at last, the dying had begun.

While I was there beside the near empty bed with its tiny bundle in the middle, barely denting the pillow, I put my hand on hers. Unexpectedly she opened her eyes, an expression of bewilderment in them. With both hands she grabbed mine. She didn't say anything, I'm not even sure that she knew it was me, but she held me in her grip and would not let go. Holding on, it felt, to life itself. Holding on, in the face of hell itself. I thought of my own attempts at holding on, my writing, these notes I am so compulsively making. Impossible to let go, because all will then be lost.

She was mouthing something. I held my ear to her face. The voice was less than a whisper. All I thought I could make out, if that was what she muttered, was, 'I don't want to go, Boetie. I don't want to go. Don't let me go.'

Holding on. After a hundred and two years. What could unleash such ferocity? What was there in life that could possibly make it worthwhile to hold on so desperately? The mere need to be in touch, to reach for another hand, to escape the terror of being left utterly alone?

My own life again. All my women, all my loved and lovely women. Just part of this paroxysm of holding on? To touch the hand of someone else, to know that at least there's *someone*? To plunge into that small sheath of flesh, that little abyss, that shimmering darkness of beginnings and origins, to lose myself in the illusion or the hope of another? Poor, poor Don Giovanni. This hell, I think, is worse than the conventional one of fire and flames into which he was plunged. To be alone is unbearable.

'Goodbye, Mam,' I whispered in her ear. I could no longer handle it. I loosened the grip of her little claws from my wrist. I knew it might be the last time. It was worse than abandoning her: it felt like a betrayal.

I TRIED TO lead a more exemplary life after the shock I had with Frances. Not exactly monastic, but I avoided any real involvement with women, knowing now that it would expose me – and them – to unnecessary, probing attention. A few fleeting flings – I could not possibly become a total recluse – but nothing to remember. Some of their names found their way into a notebook, but none really lingered in my memory. The only exception was Abbie. She was something special from the moment she approached me for an interview after a reading I'd given at a college in Johannesburg. I invited her for a drink in my hotel room; she stayed for three days. The only reason why we emerged after that, was the discovery that she was also from Cape Town, up north on an assignment for her newspaper; which meant that we could fly back together and continue here in the south without a break.

After what had happened with Frances, we had to be very careful. Not just because of the constant surveillance, but because Abbie was coloured. At that time, the Immorality Act had lost its edge; as a result of so many mounting pressures, particularly from its own ranks, the government had started turning a blind eye. But that didn't mean we could do what we wanted (and we wanted, all the time): a charge under the practically defunct act could easily be laid as a simple strategy of intimidation, just to warn us that I was still being watched. It meant that she seldom stayed over at my house, even though we'd found a convenient alley through which she could approach, unseen, from the back.

We developed a very complicated system of communication. Two rings on her telephone would mean that she had to be at a particular public call box half an hour later; three sent her to another box. My own calls would always be made from a public telephone. We would meet at out-of-the-way places, and drive long distances to remote hide-outs. This cloak-and-dagger business became part of the adventure, exotic spice to the relationship. And Abbie loved it. Some of her plans made Huckleberry Finn's attempts to set Jim free look simple.

On the nights I spent at her flat, I would have to set out almost an hour in advance, taking the most elaborate precautions to shake off would-be stalkers. She would be even more circumspect in her approach. Which meant that by the time we met, we would both be so highly charged that we could detonate the moment my hand moved between her thighs, or hers between mine. She had the most eloquent fingers. Her tongue was a small wet lizard. Even her hair was articul- ate – long and black and dense, a rope fit for hanging, a most consum- mate death.

It was much more than sexual. While we were together, she put in an impressive effort to read everything I had ever written, beginning with *A Time to Weep*, the Sharpeville novel that had triggered it all, up to the most recent one, from which I'd done the reading in Johannesburg. Most flattering: but her intention was not to be a doting acolyte at all. She was invariably incisive and provocative in her comments; in particular, she could be scathing in her assessment of some of my female characters (especially those with the small breasts) – but she had the knack of doing it in such a way (rare in one so young: she was not yet thirty) that it did not rile me. We had endless discussions about the books: apart from the fiction itself, she was fascinated by everything that had gone into it. Where did you get the inspiration for this character? Is this episode based on fact? I bet you really loved this girl? Did this actually happen to you or to somebody else . . . ?

Intellectually, she was a constant challenge. And politically, she was a delight. Her opposition to apartheid was ferocious, born from the most personal experiences – of her parents whose early links to the SACP had landed both of them in detention for shorter and longer spells; of her older brother, who had left the country after 1976 for military training in East Berlin; of herself, who had been detained during the first state of emergency and humiliated and abused by her interrogators. She was the one who kept on at me: to do more, not to be content with writing as a form of opposition, but to get more 'involved'. As a political journalist, and within the UDF, she was someone to be reckoned with.

Abbie was tall and slim, a high-tension wire charged with electricity. Merely looking at her as she walked about naked in my house or in her flat, could make my knees tremble. She had the most perfect shoulders, her buttocks had the dimples of a little girl, her navel would have sent King Solomon into raptures about a round goblet which wanteth not liquor. She had the most charming love-mound, shaped for a cupped hand, with a small wisp of sleek, black pubic hair, a perfect little cowlick. Her breasts were topped with unusual, elongated nipples, almost purple in colour, and – it seemed – eternally erect. I was in Paradise.

And yet those were difficult times. As if it wasn't hard enough to avoid the constant surveillance, there were always 'things' to be done: to help comrades passing through Cape Town clandestinely to remain unnoticed, to put them in touch with the people who fabricated false passports and IDs and licences, to provide them with a place to stay overnight – never more than one night in one place.

From time to time I was tickled by an amusing memory: of Father, sheltering his far-right friends from the police during World War II. Now I was doing the same, at the other end of the spectrum. Perhaps we were not so different after all. I began to wish that I'd known him better. Now, as always, it was too late.

The end came very suddenly. Abbie was supposed to come over and spend the night, after a particularly tough week with 'customers', but at six that evening in October she telephoned to say, in our coded language, that 'the new chapter of the thesis will not be ready in time; perhaps tomorrow?'

Rather disconsolately, I spent the evening on my own, putting the final touches to the revision of a new novel. But it could not take hold of me, and in the end I put it down and went to bed with a book. Afterwards it took hours before I fell asleep. And promptly at three o'clock the front doorbell rang.

It was the wake-up call I had been expecting for years, but had begun to give up on. As I opened the door, six men burst in, crowding the whole entrance hall. I was in my pyjamas, which I would not have been wearing if Abbie had been there; they were in flannels and sports jackets, two of them in safari suits.

For the next four hours they ransacked every inch of the house.

'If you could tell me what you have come for,' I said after the first hour, 'I shall be happy to help you.'

'Don't worry, Mr Minnaar,' said the officer in charge, Captain Willemse, a sugar-coated threat. 'We shall know it when we see it.'

In the end they filled two wine boxes with letters, drafts of manuscripts, newspaper cuttings, notebooks. The only thing that really upset me was that they also took my only two copies of the new manuscript, *A Touch of Yesterday*. I used to be very meticulous about keeping copies of all my writings (I was still working with carbon paper), but lately I'd become rather more careless. Also, that evening I had set out the carbon copy for Abbie to read, and did not bother, when she couldn't come over, to put it away again.

'I hope it will keep you busy for a while,' I said as they prepared to leave.

Captain Willemse gave what I presumed was intended to be a smile. 'You will be coming with us, Mr Minnaar,' he said amicably in his broad Afrikaans accent. 'You may get dressed if you want to. But you will of course understand that one of my men must go with you. Just in case, you know.' He gave me a conspiratorial wink.

It was only four or five days later, during my solitary confinement, that the full horror struck me. Abbie. All those interminable questions about the background to my books. Her involvement with providing accommodation for our 'customers'. Her last-minute excuse for that night. I couldn't, wouldn't believe it. It was not possible. I had so unreservedly, unquestioningly, trusted her. For God's sake, I *loved* her.

But as my detention lengthened into weeks, the tenor of their questions and comments during interrogation made it clear beyond all doubt that they knew every minute detail of my recent life, most of which I hadn't discussed with anybody else at all. Only with Abbie. Betrayal never comes easy.

THERE WAS A curious interim, between 5 January when you and George came back from the Drakensberg, and your birthday on 28 February. Living in limbo. Decisions had been taken but had not been acted upon yet. George left for Kuwait only a few days after your return. You said the briefest of goodbyes while I waited at the door to take him to the airport. You did not come out to the car with us.

As I moved in next to George, I asked, 'Will she be there with you?'

'She?'

'The woman you spoke of.'

'Danielle?'

'Yes.'

'I'm not sure yet.'

'There's no need to lie to me, George,' I said. 'Just say you don't want to talk about it, or anything else. But don't lie.'

'I really don't know. I haven't tried to set up anything.'

We drove to the airport in silence. As I stopped in front of International Departures, he suddenly put his hand on my shoulder. 'I'm so sorry about all this, Chris.'

'So am I,' I said gloomily.

'I had never meant this to happen.'

'You could have avoided it.'

'Are you blaming me?'

'Yes.'

He took a deep breath. 'Will you look after Rachel for me?'

I looked straight ahead. 'No. I will look after her, but not for you.'

'You don't have anything to say to me, do you?'

'What is there to say? All our lives are falling apart.'

'Not yours.'

'What would you know about that, George?'

I did not mean to be hard on him. But I could not help myself. Everything inside me was in turmoil: but was that enough reason to turn my back on someone who had become so dear to me? For all I knew we might never see each other again. If that bloody war in Iraq materialised . . . But it seemed so far away, so unreal. (As it still does, and even more so now, in spite of – or because of? – the nightly spectacle.) And he seemed just as far away, even though he was sitting next to me. What had happened? What was happening?

'There is a single thing I'd like to ask you,' he said.

'What is that?'

'I know you are blaming me for a hell of a lot, and I suppose I deserve it. But is there one thing I have done which you have never done, or would not have done?'

I had no answer to that. What choked me, as if a hand was tightening around my throat, was the question whether my obsession with you had so blinded me that I could no longer recognise or acknowledge a true friend? Was this the real reason – that in turning against him, I was really blindly trying to condemn myself, expressing all the fury against myself that I'd been accumulating all my life without even being aware of it? I remembered something you had said the very first time I'd had a meal with the two of you, something to the effect that nobody ever blamed George for anything. Now everybody was, I more than anyone else.

'I'm sorry, George,' I said at last, and gave him my hand. 'I have behaved despicably towards you.'

'We have all three been through a rather bad whirlpool,' he said. 'Let's not dwell too much on that, but try to go on.'

'Please come back,' I said, trying to contain the sudden surge of emotion. 'In the meantime, take care.' I really meant it.

And then he went into the building, and I have not heard from him since. I don't even know if he is still alive.

On the way back to Camps Bay I stopped at the top of Kloof Nek and sat there for a long time, looking out over the city on the slopes below me, down to the sea. I did not know how I would face you. All I knew was that it had to be done.

You were surprised to see me.

'I thought you'd go straight home.'

'Too empty.'

'There's no need for you to sleep over now,' you said.

'I know. But tonight . . . Just to help you over the threshold.'

'Is it for my sake or for yours?' There was a touch of mockery in your voice.

'I have no doubt that I need it. I was hoping you might too.'

You nodded, then gave a pensive little smile. 'Thank you, Chris. I appreciate it.'

You made a simple salad for supper. Tomatoes and mozzarella and basil leaves. Neither had much to say, but we were reluctant to go to bed.

'It will take some getting used to,' you said after a long silence. 'I mean, George being gone.'

'His stuff is still here.'

'We agreed he could leave it. Until he comes back. *If* he comes back.'

'George always comes back.'

'It's different this time.'

'I'm afraid so. Now it's only the two of us.'

It sounded portentous; I hadn't meant it that way. I sat looking at you; you went out towards the night-blackness beyond the dark balcony, where the bars faintly caught some light from inside. There had been other nights too, I thought, when we two had been alone. But not like this, because in the back of our minds there had always been George.

Now only you and me, woman and man. And space; and time, lots of time.

I thought then, as I remember now, that I had seldom seen you look quite so beautiful.

When we went to bed later, you to your bedroom, I to mine, it was still unresolved. It did not concern something that might have been and now was lost; for perhaps it had never been possible at all. I know for certain now, that the love I felt for you in the silence that followed George's departure was one of the purest feelings I have felt in my life. Without desire.

And nothing of this changed during the weeks that followed. Occasionally I spent the night at your place, usually for a pre-arranged meal, or an impromptu drink, or when you phoned to say you'd seen some unsavoury characters loitering in the street above and felt apprehensive. A few times you even came over for dinner at my house and then slept over, in the spare room. Frederik always found a small bunch of flowers – nasturtiums or delphiniums – from the garden for your bedside table. Otherwise we led our separate lives. After a few weeks you even started working, tentatively, on a few ceramic sculptures again. There was nothing 'wrong' with them, not technically, but nothing striking either; and some time afterwards you destroyed them all. As for me, I felt as far removed from writing as I'd been for the past eight years. Yet we both dutifully promised each other that we would start again, soon, soon.

I began to make preparations for your birthday well in advance. We would drive out to Franschhoek and have a quiet but classy celebration there at Haute Cabrière. I took a small painting from my bedroom wall and wrapped it for you: a Czech primitive, which I'd had for many years and which you'd loved at first sight. And a French perfume which I knew, by now, you liked. And a book on last year's big Picasso/Matisse exhibition in Paris. And a long dark green skirt which I was sure would suit you perfectly. I couldn't wait to spoil you.

But on the morning of the 28th you phoned to say you couldn't go.

'What has happened, Rachel?'

'Nothing. I just can't go. I don't feel right. One cannot celebrate if there is nothing to celebrate.'

'It is your birthday.'

'I'm thirty-seven instead of thirty-six. There's nothing memorable about that.'

It was clear that nothing would change your mind. Instead, I proposed that I'd come over and make dinner there, which we could have quietly, privately, by candlelight. I could sense that you were still reluctant. But at last you accepted, even though I suspected that it was more for my sake than for yours.

I drove to Camps Bay by mid-afternoon and set to work in the kitchen. On your insistence, it was nothing elaborate, but still needed some attentive preparation. We interrupted the cooking for the presents to be opened. You fell in love with the skirt, as I had hoped you would. And promptly stripped down to your bra and tiny white knickers before me, to try it on. I briefly felt an old, familiar flush come over me. I went over to you and kissed you. For a moment you hesitated, then you kissed me back. You briefly rested your head against me; looking down I noticed, almost absently, as once before, the streaks of grey in your hair, added like an afterthought. Then you deftly twisted out of my reach. But you laughed, and I saw light in your bitter-chocolate eyes.

Minutes before I was ready to dish up, you discovered that you had run out of cigarettes.

'Can't it wait?' I asked.

'No. It will only be a minute anyway. Just up to the little supermarket.' Your smile was suddenly generous and carefree. 'Where I found you that first New Year's Eve, remember?'

How could I not remember?

I offered to go for you, but you were adamant that I should remain to keep an eye on our dinner in the kitchen.

You kissed me again, a wise little kiss on the cheek, that left me light-headed. You skipped out of the kitchen. I heard the tinkling of your keys as you picked up the bunch from the small table in the hall. Heard the front door slam and your car pull out. And heard no more at all.

MAM DIED YESTERDAY. The old-age home telephoned just after four in the afternoon. I don't know whether they meant to be considerate, or whether it was sloppiness, but by the time I got there she – now referred to as 'the deceased' – had already been taken away by the undertakers. My last visit had turned out to be a farewell. Perhaps it is better that way.

The matron was eager for me to remove her 'effects'; I had the impression that they already had someone else waiting to occupy her room, although all her fees had been paid until the end of the month. The formidable woman appeared upset when I told her I would come back in a week or so, but she could not very well have pressed me to hurry up.

I asked to be left alone and sat in the room by myself for some time. The empty space was oppressive. I felt like an intruder, although I'd come to know that severe, pale green room so well over such a long time. Absence can weigh more heavily on one than presence. The place still smelled of her. Yardley's talcum powder, some cheap scent (I'd often bought her perfume, but she never used it and persisted with what she'd been using for nearly a century), mothballs and pee.

Every time I tried to think of Mam, you were the one who came back. It was perhaps not so baffling: it is with such intense concentration that I have been avoiding that morning in the hospital. I am still not ready for it, although I know the time is fast approaching. What I have been writing in these notes over the past month – it is just about a month now, since the outbreak of the war – has been as much a grasping at straws from the past as an avoidance of that terrifying moment. Everything I have written has been penned by virtue of that silence which I have tried to postpone for as long as possible. Even now. Especially now.

The matron interrupted my thinking with a cup of tea. Was it an act of kindness or a gentle reminder that it was now time to go?

I stayed. I have age on my side.

Much later, without bothering to tell the matron I was leaving (in case she tried again to persuade me to clear out the room), I went out through the side door and drove to the undertaker's place in Woodstock. A run-down old Victorian building with flaking paint and graffiti on the walls. It was already closed but there seemed to be movement inside, so I knocked. There was no response, but I distinctly heard something. I knocked again. This time a small shutter in the door was opened and a disembodied red eye looked out. Then heavy bolts were drawn and the door was pulled open from inside without anyone appearing. It was a Dickensian encounter. In the dusky passage stood an unbelievably thin, cadaverous man with a completely bald head, like a shiny pink skull. His feverish eyes were ringed in red, and he had no eyebrows. He was dressed in a very old black suit, with a wilted white carnation in the buttonhole and some remains of his lunch on his lapels.

'You are too late,' he said in a low, half-mournful, half-accusatory voice. 'We are closed, sir.'

'I'm sorry,' I said acidly. 'I should have asked my mother to die earlier.'

'Oh.' The disapproval on his miserable face was displaced by professional commiseration. 'My condolences, sir.' He put out an inordinately long bony hand. The fingers were cold. 'Now who might be your late mother?'

'Mrs Minnaar,' I said sternly. I gave him the name of her old-age home. 'You collected her before I had time to see her off.'

'Oh dear.' He sighed, emitting a blast of very old, very cold air. 'That is most untoward.'

'Very,' I agreed.

'Come through,' he said, as if inviting me to a beheading. 'I was just busy with a cadaver. Excuse me.'

Involuntarily, I thrust the hand with which I'd greeted him into my pocket and tried to wipe it. For a moment I had a sickening present-iment that the cadaver he had been working on might be Mam's; and

I wondered, obscenely, what his 'business' with the dead entailed. Perhaps he had a solemn habit of fucking his corpses to see them off. He took me past a closed door on the right, behind which I thought I could hear movement. It could be an assistant finishing off his job on the cadaver. Unless his business on the corpse had been so invigorating as to have revived the dear departed. In this place anything was conceivable.

But the *chapelle ardente* to which he led me was less intimidating than he'd led me to expect. It was gaudily decorated, with plastic flowers and fake electrical candles, like a Christmas gone wrong. There he made me wait while he went to a room at the rear, and after a while he wheeled in a trolley on which lay a very small bundle covered by a stained sheet.

Again he said, 'Excuse me, but I wasn't expecting you, so I haven't had time to do her yet.'

Thank God, I thought; I wouldn't like to see her after he'd done her. As it was, I didn't think I'd want to see her at all. I had already taken my leave a week ago, and she'd been dead enough for me then.

I placed my hand on what I presumed to be her head, like one of Aunt Mary's small gem squashes, through the sheet; but drew it back. It was so cold, from the refrigerated room in which she had been meekly awaiting her turn. I remember, on Uncle Johnny's farm, the cool room behind the kitchen, where all the meat and milk and butter were kept. The outside walls had been covered with a netting of chicken wire, holding in place a layer of small charcoal pieces, watered down once a day to keep it cold. That would have been a good place to keep one's dead waiting to be 'done', or for eventual resurrection; I was grateful for not having thought about it at the time.

'If you don't mind,' I said, 'I'd rather not look at her again.'

'A man needs closure, sir,' he said in a prissy sort of way, with solemn emphasis. 'But it is entirely up to you.' (Your own choice, his demeanour suggested: heaven or hell.)

'I prefer it this way. I have already said goodbye. I just came to discuss the arrangements with you. I'd like to have her cremated.' (I couldn't help shuddering; it was like a macabre lunch order: I'd like her parboiled – sunny side up – well done – crisp on the outside.)

'I see.' He seemed genuinely disappointed, but resigned himself to the inevitable with what must have been encrusted grace.

Half an hour later (nothing could hurry this man, acclimatised to death and eternity), I left again, having this time pointedly overlooked his outstretched bony hand. I drove around in the deepening winter dusk for more than an hour, unable to face the silence of my house. (Frederik would be in his cottage, but I would not want to disturb him.) When at last I returned home, I went to the study and poured a glass of port, but took only a single sip. *Peach and elegant toasted oak* ... Then put it down, almost with distaste, and just remained sitting. I did not even attempt to smoke. Since the night of your birthday when you'd gone out to buy cigarettes and did not return, I have definitely given up smoking. I just sat, through the night, a very silent wake. *Sometimes I sits and thinks and then again just sits.* I may well have dozed off from time to time, but I was not really conscious of what was happening. Perhaps I was already drifting away slowly, like Mam. None too soon.

In the morning, this morning, I drove away. Inasmuch as I had any thoughts in me, I felt the impulse to drive to Camps Bay, to resume my silent sitting in your studio. But I could not do that. Moving from one death to another. I drove on, the long way round, to Cape Point. It was not a conscious decision, but I suppose I felt a need to find myself at a geographical extremity. Although I knew, of course, that this was not the southernmost promontory of Africa, it looked like an ultimate outcrop, it had the feel of an end and an ending. Hard earth under me, sea in front of me, sky above. Only fire was missing, but that I could supply from my mind, where Mam already burned. I needed this elemental severity, the cleanness and unclutteredness of it. The absolute aloneness of the moment, made even starker by the turbulent weather. A cold, blustery wind, masses of dark, banked cloud, a restlessly heaving and crashing sea, blue-black, wine-dark, with the smell of all the women I have known in my life. Years ago, on this same spot, I had met a girl in the wind. What was her name? Kathy, I think. Yes, Kathy. Today there was no one. But the urge remains. Always the urge to return from the dead to the living.

Now I am back. I haven't worked on these notes for days now. It is time to take them up again. *A man needs closure, sir.* Yes. Let us set to work on our cadavers.

THE DESPERATE NEED to find a human face in war. For several nights now, in between the spectacle of destruction and carnage and madness, there has been footage on the twelve-year-old Iraqi boy Ali Ismail Abbas who lost most of his family — father, pregnant mother, brother, aunt, three cousins, three other relatives — in the war. He also lost both arms. From a landscape far beyond emotion he stares into the camera. Not understanding. That above all. Not understanding.

But is this really for the sake of the human face, or is it just a huge propaganda coup aimed at the hearts and minds not yet petrified with cynicism or shattered by violence? Is it not yet another form of betrayal, more subtle than the war, but in its own way more deadly?

WHAT FOLLOWED MY betrayal by Abbie — the solitary confinement, the interrogations, the threats, the sounds of beating and screaming from elsewhere in the building, the pangs of hunger, the release at last — was of decisive importance for my life; but not necessarily for my relations with women. And so I shall not dwell on it here. It was hell: that is the short description. Yet I tried to fall back on what I'd learned during my years abroad, all the little strategies of survival, of not losing my bearings, of trying to make the best of even the worst situation. It turned out to be much more excruciating than any simulation Siviwe and the other instructors in Paris had ever conceived. In the long run (and thank God it turned out to be not such a long run after all, six weeks; otherwise I might not have made it) my salvation lay, not in anything I had been taught or trained to do, but in a device of my own, derived from writing.

I imagined myself in a story, in a play. That imposed a distance between myself and what was happening to me. Taking that one step back to observe myself, as it were, as over the years, even in the most intimate moments, I had always been conscious (often infuriatingly, sometimes desperately) of a double vision – for argument's sake: me, here, making love, moving towards the climax; but at the same time, me, there, observing, reminding myself to remember this, not to forget that. And sometimes, literally, making notes afterwards.

It was less unsettling, more constructive, in prison. In the beginning, in Caledon Square, where I spent the first ten days; and afterwards in Oudtshoorn, where I was taken one night – undoubtedly the worst part of the whole experience, as a hood was drawn over my head and face (there was the constant fear that I might suffocate), so that I had no idea at all of where I was going. It was only when they released me at the end of it, without prior warning, and simply turned me out on the streets, without any information about where I was, with no money, filthy (I had not been allowed to wash or change my clothes for six weeks), half hallucinating from loss of sleep, that I painfully established my whereabouts. At least it kept my imagination going by imagining the lives of the two-dimensional characters who brought me food or interrogated me, to devise a plot into which I could insert them, to find plausible solutions to an utterly implausible situation. There were times when I faltered; times when I felt so totally forsaken that it was as if my whole world was caving in on me. But I battled with every pulse of energy I could summon, not to lose my grip altogether, not to let them have their way, not to give in. Every fibre of my body was taut with the memory of Antigone's eternal cry: *No. No. No.*

When I was not working on the fabrication of my own story, I lay on my bunk bed or on my cell floor, or sat when I could, or stood when I was ordered to, often for uncountable hours, trying to turn my memories into narrative. Most intriguingly, most successfully, my memories of women. Rather than lament the loss of all I had known, I tried to reimagine every love that had ever come my way, trying to discover the structures and sequences, the moments of illumination, the set pieces as it were; but also the lesser moments, the links and bridges – between one woman and another; between the different memories that constituted a single woman. Her looks, her sounds, her touch and smell and taste, her face at the moment of orgasm or in sleep, or simply relaxed, or tense with expectation, or flushed in anger, convulsed in laughter.

Inevitably, much of my time went into rethinking the relationship with Abbie. In the beginning I recoiled in revulsion and refused to dwell on it. But I could not possibly evade it. Her betrayal became the point of convergence of so many liaisons of my life. Betrayals committed by others, and most excruciatingly (often even unwittingly) by myself. Only, hers was worse because it was so flagrant, and all the more so as it was so completely unexpected. I had trusted her all the way. How could she, a coloured woman, have been lured into infiltrating the UDF and spying on us for the apartheid government? Endless questions, all futile. All that mattered was the stark fact of it. This was what, after days and nights of searching all the recesses of my mind and memory, brought me to make some kind of peace with it. I couldn't ever forget it; if one day in the future I ran into Abbie again, I might yet explode in rage and feelings of revenge. But as time went by, I remembered it no longer as an unnatural or incomprehensible act. On the contrary, it became all too familiar, domesticated. Betrayal was woven into the tapestry of my time, my country. Look at me, I thought: here I am, the outcome of the history and the space of this land. Every turn and convulsion and shiver of history over the last century, I could mark with the memory of a woman. I bear them upon my body like scars and bruises – from the Great Drought that brought Katrien to my bed, past Anna in the elections of '48 to Abbie in the convulsions of the present states of emergency.

Through Abbie and her betrayal I reached out towards all those who had preceded her. I tried to be as precise in my memories as I could: Katrien's wriggling warmth; Driekie among the sandpapery fig leaves, the red stains left by my hands on her thin white thighs; Daphne's crazy dance in the moonlight; Bonnie thrashing her head to and fro on the office floor; Melanie covered in sea spray; Helena in her Madonna pose, holding little Pieter's small naked body against her after they had come from their bath and I approached them with a soft white towel to wrap them in; Marion on the beach by moonlight, and in the harsh morning light at the door to her parents' bedroom; Nicolette on a Paris morning in a shaft of sunlight; Tania naked in a wine barrel in

Bordeaux; Nastasya Filippovna as white and still as marble in death, with the fly buzzing over her bare foot and prone body under the sheet to settle at her head . . . Enough to feed on for a lifetime, let alone six weeks.

Being in solitary confinement actually made it easier. *Hell is other people*. Not that I myself was necessarily good company – I was not even strictly predictable; often in those days I discovered with horror, but never without some fascination, that I had become, or had always been?, a stranger to myself – but it was preferable to the irritations, the invasions, the depredations, the sheer boredom of the company of others. Which was something my captors had not bargained for; I did not readily respond to any of their meticulously assembled stereotypes. Also, I was no callow youth. Two months earlier I had turned sixty-three (what a birthday celebration Abbie had laid on for me, the little traitor). I'm sure I wasn't indulged in any way because of my age or – shamefully – the fact that I was white (that had not prevented them from murdering Dr Neil Aggett not so long before); but it might just, at least occasionally, have prompted some tiny forbearance in one or other of my tormentors. Most pertinently, I had by then seen enough of life to be at least in some measure prepared for whatever they could come up with. How many scenes of detention, incarceration, torture, even judicial murder, had I described in my books over the years? It was almost salutary to compare my fictions with these new, lived facts. Material for a new book . . . ?

Certainly, being there, being held by them, was in some ways easier to bear than the long years of constant anticipation and fear, all the maddening questions about when it would happen, and how it would turn out. Here, at least, my life was clear and hard and circumscribed within the four dirty walls of my cell. Even the graffiti on them were a source of entertainment and intrigue.

But this makes it sound almost flippant, far too easy. There were indeed days, hours, moments when I came close to breaking. If only they had known. But the last vestiges of some kind of savage pride helped me to conceal it. Another month, another week, perhaps only another day, might have taken me beyond the point of no return, beyond the thin red line the Americans in Iraq were so obsessed with;

but something was working in mysterious ways to ensure that they stopped short of the *coup de grâce*, without even realising it themselves. And so I was decanted on an unmercifully white-hot day on the streets of Oudtshoorn, shaken, but not broken. I found my way to a bookshop where I could count on being recognised (even in spite of my filthy and dishevelled appearance), and ask for help, and be offered a temporary home to sleep, a friendly place to recover in, eventually even a lift to Cape Town.

What had made them give up? They could so easily have kept me for a year; for however long it pleased them or their mad master. I heard afterwards about protests and petitions, not just locally, but by PEN, by Amnesty International, by publishers' associations in Europe and the US. But that neither guaranteed nor explained anything at all. In the past such actions had often had the opposite effect. It is more likely that the delicate negotiations the imprisoned Mandela and the apartheid government were engaged in at that very time, without anyone outside as yet suspecting it, might have contributed to a general softening of attitudes. I still have no way of telling. I don't even know whom to thank. I had my life to get on with. I had a book to finish (my manuscripts had been restored to me soon after my liberation); I was a driven man. Before the end of the following year – that momentous year when the demented old emperor was laid low by a stroke and his eager successor, desperate to shake off his right-wing reputation and become the blue-eyed playboy of the Western world, prepared to mount the horse of change already saddled by others – the drastically rewritten *A Touch of Yesterday* was published. Then, for the first time, I could catch my breath. Then, for the first time, I realised just how exhausted I was.

It was in that state of exhaustion that I met Andrea.

DURING THE YEAR between my release and the publication of my book at the end of 1989 I had lived as close to a monastic life as I knew how – an experience I should never wish to repeat, although, ironically, I believe it did me some good. There were a couple of brief and superficial encounters, but after having been bitten by Abbie I was too diffident about any real involvement; and one of those, with the blonde Jessica, ended dismally in a humiliating show of impotence, after which, despite her eagerness to help me through it, I was too crestfallen for some time to try again. But with Andrea, wholly without warning, the old frisson of the spine was there again. For that very reason, remembering Abbie, I held back. Not again. It was, however, such an extraordinary time, those last months of 1989, that I could not steel myself for long. It was the time of the great marches. With P. W. Botha out of action, hopefully for good, there were massive demonstrations all over the country, an outbreak of wild enthusiasm for a new beginning – fired, indeed, by what had been happening in Europe, in Prague and Warsaw and Budapest and Leipzig and Berlin. Everybody took to the streets, in a local re-enactment of the '68 student revolts all over the world, when – however briefly – all the old clichés and rules and taboos were swept away by youth and rage and joy.

That was how we met, in the first great march in Cape Town, thrown together by the frenzied, jubilant crowd, when suddenly nothing seemed far-fetched any more. The same flame which has illuminated every new love in my life – that moment of elation, of discovery, of acknowledgement, of celebration – was burning in that march, and in all the other outbursts of public passion that followed. And, out of the blue, Andrea was in it with me. One moment there was just the exuberant jostling of the crowd; the next she was right beside me, striding along – Andrea never walked, she strode with long-legged ease and conviction. We were swept up in song, we waved our arms and shook our fists – *Amandla! Amandla ngawethu! Viva! Viva! Viva!* – in a wave of joyful madness that made me feel fifty years younger. At some stage we discovered that we were holding hands. And later, after the seething streets had come to rest under the benign and unshaken mass of the mountain, we were washed out by the day's waves in the small cottage where she lived in Observatory.

She made something to eat – curried chicken, I seem to remember – and we drank much too much cheap red wine, and laughed and talked into the night. (Through all these years, the relationships that stand out have been those in which we could travel through days and nights in conversation.) We did not go to bed; I don't think it even occurred to either of us. There was too much to catch up with. And she was so beautiful that I felt it was, for the moment, enough just to look at her: those very dark wide-apart eyes with an almost Oriental slant to them, her long dark hair (she told me of the battle, every weekend in her childhood, to strain it into curlers), her tall lean body, her long legs, her bewitching hands. She was in her late thirties, with all the radiance of a fully mature woman happy in her body.

Perhaps the trigger was the discovery that she, too, had lived abroad, in France, in Paris. For something like eight years. I listened spellbound – she was a wonderful storyteller (a gift she got from her fisherman father, she said) – to her account of those turbulent years, the early ones of which actually overlapped with mine. There was nothing strange about our ways never having crossed there. 'I just didn't want to have anything to do with South Africans those days,' she said. 'I'd run a mile to avoid them. Even after I shacked up with a South African. He was a writer too, like you. Paul Jordaan. Quite a name, I found out, especially in the film world. But he steered clear of politics, which suited me, because I'd had enough of that.'

She had left the country, it transpired, with a young English lecturer at UCT with whom she'd had a passionate affair. But then they were caught for Immorality: Andrea was brown. They wanted her to testify against her partner – Brian, if I remember correctly – but she refused, even when they threatened her with prosecuting her younger brother, a very angry young political activist. In the end, presumably because of pressure from the British Foreign Office, Brian was deported and she was given an exit permit.

She told me a harrowing story of their last journey from Cape Town to the airport in Johannesburg. The agony of saying goodbye for ever, which was what she believed it to be at the time; the numbness of rage and pain which made her take her leave of everything she saw along the way, everything she had ever seen, or heard, or smelled, or touched, or tasted. And then the sad, slow crumbling of their relationship, once they were safe in France. Their desperate lovemaking. 'The thin man with the big cock,' was how she described him.

'He just wanted to get deeper and deeper into me, to be more and more violent, to hurt me more and more. As if that would vindicate everything. I once told him – that was the lowest blow of all – that he'd never cared about *me*, he'd only started the affair with me to strike at the underbelly of apartheid.' She shook her head. 'Poor Brian. He really meant well, you know. He just couldn't take the pressure.'

'And then you met your writer?'

'Quite a few years later. I tried my best to avoid him, precisely because he was South African. But –' she gave an eloquent shrug – 'in the end I gave way.' She sounded almost apologetic. 'He was a wonderful lover. But you know what . . . ? I think he never really knew anything about love. The only thing he ever loved was his writing. His films.'

'That is a terrible accusation.'

'But it's true, I promise you.' A long, searching look. 'Do you think all writers are like that?'

'There's only one way to find out,' I said lightly.

'Oh no.' She smiled, but I could see she was very serious. 'I shall never have anything to do with a writer again.'

I took the blow in the balls; but there was so much about her that captivated me, and all I knew was that, particularly after the relatively lean years I had behind me, I wanted to be with her.

'How did it end with your Paul?' I asked. 'I'm fascinated by beginnings and endings.' These were the two questions that always intrigued me most: *How did it begin? Why did it end?*

'Well.' She seemed to think it over before she answered: 'Paul was pushing me to get married. And I knew my time for having children was running out: I was just turning thirty then and didn't want to put it off for too long. And I really *wanted* children. Lots of them. But I knew that if we got married, I would never again have the choice of coming back here. Before that, I never thought I'd come back; but it was my choice. Now my throat seized up at the thought of never having a choice again. You must remember, those were very dark times.'

'So you decided to give up the children and rather come back?'

She shook her head very emphatically. 'It wasn't as easy as that. No, what happened was that I met another man. Mandla, a black South African. Actually, it was Paul who introduced me to him, and in the beginning we couldn't stand each other. He was an activist in the trade unions, I didn't want anything to do with politics. That made him furious. I remember how he would put his arm next to mine and say, "We're the same colour, sister. How can you deny that?" But then . . .' Her dark eyes held mine in their spell. 'We fell in love. And then he was killed.'

'Killed?'

'We never found out how. But there was reason to suspect that the South African Security Police had a hand in it. They were active all over Europe at the time, particularly in France.'

'And then?'

'I just knew, when he died, that I couldn't go on living in a kind of splendid isolation with my white lover, ten thousand kilometres away. Always, all my life, as a coloured person, I'd felt in-between. Not white, not black. Mandla made me realise that I had to make a choice. That was when I came back.'

'Do you still think you made the right choice?'

'Today I'm certain, yes. At last. But Jesus, it has taken me eight years. Of hoping against hope. It wasn't easy . . .' Her voice trailed off. Only later, in our subsequent conversations, did she consent to talk about it. The first tough years, trying to find a foothold. The suspicion from both sides, white and black. Until finally she became accepted in the UDF, throwing herself into it with the kind of total passion I soon came to admire in her. Driven by something she remembered as a favourite quote of Paul's: *The worst crime is to do nothing, for fear that we cannot do enough.* And how it landed her in detention during the first state of emergency. That was something she still wouldn't talk about. All I knew was that she was tortured. Very badly. But after two years in detention, without trial, she was released. Probably because she was in such bad shape – one of the consequences was a hysterectomy – that they thought she would either go home to die, or be so scared that she would never dare to get involved in political action again.

They obviously did not know Andrea Malgas yet.

Not all our conversations were depressing or dark or serious. What she loved was to take me on trips of discovery and rediscovery to the places she'd known as a child or a young girl. She had an obsession with District Six, where she'd been born. We could no longer establish exactly where their house would have been, but she could make some informed guesses, based on what she could remember of her father – she called him Dedda – and the route he would follow from the harbour, when his fishing trawler came in, from pub to pub, zigzagging uphill all the way to the Six.

She had memories of being perched on his shoulders as he carried her, singing at the top of his fish-bugle voice, to the Gardens, to the harbour, to the museum (where she was horrified by the plaster casts of Bushmen, which she thought were real people, stuffed like the animals), or on bus trips to Hout Bay, to Kalk Bay, to all the places of the Cape. She took me to Onrust, where Brian had taught her to skin-dive, and to Steenbras where they had made love in a smelly shallow cave, and to Cool Bay where she had nearly drowned as a little girl, running away from the police who had arrived with dogs to clear the beach of coloured 'intruders' on a holiday. She could tell endless stories about Dedda with his smell of sweat and drink and male animal. And of his death at sea. And the funeral wake they had for him, with the whole of District Six turning up to celebrate uproariously right through the night.

Her eyes were ablaze with light when she spoke about her youth. She was really the Prodigal Daughter, returned to rediscover what she had once given up. And taking me with her on these trips, through her astoundingly acute memories, was like discovering my own city for the first time. There was a life and a liveliness in her which seemed to offer me, too, an elixir to guarantee eternal youth. And when we kissed or embraced, she was almost greedy in her expressions of passion. But she would not consent to make love. It might have been my whiteness which, after her lover Paul, interposed itself between us. Or, just as likely, her suspicion about my being a writer. Both, I urgently reasoned with her, could, surely, be overcome. But there was no part of Andrea's No that could not be understood.

For months it went on: the constant joy of our journeys of discovery, our breathless conversations; and the never-ending hidden battle to find a way past, or through, her No.

Until that day. We were watching TV together on 2 February 1990, when parliament listened, in a state of shock, to the announcement of a new deal that would relegate every vestige of the old South Africa to the rubble of history. (At last, after decades of hell, the much vaunted 'winds of change' had swept through everything in their way.) We kissed, and embraced, and laughed, and cried together. And drank ourselves into the kind of stupor her father had been famous for. But that was that. For the moment.

Less than a fortnight later Mandela walked out of prison. We were there. For hours we waited in the scorching February sun beside the road through the dark green vineyards that surround Victor Verster Prison. And then the unbelievable happened, the impossible came true. Afterwards we joined the tumultuous cavalcade into Cape Town, to the parade flooded by a sea of people.

And that night, when we reached her little house and closed the door behind us to shut out the raging, jubilating streets, there was only one conceivable conclusion. Mandela had done it for us, just as, so ironically, Verwoerd had thrown Helena and me together a quarter of a century before. They had not just set us free to each other, but had also drawn us, without our asking, even without our knowledge, into the memory of the country.

She said, when we woke up sometime the following day, 'You know, Chris, I think I'm home at last.'

I knew exactly what she meant.

Some time afterwards, Andrea moved on: by the time the election of '94 brought our relationship to a formal end – that unreal, miraculous day when both of us found new partners at our polling stations and brought them home – we were already heading in different directions. (In due course she was even elected to parliament, and her life is now too hectic for any long-term relationship, although we still occasionally meet, have a meal, talk for hours.) Still, as through the years since then I've moved through what time has remained for me, at a gradually slowing pace, from the unthinking arrogance of full potency to a declining reliance on hope, her taste still dreams on my tongue and my mind.

* * *

AGAIN, I HAVE not kept my notes for days. I have lost track of the war in Iraq. When I turned on the TV last night, it was just in time for the announcement that the war was over. They were careful not to call it a victory; not yet. But all the trappings of triumph were in place. There was little Mr Bush with his gimlet eyes, striding out like one of those sad, bad, late-Roman emperors who ruled the world while in secret they shat themselves with fear of all the barbarians lurking in the dark. (The Roman reference is not entirely out of place. If the Emperor Caligula could appoint his horse as a consul of the empire, perhaps America's choice, in the period of its own decadence, of an ass as president, need not be surprising.) The scene on the US aircraft carrier *Abraham Lincoln*, where he insisted on appearing in a pilot's uniform. Draped from the bridge of the carrier the banner proclaiming, with crude simple-mindedness, *Mission Accomplished*. Some mission, some accomplishment. The crowning illusion to a massive invasion masked as an act of liberation, waged by the politics of the extreme right and inspired by pure fantasy. As in Afghanistan, a vast country has been laid waste under the pretence of saving it from itself; and all we can still look forward to is the feeding frenzy of the conquerors.

The real war lies ahead.

WHAT WORRIES ME is how I will now spend my nights without a war to watch. It has been the context and condition of my memories of love. My thousand and one nights have ended. The stories now are over, *finita la commedia*. My darling Scheherazade will have to wrap it up. We must put our precocious little Doniziade to bed. (What has she learned of love from us? What have we learned from her?) Because it was not the war as such that held me in its evil spell, but the telling of it. By all those embedded journalists.

It is nearly time to wind up. I can feel that it is almost done. Mam has been laid to rest. On the appointed day I went to the crematorium. There were five or six people from the old-age home; she had outlived all her contemporaries.

The crematorium official in charge, obsequious and rubbing his hands, recognised me from the last time, barely a month ago. 'Sorry to see you here again so soon,' he said. His tone of voice suggested, *Welcome back*.

That was what provoked me to retort, 'I burn all my women.'

He found it difficult to digest, but kept a brave face. *It takes all kinds*, his attitude conveyed.

I was supposed to collect the ashes later, but so far I haven't. I haven't even disposed of yours. Perhaps I'll go to the sea, one day, to scatter them all and hopefully choke a gull.

This is it, then. I cannot postpone it any longer; I am approaching the end. In the beginning, and all my life, I think, I believed that I was writing to hold on, not to let go, not to lose it all for ever. But through Mam's death — and through yours, which I am now approaching — I know that the opposite is true. We do not write to hold on, but to let go. I am learning, I hope, to loosen my grip, to set memory free, to let myself be: myself and all the women who have allowed me to be what I am now — whatever that may be.

There is only this last moment and then I can leave it all. No need to write again. This much I have done for you. The rest is silence.

Viva la libertà! sang the chorus in *Don Giovanni*, remember? Mozart knew more about freedom and love, after all, than we tend to give him credit for.

AFTER YOU HAD gone out for the cigarettes I waited for half an hour, then went outside. A peaceful February night. The glow of the city was washed up against the sky from the other side of the mountain. This side the sky was black and clear, dusted with stars scattered like ashes. My car was there. Yours was gone; the garage still stood open. I felt a brief shiver, although the night was warm. Perhaps you'd met a friend or a neighbour at the supermarket, I told myself. I should wait a while longer, hoping the dinner wouldn't get spoiled.

After an hour I drove up to the little supermarket where I had first met you. The completion of a circle. (What had I once said, to whom, about circles endlessly covering one another? Such a plausible pretext.

But a pretext nevertheless.) The place was still open, but the half-asleep man inside could not remember seeing you; he was more interested in a soccer match on TV anyway. An hour later I went to the police. The constable on duty was busy taking down particulars of a rape from a young woman who was sobbing hysterically. He had problems with his spelling. By the time he had arranged with a colleague to take her to a district surgeon, he was clearly fed up. ('Why do women always choose such bad times to get raped?') What did I expect him to do? he asked. I gave him the details of your car, but those didn't interest him.

'Come back tomorrow,' he said, obviously fed-up.

I drove up and down Camps Bay, exploring every street and alley and cul-de-sac, but there was no sign of you. Just after two I returned to the police station. The same constable was on duty, and sent me away in the same gruff manner. In your house I put the food away in the fridge, and went to sit in the studio waiting, against all hope, for you to return. I had time to retrace all our steps since that first night. The endless conversations. Meeting George. The things we did together. Our excursion to the Cedarberg: how I had gone in search of you in the night and heard you making love; how we had come down the mountain as a threesome, I hobbling between the two of you, bound together – as it then felt – for life. That morning in the studio, when you had shown me the photos George had taken of you.

The day was slow in dawning. Before the sun came out I had a bath in your bathroom – remembering those early nights when I would lie awake listening to every sound you made; and how you would later bring me a cup of tea or Milo. I was still expecting you to come back at any moment. How could you *not* come back?

Just after nine I returned to the police station. This time there was a new man on duty. He took my statement (at least he didn't have so many problems with his spelling), and said they would keep their eyes open. But he didn't hold out much hope of any quick development.

However, just before noon he telephoned. They might have something for me, he said.

The car had been found in Khayelitsha, near the turn-off George used to take on his way to his photography workshop. What memories that brought back: George with his brightly coloured plastic boxes of food for the boisterous youngsters; the eagerness with which they learned everything he wished to teach them, to equip them with skills for their own lives. (I remembered how I'd once asked him whether he would ever retire; and how he had responded with his bright, boyish smile that he might follow Cartier-Bresson's example and continue taking photographs even when he no longer needed a camera. With a pang of loss I wondered where *he* might be now.) For a moment, wholly without any reason, it made me hopeful again. But when I arrived at the station and the constable gave me the details, the last hope evaporated. The car had been wrecked and burnt out. No sign of any occupants. No reports about how or when it could have happened. But there was another piece of the jigsaw to be fitted: the body of a young woman had been found beside the N2, just after the airport, near the turn-off to Crossroads. She was still alive, but in a serious condition in the City Park Hospital. They guessed that she had been thrown from a fast-moving car. So far, they had been unable to identify her. But if I cared to accompany the detectives on the case I might be able to help them.

Of course it was you. One side of your face barely recognisable. But how could I *not* recognise you? I spoke to two doctors. They could still not provide any reliable prognosis. Extensive brain injuries by the look of it. They were on the point of doing some scans and taking X-rays. I told them I would wait, no matter how many hours it took.

In the late afternoon a neurosurgeon came out to talk to me. It was too early to tell with any certainty, he said. But it didn't look good. In these cases there was always a chance of recovery, miracles do happen; but frankly, man to man, the brain injuries were so extensive that he couldn't hold out much hope. He put a comradely hand on my shoulder – at that stage, for some reason, he still assumed I was your father – and told me not to give up hope.

'Do you think,' I asked, hearing my own voice coming to me as from a great distance, 'the worst may happen?'

'Sometimes,' he said, 'the worst is the best that can happen.'

I stayed there, throughout the night, beside your bed, until a sympathetic but no-nonsense, middle-aged sister firmly ordered me to go home and get some rest. I thought it would be impossible to sleep, but I passed out the moment I fell down on the bed without even taking off my clothes. By the evening I was back. Over the next few weeks they got so used to my presence that I was being treated as an honorary member of staff.

You were, they assured me, 'stable'. They had drilled a small hole into your skull to relieve the pressure on the brain. They had to shave off the hair from a patch on your head. Your face was still unrecognisably swollen, bruised in all colours. (Was this, I thought in a sacrilegious rage beyond shock, what the Rainbow Nation really looks like?)

Two days later they operated on you. Too gruesome to think about: the top part of your skull had to be removed, like a lid from a casserole, to reach the brain, and then replaced, the surgeon explained in the graphic terminology a layman like me might (but would not) understand. As a precaution, you were attached to a ventilator. But because the brain stem which regulates breathing had not been damaged, he painstakingly made clear, this could be removed after a few days. What remained was a tangle of IV tubes and wires to sci-fi monitors which finally dehumanised you: a small spaceship readied for a moon launch. But you remained in a coma, and I remained at your bedside.

Three weeks. You seemed to be shrinking every day. I remembered what you once told me about sculpting a horse from marble: chipping, chipping away until everything that was not a horse was removed. If you were marble, I thought, and you were indeed becoming whiter all the time, you would now be very close to being nothing but you. And at the same time, God knows how much weight I'd lost myself. Whenever I happened to pass a mirror, I was shocked by my reflection. It didn't look as if I'd seen a ghost but as if I *were* a ghost. All that mattered was to be with you every available moment, watching intently for the slightest flickering sign of life: an eyelid quivering, a finger twitching. Your breath was shallow, but it came evenly. The bruises started fading, the worst swelling subsided. But nothing happened.

On Wednesday 19 March they did more scans. Impossible to say anything, the specialist concluded. You might stay in that coma for many more weeks, for months. Your vital functions were, still, 'stable'.

But the brain . . . ? The doctor breathed in slowly and deeply, and shook his head. 'I'm afraid the damage is irreparable. Even if she wakes up, she will probably be catatonic for the rest of her life.'

That night I spent in my bed, propped up against the pillows, watching television. It was the first night of the war. At that moment everything might still have happened. The thin red line was still intact, if invisible. The forces of evil were marshalled against the forces of evil. Tonight, as I sit here writing my last notes, it is all clear, and all but over. With a kind of tortured lucidity I can see it all. But then? The screen was merely a flat surface to focus my eyes: my thoughts were elsewhere, with you.

I already knew then what I would have to do. But it was not easy.

This was what it had all come to, I thought, lying back against the pillows, weaving your thin, pale moon-cloth in my mind. Here I was, on the night before your death, in a solitude as utter as anything I had ever lived through. I had no child, no family, nobody. (Mam was still alive then, but already slipping away, out of reach.) I had an irrelevant and irreverent thought: How lucky Don Giovanni had been, to be plunged into hell. And so young. I thought: Can anyone imagine Don Giovanni old? What we know about him is that he can never be old. He can move from youth to early-middle age – it is his in-betweenness that defines his position – but no further. There is a beyondness about being old which cannot be reached even by pain.

You had once said, I thought, *Poor Don Giovanni*. And I had replied, or perhaps merely thought to myself, *Then you are lost. Once a woman pities a man, she is lost*. What had not occurred to me then was that he was lost too.

I thought: Rachel, I love you. At this late hour of my life I know at last what it means. And what I am going to do is because I love you. But even as the thought moved in me, it reminded me, in a sickening way, of my father, in my boyhood, of the pious words and prayers and readings from the Bible and which would precede the order to uncover my backside so that he could punish me. Because, he said, he loved me and had to hurt me for my own good. What did my words really mean, what did they amount to? Never enough.

From my vantage point, beyond everything that mattered, there was only one thing I could still do to intervene. The ultimate I-love-you. Could I face that? How could I not?

And the next morning, very early, when I returned to the hospital, I was incredibly calm. At last everything was clear.

As I bent over you, at seventeen minutes to ten, holding the pillow in my two hands, I knew that this was the only way in which I could still, possibly, say those dark words: *I love you*. Even if it seemed like an ultimate betrayal.

But as I sit here writing this, approaching the end, I know with even greater clarity: We betray those we love by loving them.

When we love, we transform the one we love into the one we should love to love. That denies the reality of the one we love. And this is the first betrayal which leads to all the others. I don't even know if this makes sense; but I am beyond sense, as love is beyond it, thank God.

The moment is still with me and will never let go.

As I lower the pillow over your face something restrains me. I stop to look at that deathly white face which is no longer yours. I can see no sign of breathing. I bend over to listen very closely. Not the faintest hiss or rustle or flicker of life. I reach out to take your hand, to feel your pulse. It is not yet cold, but no longer warm. You must have died mere minutes ago.

I put away the pillow. It is no longer necessary, it has been taken out of my hands. It was George who said, If it must happen, it will happen.

But the decision has already been taken. I am as guilty as if I have done it. It is not my fault that I have come too late. Like Rogozhin, I killed the thing I loved.

I have to stop writing. It is the end. But it is never the end. I must now go on living, that is not done yet. Yet nothing remains as it has been. For the first time I can imagine Don Giovanni old. He is still woman-struck, a man possessed by love and loving. The only difference is that he no longer needs a camera.

Acknowledgements

Luigi Malerba's words on page 20 come from *La Pianeta Azzurro* (Milan: Garzanti, 1986).

The Frenchman who dined well, also on page 20, was Jean d'Ormesson's grandfather, who dies in *C'était bien* (Paris: Gallimard, 2003).

The brief comment on war by Chris Hedges on page 6 is taken from *War is a Force that Gives Us Meaning* (New York: Anchor Books, 2003).

For my reading of Nastasya Filippovna, I quite extensively used the David Magarshack translation of Dostoevsky's *The Idiot* (Harmondsworth: Penguin Classics, 1965).

The image of Antigone was, of course, inspired primarily by Sophocles, but also by Anouilh's version, from which some lines and the scene of her brother Haemon's paper flower were borrowed.

Two of the women in the book made their first appearance in some of my earlier novels: Nicolette in *The Ambassador* (1983), and Andrea in *The Wall of the Plague* (1984).

Thank you to Colette Gordon for her understanding of Scheherazade.